VOWS FORGED IN BLOOD

K. D. MILLER

To Amanda.

Thank you for letting this weird little indie author you found on the interwebs latch onto you like a giant (but kinda cute?) barnacle and force her friendship on you for forever.

Also for being a freaky naughty artist and somehow taking my half-articulated ideas and creating absolutely beautiful things.

I love you. Enjoy your sexy vampire warlord 😉

CONTENTS

You are cordially invited to the two hundred forty-seventh Choosing. In honor of the Blood Peace and the continued harmony and friendship between the humans and vampires, each noble house, if able, will present one of-age Potential Consort for consideration by a Prince of the Montclare Clan. May the Goddess of Luck smile upon you.

CHAPTER 1
ALARIC

"It's fucking ridiculous!" I spit as I pace furiously in front of the hearth in my study. The wind howls outside, rattling the windows. A fierce storm has blown in from beyond the Sisters, the hulking twin peaks of the Black Mountains that guard the whole of Braxhelm from the threats just outside. The sky is a deep, churning gray, the color almost as dark as the blade of Night's Fury, my famed—and feared—longsword. Thunder rumbles in the distance and lightning streaks through the clouds every few minutes. It's foul weather, perfectly matching my foul mood. I'd been happy with Sebastian's unexpected visit to my war camp, but the reunion with my favorite brother quickly soured when the true reason for his sudden appearance was revealed: the demand that I come home and choose a Consort.

"It is tradition," Sebastian replies, ever calm as he sips his blood-laced wine and studies me with the golden Montclare eyes we all share, though his have always seemed to see more than the rest of us, to see to the very heart of things. A small, indulgent smile plays on his lips as I run a hand through my unruly hair. He used to ruffle it when I was a child, much to my chagrin (and secret delight), and I wonder if he still sees me that way even after centuries, still as a child running through the grand Montclare palace in the heart of Braxhelm, wayward curls and baby fangs, wooden sword in my hand from the time I could toddle.

"There are eleven other princes. Make one of them the grand master of this ridiculous ceremony." I know I sound like a petulant child, but I can't help myself. I *feel* like a petulant child, even having the urge to stomp my foot. I don't want a fucking Consort. I don't want anything to do with this part of being a Montclare. I love my life of blood and battle. It sings in my veins. It makes my heart thunder and my soul come alive as nothing else can. I am a prince, but I don't want the life of one. I never have. Fighting and protecting —*that* has always been my purpose. I know I should be grateful that Sebastian allowed me to join the army at all—our father surely never would have—let alone *lead* it all this time, and I am, truly. I'm grateful to my brother for all that he has allowed me, the way he stood against some of the others who said it wasn't the place of a prince to fight or to be a warrior. But as grateful as I am, right now, I want to toss him out into the raging storm, ass first. What the hells will *I* do with a Consort here in my fucking war camp?

"You are the only prince who does not have a Consort, brother."

"Cillian has no Consort," I point out to be contrary, though I know that avenue is a futile one. Sebastian arches a light brow.

"Cillian has a mate. You know those with mates do not take Consorts." Of course I know that. Mates are exceedingly rare for our kind these days (though no one quite knows why), but the laws of mates are held above all else. Vampires rarely take blood from other vampires, but a mate is the exception to that rule. Something in the bond between mates changes things, somehow causes their bodies to sustain each other in a perfect harmony of give and take, fulfill and be fulfilled. Once the bond is forged, mates only take blood from each other, save a life-or-death situation, I suppose. Cillian is the only prince with a mate, but the rules have been set in stone regarding princes and Consorts and mates from the moment he bonded. A mate above *all* else.

Sebastian's lips quirk up in a sardonic smile.

"Would you rather have a mate then, little brother?"

"Be serious," I snap, making Sebastian chuckle into his wineglass. Having a Consort will be headache enough. Having a mate would be a nightmare. Being tied to another in all ways, so entwined that our very lives depended on one another? *No fucking thank you.*

"Alaric, you are the only one of us who has *never* had a Consort. Cillian had three before he found Lyanna. We've overlooked it all these years because of your choice to lead the army, to wage war on our enemies—a noble endeavor that we are very proud of, mind you —but now that the war has calmed, it is time for you to participate in one of our most exalted customs."

"There are still battles to be fought, Bastian. Every fucking day we fight." I fling an arm out, gesturing towards the shadow of the Sisters in the distance, where, on the other side, a hoard of dark, evil creatures waits and plots, their only goal to destroy Braxhelm and everyone within it. It has taken *centuries* of battles and strategy and death to finally beat the majority of the Revenants back beyond the northern borders of Braxhelm and for the continent to feel relatively safe.

Even so, the war is far from over. Kilgren, the Revenants' leader, is ruthless and relentless and will never stop trying to find his way back through my army. The wide, barren expanse just outside the pass has seen so many battles that the ground is permanently stained nearly black with blood, and it's been named the Obsidian Plain.

I shake my head in frustration and disgust.

"We have beaten them back, yes, but the war is far from won, and farther still from over." I'm not sure it will ever truly be over, not until every last Revenant falls, but I will spend my eternal life seeing that it happens.

"I understand that, but the fighting *has* calmed. You control the pass, do you not?"

"Yes, but—"

"And attacks inside of Braxhelm's borders have diminished drastically, correct?"

I sigh. "Yes, the nests are being found fewer and farther between, but—"

"And is your camp—the camp of one of the greatest warlords in all of history—not secure?" I narrow my eyes, knowing exactly what my brother is doing.

Through gritted teeth, I say, "Yes, it is, but—"

"Then there's no reason why you cannot choose a Consort and bring them here." Before I can protest, Sebastian holds his hand up to halt me. "It is done, Alaric," he says, a note of iron authority ringing in his voice. An authority that despite having every right to wield as head of the Montclare Clan, he rarely uses. It's one of the many reasons that Sebastian has always been my favorite sibling. He's always been protective over me, the youngest of the family, and the two of us have been closer than any of our other seventeen siblings. Even after he became the head of the Clan when our father died almost two centuries ago, Sebastian remained ever the loyal, protective brother, not just a tyrannical leader who threw his authority around at will.

Thinking of all of my siblings, I curse in annoyance at the fact that my sisters have never been forced to take Consorts, but alas, such is a right—or curse—only bestowed upon the princes for ridiculous, outdated notions regarding the difference in the sexes. Some of my most brutal warriors are my *female* soldiers. I have no idea why men and women aren't seen as equal in all ways, in all matters, but there are many who don't have the same views as I do, who think that women should still be seen and not heard, that they should act only as ornaments to be shown off and the bearers of children as they had been thousands of years ago. I think about bringing this up to Sebastian, insisting that our sisters start taking Consorts of their own, but I know now is not the time, and, in any event, it will not stop this from happening.

Softer, Sebastian adds, "it isn't so bad as you're making it out to be. You'll come to the Choosing, you'll pick a Consort, and you'll have fresh blood until they perish and it is time to pick another. You do not have to...socialize with them, should you not wish to," he glances around the study, his handsome face pinching slightly, "though it will be a bit harder to avoid them in this small space than it is for the rest of us I suppose."

I snort, something between a laugh and an exasperated huff. I can see the whole of my cabin in my mind's eye and barely stifle a shudder. Though larger than any other cabin at the camp, there will be no escaping each other here. I suppose I could have a separate cabin built for them, but it is tradition for a Consort to reside with their prince—though usually in a completely separate wing of a damned *castle* with plenty of space between them. And, I have to admit, that I feel a small pang of sympathy for the human, the nameless, faceless man or woman who is going to be pulled from their life of luxury as a noble and forced to live in a war camp in the often-times harsh Northlands. I don't think it would be very becoming of me to force all this on them and then have it said that I'm not treating them with the respect the position deserves. I may think the entire notion of Consorts is ridiculous, but I am a man of honor and duty above almost all else, and Consorts are one of the most respected titles in all of Braxhelm.

So, no. We will...*share*. I nearly put my fist through the wall at the idea. Sebastian rises and grins, knowing that I'm resigned to my fate, and claps a hand on my shoulder.

"All will be well, brother. Perhaps you might even like them. Several of my Consorts were very amenable."

"And the others?" Sebastian wrinkles his nose, his golden eyes twinkling.

"Those are the times when I was thankful for the separate

wings." I shake my head, huffing out a strained laugh and Bastian squeezes my shoulder.

So, I order that an addition be built onto my cabin—a separate wing for my Consort and her Keeper, as is expected—another, separate cabin built for his or her chef and any other staff that may be sent, with all the necessities a human might need, and reluctantly set off to Astoria's Keep.

CHAPTER 2
DAHLIA

"Dahlia Clayburn," the low, velvety smooth voice of Alaric Montclare rings out in the silence of the grand ballroom.

My head snaps up, my eyes wide in shock and confusion. If I wasn't kneeling before the dais with the rest of the Potentials, I probably would have fallen over. A soft, collective gasp of surprise ripples through the line of Potentials, all of them just as confused as I am. There is no possible way he's chosen...*me*. It has to be some sort of mistake, or a cruel joke, or perhaps I'm dreaming. Yes, all of this is just one big, terrible nightmare. It *has* to be.

But as my gaze collides with the cool, golden stare of the prince and High General, I know deep in my bones that it's no mistake, no dream. I swallow hard as the thought settles inside my mind.

This is real.

And I've just become Alaric Montclare's Consort.

Well fuck.

Annalise Whitehollow stiffens beside me, muttering a low curse beneath her breath that I'm honestly surprised a daughter of a noble even knows. Though her head is still bowed, she cuts her eyes towards me, glaring daggers. On my other side, Wilhelm Vandrose turns to openly gape at me, looking almost accusatory. They're acting as if I'd meant for this to happen! As if I could possibly *want* to be a Consort like the rest of these damned fool Potentials, when, in fact, I want nothing to do with the entire affair.

No, no, no. This can't be right. Maybe Alaric misunderstood what he was meant to do here. It's his first Choosing, after all. Perhaps he thought he was selecting the most *lacking* of the nobles, one to be sacrificed on some alter to one of the gods—though I'm far from a proper virgin sacrifice. I almost laugh at the thought, my head suddenly feeling light, my blood pumping through my veins too quickly, my thoughts scattered and frantic and becoming a bit hysterical.

I shouldn't even really be here. This *has* to be a fucking mistake.

"Rise, Dahlia Clayburn," the Magister, a burly vampire with long, white hair and a matching beard that hangs to his chest, says in his booming voice. He's a turned vampire, not born, and looks to have been in his forties when he'd been changed. A bit later than most, but there had to have been a reason, I suppose. Vampires don't turn just any human. Or *attempt* to turn them anyway. It doesn't always work and there is great risk in the transformation process—since the catalyst is death.

I stay on my knees, frozen for a long moment before sense and self-preservation win out over shock and denial. You don't disobey the vampires. The humans and vampires have been living in relative harmony for nearly six hundred years now, but they're still *vampires* and I need to do what's expected of me.

Slowly, I rise, a cold sweat breaking out on the back of my neck and my heart thundering loudly in my ears. Can they hear the wild beating? *Of course they can.*

"You have been honored above all others this day," the Magister decrees to the gathered crowd, a mix of vampires and human nobles. "Ascend the dais."

I don't make the decision to move, but somehow I'm gliding

forward, up the stone steps of the platform, careful not to trip on the skirt of my gown. I'm not used to wearing them, truth be told, especially nothing this fine or formal. It would be my luck to fall in front of the gods and everyone after being chosen as a Consort, the highest honor that could be bestowed upon a human, more coveted and revered than even the Dukes. I idly wonder if it would negate my selection. Would they make Alaric choose someone else, someone who could walk up a set of stairs without falling over? Consorts are supposed to be regal, after all, refined and polished and the epitome of elegance. I am exactly none of those things, and don't particularly care to be.

Before I can seriously consider falling on purpose, just to see if it will somehow end this nightmare before it truly begins, the rest of the princes and princesses stand from their gilded thrones. Sixteen pairs of golden eyes fix on me as I slowly make my way across stage —for that's what it truly is, isn't it? A stage for this ridiculous play? —towards Alaric Montclare. I can't remember if I'm supposed to avert my eyes, but even if I am, I don't think I could possibly manage it. Alaric is the most handsome man I've ever seen, could ever possibly even conjure in my most delicious and secret dreams. All of the Montclares are beautiful, of course, but Alaric is more so than any other. But even more than beauty, there is something else that calls to me, something deep inside my soul flaring inside my chest for a moment as I look upon him. I shake myself, forcing the strange thoughts away as I continue to stare at him.

He is beautiful, yes—and absolutely *terrifying.* Icy fear skitters down my spine, an instinctual fear rooted deeply in the core of my being, passed down from ancestors long-dead. Even so, I press on. I remind myself to breathe as I continue towards him, my legs trembling slightly. He towers over me, the top of my head reaching just above the bottom of his chest, a chest that's broad and brawny and seems to be straining the fabric of his dress tunic. The sigil of his Coven, a great snarling wolf's head, is emblazoned on the front in golden thread. We had to learn all of the royals' sigils in school, of course, and Alaric's had always admittedly been one of my favorites. His hands are clenched into fists at his sides, his knuckles scarred faintly, years of training and battle evident on his skin and setting him apart from the rest of his nearly-perfect siblings.

I crane my head upward as I approach. His hair is black as night and falls in unruly curls to his collar, and his face is unreadable, though his square jaw is clenched tightly beneath his thick scruff, his lips pressed into a hard line. I get the distinct feeling that he has no desire to have a Consort and this entire thing is an utter annoyance to him. I'm not sure that bodes well for me. As his Consort, I'm bound to remain with him. For most Consorts, that means residing in one of the luxurious Montclare castles spread throughout Braxhelm, in their own dedicated wing, with their own maids and butlers and chefs and everything else one could possibly imagine or want, only seeing their prince on social occasions or should he care to take the blood from her veins into his cup himself—which I've heard is quite rare. Usually a servant just fetches the blood and that's that.

The Consorts and their princes live largely separate lives. The title, even this ceremony, really, are all just for show, a stupid fucking tradition that began hundreds of years ago as a way to celebrate the thriving Blood Peace.

But Alaric Montclare isn't like the other princes. He's High General of the vampiric army, and he doesn't just lead them from afar, making decisions from the safety of a castle and letting his men do the work. No, he fights beside them, bathes his own famed blade in Revenant blood as often as possible, riding in at the front of almost every battle if rumors are to be believed, and he lives in the permanent war camp in the Northlands. There will be no separate wing in a castle for me. Perhaps a separate tent? Do they even sleep in tents? Or maybe just in bedrolls on the ground? How big is a war camp anyway? Can we really escape each other totally?

I know my thoughts are spiraling but one keeps ringing in my ears: *war camp*. I'm going to be living in a fucking *war camp*, surrounded by thousands of vampire warriors. What in the seven hells is that going to be like? Dark and dreary, filled with blood and screams and rage? I shudder. Is that really to be my life from now on? I know that his men will be under strict orders not to harm me, of course, but...well, the vampires in the army are very different from the ones who live and work side by side with the humans in the cities and villages, and leagues away from the ones of the noble Covens—those vampires who are part of the bloodline of each prince or princess, and all who are selected to serve them. The vampires in the army are warriors, living for bloodshed and battle—how will a human girl fair among them?

I shake myself again, trying to focus on what's happening now instead of dreading the future. I stop before Alaric, the two of us facing each other before the rest of the Potentials. They all still kneel just before the dais, and I can practically feel the resentment drifting from them. The nobles sit in neat rows behind the Potentials, and the rest of the vampires look on from the gallery above. Hundreds of eyes watching down like angels from the heavens, a mix of members of all nineteen Covens, though the majority of Alaric's Coven is, in fact, his army, and are not present here.

The princes and princesses stand in a line on the dais, and I dare a glance at them. They're all so...*imposing*. I've been around vampires before, of course, but never the royals, and now I understand why everyone always says they're different than the other vampires. A raw, unearthly power emanates from them, a quiet, but lethal ferocity and authority, something preternatural that my human mind can't completely understand but instinctually knows to fear.

They all vary in coloring and looks (their father had many, *many* companions, so they almost all have different mothers)—some have skin as pale as ivory, others dark as onyx; some blonde, some brunette, some with hair as red as fire like my own; some with delicate, aristocratic features, others more rough-hewn—but all share two similarities: they all have the unmistakable golden Montclare eyes, and they're all devastatingly attractive. All born vampires are beautiful, and even turned vampires have a certain allure about them, something that draws people in. I suppose that's a bit of the point, isn't it? Vampires at their core are predators, and their looks draw in prey, the way some of the most poisonous flowers are the most beautiful to look at. They beckon with that beauty, but the price for coming near is a dire one.

Or, it *could* be. Though the vampires and humans have been living in peace for over five hundred years, it wasn't always the way of it. There was a time when the vampires were the beasts to be feared alongside the Revenants, attacking humans, feeding and killing with a brutality that nearly destroyed the entire continent.

Until Etienne Montclare.

The patriarch of the Montclare Clan, older than any vampire I've ever heard tale of, Etienne was the one who changed the history of our entire world. The Montclares hadn't always lived in Braxhelm. Other far less civilized vampires resided here first and spread their terror through the lands. The Montclares migrated here after the Great Flood destroyed many other continents in this world, arriving in the midst of a raging war between vampires and the Revenants. The stories say that the Montclares quickly took control of the vampire contingent, either defeating the others or making them vow loyalty to the Montclare line. Even so, the humans were already verging on extinction, caught in the crossfire between the two sides for far too long, and so the vampires were losing their food source. It was a bleak future all around until Etienne put a stop to it, seeing a better way for survival for the vampires and the humans alike, and a path forward to ending the Revenants.

Etienne proposed a deal: the vampires would protect the humans and vow that no vampire would hunt or kill a human without provocation again, so long as the humans agreed to provide blood slaves to the Montclares and offerings of the strongest among them to be turned and join the vampiric army. No more fighting, no more bloodshed, no more living in fear.

Peace.

Etienne Montclare offered peace, after so many years of unrest and death. The human king of Braxhelm at the time agreed. He knew that the humans would eventually fall completely, whether to the vampires or the Revenants, and the sacrifice of some was outweighed by the survival of the many.

And so, the Blood Peace came to be.

To much surprise, it *worked*. The Montclares, their army bolstered by the newly turned humans, began to overtake the Revenants, to drive them farther and farther north. The humans provided blood slaves to sustain the vampires and, as promised, all attacks stopped. It was a tenuous truce at first, of course, but it grew in strength and soon they were true allies, the blood slaves being looked at as glorious martyrs and treated with great dignity. It was an *honor* to be chosen to serve and sacrifice, many humans volunteering for the duty to bring glory to their family names. The two species grew to respect and care for each other, great friendships and even romances evolving over time.

It was even a team of human and vampire alchemists, working together, who discovered how to replicate human blood, all but removing the need for the blood slaves at all—but the human nobles and Etienne Montclare had other ideas.

That is when the Choosing came to be. Instead of blood slaves giving blood to the entire Clan, a single Consort would be given only to each prince (why the princesses didn't get to be a part of the fun, I don't know, but this is the way it has always been). A Consort would be chosen from among only the noble human families, as a continued symbol of the alliance between the vampires and the humans of Braxhelm. The Consort's blood was only given directly to their prince, and it was expected that the prince would only have his Consort's blood, no replications and no others. When a Consort died, another Choosing ceremony was held for that prince to find a replacement.

It's a stupid, ridiculous custom that only makes the rich even richer since the Consort's family is given a hefty dowry in exchange for their service, and I've always hated the entire notion of it. I never dreamed I'd ever be a part of it, let alone a chosen Consort, it's so asinine and—

"Your wrist," Alaric hisses in a low, gruff whisper, startling me from my thoughts. I glance up and from the expectant look on the Magister's face, I realize that he's asked for my hand already, probably more than once.

"Fuck," I mutter quietly and the Magister's eyes widen in surprise. I bite my lip, forgetting myself as usual. Noble girls don't curse. Or drink. Or dance on the bar tops in taverns. Or do anything fun, from what I can tell, honestly. I think I see Alaric's lips twitch ever so slightly, as if amused, but his stoic look is back in place again so quickly, that I decide I must have imagined it. I take a deep breath and raise my hand, and almost quicker than I can track, the Magister slices my wrist with a beautiful dagger, the blade inlaid with golden script in a language that I can't read, and the hilt bejeweled with rubies, their color only a few shades darker than the blood welling from the cut on my skin. I gasp, more from surprise than pain really, and the Magister tilts my hand so that the blood drips into a small crystal goblet. He hands it to an attendant and Alaric proffers his own wrist.

My stomach churns as the Magister repeats the process, slicing Alaric's wrist and capturing the blood in an identical goblet, though Alaric shows no reaction whatsoever. I'd nearly forgotten this part of the ceremony. Admittedly, I hadn't paid all that much attention to the particulars when I'd been forced to learn the etiquette and what was to be expected of me during the Choosing. Never in a million years would I have thought I'd actually be selected. There was no need to know what happened after the Consort was chosen—it would never be me.

But now, as the Magister hands me the goblet of Alaric's blood, and him the goblet of mine, I remember: we are to exchange blood, this one time, to bind us together. The thought of drinking blood makes bile rise in my throat, but I force it away. It won't do well to toss my breakfast all over the Magister's fine robes—though it may be fairly comical, I have to admit.

"And now, with the exchanging of blood, the prince and his chosen Consort shall be bound, now until one shall perish."

I hesitate. I stare at the glass, the liquid within so dark it's nearly black. *Just do it. Just get it over with.* I inhale deeply and then bring the goblet to my lips. I toss the contents back, like I might a bit of whisky, and squeeze my eyes shut, expecting it to be horrid. It's salty and metallic, but something else stirs beneath that, something that slams into me like a fist to the chest. Power. Strength. Endless knowledge and life eternal. I gasp quietly as it surges through my veins like fire, but it isn't a fire that consumes and destroys. It's a fire that tempers and forges something new, something better and stronger and dangerous. I feel almost drunk with the flare of power, nearly toppling. It ebbs finally, but I can feel the shadows of the fire still thrumming through my veins, like the smoldering coals left after the flames have died out.

When I pry my eyes open once more, Alaric is pulling his gaze away from me and handing his now-empty goblet back to the Magister. His body looks as if it's been carved from stone, every muscle tight and rigid, his jaw clenched so hard I think it might shatter at any moment, but his eyes seem to be *burning*, the irises churning like liquid gold.

"Alaric Montclare, you have Chosen. Dahlia Clayburn, you have been Chosen. You are bound."

With that, every vampire in the gallery above bows their heads, a sign of acceptance of me as one of their own, as a member of the Montclare Clan, as a Lady of the Coven of the Wolf.

As Alaric's Consort.

Fuck.

CHAPTER 3
ALARIC

I'm not quite sure what to make of all that has transpired this day. It hasn't turned out at all as I'd been expecting. Or dreading, rather, I suppose. I still can't believe that I'd actually been forced to take part in the ridiculous ceremony at all, after two hundred years of avoiding it, but what had happened during it was... interesting to say the least.

The entire palace had been a flurry of activity since the moment I arrived, and I immediately felt as if I were suffocating. I missed the crisp, biting air of the mountains, I missed the rolling hills and the roar of the river and the smell of the snow far in the distance. It had been good to see my siblings—most of them, anyway—but if I were congratulated one more time for "finally becoming a real Montclare" I was going to start cutting off limbs. Ahmed especially seemed to delight in my misfortune, grinning like a snake behind his wine glass and reminding me all over again why he's my least favorite brother.

I'd been forced into formal attire (which I hate), been told to leave my weapons in my chambers (which I despise), and one of my sisters had been chasing me around all morning hellbent on taming my hair (which is entirely impossible). Ever the brilliant military tactician, I'd evaded her, of course, but when Fiona gets something in her head, she's a determined little devil. The two of us are only a few months apart in age, but she constantly likes to remind me that she's older. I love her more than most anything else in this world, but I refuse to be treated like a doll. So, I'd ducked into a hidden corridor in an attempt to escape the madness and, admittedly, hide until the cursed ceremony began.

I walked along the hallway, trailing my fingers along the cold, rough stone, smiling faintly at the remnants of the places where I painted on the walls when I'd found this hiding place as a child. Voices flitted to my ears and I ground my teeth in annoyance, realizing too late that this corridor ran behind the smaller ballroom that was used as the preparation area for the Potentials.

"Fucking perfect," I'd groaned as I continued on, listening to the inane chatter.

"You must be chosen, Halda. Your father's gambling…well, you just must."

"Lace your corset tighter. That's it."

"Is this truly his first bride?"

"Drink this. The glendine root brings the blood to the surface. It will attract his attention."

I rolled my eyes and my fangs slid out in irritation. I hurried along the corridor, wanting to get away from these humans as quickly as possible. They were all vapid and spoiled, trained to be Consorts since birth and look down their noses at nearly everyone— and I can't stand the lot of them. It's one of the many reasons I've chosen the life I have. I prefer blood and battle over…well, pretty much everything else, but definitely over high society bullshit. I'd hated having to attend balls and soirees as a child, even then hating how the Consorts acted to everyone around them, hating the idea of someday having to take one of my own.

"I cannot believe you're wearing that." Another voice had filtered through the stone, followed by a snort of a laugh.

"Have you met me?" This voice had a slight husk to it that made me slow my steps. It was...pleasing to my ears.

The first girl laughed lightly. "Ok, so I *can* believe it, but still. You know damn well that most Potentials wear *white*...and far more modest dresses. It's tradition." Her voice was softer than the other girl's, higher pitched but gentle.

"It's fucking stupid is what it is."

I blinked in surprise. I was honestly shocked a Potential even knew the word *fuck*, let alone would say it so casually.

"Dahlia," the girl hissed in a warning whisper, though there was amusement there as well. *Dahlia.* A pretty name, I supposed. The flower she was named after grows high in the mountains, near my camp. Some might say that this was a sign of sorts, but I didn't believe in signs. At least, I didn't when I was in that hallway...now, I'm not sure.

"What? You know as well as I do that I will never be picked, regardless of what I wear. We shouldn't even *be* here, Enid." I moved towards the voices, leaning my shoulder against the wall, imagining what might be happening on the other side of the stone. I knew that a small room had been partitioned off for each Potential Consort to dress and prepare in semi-privacy within the ballroom.

Why shouldn't you be here? I wondered, despite myself. As if in answer, the girl—Dahlia—spoke again.

"I'm only here because Lord Burren hated his worthless son and left his entire fortune and title to da instead. We're technically a noble family now, but in what world does a blacksmith's daughter *really* belong here?"

My brows had flown up at that. *A blacksmith?* I wondered...but it couldn't be...could it? I can admit that my interest was piqued, something strange simmering in my blood.

"That may be true, but we *are* noble now. So, you could at least pretend to be a lady."

"Again, I must ask: have you *met* me?" Dahlia asked incredulously.

I'd barely stopped myself from laughing. Enid did laugh, seemingly despite herself.

"Alright, fair point." I heard a rustle of fabric, and when she spoke again, she sounded closer to the other girl. "Mum would roll over in her grave if she could see you right now."

"I think the dress would be the *least* of her worries about me."

"You mean like you in the stables with the Roland twins last week?" Another round of soft laughter, and, damn it, I couldn't curb my curiosity. What in the devil's name had she done in the stable with these Roland twins? And had she done whatever it was with *both* of them?? For reasons I couldn't fathom, I was entirely intrigued, and yet...bothered?

Enid sounded thoughtful when she'd said, "But of *all* the princes to be Choosing today and *this* is the dress you wear..." Dahlia made a sound that was part groan, part sigh.

"I know. I know. But don't read anything into it, Enid. You and your signs from the gods." I could practically hear the girl rolling her eyes. "It doesn't matter what dress I'm wearing, I won't be considered for even a moment as a real option. They're given dossiers on every Potential, you know. He'll take one look at our family history and toss mine into the fire, I assure you. So, nothing to fret about."

It was true that I'd been given information on each of the Potentials. Names, family lineage, any previous Consorts from the house, languages spoken, instruments played, special skills—none of which I gave two shits about. So, I hadn't read any of the files. I honestly wasn't sure how I was going to pick at that point. Perhaps I'd toss a pebble and whomever it hit was the winner. Or loser, I supposed, depending on how one chose to look at it.

Enid didn't sound convinced, giving a simple noncommittal "mmm" but chose to let the topic drop and move on to the more interesting one of *me.*

"So, do you think he'll come back from the war now that he's choosing a Consort?"

"I don't think so," Dahlia had responded. "He's a warrior. He won't be content to be caged in some castle drinking blood-laced whisky or wine, having courtiers fawn over him and companions falling over themselves to get into his bed—well, perhaps he'd like that bit, actually. But he's been free," she added in a wistful sigh, "he couldn't give that up any more than he could stop breathing, I'd bet." I leaned away from the wall, stared at the stone as if I could see past it if I only concentrated hard enough, that I could see the girl on the other side. The girl who, somehow, had me dead to rights without ever meeting me. Leading my army, the thrill of battle, riding my warhorses over the rolling hills: it *was* freedom. A freedom I couldn't imagine giving up. It was a part of me, as much as a limb. I could survive the loss of it, surely, but it would be a constant pain that I could never escape, knowing my men were out there fighting without me.

"Well, I'm sure his Consort will love being toted off to some war camp in the mountains instead of a lavish castle," Enid added with a laugh.

"Oh gods, can you imagine Nicoletta Hargrave out in the Northlands, surrounded by an entire army of vampires? Do'ye think she would shite herself first? Or just die on the spot?"

The girls both laughed, and I felt the corner of my mouth curl upward, partly in amusement at her words and partly because of her accent. The brogue of the mountain lands to the east slipped through a bit thicker as she joked with Enid. I'd always liked the sound of it, something a bit...wild and untamed associated with the lilting melody. The girl couldn't live there, I knew, her accent not nearly thick enough for that to be the case, but perhaps her parents had. Many of my men were Rykhurst born, and hearing the brogue brought back memories of them sitting around campfires, drinking and telling tales, of comradery and friendship...and the bitter tang of loss as I remembered the ones that had been slain over the years.

I suppose it was then that I'd decided that she would be the one, but everything had shifted so completely when she'd entered the ballroom, any doubt or questions melting away like snow at the edge of winter. She was absolutely stunning, more beautiful than I could have imagined, and I watched raptly as she took her turn to be presented, walking down the center of the enormous room, shoulders back, despite her thundering heart giving away her nerves. Flaming red hair and startling green eyes, the color of jade. She was tall for a woman—though she would still probably only reach my chest, if that—and she was lithe and shapely, the material of her dress hugging her curves in a way that made me crave...things. Things I had no business craving, at least not from the likes of her, and things I promptly told myself to *stop fucking thinking about.*

But besides her beauty, I'd taken note of the quiet ferocity and strength about her. The other Consorts reminded me of the delicate petals of a flower, but Dahlia was like a rose: beautiful, but with thorns one should mind.

When she'd moved ever closer to the dais, I'd felt it. Like a small explosion in my chest, everything around me seemed to flare brighter for a moment, rocking me back on my heels. My entire world seemed to tilt and change its focus, now revolving solely around the girl before me. My heart thundered, my fangs shot long without thought, and my blood felt as it was boiling in my veins. At first, I had no idea what was happening, no idea why my body and soul seemed to be pulled to her, as if she were my sole purpose in life, as if she were the sun, as if—

No, I'd thought, horrified by the possibility even as part of me reveled in it, soared with a joy I couldn't explain. *Keeva,* my mind whispered in our ancient language. *Mine.*

No, no, no. I refused to accept the truth of what I'd felt, even as instincts flared to life, instincts I never thought I'd hear inside my mind. My entire being screamed at me, screamed things I didn't want to hear. I forced my body into immobility, forced my mind to quiet. I would not obey these instincts. I would not accept this fate.

I'd been the first Montclare to leave the life of luxury and join the army.

Now I would be the first one to forsake his mate.

She. Is. Not. Mine. I growled the thought, over and over, determined for it to become fact by sheer force of will. Even so, her name left my lips without thought when the Magister asked for my choice. As much as I was determined not to accept this ridiculous idea, I also refused to leave this place without her.

The binding had been a special kind of torture, but if there was one thing I've mastered in my three hundred and fifty years in this world, it's complete discipline over my body. Even so, I barely held myself still, barely stopped from yanking her to me, sinking my fangs into her throat and drinking what the gods had deigned was mine by rights. Her blood was...ecstasy. Never had I tasted anything so sweet, so full of life, so addictive. It drove me nearly mad, made my pulse race and my cock ache and strength flood every inch of me. With but a few drops, I felt as if I could destroy all of the Revenants single handedly.

Mate or not, with the taste of her on my tongue, I could understand why the elders had decreed that taking straight from a living source was to be avoided by the royal line. My baser desires and instincts flared to the front, my fangs shooting ever longer, my nails flaring and sharpening into claws, the urge to bite her tender flesh startling me in its fierceness. My muscles tensed, bulging as my body prepared to strike. I could snap her like a twig, could turn her bones to dust without even trying should I lose control. I heard my brothers chuckling low behind me and I knew that the bastards knew *exactly* what I was thinking and feeling—at least to an extent. I feared that what I was experiencing was even more intense because of the fact that she was...No. Again, I refused to even think it.

I also understood now why so many of my men frequented the blood house in the village to the west of the camp. I was suddenly envious of my men, envious of their lack of title, the lack of expectation to be above such desires and to abstain from ever taking blood directly from a human's body, of doing...other things with a human. The idea of sinking my fangs and my cock into Dahlia...I'd shuddered violently and locked every muscle into place, commanding my body to obey.

In addition to the bliss of her blood, I felt a connection between us snap into place as soon as our glasses were drained. It was as if a cord tethered us together now. A thin cord, given the small amount of blood, but a cord nonetheless. I knew the cord would only strengthen for me each time I drank her blood, and I scowled at the thought. This was going to be difficult enough as it was, but being connected to her in this way was going to make everything that much harder.

"This concludes the Choosing," the Magister's voice rings out now. All of the vampires bow their heads. The other Potentials finally rise from their kneeling positions in front of the dais, some wearing expressions of shock, others of devastation, and still others of disgust and anger. One girl in particular sneers at Dahlia with such contempt that I'm glad that looks cannot kill or my new Consort would be dead on the spot. Instincts flare and for reasons I can't quite understand, I shift to put myself between Dahlia and the girl, to shield her, to...protect her. The girl shifts her gaze upward and whatever she sees on my face has her paling and quickly averting her eyes, scurrying out of the room behind the other humans like a rat fleeing a sinking ship, her heart thundering in her chest, fear thick and acrid in the air.

I turn, intending to say something to Dahlia—though I admittedly don't know what—but the Magister's attendants are already dragging her away from the dais and out of a side door, the girl looking utterly dazed. From my blood? Or from the situation in general? Her entire world has just been upended, after all, of course she might be a bit out of sorts. Sebastian clamps a hand on my shoulder as I stare after my Consort. The word feels strange in my mind. I will not even *think* the other. She is my Consort only, nothing more.

"See, not so bad, was it? You chose well, brother. She's quite stunning. And that *dress*." Sebastian shakes his head, squeezing my shoulder. "A bit unorthodox, of course, but...my gods." Princes do not engage in physical acts with mortals—at least not officially. Unofficially, I know damned well that plenty of them partake, it's simply not spoken about and hidden away—but that doesn't mean we can't...appreciate the view. And it's true: the dress is unlike what any other Potential had worn. It was *evocative*. While the others wore white or pale shades of pink or blue, in tulle and gossamer, flowing away from their bodies and making them look like, in my humble opinion, large puffed pastries, Dahlia's dress was midnight blue silk that flowed over her body like water, hugging every curve as if had been painted there by an artist's skilled hand. The straps over her shoulders connected with links of metal, and the front dipped daringly between her breasts. At first look, it appeared that an overlay of black lace ran along the bodice and down the skirts, flowing out behind her in a small train, but upon closer inspection, I found that it was thin, intricately designed chainmail. *A dress befitting a blacksmith's daughter*, I muse. *And a dress befitting the mate of a warlord*...I scowl at that, banishing the thought away.

"She is of a new noble family, so she was not raised in this life. But," Sebastian studies me for a long moment, searching my eyes in that way he has, "I think that might suit you perfectly. And hells, if she has more garments like that dress, sharing a cabin may not be so bad..." My brother waggles his eyebrows in a manner that's very unbecoming of the head of the Montclare Clan, grinning like a horse's ass.

"You could have warned me about the blood," I hiss, changing the subject from the way Dahlia had looked in that sin of a gown, and ducking out of his grip to shove him hard in the shoulder.

Sebastian chuckles. "Now where would the fun be in that?" I narrow my eyes but that only makes Sebastian's grin widen. "We knew that you could handle it, oh great warlord." I roll my eyes and he laughs, that deep, booming laugh that warms my soul. Fiona bounds up then and immediately frowns at my hair.

"I cannot believe you went through your first Choosing looking like that. I could have—"

"No, you couldn't have, Fi. My hair cannot be tamed."

"Just like your heart," she says with a roll of her golden eyes. She wraps her arms around me and I hold her close, squeezing her tightly. I've missed her. I know I should come visit more often, but it's hard for me to be away from my men, to keep the war from my mind for any real amount of time. As if reading my thoughts, Fiona sighs.

"Will you stay and celebrate?" she asks, though she already knows the answer.

"I want to get back to my men."

"Why you choose to spend all your time among smelly, dirty vampire soldiers is beyond me," Fi says with a dramatic shudder.

"*I* am a smelly, dirty vampire soldier, dear sister," I remind her, placing a swift kiss to her temple.

"I am proud of you, little brother," Sebastian tells me with a ruffle of my hair. "Your Consort is being escorted home to collect her belongings and then she'll be brought back for you—"

"I'll go to her," I interrupt. Sebastian's brow furrows and Fiona rolls her eyes again.

"Do you not know who her father is, Bastian?" she asks. Of course she would know. Fi would have studied the dossiers on all of the Potentials, probably knows their family histories going back centuries and learned it just for fun. She's always been the scholar of the family, retaining information in ways I can't even fathom. Bastian thinks on it for a moment and then his eyes light with under-standing.

"Ah, *Clayburn*. The smith. Of course you want to meet the man in person. Is that why you chose her, then? Because of her father?"

"Partly," I admit, though it isn't completely true. It's a perk, to be sure, but I'd chosen Dahlia for a host of other reasons that I need more time to fully analyze and understand, reasons I most certainly can't explain to Sebastian. To tell the leader of the Clan that I'd found my mate in a human? He'd be...concerned to say the least. It's unheard of. Mates are *never* human. The loss of a mate is too traumatic for a vampire to bear, his or her life and soul too entwined with the other to continue alone. Humans are entirely too fragile, their life spans too short. The gods would never play such a cruel joke as to pair a prince with a human. Except, apparently, they have... if I choose to accept it, which of course, I won't.

Of course, if somehow a mate *was* human, they could be turned... but the catalyst for turning is death. It would be almost too much for any vampire to handle, even for the short time between death and the transition, but princes felt things stronger than other vampires. It would be agony to wait, to feel the loss of his mate, even for a few hours.

And the turning doesn't always work.

I shake myself, not wanting to continue down this particular line of thinking.

"I wonder if the great smith has received all of your declarations of love in the post," Sebastian muses in a teasing voice. "Perhaps he'll agree to be your Consort in his daughter's place."

I shove my favorite brother harder this time and he laughs heartily.

"Fuck off, Bastian," I mutter, though I can't help the small smile that curls my lips. For all that I love my camp and my soldiers, love the mountains and the snow and the thrill of battle, I do miss my family (most of them—Ahmed can fuck off) dearly. Though I plan to go collect Dahlia, I take a few minutes to visit with the rest of the family. I meet several nieces and nephews for the first time—the fact that they aren't infants makes me realize how long it's been since I've made an effort to see most of my siblings. I have the excuse of fighting a constant war that keeps all of them, the entire *continent*, safe, but I know that I should do better. But, in truth, I've always felt so different than any of them, so on the outside. Bastian and Fi are the only ones who seem to actually understand my choices and my decision to join the fight rather than take the mantle of a true royal

—and don't judge me for them. Even still, I should at least write to the others more often, send gifts for the children.

"I'll come visit soon, to check in on…things," he says, slapping me on the back.

"Well, I won't come visit that terrible camp, but if you decide to go to Ashcliff, I will gladly come see you there," Fi says with a pleading smile. She's always adored my manor—a castle, really, I suppose, but I hate using that term—overlooking the Lyranian Sea. I rarely go there, haven't been in…almost twenty years, I think with a frown. *Perhaps Dahlia would like…*

I shake myself, pushing the thought away.

"If I make a trip to the coast, I will let you know," I promise her. "And my camp is not terrible," I add. She gives me a look that says she would rather lose a limb than spend time there and I smile. "I'll see you soon, brother," I tell Bastian. I glance towards the rest of my siblings and catch Ahmed glaring my way. I glare right back, itching for him to try something. Bastian follows my gaze and rolls his eyes.

"It was more than two hundred years ago, Alaric. You've got to let it go."

"I most certainly do not. Isn't that one of the perks of being immortal? I can hold a grudge for all of eternity if my prick of a brother deserves it?" He sighs and shakes his head, knowing I won't be moved from this. Let *him* be buried alive in fifty feet of snow for *weeks* by his own brother and see if he's quick to forgive. Ahmed claimed later that it was a harmless prank, but I honestly believe he was trying to kill me. *All over a barmaid who found her way into my bed instead of his*, I think with a roll of my eyes.

"Goodbye, Bastian," I say again, hugging him tightly once more time.

"Good luck," he calls with a laugh as I stride off the dais and through the palace, suddenly desperate to find my…Consort.

CHAPTER 4
DAHLIA

"I can't believe it," Enid says for the tenth time in as many minutes.

"I know," I sigh, putting my sketchpads into the large trunk on top of my books and clothes. Apparently new ones will be made and sent to the camp for me, ones befitting a prince's Consort, I imagine, but I still don't like the idea of leaving home without anything of my own. I look around my room, the one that, despite having plenty of space in our new home, I still share with my sister as we always have. I'm leaving it forever today. I'll never lie in the bed across from Enid and talk in whispers well into the night again. I won't be there when she wakes from nightmares or when she can't sleep because of storms rolling through. *I won't be here for her.* Tears prick my eyes, but they aren't tears of sorrow. They're tears of absolute rage, surging hot and bitter in my chest. How had this happened? *Why* had this happened? It doesn't make sense! And it isn't fucking *fair*!

"I don't know what he was thinking!" I snap, slamming the lid of the trunk down. "Why would he...He's so...How could he...UGH!" I kick the trunk several times while I scream in frustration, and then finally sit heavily on top of it with a long exhale as the anger drains out of me as quickly as it had come. Enid is there then, wrapping her arms tightly around me, rocking us slowly back and forth.

"It will be ok, Lia," Enid says quietly. "You'll be treated like a queen, even within a war camp." I pull away, scrubbing at my eyes before the tears can fall.

"It's not *me* I'm worried about, Enid." I search my sister's eyes. They're warm brown, like melted chocolate, just like our mother's had been. I'd gotten our father's coloring with my green eyes and red hair. *My little firebrand*, he'd always said with a doting smile. I'd driven our mother crazy with my antics—gods rest her soul—with my lack of "feminine sensibilities," whatever the hells that means, but da and I have always been thick as thieves.

He hadn't been surprised that I'd wanted to spend my days beside him at the forge, had never thought me strange or decided it was not something for girls. He taught me everything I wanted to know, let me try and fail and try again. He'd made me strong and fearless and headstrong, just like him, but I am who I am because of my father. I can't imagine not seeing him every day, not working beside him in the shop, not seeing his eyes shine with pride when I show him some new design or when I best the boys at the tavern in dice.

My chest feels like it's going to split open, my heart bleeding and broken.

"I know," Enid says with a smile. "But we'll be ok, too, you know." She takes a deep breath. "I know you've always felt like you had to take care of me, Lia, and for a long time, you did, but you don't have to anymore. Let me be the older sister and worry about you for a change. Da and I will both be alright, I promise."

I let out a long, shaking breath and try to smile. "I know you will. At least we have a cook now and you don't have to rely on da's... concoctions." I wrinkle my nose and Enid pretends to vomit, both of us laughing at the memories of our father's awful attempts at cooking. Gods bless him, he *loves* it, but the results are often less than appetizing. In fact, they usually aren't actually edible at all and Enid and I made games out of finding creative ways to hide the evidence so as not to hurt his feelings. One of the best things about becoming noble was that we inherited Lord Burren's staff, including Mrs. Drury, the phenomenal cook. She politely, but firmly, told da that she would be taking over the cooking duties from now on when we first arrived and he'd attempted to make something with a chicken that turned out somehow burnt and raw at the same time.

Our laughter slowly fades and Enid sighs.

"It should be me," she says softly.

"Hey, none of that."

"It's true. If I had pure blood, I would have been the one at the Choosing today, not you." Enid is the oldest by barely a year, so technically she's right: she should have been the first child put to the Choosing, but when she was young, she fell very, very ill. She was diagnosed with a disease of the blood that, thankfully, was able to be treated, but she would never be eligible to be a Consort because of it. Which is just fine with me. She may be older, but I have always been the one to take care of her. She was so frail for so many years, I always felt so protective, like it was my job to watch over her and make her stronger somehow, pushing my own strength into her by sheer force of will.

So, I'm happy she'll never have to go through this, that I will be the first and only Clayburn to ever be a Consort, but gods will I miss her. I pull on the end of Enid's braid until she meets my gaze and, after a few moments of silent communication between us, she gives me a small smile, accepting that there isn't anything either of us can do. Da always says that the only way forward is forward. So, we'll move forward and make the best of whatever is to come.

"I'm going to go find da," I say, standing and brushing the tears from my eyes.

The goodbye with my father is quiet and reserved, and quite possibly the hardest thing I've ever done. He's a big man, his arms and chest bulky and muscled from years at the forge, with a thick beard and braids in his long, red hair, the way of the old Rykhurst warriors. You wouldn't know by the look of him that he's as sweet as a kitten, and as gentle as one with everything but the metal in his shop.

I can barely speak, but da seems to know the words I'm trying to say without having to hear them.

"I'll miss ye too, little firebrand," he says, voice thick and rough with emotion, his rumbling brogue making me feel safe and warm. "But ye'll be taken care of, I'm sure of it." He shucks me under the chin, forcing my eyes upward. "We knew this was a possibility. When I took the title, we knew..."

I let out a rough exhale. "I know. I just...well, I didn't expect it to ever actually happen is all."

"Aye," he says, nodding, "I know it's a shock, and I'll miss ye with every fiber of my being, but all will be well. I have faith." He eyes me until I relax slightly, nodding. If he's sure of this, if he's able to be strong and accept this, then I can too. "I'll be right back. I've got something for ye." He grins as my eyes light up with excitement and suspicion. I adore surprises, but Arwan Clayburn is known as a lover of jokes and tricks. He could come back with a heartfelt gift that will make me cry...or something ridiculous to make me laugh. The odds are evenly matched on the outcome.

While I wait, I stand before one of the high work tables lining the walls of the large room. *My* work table. When we'd inherited Lord Burren's wealth and title, da had been able to build a much bigger and better shop, hiring one of his apprentices on as another smith, and taking on several new apprentices as well. It had always been his dream and the fact that it had become a reality was all I could ever want. He'd made a special work area within it, just for me and my projects.

I run my fingers over the polished table top, thinking on the hours upon hours I've spent here, the heat and the sounds of clanging and the smells so much a part of me that I don't know how I'll survive without them. I pick up a gauntlet I've been working on, turning it over in my hands as I squeeze my eyes shut against the pain.

"He made my sword, you know." I gasp and whirl, dropping the gauntlet. "Your father, I mean," Alaric Montclare clarifies from the doorway. He's changed from his formal dress, now clad in what looks like military gear: black leather pants and vest over a black tunic, a weapons belt slung around his hips and the hilt of a giant sword peeking out from behind his back. I grip the top of the work table behind me, my pulse thundering as he slowly makes his way into the large space. The blood we shared during the Choosing has connected us in some way, I think. His mere presence here has my heart racing and the blood in my veins singing, a longing to be near him rearing inside my chest...*like a hound longs to be near its master*, I think coldly. That's what I am now. His pet. His property. The thought cools some of that longing, but there are still embers burning beneath the smothered flames.

He eyes me curiously as I try to regain my composure and bend to quickly scoop up the gauntlet.

"You need not fear me," he says smoothly.

"I'm not afraid," I say a little too quickly, my words belied by my thundering heart that I know he can hear. He arches one dark brow, but otherwise doesn't comment. I lick my dry lips and swallow hard. "What are you—" I stop, remembering myself at the last moment, and instead bow my head. "Your highness," I amend, "I was told I'd be brought to you after I collected my things. I...I didn't expect to see you here."

"I am not like the other princes," he says, ignoring the rest. "I care for no titles other than High General, and that is only for my men. You..." He takes a moment, almost as if he's steadying himself, before he speaks again. "You may just call me Alaric."

I have no idea what to do with that. I never imagined even being in the presence of one of the princes, let alone calling him by his given name. I wonder yet again if maybe I'm dreaming, that this is all in my head and I'll wake up any minute.

He begins to stroll around the space, inspecting tools and running his long fingers along weapons and scrap pieces of metal. I watch him in silence, my pulse racing as I take the opportunity to openly study him. He's utterly terrifying and incomprehensibly handsome at the same time. Tall, with a broad chest and shoulders, thick, black hair in a devil-may-care disarray that makes him even more attractive. It's the kind of hair that you long to run your fingers through while you do all manner of sinful things—and looks like perhaps someone already has. It's unsettlingly how gorgeous this man is.

His features are hard and sharp, as if he's a sculpture brought to life. He looks to have stopped aging around thirty-five or so, but I know he's much older than that, three hundred at least, maybe more. Despite him looking regal and breathtaking in his finery at the Choosing, I have to admit that the dark fighting leathers suit him much better. There's a rugged wildness about him that makes my breath shallow and my blood heat. Something about him calls to me in a way I can't describe. It has to be the blood we shared, doesn't it? Or is it just his preternatural allure, the vampire prince in him working its wiles on my mind and body?

"Alaric," I say, testing out the name. His eyes seem to darken slightly at that, the gold flashing a deep amber for a moment. "I thought I was to be delivered back to the palace. Why..." I trail off as he runs his fingers gently, almost reverently, along the blade of a sword hanging from a hook on the wall, and realization dawns. "Oh. Of course, you want to meet my father. He's just inside, I can go fetch him for you."

"What's that you've got there?" Alaric asks, gesturing to my hands.

"It's nothing," I say hastily, moving to put the gauntlet down, but suddenly he's here, right in front of me, only a few inches separating us. I gasp in surprise, eyes flying wide. *Dear gods he's fast.* Vampires are all fast, of course, faster and stronger than humans, but Alaric is like lightning. He hadn't made a single sound, just seeming to materialize before me in an instant. I have a feeling seeing a prince using his full abilities would be something to behold—and to fear. No wonder he managed to drive the Revenant army almost totally out of Braxhelm. No wonder his very name strikes fear in the hearts of any who hear it. No wonder I'm trembling ever so slightly at his nearness.

He plucks the gauntlet from my fingers, turning it over in his hands. As if to himself he murmurs, "beautiful workmanship. It's light as a feather, and yet—" He flicks his hand, his nail suddenly claw-like and sharp as a razor, and rakes it down the side of the gauntlet. "—nearly impenetrable. Remarkable." His brow furrows. "What's that there?"

It takes me an embarrassingly long moment to find my voice, unnerved as I am with him being so close and with his blood singing in my veins, but I somehow manage to say, "it's a mechanism to release a set of hidden blades. If you press just there," I point to the small release, nearly unnoticeable "you can see."

He does, his eyes alighting and his lips *almost* quirking into a smile, I think.

"Clever." He studies the gauntlet closer. "The blades are completely undetectable. And I assume when worn, the mechanism could be released with a certain movement of the wrist." I blink, pleasantly surprised by his deduction.

"Yes, exactly." He nods and hands it back. I take it, careful not to touch his fingers as I do, very aware of his body and how close he is to me. I inch backwards as I put the gauntlet back on the table.

"I don't suppose your father would be willing to part with them? And perhaps build several more sets?"

I should say *of course, anything for the High General and a Prince.* But instead, when I open my fool mouth, what comes out is, "It's mine, actually."

Alaric's brows rise in surprise and he tilts his head slightly, in question. I inwardly kick myself, cursing so colorfully my mum is definitely aghast in her grave. Being so close to him, alone with him, is…unnerving. I'm not thinking clearly. But he stares at me, waiting for an answer, so I sigh and go on.

"My design. My work. I've been learning from my father since I was old enough to know not to jump headlong into the forge," I say with a small shrug. Why am I telling him all this? I blame being so close to him, the strange connection between us, my blood practically screaming at me to move closer to him, to do…other things I dare not give thought to. What is wrong with me? Before I can stop myself, I add, "Discrete weaponry is a bit of a hobby, you could say."

I've always been fascinated with the idea of unassuming weapons, things that may not appear to be a threat but suddenly are. Perhaps it goes back to Enid and her illness. She was often teased and taunted by the other children when we were young and I always wished that she could feel as strong as I knew in my heart she could be, to have those boys who pulled her hair or pushed her in the mud believe her to be as weak and delicate as they imagined—and then have them regret it.

I've designed corsets and vests outfitted with hidden sheaths for daggers, hair pins that doubled as throwing stars, walking canes with spring-loaded swords hidden within them, parasols with razor sharp edges hidden beneath lace and silk. Of course, I have no idea how to actually *use* any of those weapons, so they aren't exactly helpful for me, personally, but still, I love the art of them, the way my mind seems to relax as I sketch my designs. And da has even sold a few things to some of his patrons, so it's not as if all my tinkering is for nothing.

Alaric studies me for a long moment, as one might study a particularly interesting looking insect. His face remains as unreadable as the surface of a lake, no clues at all as to what may be churning beneath. He opens his mouth to speak, but da walks in. Before I can even let out my breath, Alaric is suddenly a few feet farther away, moving again like lightning.

Da's face is stoic, the set of his shoulders tense. He has a small box in his hands and he sits it gently on the table behind him. He bows to Alaric, eyeing him sternly when he rises. What does a man say to a vampire prince who was taking his daughter off to a war camp to drink her blood? *Thank you? Best of luck? Fuck you?* Alaric surprises me by speaking first.

"Duke Clayburn. I wish we had met under...different circumstances, but I wish to extend my thanks." Da's thick brows arch upward in clear surprise.

"Thanks?" he repeats, confused.

"I'm not sure if you remember, but you forged my blade—"

"Night's Fury," he finishes, eying the hilt over Alaric's right shoulder. "Aye, I remember every sword I've ever forged, your highness." He extends his hand and Alaric unsheathes the blade from his back in a quick, practiced motion that's smooth and graceful...and oddly attractive. I realize I'm biting my lip before quickly shaking myself. *What in the seven hells is wrong with me?* I rub the back of my neck and am entirely grateful that no one is paying me much attention at the moment. I know it must be because of the blood we shared, but it doesn't make it any less embarrassing.

Alaric inclines his head as he presents the sword to da, hilt first.

My eyes widen as I take in the sword. I've heard stories of the blade, of course, everyone has, but I've never actually laid eyes on it. Da had forged it years before I was born. It's gorgeous, with the grip and cross-guard black as pitch, the wolf sigil of Alaric's Coven on the pommel, eyes set with gleaming rubies and teeth bared in a fearsome snarl. The blade itself is such a dark gray that it's nearly black as midnight, with silver stars inlaid along the blade. *Real* silver.

Silver is poisonous to vampires and Revenants alike, could even be deadly, but most of it had been used during the bloodiest parts of the war. The remaining stores, small as they are, are closely guarded. The fact that Alaric commissioned a sword with actual silver in the blade is...well, the barkeep at the tavern would have said that Alaric's bollocks were as big as boulders for it. I have to agree. It could harm his enemies, of course, but it could just as easily harm him, *kill* him even, if someone managed to turn his own blade against him.

I watch, fascinated, as da takes the sword and looks down the long blade. The lights spark off of the dark and light metals, the wolf's eyes glinting brightly. I idly wonder how the two men can possibly even hold the massive thing, let alone how someone might actually wield it in battle. It's nearly as tall as I am and I can only imagine how much it must weigh.

Da twists it this way and that before running his hand along the metal, fingers gently skating over the stars.

"This may well be the most perfectly balanced blade I've ever made, and I daresay the most beautiful." He hands the sword back to Alaric, and he quickly slides it home with a quiet *schnik* sound. "I hope it has served ye well."

"It has. Its name is enough to strike fear into the heart of our enemies." Da's lips curls at that. He's always been proud of his work, and having it complimented by the High General, the famed Alaric Montclare, is something indeed, regardless of the strange situation we've found ourselves in.

"And the bearer of the blade would have little tae do with that, I'm sure," da muses, seemingly untroubled by speaking with a prince, by having him so near. Alaric doesn't smile, but his features soften slightly, perhaps the *ghost* of a smile curling his lips ever so slightly. I wonder if he *ever* smiles. Perhaps when he's cutting down Revenants on the battlefield.

"Only a little, I assure you." Da grins at that, chuckling lightly, but Alaric's features harden once again and he seems to steel himself. "I...Your daughter will be safe with me. I vow it." My mouth drops open and I realize that I'm openly gawking, but I can't stop myself. A prince is not only conversing with my father as if they were equals, but is *assuring him of my safety*? Alaric doesn't owe us such a thing. He doesn't owe us *anything*. Why is he doing it?

I huff out a tiny laugh, one so soft that my father doesn't notice, but Alaric cuts his eyes to me for a moment and I'm sure he does. I realize that he truly doesn't know how to act like a prince. He might be one in title and blood, but he isn't one in his heart, doesn't hold with the notion that he's above anyone and everyone because of the family he'd been born into. I can't deny that I like that about him, that it makes this whole ordeal slightly easier to bear for some reason. We're strangely alike in that respect and I feel that connection between us seem to tighten, almost as if someone's tugged the cord, trying to pull me closer to him.

Da takes a deep, shuddering breath. He looks to me, a sad smile on his lips and so much love and tenderness in his green eyes, so like my own, that my heart splinters. He turns back to Alaric, studying the vampire for what feels like an eternity, and Alaric lets him, though of course he doesn't have to.

"If she has tae go, I'm glad it is with you and no' one of the others," da finally says quietly. Alaric's brow raises ever so slightly in surprise, but he otherwise shows nothing. He inclines his head and the two of them begin to talk battles and weapons, da pulling out parchment and pen to write down some requisition requests for Alaric and his men. There are other smiths that supply the bulk of the weapons to the army, of course, at least one at every camp, but the High General and his lieutenants get special items. I slip out of the shop without another word, deciding to come back after they're done to say my final goodbyes, but I swear I can feel Alaric's eyes on me as I go.

And damn it all, my heart races because of it.

CHAPTER 5

ALARIC

The journey back to the Northlands takes us five fucking days. I'm not used to traveling with anyone but my men and most certainly not accustomed to having to slow my pace to accommodate oversized carriages full of who knows what. The Magister had tried to send an entire cadre of maids and butlers and even a hair attendant. What in the actual *fuck* is a hair attendant? Literally a being whose entire purpose in life is to attend to my Consort's hair? It's utter insanity. I made the concession to take a Consort, but I will not have such other nonsense in my camp, duty and honor be damned. Dahlia will have her Keeper and her personal chef to attend to her meals, but that is all. And honestly, I'm fairly sure Dahlia wouldn't want much else if she had the choice. She doesn't strike me as the type to *want* to be waited on hand and foot. She'll have all that she requires and will be treated with all her due respect, but I must draw the line somewhere—and I draw it at a fucking hair attendant.

The Magister looked aghast when I'd made my decree, clearly uncomprehending how a Consort could possibly survive without such things, but after Sebastian's blessing, he let it slide.

I haven't spoken a word to Dahlia since we left Astoria's Keep, have barely even seen her really over the course of the trip. To say that I'm conflicted and confused is an understatement on the most epic of scales. Part of me longs to be near her, the pull nearly undeniable, but the other part refuses to accept this fate and is cursing the gods to the depths of all seven hells. Why would this happen? How can it even be possible? It has to be a mistake. Perhaps something went wrong during the binding and whatever these confused instincts are will fade in time...though I don't see how that's likely if I'm going to continue taking her blood. I suppose I could simply continue with the replicated blood I've been surviving on for the last nearly four hundred years, but even as the thought forms, my mind rejects it. I sigh, admitting that part of me wants to take her blood. Not just wants, but *aches* for it.

I'm beyond irritable by the time we stop for the final night before arriving at camp tomorrow. Partly because I do need blood, and partly because the reality of the situation is settling upon me like a thick, suffocating blanket. She's going to be a part of my life, in some capacity, for the foreseeable future. Regardless of the fact that my instincts are demanding that I do it anyway, I vowed to her father that she would be safe with me, that I would take care of her. And I keep my vows. Always.

But humans are so fucking *fragile*. I'd mused on that fact as we'd ridden, my mind wandering. Sickness, injury, drowning, an ill-timed cross beneath a snow-covered peak. Hells, even a fucking *bee sting*. Any little thing could kill her kind so easily. And if she *is* somehow truly my mate, my life is now tied to hers. I won't be able to survive without her...

No. Fuck that. I'm Alaric Montclare. I'm the greatest warlord in history. If anyone could survive the death of their mate—a mate I don't plan to even acknowledge, mind you—it would be me. Even still, I'll do my best to protect her, to uphold my vow and keep her safe.

"I want a list of your recommendations for a personal guard for my Consort," I tell Elias, the phrase still feeling strange on my tongue. "Four—no six."

Elias, my most trusted and valued lieutenant and friend, nods. He'd ridden to meet us at the inn, knowing that I would be anxious for updates from the camp. And, knowing him, he was dying to get a look at my new Consort before anyone else.

"Six seems...excessive..." I arch a brow, telling him that I'm not in the mood, and he holds his hands up in surrender. "Of course. I'll have a list ready tomorrow upon your arrival."

"Good. And the additions to my cabin have been made?"

"Yes, all as you requested—with a few changes."

"Elias," I say, half warning, half exasperation.

"She'll love them, I promise. Who has more experience with human women and what they want and need?" Elias arches a golden brow, smirking, and I grind my teeth. The bastard is right—I know next to nothing about human women, while Elias spends plenty of time surrounded by them in blood houses, doing all manner of things that, up until five days ago, I had no interest in.

"Go away," I growl, which only makes Elias' smirk turn into a full-fledged grin.

"As you wish," he says with an exaggerated bow. "I'll see you tomorrow back at camp and we can...catch up more fully." He gives me a pointed look and I know he wants to know all the gory details about the Choosing and my new Consort. I can't tell him about the potential mate issue, of course, but since I'm going to refuse the bond, it doesn't matter. I wonder how many times I need to say that to myself before it becomes even close to true.

Elias rises and claps me on the shoulder before leaving the room, nearly knocking into Dahlia in the hallway just outside the door.

"Oh!" she exclaims. I shoot to my feet, but Elias reaches out to steady her easily.

"Alright then?" Elias asks, giving her an easy smile. Her eyes widen slightly, her cheeks flushing, and I can hear her heartbeat speed its rhythm. I can't say that I'm surprised—all women, mortal or otherwise, nearly faint at the sight of Elias. Golden hair, square jaw, eyes as blue as the ocean after a storm—but I *am* surprised by the surge of jealous annoyance that rips through me.

"Y-yes," she breathes.

"Have the men from your list assembled for inspection upon our arrival," I call, a hard edge to my voice that I rarely use with Elias.

"Of course, sir," Elias says, unfazed, giving me a quick, appraising look before inclining his head. He flashes Dahlia another quick smile—and a fucking *wink*, making me clench my fists so tightly my knuckles turn white—and heads down the hallway, whistling as he goes. If I didn't love the bastard so much, I might hate him. Dahlia blinks and watches him go, eyes glued down the hallway.

"Is there something you needed?" I bark, making the girl flinch. Fuck, *I really am irritable*. I should—

"I-I was told you might need...blood?" she stammers, pulling her gaze away from Elias' retreating form and stepping cautiously through the doorway. I can see the pulse point racing at her throat, and my fangs extend, practically throbbing with the longing for blood. *Fuck*. That hasn't happened in centuries, not since I was a boy, learning to quell my natural instincts to hunt and feed.

"Come in then," I say gruffly. I do, in fact, need blood, and I'd better get used to this, I suppose. Perhaps it could improve my mood. I pluck an empty tankard from the table and beckon her forward. She obeys, the fabric of her skirt swishing as she walks. I slowly rake my gaze over her. The dress is simple, nothing like what she wore to the Choosing, but form-fitting, the tight bodice giving her body an hour-glass-shape that's admittedly attractive. *Exceedingly* attractive. My eyes linger on her chest, the delicate lace wringing the edge of the neckline rising and falling against her sun-kissed skin with every shallow breath she takes. I yank my gaze away as unwanted thoughts flood my mind, making my mood even more foul, but just as I look away, she stumbles, her toe catching the end of her skirt. I reach out and catch her before she tumbles into the table and she gasps, clutching my bicep as I steady her. Our gazes meet and though there's a bit of fear in her eyes, there's something else there as well. Something unexpected and unwelcome. Part of my mind taunts me, calling me a lying son of a devil: *Unwelcome my fucking ass.*

But princes are not supposed to fuck their Consorts. Other vampires sleep with humans, of course, but never the royals. All vampires are strong and can easily kill a human, but the Montclare royals are stronger still. The risk of death is far too great where we're concerned, and so we do not drink from, or fuck, humans. *Officially.* I know it happens and I know how often a mess has had be to cleaned and covered up when one of my siblings felt the need to stray from the decrees of our father. But even though the others might do it, I never have.

And that has never bothered me, has really never even entered my thoughts before this moment. My men go to the blood houses, drinking and fucking any human who is willing and amenable, but I've never once longed to join them. But now, all I can think of is sinking my fangs into this human's neck, exploring every inch of her body with my fingers and tongue, hearing her cries in my ears as her blood slides down my throat and my cock slides into—

I shake myself, forcing the thoughts away. Grinding my teeth, I let her go quickly, not entirely trusting myself to keep my hands on her without doing more. Much, *much* more. I manage to remain gentle as I push her away, though my roiling thoughts are anything but. She clears her throat quietly, blinking away whatever had been in those piercing eyes a moment ago.

"Do you always have this much trouble walking?" I snap. "You nearly tumble in the hallway and now you can't do something as simple as walk across the room?"

She blinks again and then narrows her eyes, the green seeming to burn, all vulnerability and fear gone in an instant. *Interesting...*

"First off, *he* ran into *me*, thank you. And I can walk perfectly fine, it's this fuc—this dress," she quickly corrects, stopping herself from cursing. It *almost* improves my mood by a fraction. She pulls her lips in as if she can't believe she's just let the words escape, as if she can't believe she snapped back at a prince, at *her* prince, but, to my surprise, she doesn't cower. She has fire inside her, that's for certain. I find it commendable…and, yes, attractive. Exceedingly so. I can admit that much. Finding her attractive isn't against any law. *Technically, bedding her isn't against an actual* law *either, it's more just an understood expectation…*

Get a hold on your fucking thoughts, I snap silently to myself. I need to stop thinking about fucking this girl, because the more I think, the more vivid my imagination becomes, the more my instincts fire and scream, demanding that I claim her, sink my fangs deep into her tender flesh while I sink my co—

"What is wrong with the dress?" I ask, cooly, stopping the thought in its tracks once more. She clenches her jaw several times and seems to be trying to rein in her temper before replying.

"I'm not used to wearing them," she finally says, equally cooly.

"Then why are you wearing one now?" I ask, too tired and annoyed to hide my confusion, brow furrowing. A small v forms between her own brows as she glances down at the garment in question, running her hands down her front.

"I was told that I should—" I hold up a hand up and roll my eyes, realization hitting.

"Your Keeper is used to Consorts in the castles, Consorts of true princes," I say with a shake of my head. "Wear whatever the fuck you like, and tell your Keeper that is my decree. In fact, trousers will be much easier for you in the Northlands and within the camp. They'll keep you warmer and when the rains come, you won't want to be dragging around a dress with mud coating the skirt everywhere you go." I suppose I'll have to speak with her Keeper and ensure that proper clothing is acquired for her, not the typical wardrobe of a Consort. Had no one thought of how impractical a bunch of ball gowns would be in a fucking war camp?

"Oh," she says, clearly surprised. "Alright then."

We stand in silence for a moment. Surprisingly, it isn't entirely uncomfortable, but as I watch her pulse beat at the base of her throat, my fangs ache and I'm reminded of my need. I gesture impatiently for her hand and she offers it up, a curious look on her face. She doesn't seem afraid, merely interested and maybe a bit nervous. I know that simply being around me is unnerving for her, as it is for most humans who don't routinely encounter the royals. All vampires give off something unworldly that humans can instinctively perceive, instinctively know to fear, but the royals are something else entirely. We are the apex of all predators, innate power flowing in our veins that makes humans both enamored and terrified.

I use my nail to slice her wrist, trying my best to be gentle and cause her the least amount of pain as possible. She hisses in a sharp breath but doesn't try to pull away. My mouth waters and my fangs throb as the sweet, heady scent of her blood hits me. I've never smelled human blood so alluring, so full of life. I watch as it spills into the tankard, commanding my body to remain still and under complete and total control. I make sure not to take too much—I know that it will take time before her body grows accustomed to the loss. Even now, her skin pales and she sways slightly.

"Sit," I command, voice rough and full of authority as I release her hand. I suppose I'm used to addressing my soldiers and wait for her to flinch away, or hells, maybe push back, but she obeys, blinking rapidly as she sinks heavily into the chair. Perhaps I took too much? I quickly grab a cloth and press it to her wrist. She holds it there as I step away, looking a little dazed. I rummage in one of my bags for the tonic the healers had given me for just this purpose. I uncork the bottle, the sweet scent of honey and the spice of underlying herbs hitting my nose.

"Drink this." She takes the bottle, eyeing me a little warily. "It will help with the dizziness you're feeling from the blood loss. That will lessen over time, I'm told, and there are pills that will help replenish your blood more quickly. A supply of them should be in with your things packed in one of the carriages."

She nods and drinks, wrinkling her nose as she swallows and then glaring at me as if I tricked her into drinking poison. I almost laugh. Gods, the nonstop war inside my mind between irritation and interest, between amusement and loathing, between instincts and what I refuse to accept, is making my head ache. I feel a bit as if I've been caught within one of the deadly cyclones out at sea, being thrown this way and that and back again, never able to find my footing before being thrown yet again. I don't know how to act or what to say or think or do. And I don't like not knowing.

"The whole thing," I say, gesturing to the bottle. She sighs but lifts the vial to her lips once more.

"So, it's true then," she says quietly, taking another small sip, "that the princes don't take straight from the flesh."

"Do *you* sink your teeth directly into the cow or chicken?" I ask, sarcasm thick in my voice.

"Only when I'm *really* hungry," she replies dryly, almost absently, and I smother a laugh. She rubs her temples, still pale, a thin sheen of sweat covering her forehead. I frown, wondering if there's something more wrong than simple blood loss. Shouldn't the tonic have started working by now? What is this incessant worry clawing at my throat at the idea of something being wrong with her, or her being hurt? *Fucking hells.*

"Why not? I know other vampires do."

"And how, exactly, do you know that?"

She huffs out a laugh. "I didn't grow up in the noble district, as I'm sure you know. I'm well aware of what goes on in a blood house."

"Are you now?" I ask in a silky voice, despite myself, brow arched in something dangerously close to teasing. Some color comes back to her cheeks as she blushes.

"I mean, I'm not *well* aware. I've never...I mean, I haven't *personally*...but I've, uh, heard stories...maybe spied a bit from a tree outside..." I tilt my head, surprised by her confession. Surprised and amused and maybe even a little aroused, though I can't explain why. Her eyes fly wide and she puts her head in her hands, whispering, "I cannot believe I just said that out loud."

I turn away to hide the smile pulling on my lips. I walk to the hearth and stare out of the window just beside it into the darkness for a long moment. I turn back to her, leaning a shoulder against the mantle. I'm honestly not used to conversing with humans casually, save the few that work in the camp, but even then we aren't, what does Elias call it? Shooting the shit. But one of the many reasons I'd chosen Dahlia (at least the reasons that I'll admit to at this point) was because I thought I might be able to hold a conversation with her without wanting to claw my own eyes out. So far, we've managed fairly well. The few moments we spent in her father's shop after the ceremony had been…pleasant. I originally thought that I'd keep myself closed off from her completely, but with her here now, I find that I…want to talk to her? *Fuck. Might as well give it a shot, I suppose.*

"Princes do not take from the flesh partly because my father decreed that we were above such baser desires long ago, and we adhere to his instructions still. Though they are not absolute law…" Why the fuck did I say that? I will not be bending this rule, this non-absolute law. *I. Will. Not.* I clear my throat lightly. "But we also refrain because the princes are different than other vampires, as I'm sure you are aware." She nods gravely, a small shudder running through her body. "All vampires are strong and can kill a human while feeding, but the princes even more so. Our strength is beyond compare. We could easily snap your bones to twigs, grind them to dust, drain you as dry as a corn husk." And it isn't just because of the feeding. Lust and bloodlust often get roused together for vampires, the intensity and aggression and wanting all mixing together, and the outcome can be disastrous if the vampire loses control. But if a *prince* were to lose control? There could be literally nothing left of the human but a memory.

"Easily?" she asks, voice shaking ever so slightly, though I can tell she's trying her best to hide it.

"Easier than breathing," I respond without thinking, only realizing how harsh it might sound when she swallows hard. I'm not used to mincing words or trying to be mindful of someone's feelings.

I'm not harsh with my soldiers—unless it's warranted, of course—but I am direct. I feel the tiniest bit of guilt when I see fear flare in her eyes, guilt and a feeling of utter wrongness in my bones.

She should never fear you, a voice whispers in the back of my mind. *You are meant to protect her, to ease her fears, to put her above all else and make her happy.* I scowl at the voice and she tears her gaze away, looking down at her wrist. The cloth is stained red with her blood. She tentatively pulls it away and inhales sharply.

"Seven hells," she whispers. "It's...it's almost healed already!" She looks at me again, confusion and question in her eyes. I notice the striations of gold within the green that most humans wouldn't be able to see at all. They are utterly captivating.

"It's because of the binding. Our blood has healing properties. The effects will wear off for you after a few weeks since such little blood was exchanged, but you will heal quickly, be a bit stronger and faster than usual, possibly even sense my emotions, if they're strong enough, I suppose, though I doubt you took enough for that."

"What?" she blurts, incredulous. I shrug.

"It is one of the effects of sharing blood." With such a little exchange on her part, it is unlikely she'll be able to sense anything from me, but I, on the other hand, won't be so lucky. I asked Bastian about it, and he confirmed that yes, they all can feel their Consort's emotions at times, but the physical distance helps and they all learned to ignore them long ago. It would just take time for me to as well. Yet another thing I'm going to have to deal with.

The clever girl comes to the same conclusion on her own.

"So...so you'll be able to feel what I'm feeling all the time then, since you'll be drinking my blood often?"

I hike a shoulder. She mutters a soft *what the fuck?* that I'm sure she doesn't realize I can hear and runs a finger over the small pink line where I'd sliced her skin only minutes ago. Her color has thankfully returned, a warm glow beneath her sun-bronzed skin. My fangs lengthen and throb once more and I realize I haven't actually fed yet. I steel myself and then quickly cross back to the table, grabbing the tankard and draining the contents. When her blood hits my tongue, my eyes slide closed and though I try to lock my muscles in place, the taste hits me like a physical blow and I take one staggering step back. A low growl rumbles in my chest and a glorious fire tears through every inch of me, flooding my veins. I'm more prepared this time, but *dear gods* it's still an intense rush that I don't think I'll ever fully grow accustomed to.

When I open my eyes again, everything in the room looks suddenly brighter. The smells are stronger, the sounds sharper, the colors more vibrant. Everything is just...*more* somehow. *Fuck me.* Is it always like this with fresh blood from the vein? Or is it only because of...?

I focus my gaze back on Dahlia to find her staring.

"Is it different?" she asks, "than the replicated blood?"

"You have no idea," I mutter quietly, not really meaning to let the words slip free, but not particularly caring at the moment either. I feel almost drunk, as if I've been drinking blood-laced ale or whisky all night. My blood feels practically molten, pumping faster through every inch of my body, my muscles tensing and strength coursing through me like a storm. I inhale deeply and Dahlia's scent hits me, stronger than before. The sweetness of her blood mixed with a wild, floral scent—*how apt*—that inexplicably makes me aroused as hell. I've always managed to keep lust and bloodlust separate in my mind, never truly understanding how the two get so mixed up together for so many vampires, but now...

My fangs ache, my nails sharpen and curl into claws, and my cock is suddenly as hard as the steel of Night's Fury. I move across the room quicker than she could possibly track, putting as much space between us as possible. I'm breathing hard, instincts and desires screaming in my head. Over the tumult, I can hear her thundering heart, can smell the fear tinging the air. *No. No, I'm scaring her. I could hurt her. I could* kill *her.* The thought sends a tendril of fear and disgust through my body, strong enough to clear my thoughts and allow me to regain control. By sheer force of will, I lock my muscles into place and clear my throat, willing my mind to blank and forcing my body under my command. Regardless of my determination not to formally accept her as my mate, my priority will still always be to keep her safe.

Especially from myself.

"That will be all, Keeva," I bite out in a low, rough voice.

"Keeva?" she whispers.

I turn back to her. Her eyes are wide, her pulse racing at her throat. With more composure than I would have thought myself capable of in this moment, I wave her question away airily.

"It is simply your name in my language," I lie.

She nods, rising and practically fleeing from the room. I collapse heavily back against the wall, breathing as if I've just come from the battlefield. I rub the heel of my hand against my chest, just over my heart.

"What in the fucking hells am I going to do?"

CHAPTER 6

DAHLIA

I'm honestly not sure what to make of, well, any of this really, but especially last night with Alaric. He mostly ignored me for the entirety of our trip north, but my Keeper—a young turned vampire named Takara who is basically my right hand for the rest of my life—instructed me to offer blood on the fifth day, so that's what I'd done. I don't exactly enjoy being ordered around, but I know what's expected of me as a Consort, and no matter how much it may irk me, I will do my duty.

So, I'd been a good little Consort. I'd gone to his room at the inn and offered him blood. It had been...interesting. Being around him again after four days had made my head spin, my entire body coming to life in a way I couldn't explain. He's just so...*Alaric*. So handsome, so stoic, so strong, so intimidating, so confusing. It's too much all at once, like his presence, his very being, just engulfs me completely and makes it impossible to see or feel or think about anything else. For the hundredth time, I tell myself that it's merely the binding, our shared blood telling my mind and body that it's connected to his, but a small voice in the back of my mind keeps whispering that it's more than that. That voice is obviously drunk or very, very misguided, so I tell her to shut her trap and she fades away into nothingness.

He doesn't seem to know how the hells he wants to act towards me, being civil and almost gentlemanly the day we left Astoria's Keep, then short and irritable last night at the inn before he drank my blood, and then different yet again after that. He seemed almost intoxicated by the blood, and for a second I would have sworn he wanted...more than blood. I know that often times feeding and sex go hand-and-hand for vampires, but not princes with their Consorts. Never that. *Plus he can apparently kill me with little more than a look.*

Thankfully, he hadn't seemed to be offended or irritated when I'd snapped at him. Some princes may have had my head for that, but Alaric actually seemed a little impressed, if not amused. Enid had begged me to watch my tongue before we'd departed, reminding me that, though he may not act like it, he *is* a Montclare prince.

"Be...not so much yourself, maybe?" Enid had said, scrunching her nose in that way that always makes me laugh. Now, I nearly cry thinking of it. It's only been a few days and already I miss home so badly it feels like a part of myself has been ripped away. A leg, or an arm perhaps, something I can survive without, but something that I'll forever feel and miss with a longing ache.

Today, we'll reach my new home. Not for the first time, I wonder how hellish the camp is truly going to be. Will I be sleeping on a pile of furs on the ground? Will I have my own tent, or will I be expected to share with Alaric? Are there *baths*? One of my favorite things in the world is to soak in a hot bath until my skin wrinkles or Enid yells at me to get out, and the thought of having to bathe in a cold river somewhere makes me shudder.

"Are you cold, my Lady?" Takara asks, startling me.

"Oh no, I'm alright." I'm far from used to being addressed as "my Lady." Honestly, I don't think I ever will be. I don't feel like myself when people call me that. I don't feel like the girl who'd grown up in a small three-room house with a thatched roof, the one who spent hours at the forge with my father, who constantly had soot or dirt smeared across my nose. The one who, when I was older, liked to run wild with the boys in the village, swimming naked in the lake, and sneaking kisses—or more—in the stables or the caves. *That*'s who I truly am. But Lady Dahlia? I don't know that girl.

I sigh and stare out the window of the carriage, toying with the ring da had given me before we'd left. It was a round stone of polished obsidian, vines of gold wrapping around the edges and holding the stone in place.

"Just in case," he'd whispered in my ear, hugging me after I'd slid the ring on my index finger, and I'd heard both the grin and the seriousness in his voice. When I looked closer at the ring, recognizing the design, I opened my mouth in confusion, but he'd cut me off. "Doona ask," he'd said with that mischievous glint in his green eyes, so like my own, "just keep it on ye at all times, my firebrand."

"We're nearly there," Takara says, pulling me from my memories. I straighten in my seat, squinting out the window but seeing nothing ahead.

"Have you been to the camp before?" I ask.

"No, my Lady, but I can hear the men training."

I, of course, can't hear anything of the sort. I can't deny I marvel at the idea of being able to hear or see things miles away, to be able to run like the wind, to be strong enough to fell a tree with little thought or trouble. I almost ask Takara what it's like, if she's happy with her transformation or if she misses anything about being human, but think better of it. We hardly know each other and that seems like a very personal question.

Though, to be fair, she has asked me insanely personal questions from the moment she was introduced to me just after the Magister whisked me away from the Choosing ceremony—about my diet, the schedule of my monthly cycles, sexual preferences and if I had a partner I wished to accompany me to the camp, or perhaps partners—plural—that I wished to join in my harem. A *harem*, for gods' sake. Apparently it's quite common for Consorts to keep them, getting their jollys off with as many folks as they wish while they luxuriate in their castles. Though I'm the farthest thing from chaste or a prude, the idea of keeping a whole host of men around to bed whenever I feel the need seems...scandalous, even for me. *I suppose it* could *be fun, on rare occasions after a lot of ale...*

By the time we finally reach the camp, I'm practically vibrating with tension, my stomach twisted into tight knots. This is it. I'm about to get the first glimpse into what will be my life from now on. I've been coming to terms with things over the past few days, but now that it's truly here, I can't seem to shake the nerves. I try to control my breathing, but it begins to come in quick, shallow bursts, my heart racing inside my chest.

"Easy, my Lady," Takara says in a surprisingly gentle voice. She hasn't been unkind before now, exactly, just...distant. Respectful, but a little cold. I assume that's just how most Keepers and Consorts are together. After all, most Consorts have been raised since birth to see staff of any kind, vampire or otherwise, as beneath them.

"I'm...how can you tell?"

"I can hear your heart racing. You have nothing to fear from these vampires. They would just as soon slit their own throats with a silver-tipped dagger than harm you." I want to tell her that it isn't about being fearful for my life, it's the ache of missing my home and my family, the thought of living a life that will never truly fulfill me... but I don't. I can't find my voice and I'm not sure I can really explain it to the vampire anyway, so I simply nod.

The curiosity outweighs the nerves and I open the window of the carriage, sticking my head out to take it all in. I think I hear Takara laugh lightly behind me. We roll through a towering stone gate, guards standing like statues on either side. They incline their heads as the caravan makes its way through, slamming their closed fists over their hearts when Alaric rides past. A clear sign of respect. I wonder if it's a true respect, born out of admiration and love and loyalty—or respect brought by fear. I think about how deadly Alaric can be, how menacing I imagine he must look on the battlefield,

Night's Fury in his hands, the silver stars shining brightly against the dark blade. If his men don't fear him, at least a little, they're fools.

Takara clears her throat lightly and I reluctantly pull myself back inside the carriage, though I continue to watch raptly as we move through the camp, my mouth practically hanging open in shock. It's nothing like I expected. Groups of soldiers train in large fields on either side of the main path—which is an actual *road* made of cobblestone—and the sounds of metal clanging against metal ring out all around. Grunts of pain or exertion, cheers and jeers, barked commands, hearty laughs. The camp is *loud*, but I don't mind. The clash of metal reminds me a bit of da's hammer, the laughter and chatter reminding me of the gatherings in the square outside the tavern before we'd moved to the noble district. It's comforting but makes my heart ache, all at once.

I rub the heel of my hand against my chest, trying to ease the ache, and Takara says quietly, "It will get easier." I turn to her, blinking away tears.

"What?"

"Missing your family. It will become easier over time." There's a flash of profound sadness in her deep brown eyes, so dark they look almost black, and I can't help but ask.

"How do you know?" She looks to be debating if she should answer, and I sigh. "Do Keepers not usually speak with the Consorts? Is that it?"

The vampire purses her lips. "Not in a conversational way, no..." She studies me for a long moment, and then sighs, seemingly making some sort of decision. "But I suppose our circumstances are a bit different than most Consorts and their Keepers, aren't they?" I see the rigidity thaw out of her, and I have a sliver of hope that maybe I'll have a friend here after all. No one can replace Enid, of course, but having someone to talk to, to laugh or cry with? Well, it will be a blessing in the midst of this nightmare.

"You are my first assignment as a Keeper," Takara says, the words almost sounding like a confession.

"I'm sorry that your first is...well, *me*." If I'm stuck in a war camp, then so is she. I'm sure she would rather be in a castle somewhere.

"I'm not," Takara says, surprising me. "Like you, I was not born to that world—and I don't particularly care for it, if you don't mind my candor. The rich accommodations and fine silks are nice, of course, but the rest of it—" She waves her hand airily to encompass what I assume is the politics and social standing and court drama nonsense. "—I can do without any of it." My lips quirk. Maybe Takara and I have much more in common than I ever thought possible.

She takes a deep breath, letting it out slowly. There have always been stories of vampires, myths and legends told around campfires from long before the Blood Peace, when vampires were still monsters hiding in the shadows. For some reason, all the stories claimed that vampires didn't breathe. Though it's true that they can hold their breath for extremely long periods of time, they *do* breathe, and I've always wondered where that particular false characteristic came from. Of course, there were plenty of other silly ones to go along with that: an allergy to garlic and sunlight, the inability to cross bodies of water, a lack of reflection in mirrored surfaces. Perhaps I can ask Takara...or Alaric? *No, that's ridiculous*, I chide myself as I push the thought away. I know that once settled in at the camp we won't be speaking very often, if at all. We certainly won't be discussing the origins of vampire mythology over a pint.

"I had a husband and a son," Takara finally says quietly, pulling me from my thoughts. "Long, long ago. They died in a Revenant attack and I was gravely injured. One of the vampires found me, one of Alaric's men, actually—it's the reason I was selected as your Keeper, I believe—and he gave me the choice of attempting the turning or ending things mercifully for me. I chose the turning." She hikes one slim shoulder, making the gesture look ridiculously elegant as her sleek black hair shifts to the side. "At the time, I had grand notions about seeking revenge, deciding that living on as a vampire would be the only way I could avenge my family and then join them, but…well, I wasn't made to be a soldier." Her lips curl upwards. "I did two days of training and promptly decided to serve the Montclares in other ways instead, that my service to the family would be payment to Alaric and his Coven for taking my revenge for me." She glances to me and adds with a scrunch of her nose, reminding me so much of Enid in that moment that my heart cracks, "The training involved lots of dirt and physical exertion—and *not* the fun kind."

I bark out a surprised laugh and Takara chuckles softly, the tips of her small fangs peeking out as she smiles.

After a few moments, I say, "I'm sorry. About your family, I mean."

"It was almost a hundred years ago now," she says in a tone that tells me the subject is closed for now. I nod and turn back to the window, watching as we move farther into the camp. I frown. Buildings are scattered all over. *Actual* buildings, with walls and roofs and even chimneys, and soon there are hundreds of them, thousands maybe, spread out in neat rows. The lines fan off in both directions as far as I can see, vanishing in the distance.

"What the…?"

"Those are the living quarters, my Lady," Takara answers. "Not to worry, I've been assured that the High General's cabin is much larger than these."

"I…well, I honestly expected to be sleeping on the ground in a tent." Takara looks horrified.

"Absolutely not, my Lady. And besides," she adds, "even if they did live in tents, we would have demanded a cabin for you. For *us*," she amends. "A Consort and her Keeper do *not* sleep in tents."

I laugh lightly at the disgust in Takara's voice at the thought of sleeping in a tent. The rows of cabins finally stop, but we continue on the road. Apparently, the High General's quarters are set apart from the rest, up a small rise with an admittedly stunning view of the dark mountains in the distance behind it. We finally came to a stop in front of the cabin and exit the carriage. I roll my shoulders and neck, barely stopping myself from rubbing my ass. It's entirely numb from sitting for so long, despite the thickly cushioned seats.

I eye the large cabin in front of me with interest. Though simple, it's beautifully crafted, with motifs of battle scenes carved into the four thick columns flanking the oversized front doors. The doors themselves are each carved with Alaric's sigil, the snarling wolf seeming to look right through me.

It's at least five times as large as any of the other cabins I'd seen, made out of a deep, red wood and gray stone, with wings extending to each side, angled slightly back towards the mountains. I wonder what the inside of a vampiric warlord's personal quarters might look like. Sparse and utilitarian? Rich with spoils of war? Maps and weapons strewn across every surface? From the little I know of Alaric, I would guess the first, but I can't deny that I'm curious to know the truth. Will I ever be invited inside? Will I go there to provide blood? Or will he simply send someone to collect it from me from my own cabin now that we're at the camp?

Off to the right and slightly lower down the hill, another cabin stands, much larger than the other living quarters for the soldiers, but not nearly as large as Alaric's. It looks new—built after Alaric learned he'd be bringing a Consort back with him? This must be for me. It's customary for Consorts to reside with their princes, technically in the same home, though they usually have their own wing and completely separate life for the most part, but I'm not surprised that Alaric would only make so many concessions. Being forced to take a Consort after all these years is one thing. Sharing his home is another.

And that's completely fine with me. I'm perfectly content to live in the smaller cabin with Takara. A chef had also been sent from the palace, though I know there are cooks here at the camp who prepare the meals for the humans who serve the army, so why I need a personal chef is beyond me. I mean, I know exactly why—to most, the Consort is one step below royalty, someone who deserves and needs special attention—but I still think it's silly. My palate is decidedly unrefined and I'd be more than happy to eat whatever the rest of the humans do. I'd probably prefer it, actually.

Either way, I wonder if Reginald will reside with us in this cabin or if he'll stay with the rest of the humans. Where are the rest of the humans, anyway? Do they all live together, or do they get their own quarters like the soldiers apparently do? What do they *do*, exactly? Wash and mend clothes, and clean up around the camp, I imagine. Will I be allowed to mingle with them?

I puff out my cheeks and let out a long, slow breath. I'm getting extremely tired of not knowing what's going on or what's to come.

The wind blows in, and though it's cooler than what I'm used to farther south, it isn't the utterly bitter cold I'd been expecting this far into the Northlands. It feels nice, actually, and I raise my face to let it kiss my skin, blowing wisps of hair away from my face.

As if reading my thoughts, Takara says, "winter is still months off yet. When that comes...well, we'll be sure you have proper clothing before then, not to worry. I'll return shortly." With that, she glides away in that eerily graceful way that vampires have, almost as if her feet aren't even touching the ground. I'm admittedly a bit jealous of it.

I watch her go, and then glance around at the rest of the party who have all dismounted and are talking in small groups or unloading things from the carriages or saddlebags. No one seems to be paying me much attention at all, so I just stand here alone, a bit awkwardly, unsure what I should be doing. On the one hand, I'm a Consort and that means I can do mostly whatever I please, but on the other, I've just entered a war camp, the most notorious war camp in all of Braxhelm to be exact, and am surrounded by vampire warriors. Though they'll be respectful of the title in that I'm sure they'll incline their heads when I pass and not hurt me in any way, I have a feeling they won't really give two shits about who I am or what I'm doing there. These people have far more important things to worry about than some ridiculous, ancient custom and made-up title. Little things like preparing for battle and protecting the entire continent from Revenants, for example. I shiver a little at the thought, cutting my eyes to the mountains far in the distance. I know that the Revenant army lies just beyond, always at the ready, always plotting and planning and trying to find a way through Alaric's forces and back into Braxhelm.

I tear my eyes away from the mountains, disliking the fear that skitters up my spine the longer I look at them, as if I stare long enough, I'll see the enemy just beyond. There's a large stable set off to the left of the cabin, and, without having anything else to do, I wander towards it. I've always loved horses and have been shoeing them for years at the shop. I walk slowly at first, waiting for someone to tell me to stop, but no one pays me any mind, so I shrug and quickly speed inside. An absolutely massive horse stands in the center of the aisle between the rows of stalls. I know immediately that he's Alaric's horse, though this is as close as I've been to him throughout the journey north. He's easily the largest horse I've ever seen. I've heard rumors that Alaric's army is full of massive beasts, war horses bred for battle and to withstand the harsh northern climate. Though a little frightening, he's absolutely beautiful: black as midnight save a silvery-gray patch in the shape of a star on his right flank. He reminds me of Night's Fury and I wonder if Alaric had chosen the horse for that reason, or if it was just a happy coincidence. His mane is just as a dark, flowing thickly down his neck like spilled ink.

"Hello there," I say softly, and the horse whickers quietly in response. "*Please* don't kick me..." I add as I approach. I gasp quietly when the horse turns his head to give me a measuring look. His eyes are a glittering crimson with a starburst of silver around his pupils. It's unlike anything I've ever seen before. It's...menacing. I can only imagine how terrifying it would be to see this horse riding into battle, red eyes gleaming, and Alaric Montclare on his back, blade raised and thirsting for blood. I swallow hard and wait for a moment, letting the horse make a decision, and then ease forward when he lowers his head slightly, telling me that he's going to tolerate my presence, at least for now. I let out a slow exhale before reaching out and trailing my hand down his side and up his neck as I come around to his front.

He eyes me, but the more I look, the less menacing the red becomes. His eyes are soulful with an incredible intelligence within, something otherworldly and powerful. I can't help but smile as our gazes hold for long moments, and then he presses his nose into my hands, demanding attention. I laugh lightly.

"Beautiful boy," I say, rubbing his nose. "Ack, but you know that, don't you?"

CHAPTER 7

ALARIC

I watch from the shadows of the stable as Dahlia cautiously makes her way towards Xanthus. Cautious, but not afraid. She's braver than most humans, I'll give her that. I watch for a few moments more as the two share a long look before Xanthus finally decides that he likes her and shoves his nose into her hands. She murmurs nonsense to the horse, stroking his nose and his ego all at once, laughing lightly when he pushes his big head into her shoulder for more attention when she stops rubbing him for a mere second. *The big baby*, I think, almost smiling. She seems so at ease here, genuinely happy for a precious moment. I can only imagine what she must be thinking now that she's seen the camp, seen the life I've condemned her to. Will she hate me for it? I scowl, reminding myself that it doesn't matter. It would probably be better if she hates me, honestly. It will be easier to keep distance between us if she has no desire to be near me.

Her hair is in a thick plait over one shoulder, but a few strands have escaped and curl softly against her temples and cheek. I roll my eyes as the insane urge to brush them away rushes through me. *Fucking ridiculous.* She took my advice about her wardrobe and instead of a gown she's in tight leather britches that look as if they've been molded to her body and a leather corseted vest, lacing up the front. I try to stop the thoughts but I'm powerless: I imagine tearing those laces free, ripping the leathers from her and taking her hard against the stall door just behind her. I imagine the feel of her lips on mine, the thrum of her pulse beneath my tongue as I lick her throat before biting, sinking my aching fangs into her flesh and drinking deep. I imagine her hands in my hair, her gasps and cries, imagine lifting her up and slamming my cock—

"He likes you," I say, striding out into the light before my imagination drives me mad. She yelps and leaps away from the horse, her back hitting the stall door. I clench my jaw, the image from a moment ago, of her against that very door with my body flush against hers, searing my mind and blood once more. Her heart thuds loudly in her chest and the sound makes my body feel as if it's on fire. "Calm your heart, Keeva," I bite out through clenched teeth. Every beat is like a hammer against my control, daring me to break. I will beat this, I *will* master myself, but I need time. She swallows hard and straightens.

"You can hear it?" she asks, a little breathless. I merely arch a brow in response, striding forward. She eyes me a little warily, but doesn't move away.

"His eyes?" she asks, having to clear her throat quietly before the words will come out. Does she truly fear me? I know she must on some level, but she doesn't believe that I'll harm her, does she? Consorts don't fear their princes, as a general rule, and I have no desire for Dahlia to feel that way about me. In fact, a part of my mind recoils at the idea of it. She should never fear me. She should lo—*No*, I growl at the voice echoing in the back of my mind. *She should not.* I clench my jaw at this confusing, fuck storm of a situation that, for the first time in all my life, I have no idea how to navigate.

"He's immortal, turned by me years ago, and given a bit of my blood every week. It bonds us and makes him an asset in battle. He can read my intentions and emotions, knowing when and where I need him, or can help him to find me quickly in a melee. We aren't sure why their eyes change. Obviously turned humans don't have that reaction."

"What's his name?" She eases forward again, her heart slowing, the pulse point at the base of her throat beating in a steady rhythm again.

"Xanthus," I say, turning to take the saddle from the horse's back. "His brother, Xerxes, is in the stall in the back." In answer, an annoyed huff echoes through the stable and I roll my eyes.

Larken, one of the stable hands, comes to assist. The young vampire bows his head as I hand him the saddle, but not before I catch his eyes widening slightly as he takes in Dahlia. She nods at him a little awkwardly, clearly not quite sure how she's supposed to interact with others in the camp. I should offer her guidance, but I'm not sure how she should act either, really. A typical Consort would hold themselves above everyone save their prince, would barely deign to look at anyone, much less speak to them unless issuing commands.

But Dahlia is not a typical Consort, and further, this is no typical circumstance. I want her to feel welcome in my camp. Safe. My men are like a family and she should feel a part of that, in as much as she wishes to. I imagine she must be feeling exceptionally alone at present, torn from her family and friends and home. Before I can open my mouth to voice some kind of advice, telling her she should feel free to be informal with the soldiers, if that's what she wishes, to interact with them however she likes, she makes her way towards Xerxes' stall.

"Careful," I say quickly. "Xerxes is a bit more...headstrong than his brother. Stubborn bastard, really," I say, almost to myself and she huffs out a quiet laugh, not taking her eyes from the horse. Xerxes eyes her, nostrils flaring, and I brace myself for her scream when the horse inevitably stomps and huffs and snaps at her with his large, sharp teeth. "He doesn't let anyone but me near him most days..."

I trail off as Dahlia raises her hand towards the horse's nose in question. I move to her side fast as lightning, ready to pull her away, but I stop myself at the last second, head cocked as I watch in shock. Xerxes holds her gaze and then, to my utter astonishment, exhales roughly and lowers his head towards her open palm, bumping it gruffly in his approximation of grudging affection.

"Fucking hells," Larken mutters from across the room. "Oh, apologies, my Lady," he adds quickly at my stern glance, though I share his sentiments exactly. *Fucking hells indeed.* The horse rarely lets anyone near him like that, let alone a stranger. Perhaps it's because she's human? Or a woman? There are plenty of female vampires in the army, but none of them have been around Xerxes other than during battle.

...Or can the bastard sense the connection between his master and this woman? *Fuck.*

I don't know what to make of the interaction, don't know what to make of this girl at all or the situation we're now in, and I don't like this feeling. I'm used to being in complete control, to seeing all of the pieces on the chess board and understanding exactly what moves will be made, what counter moves and the motivations behind them. Some of my men even joke that I'm omnipotent, often being able to anticipate our enemies' moves on the battlefield with deadly accuracy. This feeling of...floundering? Of feeling as if I'm standing on a piece of driftwood in the middle of a tempest, no way to find the right footing? I do not care for it at all. Irritation flares. At myself, at the situation, at the woman in front of me, at the gods themselves.

"I'll show you to your room," I say gruffly, gesturing towards the wide door of the stable. She pulls her hand away from Xerxes, a look of confusion passing over her beautiful face, but she quickly blanks her features and nods, making her way quickly back outside. She walks past the front doors of the cabin towards the newly constructed one down the hill a bit.

"Where are you going?" She pauses and turns back, frowning.

"I thought...well, is that cabin not for me?" she asks, pointing towards the small structure.

"Consorts reside with their princes," I say through gritted teeth. Her eyes widen in shock and she swallows hard.

"Oh," she says quietly. I grind my teeth, annoyed by yet another reminder that my life is being altered by a stupid, needless tradition...even as part of me all but melts in contentment at the idea of her being with me under my roof. *Where she belongs.* I feel as if my head is going to split right in two with all of these back-and-forth thoughts, all the contradiction and confusion.

I turn on my heel and make my way towards the front doors of my cabin—*our* cabin—not pausing to see if she follows, but a second later I hear the sound of her footsteps hastening to catch up with my long strides. I walk through the wide entry area, a massive round, stone fireplace dominating the middle of the space. Hallways branch off in four directions.

"My quarters, weapons room, a training room, and war room are this way," I say with a gesture towards the two corridors to the left. "Study and guest quarters this way." A flick of my fingers to the corridor to the right. I skirt around the fireplace and stride down the newly-added hallway towards her wing. I can smell the freshly-cut timber, the iron, the churned earth. My men had worked quickly and well in my absence. I give an appreciative glance at the framed windows and arched doorways, the workmanship and detail put into the construction, and make a mental note to commend those who did the work personally.

I indicate two doors as we pass. "Sitting room and dining space." She peers inside as we walk, but since I don't pause, neither does she. She has nothing but time to explore every inch of these rooms, so she can do it at her leisure without me. Glancing inside each I see that everything within is plush and elegant and befitting a Consort, though a little much for a war camp. I wonder what instructions Elias gave whomever was in charge of furnishing the spaces and shake my head ruefully. "If you would rather your Keeper reside in this cabin with you instead of the one next door, that can be arranged as well. There is extra space down this hallway here," I say gesturing to the short corridor on the right. I see her nod out of the corner of my eye.

I open the double doors at the end of the hallway and usher her inside. The room is large, double the size of one of my soldier's cabins. She glances around the room as she enters behind me, but I can't decipher her thoughts. Is she impressed? Underwhelmed? Do I really give a shit either way? Damn me, I...do.

"Should you wish for different or additional furnishings, tell your Keeper," I find myself saying as she roams around the room. "Anything you desire is yours."

She runs a finger down one of the carved posts of the oversized bed, trailing it downward until it reaches the thick, fur coverlet. An errant thought rises in my mind, unbidden: will she take lovers here? It's her right, after all. Consorts can bed whomever they wish. Some have full harems, in fact (as do the princes for that matter). Will Dahlia? The thought is...unwelcome. I clench my fists in frustration as I stride to another door within the room.

"Your bathing chamber," I say gruffly.

Her brows rise, in surprise I think. What had she been expecting? A tent for shelter? A cold river for a bath? A bucket to shit in? I'm strangely offended by the idea of her thinking I would treat my Consort as such. Though I'm sure I've made it rather obvious that I did not want a Consort, I don't want her to think that I would act so dishonorably as to treat her with anything less than the respect her position is due.

"Oh," she breathes as she drifts over to examine the room. She brushes past me, entirely too close, her sweet scent assaulting me, the warmth of her body burning me with the tiniest breath of the touch we share as her shoulder skims my chest. I tense as she moves past, not seeming to have noticed the touch at all, and I keep distance between us, remaining in the doorway as she moves into the space.

A large, oval tub carved from the white granite found in the caves of the Sisters dominates the space, a matching basin for washing her face and teeth on one side, a large shower stall, and a privy in a small, separate room attached to the larger chamber on the other. I study the tub. This must have been one of the modifications Elias had mentioned. It's beautiful, to be sure, and I suppose it's better than the plain copper tub I'd originally requested, but it's obscenely large. Does Elias expect her to have *company* in the bath with her? I clench my fists harder, my knuckles cracking, in jealousy or wanting, I'm not even sure. My head is pounding and I could use a very large drink.

"Water is pumped from the underground hot-springs just outside the camp and will come directly into the tub from those pipes there," I say, gesturing. "Same in the shower," I add with a nod towards the stall where the pipes are visible over the half wall, tiled with red and gold gemstones. She exhales in what appears to be relief and I arch a brow in question.

"I...I wasn't expecting to have such things here," she says, fiddling with the edge of her leather vest. So she truly had been expecting awful conditions being my Consort, had resigned herself to sleeping in the dirt most likely.

"Though not a castle, the cabin will have everything you need. If you wish for something, ask your Keeper and you shall have it." She turns and meets my gaze, the green absolutely striking in the afternoon light streaming in through the high windows above the tub. We stand locked in a strange, heavy silence for a long moment. To my surprise, her gaze dips to my lips, down my chest and lower, and her cheeks flush faintly. What is she thinking? My fangs ache at the sight of the blood rushing just beneath the surface, of her pulse beating rapidly at her throat. *Why* is it racing? Fear? Or...something else? *It doesn't fucking matter.*

She pulls her gaze back to mine again and before I can say or do something reprehensible, I give her a clipped nod and turn to all but flee the room. I need to get away from her. I need time to deal with all of this, to fully absorb all of the changes that have happened in such a short amount of time. Sharing my home, taking fresh blood, being so near a human so often, having a Consort...having a mate...

I shake myself and keep walking.

"What am I supposed to do now?" she calls.

I stop at the doorway and glance over my shoulder.

"Whatever you want," I say simply, and leave her standing in the center of her room alone.

CHAPTER 8
DAHLIA

I don't do much of anything the first week after arriving at the camp. I spend the first few days grieving the loss of my family and the life I knew, and, admittedly, wallowing. I slept for a full day and a half, exhaustion from everything that had happened slamming into me almost the instant Alaric had left me in my chambers that first day, only waking to eat some of the food that had been left by Takara I assume, and to use the privy (which I'd been very excited to have—I had been fairly certain before arriving that I was going to be expected to piss in a hole in the ground).

The next day, I explored my wing, still surprised that I had it at all. I never would have thought Alaric would share his cabin. Everything was luxurious and expensive, I could tell—plush sofas and chairs, thick fur rugs, gold and crystal sconces and chandeliers, gem-inlaid cups and plates. It was all a bit much, though I suppose it had been constructed and furnished with a typical Consort in mind, and I'm anything but typical when it comes to these things. I appreciate luxuries and beautiful things, but they aren't things I'm used to or need to have to be happy or comfortable.

Alaric did say that I could change whatever I liked...maybe I'll redecorate at some point. That would kill some time and apparently that's all I have now. Time. Endless time to do...I have no idea what. Everything. Nothing. I have no purpose here other than giving blood, and when I'm not doing that, I'm not really sure what I'm supposed to do to fill my days.

Takara came the third day to make sure I didn't need anything and to see how I was settling in. I feigned more exhaustion because I just honestly didn't feel like having company. So, she left and I laid in the extremely comfortable bed, dozing and crying.

I know it's only been a handful of days, but I already miss my family so badly my chest feels as if it's been cracked in two. I pull myself from my bed and find parchment and pens in the desk in the corner of my room. It's a beautiful piece, with elegant knots carved into the legs and across the fronts of the drawers, and painted the deep green color of the forest surrounding the camp in the distance.

> *Dear Enid,*
>
> *I feel silly writing to you already when I've only just left, but I knew that you were probably falling apart without me, and my words would be needed.*
>
> *And perhaps I miss you and da a bit as well.*
>
> *The journey was long, but not too terrible. The High General's carriage is exceedingly comfortable, of course. Seeing the landscape change from city streets to rolling hills and farmland, to forests as far as you can see, snow-capped mountains in the distance, was truly extraordinary. I wish you could have seen it. The camp is...*

I frown, not really knowing *what* the camp is like. I'd seen it when we rode in that first day, of course, but other than that, I've been hiding here in the cabin, sulking in my rooms since arriving.

The camp is massive, but not nearly as primitive as we feared. You'll be happy to know that I am not sleeping on the ground or in a tent. In fact, everyone here has their own cabin. Well, actually that isn't entirely true — not everyone has their own cabin. I share the largest cabin in the camp with Alaric. I have my own wing, of course, so we're as separate as we can be, but even so, being here in the same house, under the same roof...I'm not sure how to feel, Enid. His presence is so large and all-encompassing, I can feel it from across the expanse of the house.

And we're connected in ways I can't even describe for the time being because of the ceremony. I'm told it will fade, but it's a little overwhelming. I can feel myself longing to be near him, my very blood seeming to call out to his. It's... confusing. And inconvenient. And fucking unwanted. I don't want to be near him. I want to be home with you.

Tears well, both of sorrow and anger, and I scrub them away quickly.

I'll write again soon. Give da my love and make sure he's not eating too many tarts—make sure he knows that he fools no one when he thinks he's sneaking them away from the kitchen with no one the wiser.

I love you so much.

—Dahlia

I find an envelope, wax, and a seal bearing the Coven's sigil with an elegant *C* scrawled beneath the snarling wolf's head. I run my fingertips over it.

"C. For Consort. Because I'm the Wolf Coven leader's fucking *Consort*."

I drop the seal to the desk with a heavy thud and put my head in my hands. I have to take a few deep breaths as that truly sinks in, that this is truly my life now. It is no nightmare, no hallucination. There is no escaping it. I am Alaric's Consort and will be until the day I die.

Something inside my chest feels heavy, as if my very soul is being pulled under the waves by a weighty anchor. I heat the wax and seal the letter before setting out to find out how in the bloody hells I'm supposed to send correspondence from a fucking war camp, but even as I stride from the room to find Takara, I can feel myself on the verge of slipping into a darkness that I don't know if I'll be able to climb out of.

On the fifth day, I knock on the door to the war room. I'd honestly been a bit surprised that Alaric wanted me to come to him so he could take my blood himself rather than just sending one of his squires or servants or whatever they're called here to do it for him. Surprised, but admittedly excited. *How pathetic.*

"Enter," Alaric's voice comes from within, though he sounds distracted. I push the large doors open and step inside the room. It's nearly the size of my entire wing, with a giant round table in the middle, maps laid out on top with what look like game pieces placed all around it. It takes me a moment to realize that the pieces are meant to represent the vampiric army and the Revenant one. Each of the five permanent war camps within Braxhelm is marked with a castle-like statue, and I wonder what the others might look like. Do they all have cabins and warm water? Or were others more primitive?

Alaric stands at the table, studying the map intently, his dark brows drawn down. Strands of his black hair tumble over his forehead and I'm struck again by how beautiful he is. More rough-hewn than his brothers, but all the more handsome for it, I think. I shake myself. It doesn't matter if he's handsome or not.

I stop on the other side of the table and he cuts his eyes upward to meet mine across the wide expanse of marble. The gold is the color of warm honey today, a bit darker in the chemical lamps around the room.

"Come," he says in a clipped tone, holding out his hand in a beckoning gesture. I make my way around the table and by the time I'm beside him, he already has an iron cup in his hand. I hold out my wrist and he quickly slices through my skin as if it's parchment. I'm more prepared this time, but I still hiss in a quick breath as I feel my skin open, my blood beginning to flow. Though I haven't done much else these last few days, I have been taking the pills to help increase my blood supply and recover more quickly, and the lightheaded feeling I'd experienced the last time isn't nearly as bad now.

"I trust everything is to your liking," he says a little rigidly as my blood drips into the cup. It's like he doesn't really want to speak with me, but can't quite help it. *Strange vampire.*

"Y-yes." He gives me one sharp nod and steps away, setting the cup on the table.

"That will be all."

Effectively dismissed, I turn to find Elias entering the room, grinning his easy smile, the light glinting off of his fangs. Deep blue-gray eyes, tousled golden hair and matching beard, and a dimple on one cheek when he grins—I have no doubt he makes every woman swoon. Men too, I imagine. I think you'd be hard pressed to find any being with a pulse that isn't charmed by one look at Elias.

"Ah, Lady Dahlia," he says, bowing dramatically. My lips curl despite my mood. "How are you this lovely evening?"

"I'm well, thank you." Is my voice...breathy? *Gods.* I feel my cheeks heat.

"You look it," he says in a low, smooth voice, eyes skating down my body in a way that makes my stomach tighten and my pulse jump. Is he just a shameless flirt, like so many vampires are? Vampires on the whole are a very *physical* species, to put it mildly. The blood houses are popular destinations for a reason—and not just for the vampires. I've heard rumors that sex with a vampire is unlike anything you can imagine, and being bitten is like seeing the gods. I clear my throat lightly, trying not to think about those particular things at the moment. Elias' grin widens as if he can read my every thought. Perhaps I'll find out for myself just what being with a vampire is like. As I drink Elias in, I wonder...but no, I can't very well do anything with him...can I? *Technically,* I'm free to do whatever I want with whomever I want...right?

"Elias," Alaric snaps from the table, sounding irritable.

Perhaps Alaric's lieutenants are off-limits to his Consort. I'll have to ask Takara about the rules for these things once I'm feeling more up to it. Elias winks at me and then saunters to the table to join Alaric, unperturbed by the High General's brisk tone. I get the feeling that nothing much fazes Elias Kovach.

I quickly make my way to the door, glancing over my shoulder to find Alaric's intent stare on me, the gold in his eyes seeming to burn. With what, I'm not completely sure. Anger? Thirst? Something else? My heart hammers in my chest as something swift and hot rushes through my body at that look, all thoughts of Elias swept from my mind.

I swallow hard and quickly leave the room, closing the door behind me with a loud thud.

THE NEXT WEEK is much of the same. I feel myself slipping farther and farther down into the darkness, being pulled beneath the waves of despair. I have little energy, little appetite, little interest in much of anything. I lie in bed, but hardly sleep, everything too different, my room too big and too quiet without Enid here with me. Takara seems unsure what to do to help. She checks in on me every day, makes sure the chef, Reginald, is bringing meals regularly, even if I'm not eating them, and offers to help me bathe or to style my hair, but overall, the vampire has mostly left me to find a way to work through this on my own.

The next time I go to Alaric to offer blood, I know that he notes the dark circles under my eyes, the weight I've lost in the two weeks since we arrived, but he doesn't say anything. He takes my blood and dismisses me with no exchange of words between us at all, but there's something I can't quite read radiating off of him in waves. Anger? Annoyance? I'm sure he's just put out with having to deal with a sad, sulky human, but I honestly can't quite make myself care. I'm to live with him and provide blood, and that's all. I have no duty to be pleasant or happy while I do it.

The next day, Alaric leaves with a large group of soldiers. I watch them ride out of the camp and towards the Sisters from the hill where the cabin stands.

"Where are they going?" I ask without taking my eyes off of the procession. I feel as if an invisible string connects me to Alaric and with every step that Xanthus takes, the tauter the string becomes. I know it's only because of the bonding during the Choosing, but it doesn't make me feel any better. My body only knows that it longs to be near Alaric, that it *should* be near him, and as he moves farther away from me, my veins sing with tension and unease. It radiates throughout my whole body like a soft tremor.

"Off to battle," Takara says easily. My heart stutters and Takara suddenly seems to understand. "Ah, the binding. It will get easier as time goes on and the bond fades." I only nod absently, still watching the cadre ride out. I wonder what they might be riding out to face, what kind of battle might be waiting for them. What would happen if Alaric...didn't come back? Icy fingers of dread and fear whisper up my spine. It's too much. I don't like feeling this connection to him. I don't like this utter terror coursing through my body at the thought of something happening to him. The quicker this bond fades, the better.

Takara studies me, her lips pressed into a hard line.

"A walk," she says simply. I turn to her, finally yanking my gaze from the line of soldiers disappearing in the distance.

"A what? Oh," I say, realization dawning, "No, I don't feel—"

"You are wasting away and going to a dark place," Takara interrupts. "Part of my job as your Keeper is to keep you healthy, not just in body but in mind as well. I cannot let you wallow any longer. I know that you mourn the loss of your previous life, and you were allowed time for that, but now we must look forward. It is the only way."

I inhale deeply as Takara's words—words so similar to da's—hit me. She's right. She's absolutely fucking right. This isn't me; this isn't how I should be acting. I'm stronger than this and I know it. I was allowed to feel the sting and pain of loss, but Takara's right: I need to keep going. It's time to accept the hand that fate has dealt me and make the most of this new path. Enid always says we need to look for the light in the dark things, to look for joy within the pain and the good within the bad. I know that's what she'd be telling me to do if she were here beside me now. Probably smacking me with a shoe while she said it, too. A small smile tugs at my lips at the thought for the first time in what feels like an eternity. I let out a long, slow exhale.

I am Dahlia Clayburn. I am my father's firebrand. It's time I start acting like it.

I push my shoulders back and lift my chin.

"Yes, a walk sounds perfect."

Takara smiles and inclines her head, seemingly glad to see me climbing back out of the darkness. So the two of us, accompanied by the six hulking vampires that are apparently my personal guard, make our way through the camp. Why I could possibly need a guard here within the camp is beyond me, but I don't question it. This is something Alaric was adamant about, even hand-selecting the members himself, so I'm going to have to learn to live with them. Takara assures me that the full guard won't usually accompany me within the camp, but today they're all in tow since it was my first real outing and so that I can get to know them.

The camp is absolutely massive, far larger than I ever could have imagined. There must be thousands of vampires here, ready to defend the pass at a moment's notice. The thought is staggering... and a little terrifying.

I can't help glancing back over my shoulder every so often as we walk, unused to having a lethal, vampiric shadow on my heels. Though I know they would never hurt me—they are, in fact, charged with doing just the opposite—some long-imbedded instincts put me on edge with them at my back.

"That is the great meeting hall," Takara says, pointing a slender hand towards a massive building on the southern side of the camp. A golden bracelet in the shape of a snake winds around her wrist and forearm, jade eyes staring up at me. A matching necklace loops around her delicate throat. I wonder if she has an affinity for the creatures or just liked the way the jewelry looked. "They gather there to receive orders and also for feasts and celebrations." I wonder what a vampire army celebration might look like. Total debauchery, I would imagine.

As if reading my mind, one of my guards—Viktor, I think—grins. "You've not experienced life until you've attended a celebration in our camp, my Lady." His eyes are a mix of brown and green, reminding me of the forest near the lake where I used to swim and play as a child. There's a rakish mischief in them that makes my lips curl upwards at the corners.

"Aye, it's true," another guard—Malcom?—says, his brogue thick, reminding me of da's—or my own at times. Usually if I'm very put out or very drunk. I like hearing it. If I close my eyes, I can almost pretend my father is here with me. "Descartes sings when he's into the blood-laced whisky." He hikes a thumb towards the biggest of the group, a towering tree of a man with a no-nonsense air about him that makes my smile fade. He does *not* look amused or happy to be included in the conversation, his shoulders and jaw set into hard lines. "But alas, it is no' thing o' beauty, my Lady. Truly horrendous," Malcom stage-whispers and shudders, "sounds a bit like feral cats fighting inside of a washing barrel."

Descartes narrows his eyes and my own widen slightly, wondering if Malcom is about to get pummeled or perhaps beheaded…but then the big vampire *grins*.

"I have a lovely singing voice, my Lady. Do not listen to these ingrates."

I huff out a surprised laugh and Descartes winks subtly at me before shoving Malcom so hard that he flies off of the path and into stack of crates with a yelp. I gasp and Takara exhales, something between amusement and exasperation.

"They are all children, I swear to the gods…Human, vampire, even Revenants I bet. All men are *children*."

The other guards laugh and I feel myself relax despite the unease that had settled deep in my stomach with Alaric's departure. I'd been afraid that this new life would be a bleak one, with no laughter or joy to be seen, only blood and battle and death. But with their laughter ringing in my ears, I think that perhaps things won't be so bad.

I eye the meeting hall, wondering again about the celebrations. Would I be allowed to attend? I honestly have no idea how this is all supposed to work. Again, I'm *technically* allowed to do pretty much anything I want—Consorts are above even Dukes when it comes to titles and privileges—but I have no idea how much that holds true with me being *Alaric's* Consort. Ours is a truly unique situation and I have nothing to measure it against, no precedent to rely on. Am I even allowed to come and go as I please anywhere within the camp? Should I stay away from the soldiers? I rub my temples, the endless what-ifs and questions making my head ache.

Fuck this.

I decide then that I'm going to do what I want and see what happens. I've always believed in asking for forgiveness, not permission, so why change now? If I do something I shouldn't, Takara or my guard or Alaric himself will tell me.

Takara continues to point out different parts of the camp: the washhouse, where the army's clothes are laundered; several large bathhouses for the soldiers where hot water is pumped in just as it is in my own room; training fields and sparring rings; several giant stables filled with horses; and—

"A smithy?" I breathe, rushing forward before Takara can stop me. Or, more accurately, the vampire could have easily, but chose not to, which I appreciate. The familiar sounds and scents hit me like a physical blow, and my eyes sting with sudden tears. The heat of the forge envelops me like an old friend as I step inside the open-sided building. I feel Takara step under the covered area behind me, but the rest of the guard remain outside.

I look over the stacks of weapons and wrinkle my nose, immediately feeling a tiny twinge of guilt. I'm admittedly biased, but the craftsmanship of these weapons was nowhere near that of my father's. It's understandable, of course. An army would need copious amounts of weapons, not necessarily of the highest quality. Not the beautiful instruments of war that Arwan Clayburn creates. I miss him in this moment so badly I can barely breathe.

"What the bloody hells are you doing?" a gravelly voice snaps, pulling me from my pursual of one of the blades. I gasp and leap backward, knocking into Takara who steadies me with amusement. The vampire who steps from a back room is built like a bull, with a barrel-chest and arms as thick as tree trunks, and his long brown hair is pulled back into a knot at the back of his head. His eyes are a blue so light that they remind me of ice. A long scar bisects his left eye, ending just above his lip and tattoos cover much of his skin. He looks absolutely menacing, to say the least, even more so than Descartes—which is *really* saying something.

"I-I'm sorry, I was just—"

He glances to Takara and his eyes widen. He quickly bows his head, hastily wiping his hands on his apron. I assume that Takara has already made her rounds through the camp, making sure anyone and everyone is aware of who she is and who she works for.

"Apologies, my Lady. I didn't realize." He straightens and his brow furrows slightly, clearly confused by the appearance of the High General's Consort on his doorstep. I can't blame him. I doubt any Consort in the history of the Blood Peace has ever stepped foot in this type of place before. "Can I, uh, help you with something?" For some reason, I immediately like the vampire. He reminds me of da in a way, though they don't look much alike save their muscular builds. Perhaps it's the unexpected gentleness and kindness in his eyes.

"No, no, I'm sorry I just...Well, I was missing home, honestly," I admit.

Clearly still confused, he says carefully, "and a blacksmith's work table might ease the ache?"

"My father..." I bite my lip, "I'm Dahlia Clayburn." His eyes fly wide.

"Fucking hells," the vampire breathes and my lips twitch. "Er, pardon, my Lady. I don't pay much attention to the gossip that flows through the camp and didn't realize who you were. Your father is *legendary*."

"That's kind of you to say," I reply, giving him a small smile.

"I'm Braddock." He bows his head again in introduction.

"Dahlia."

"It is an honor to meet you, Lady Dahlia." I barely stop myself from rolling my eyes or correcting him that it's just Dahlia. Another thing I need to get used to, I suppose.

"Come, my Lady," Takara says with a light hand on my shoulder. I nod to Braddock, giving a little wave as I walk back out onto the path, but then whirl, unable to stop myself. I've decided I'm going to do whatever I please so, might as well start now.

"Would it be alright if I came back? To assist you or to watch or to...to just..." I can't get the words out to make it make sense. *To feel closer to my father. To feel like myself again in this strange place. To ease the ache threatening to tear my heart to ribbons.*

"It would be my great honor," Braddock says, seeming to understand and placing a hand over his chest. A smile breaks over my face and I nod, turning to stride off with Takara and feeling better than I have in two weeks.

As we near the cabin later that afternoon, a vampire is waiting for me with a letter from Enid and my heart nearly bursts. I almost throw my arms around the boy (though I'm sure he's much older than he looks) but stop myself at the last minute. He gives me a small smile before scurrying off.

"I'll leave you to your letter and have Reginald begin your dinner, shall I?" Takara asks.

"That would be lovely, thank you. And thank you for...for today. For helping to pull me out." I know she understands what I mean. She's been in the darkness before, I can tell. After she lost her family, I can only imagine the darkness that came for her.

"Of course, my Lady." She smiles and heads down the hill. I run through the cabin and throw myself across my bed as I tear open the envelope.

Dear Lia,

Oh yes, of course, we couldn't have survived another moment without your letter. You know us so well. (I hope you can feel how hard I am rolling my eyes at you through this ink and parchment). As ridiculous as you are, I cannot lie and say that receiving your letter didn't make my heart lighten. Do not let that go to your head. The journey sounds amazing. Perhaps I'll get to make it one day.

I'm very glad that you aren't sleeping on the ground like an animal. I'm finding it hard to sleep, truth be told. The room is too big without you here. And too quiet without your snoring.

My mouth drops open in protest. "I do not snore!"

Yes, you do snore. Do not try to deny it. I know I'll get used to it, but for now, I lie awake most of the night and wake bitter and grumpy in the morning. Da even brandished a spoon at me like a sword and called me a demon yesterday. Can you believe him?

I snort. I can see it happening so clearly in my head that I laugh through the tears suddenly welling. *I should be there with them.* I sniffle and continue reading.

Da misses you, of course, and sends his love. I love and miss you too.

Now, tell me more about this bond between you and the High General. It sounds frightening. But also, perhaps, a little…exciting. Don't roll your eyes at me. It is terribly boring here without you and the idea of being connected to a sexy vampire warrior is far better than being stuck here avoiding the throngs of new "friends" who are suddenly desperate to talk to me. Such is the life of a Consort's sister, I suppose. I'm famous and shiny by association, apparently.

I'll write again soon.

Be safe.

-Enid

I turn to lie on my back, holding the letter above me and running my fingers gently over the ink. I miss them so much, but I know they'll be ok. I think about today, about seeing the camp and feeling more like myself and I smile a little.

I know we'll *all* be ok.

CHAPTER 9
ALARIC

My blade slices through the neck of a Revenant as if it was slicing through butter. Blood sprays, hot and thick, the scent of it bitter and sharp compared to the sweet, rich aroma of Dahlia's. At the mere thought, my fangs throb, my throat aching. It's only been a few weeks and already I'm all but addicted. I clench my jaw, pushing thoughts of my Consort and her blood far from my mind. Being separated from her is...uncomfortable to say the least. The bond between us makes me feel as if I'm being pulled apart, stretched so tightly I might snap at any moment. I'd felt it the moment we'd left camp. Hells, I've been feeling it every second of every day since the Choosing. I don't know how much of it is her blood and the binding, and how much is because she's...mine. It's difficult for vampires to be apart from their mates. Our entire beings crave our mates' company, and our every instinct commands us to protect and provide for and please them. I'm not doing any of that, of course, but still, being away is entirely more difficult than I'd anticipated.

The connection with her grows stronger with every sip of her blood. I can feel her more now, like a low buzz in the back of my head. Before we left, I could feel her despair and sorrow, the darkness threatening to swallow her, but I had no idea what the fuck to do about it, and despite part of me clamoring to erase her pain, the other part is beyond irritated that I'm even having to *think* about what the fuck to do about it.

So, I'd done nothing. My very soul seemed to rebel, but I was determined to master these instincts and so I'd avoided her, leaving her to deal with everything on her own. A new life, a new home, pulled from her family that she so clearly adores. I'd taken her blood when I needed it, but had barely spoken to her even then. Thinking of it now, guilt twists my chest. After all, *I'd* chosen *her*—she hadn't wanted this. I hadn't either, but at the end of the day, it's my fault that her entire life has been upended, that instead of a castle surrounded by riches and luxury, she's been forced to move to a fucking war camp surrounded by vampires...

"Fuck," I grate, moving forward across the rocky plain. I'm not handling this well, I can admit that, but things are fucking complicated. I'm not used to all of these feelings, to sharing my home, to her blood. The thought of it now makes a low growl rumble through my chest. The taste of it on my tongue, the fire it spreads through my veins, the life and vitality of it...the things it makes me want to do. In truth, that's another reason for the distance I've been keeping: I don't trust myself around her yet. The things I want when she's near, the way my body craves hers in ways I can't even explain or comprehend...*No, no, no*. I shut out the thoughts before they can spiral—and before I'm striding across this battlefield with a raging cockstand.

This Consort business is very fucking inconvenient. I sigh to myself as I add in the inevitable: so is having a *mate*. I still don't understand how it's possible, how my mate could *possibly* be human, but I can't deny the truth of it. I know it in my bones, in my soul. And I hate it. I fucking hate it at the same time that I love it. It's heaven and hell all rolled into one and if I don't figure out how to deal with all of this soon, I'm going to impale myself on Night's Fury just to end the headache of it all.

"On your left!" Elias calls and I turn just as another Revenant lunges for me. I sidestep and spin, whirling to lash out with my sword. The blade slices through the air with a low whistle before connecting with the Revenant's back, easily cutting through his armor and severing his spine. He screams in pain as the silver stars burn his body from within, and falls to his knees. He bares his black fangs as I loom over him, his crimson eyes wide with pain and fury and fear. I finish the job quickly, without hesitation or thought.

Elias jogs up, his own armor covered in blood—not his own.

"Distracted, are we?" he asks with a smug smile, out of breath but as casually as if we're out for a leisurely stroll instead of in the midst of a bloodbath.

Ignoring his jibe, I jerk my chin. "They're falling back." I survey the blood-soaked plain, searching for Kilgren, though I know I won't find him. The coward never comes into battle with his men, always instead watching from afar and letting them fall in his place.

"Do you want to press after them?" I glance around and do quick calculations before shaking my head.

"No, let them go. We'll fall back to the ridge and regroup. See if they try to press forward again or retreat back past the river." The Revenant stronghold was just over The Devil's Tongue, a dangerous, roaring river with only a single bridge across. To Kilgren's credit, it's a smart choice and easily defended, which is why we've never tried a full attack on them there. I was surprised when reports came in of a Revenant unit moving down towards the eastern side of the Sisters. They don't typically engage here as there's no real point—there's no way through the mountains here. So, I'd made a point to come myself despite the Revenant forces being relatively small. Something about this was strange, and I've been fighting this war long enough to know that strange is never a good sign.

"I'll tell the others." Just as Elias turns to head back into the thinning fray, an arrow sails into my shoulder—*through* my armor. Sharp pain sears my arm, blood pouring hot and thick. I stagger back a step from the force of the blow, gnashing my teeth.

"Alaric!" Elias cries, eyes wide in shock. "How the fuck..." He trails off as I bare my fangs in utter rage, turning to find the bastard who shot me. I find him easily, standing atop a small boulder, black fangs shining as he grins triumphantly. Another leaps from the boulder and sprints away from the battle, running so fast he's nearly a blur.

"Alaric, don't—" Before Elias can finish, I reach up and grip the shaft of the arrow, pulling as I hold the Revenant's gaze. The arrow tears free of my skin, taking a good chunk of flesh with it, and I hold it wordlessly out for Elias. He takes it and I smile at the Revenant.

His crimson eyes that had only seconds ago been gleaming with delight now flash with fear as I streak across the field towards him, faster than a lightning strike. He tries to fire off another arrow, but I'm on him before he can even get it nocked. Blood pours down my arm, my fingers coated with it, but my grip on Night's Fury is as strong and steady as ever. I knock the Revenant to his back, leaping atop him and pinning him down easily. Night's Fury is at his throat a heartbeat later and though there's still fear in his eyes, that triumphant smile returns just before I separate his head from his body.

On some signal I don't see, the rest of the Revenants turn and flee, falling back from the killing field in a wave. Elias is there a moment later, hand over my shoulder to staunch the bleeding.

"How in the bloody fuck did that arrow pierce your armor?" he asks as he hauls me up and we join the rest of the men.

"Stay alert," I tell them. "Fall back to the ridge. You six—scout at our backs." Like the well-oiled machine they are, my men (and women—the term "men" just encompasses the fighting force as a whole, of course) configure themselves into defensive lines as we draw back, ever alert. My scouts remain, fanning out and disappearing into the trees like ghosts as the rest of us retreat to our camp.

"Alaric," Elias snaps as he falls into step beside me. "How did—"

"I don't know," I tell him honestly. "I don't fucking know, Elias." It shouldn't be possible. This armor is all but impenetrable, made from a mix of Treshian steel and the scales of the last dragon to ever walk Braxhelm. It had been a gift from Sebastian when I'd first become High General. *Legendary armor from a legendary beast for a legendary man*, he'd said. So how the fuck could a simple arrow pierce it?

"Get that arrow to the weapons masters and alchemists. I want it analyzed as soon as possible."

Once back in camp, I tear through my pack to find a vial of Dahlia's blood, pulling the stopper out with my teeth and downing the sweet contents in one long gulp. My shoulder throbs and burns, but the wound isn't nearly the worst I've ever had. With Dahlia's blood, I'll heal in an hour or two. Already the pain is fading and the blood flow ebbs.

"Are you alright?" Elias asks as he ducks beneath the flap of my tent.

"Fine," I grumble. I'm not used to being injured, and certainly not used to being taken care of. I'm pissed more than anything, honestly. Pissed that I was distracted enough not to notice the archer. Pissed that he somehow pierced my armor. Pissed that all I can think about right now is Dahlia and wishing she were here beside me more than anything in the world.

"Make sure we have a watch rotation set up for the night."

"Already done," Elias assures me and settles down on the pile of furs beside me, arms tucked casually behind his head.

"And what, exactly, do you think you're doing?"

"You're injured. I'm going to stay with you and nurse you back to health, my liege."

"Fuck off."

"Oh come on now. A sexy healer is a very common fantasy, no need to be shy. I'm sure I can find something resembling the cream robes they wear, if that will help..." He waggles his blonde brows at me and I kick him in the thigh. "Oof! That hurt."

"It was supposed to. Go away."

"I'm comfortable right here, thanks." He turns his head to study me. "Unless you'd like me to bathe you? A sexy healer bathing you is *definitely* a fantasy—"

Despite my injury, I lunge for him, smothering him with a blanket. He laughs as he fights me off and I wince slightly as I settle back into the furs.

"You have such a funny way of saying 'why thank you for wanting to stay with me through the night and be sure that the arrow that miraculously pierced my unpierceable armor wasn't coated in some kind of demon venom or something and ensure I'm alright. You are a wonderful friend and the most adept and handsome First Lieutenant in the history of the vampiric army.'" I frown, not even having thought about the arrow possibly being poisoned. I don't feel as if there's anything running through my veins, don't smell any toxins, but still, he makes a good point.

I settle back, grateful for him, but I refuse to stroke his ego. I stare at the ceiling of the tent but all I see are green eyes staring back. With her blood flowing through me, Dahlia is all I can think of, filling up my entire being. I sigh, not trying to fight it, and let the thoughts of her settle my tumultuous heart. After a long bout of silence, I speak into the darkness between Elias and me.

"You aren't *that* handsome..." I hear him laugh low.

"You've lost too much blood and are now clearly delusional. Sleep, your highness. You need your rest to recover."

I chuckle and drift off to sleep with visions of Dahlia drifting through my head.

CHAPTER 10

DAHLIA

Alaric remained gone for another two weeks. One of his soldiers came to collect my blood twice to take back to him on the battlefield. Though I've grown used to it after the long days, the strain of him being gone is still there, like an ever-present thrumming in the back of my mind.

"Is it normal for them to be gone so long? For battles to take weeks?" I ask as we walk towards one of the sparring rings. I've found it quite entertaining to watch the men practice their hand-to-hand combat...especially when they happen to do so shirtless. Takara has been very supportive of my new hobby, much more than my time in the shop with Braddock.

Things have been much better since that first day that she helped me start my climb out of the dark. I still miss my home and my family, as I always will, but it's getting easier every day.

"Yes, my Lady." I roll my eyes. I've repeatedly asked her not to call me that, but she continues. I'll wear her down eventually. After all, I've got nothing but time. "Do not worry. Battles ebb and flow. It often isn't one fight that starts and ends cleanly. There are retreats and advances, one or both sides regrouping and resting."

I'd never thought about it that way. Admittedly, I always envisioned battles almost like boxing matches: beginning when someone said "go" and stopping when a winner was announced or both sides decided to call it a draw. Now I feel silly. Of course it wasn't that simple or easy.

I nod and we stop outside the largest of the sparring rings. A low stone wall surrounds the area and the ground within is a mix of sand and sawdust—better to absorb the blood, I've learned. With their enhanced healing, vampires don't take it easy on one another inside the ring. It's *mostly* good-natured, but they all fight to win, and the ground is usually painted crimson by the time any match is over.

In one corner, one of the more senior warriors is giving instruction to some soldiers who've only just graduated from the training academy on Sol Island from the looks of it, slowing his motions and demonstrating moves so they can understand the mechanics before practicing themselves. In another corner, two vampires practice swordplay.

I make my way closer to the wall, leaning my elbows against the cool stone. A tall, leanly-muscled vampire with a dragon tattooed across his back is facing off against another male, shorter but brawnier, his fangs glinting in the sun as he smirks. They're both slicked with sweat, slashes and blood marring their bare torsos. There's something familiar about the taller vampire, but I have no idea why. I can't see his face, just the mop of brownish-blondish hair, but even so, something tugs at the back of my mind.

The bigger vampire lurches forward, but the other one is too quick, sidestepping and landing a punishing blow to the other man's jaw. He staggers back, spitting blood and narrowing his eyes.

"You've gotten better, Ravenswood," he says in a booming, amused voice.

Ravenswood? My lips part on a soft gasp.

"Wesley?"

The taller vampire whirls around, his eyes going wide in surprise. A smile breaks across his face just before the other vampire slams into him. The two of them go down hard and skid several feet, dirt and sawdust fanning across the air. I yelp and slap a hand over my mouth. The bigger vampire leaps on top of Wesley and grips his throat.

"Distractions can cost you your life, Ravenswood." He glances up at me and his lips quirk. "Especially pretty distractions." He stands and offers Wesley his hand. Wesley takes it and the other vampire yanks him upward. "Five-minute break," he says, inclining his head to me and walking off to speak with another set of fighters.

I can do nothing but stare for a long moment. I haven't seen him in years, not since we were teenagers and they moved away. He rushes over, grinning a fangy grin, and the sight is jarring. Even so, I throw my arms around him and he squeezes me tightly. He's bigger now, a man, not the boy I'd known. The boy I'd been friends with, running barefoot through town and climbing trees and stealing apples, the boy who had stood up for me when the other boys had teased me and pulled my hair, the boy who'd stolen my first kiss in the loft above his father's apothecary shop. The first boy I'd ever...My cheeks heat at the memory of the two of us, all sprawling limbs and giggling awkwardness and reckless abandon on the edge of the lake all those years ago.

I pull back and smack his chest, making a face at the sweat and blood that now coats my fingers. We both laugh and it feels like I'm back home again, back in my old life where we never moved to the noble district and Wesley never left and I never became a Consort.

"My gods, I can't believe it! I'd heard from Widow Jones that you'd enlisted to be turned, but I didn't know..." I shake my head, smiling bigger than I have in weeks. "I can't believe you're here!"

"I can't believe *you're* here," he counters. "I'd heard that there was a Consort here now, but I never would have thought...how in the seven hells did this happen?"

"That's a very long story," I sigh, toying with the end of my braid. The older vampire whistles to get Wesley's attention.

"Fuck," he says, "I've got to get back to training. Meet me

tonight? My cabin is in Third Quadrant, on the south-east side of the camp, second row closest to the tree line."

"I'll find you," I say, smiling. I can't seem to stop. He grins back, slapping the top of the stone wall before walking backwards. His stomach is flat and taut, the tail of the dragon from his back curling around his ribs. My blood heats at the sight and I shake myself, waving before Wesley turns and trots towards his opponent.

"And who, pray tell, was that?" Takara whispers low in my ear.

"That was Wesley," I say as the two of us stride away from the fighting ring. Wesley keeps stealing glances my way and I don't want him to get in trouble because of me. "We grew up together. Gods, I haven't seen him in years. I can't believe he's here, that he's turned." I shake my head, trying to wrap my mind around it all.

"He is...delicious," Takara practically purrs. "Are you going to fuck him?"

I sputter, stutter-stepping and almost slipping in the mud. Takara quickly rights me and I hear a low chuckle from behind us. I cut my eyes back and see Cyrus obviously attempting to contain his smile.

"What? No!" I say turning back to Takara, cheeks flushed. "I mean...I don't know." I close my eyes, trying to get a handle on my thoughts. "Why would you ask that?" I'm flustered and I'm not even sure why. It's not as if I'm particularly shy or reserved, but I also don't typically go around talking about who I plan to fuck in casual conversation. Takara shrugs a slim shoulder.

"Simply curious." We walk a bit more and she curls the end of her shining black hair around her finger, the color beautiful against her bronze skin. "You could, you know. Fuck him, I mean," she adds matter-of-factly, like she's making sure I know I'm allowed to drink water if I wished. "Remember, as a Consort, you are allowed to have any male or female that you like. Many of them. At the same time, if you prefer."

"Yes, I know, but that's not..." I puff out my cheeks and blow out a long breath. "He's a *friend*," I say, trying to steer the conversation in another direction. Takara purses her lips.

I think the topic has been dropped, but then she says, "If you aren't going to, would you mind very much if *I* fucked him?"

I stop walking and pinch the bridge of my nose as Cyrus laughs again from behind us, not even trying to hide it this time.

"Can we *please* stop talking about who is or is not going to fuck Wesley? I beg of you."

"As you wish, my Lady," Takara says, and I can see that she, too, is smiling. My discomfort is apparently very, very amusing. I scowl, but then, despite everything, I grin too, shaking my head at both of them and feeling lighter than I have in weeks.

~

Dear Enid,

Things are better. I miss you still, of course, but I'm settling in here. I've explored the camp now. Truth be told, the last time I wrote, I had barely left my wing of the cabin. I was wallowing, I'll admit it. But, I'm doing much better now. The camp is even bigger than I'd originally thought—it took me hours to walk the entire thing, and I'm still not entirely sure I've seen all there is to see. The men are a surprise as well. Men and women, of course. I don't know why everyone refers to the entire group as "men" but no one is asking my opinions on that matter. Back to my point: the soldiers (men and women) are not at all what I was expecting either. I'd envisioned hardened, blood-thirsty warriors, and though there are some of those (who I tend to steer clear of), the majority of them are kind and funny and remind me of our friends from the old side of town.

Speaking of—you'll never believe who I found here.

Wesley Ravenswood! He's been turned, of course, but he's still the same old Wesley. Except bigger. And more muscular. And with a very enticing tattoo across his back and rib cage…I digress.

Finding him has helped ease the ache of missing home some, I think. Like having a part of my old life back with me here is grounding me in a way, helping me stay myself in the midst of all this change where mostly I feel like I'm lost, like I'm floating aimlessly at sea with no land in sight, nothing to buoy me or anchor me.

The High General has been gone for weeks now. The bond between us feels stretched, like a wire pulled too tightly, the thick anticipation of it snapping a constant thrum in my veins. I…well, I don't miss him, exactly, but the binding makes me feel as if I do, as if I'm missing a part of myself. It's hard to explain. I'm told it will fade soon and I'll be glad for it when it does. He sends someone to fetch my blood for him while he's away, so don't worry, I'm still doing my duty.

I'm going to meet Wesley tonight and catch up. I'll write again soon, but I just wanted you know that I'm doing ok. I'm doing much better, I promise.

I love you so much. Give da a hug for me.
-Dahlia

CHAPTER 11
ALARIC

We finally arrive back in the camp and the relief I feel at being near Dahlia once more is...disconcerting. It felt as if a fist had been clenching my heart from the moment we left, and its grip slowly eased with each step closer to the camp. My arm healed quickly enough, but the fact that an arrow had sailed through my armor as if it were nothing but cotton is extremely concerning. The arrowhead was something like obsidian, but neither I nor Elias had ever seen anything like it. We're waiting to hear what the weapons masters and alchemists deduce from their study.

Though important, I'll admit that all thoughts of Revenants and battle and what these new weapons might mean for us fly from my mind the moment I lay eyes on her. That fist around my heart finally releases me completely, the relief of it nearly painful. She's walking through the field behind the cabin, grabbing up wildflowers as she moves, smiling softly when she brings them to her nose. She's so beautiful it hurts to look at her, like I'm staring at the sun. Her hair flows down her back in fiery waves, the sunlight making some strands stand out golden against the red.

She looks better than when we'd left, with color back in her cheeks and the shadows beneath her eyes gone. And the way her pants and tunic hug her curves...*Fuck*. A wave of desire crashes into me so forcefully I nearly stagger. The urge to go to her, to wrap my arms around her and pull her close, to fit her body to mine and kiss her lips until she's gasping, is so forceful I actually take a few steps forward before locking my muscles in place. I'd told myself the whole ride back that I'd send for one of my companions to slack this ridiculous need riding me like a thief in the night, but at the thought of it now, my body and mind rebel. *Wrong*, they scream, and I ball my hands into fists. It's one thing to accept that she might truly be my mate. It's another thing entirely to accept that I can never fuck another because of it. *Not happening*. I'm a Montclare prince and the High General. I will fuck whomever I damned well pleased. This mate business can fuck off.

As if sensing me too, she jerks her head up and even across the great distance, our gazes lock. I can see the flecks of gold glinting in the sun and a feeling of belonging crashes through me. All thoughts of taking another into my bed disappear at the sight of her eyes darkening, her lips parting softly. I swear I can hear her whisper my name and my entire body shudders. She brushes the hair from her face and the tension in her shoulders seems to ease. Does she feel the same relief I do at being near each other again? Or has the bond faded for her after so many days? How long have we even been gone? Two weeks? Three? I honestly lost track.

Before I can do something incredibly ill-advised like run to her and take her right in the field, I nod to her in greeting and lead Xanthus to the stable. I give Xerxes a pat as I pass. The horse huffs angrily at me in return, though he leans his nose heavily into my hand. He's proud and dramatic, but I know he hates being left behind and misses Xanthus and me when we're gone. I try to alternate which one of them rides with me from the camp, each of them equally skilled and deserving of time on the battlefield, but Xerxes is far more vocal in his jealousy when it's his brother's turn.

I head into the cabin and stalk directly to my wing. I bathe and pass off my armor to be inspected and repaired. I clean and hone Night's Fury. I transcribe my notes from the battle and compose missives to some of the other generals as well as one to Bastian assuring him that all is well on the Consort front. I do everything I can to keep my mind off of Dahlia, but nothing proves successful. So, I finally give in and find myself heading towards her wing. I tell myself that I'm going to get blood, as is my right, but really, that's only part of the reason. Really, I want to see her, *need* to see her.

But she's nowhere to be found. Every room in her wing is empty. *Where the fuck is she?*

I storm back through the house in an irritated huff to find Elias leaning casually against the stone mantle of the rounded fireplace in the entrance room.

"Third Quadrant," he says breezily, cleaning his nails with the tip of a dagger.

"What?" I bark.

"I assume you were looking for your Consort. I'm told she is in Third Quadrant, has been spending quite a bit of time there while we've been away, actually. Visiting a friend," he adds when I simply stare.

A friend? One of my men? Something I can't name bubbles up in my chest, hot and angry, and I quickly try to tamp it down. *Ridiculous.* She can do whatever she pleases, wherever she pleases, with whomever she pleases. I clench my jaw.

"Why are you here?" I snap at my oldest friend. Elias scoffs, unflappable as always.

"You missed me already, I could sense it." I snort, the tension in my chest easing ever so slightly.

"I just spent three weeks sleeping and fighting beside you."

"It was closer to four, actually," he corrects. *Fuck, really?* "And yet, the hours we've spent apart this afternoon were tearing at your heart."

I roll my eyes and continue back to my own wing, Elias falling into step beside me. We settle into the oversized chairs in front of the fireplace in my study, glasses of blood-laced whisky in our hands.

"Highspear is petitioning for promotion again," Elias says and I groan. All of my soldiers are skilled—they wouldn't be allowed to remain in my army otherwise, of course—but some are far superior to others. Some are meant to lead, others to follow, it's just the way of things. Highspear is a good enough soldier, but he is not meant to lead. He doesn't have the heart or the head for it, and wants it for all the wrong reasons. I've denied his promotion requests twice before. I rub the back of my neck.

"He works hard but...he isn't sergeant material." I don't mean to sound cruel, but it's the truth, and truth is what keeps my men alive, what keeps the entire continent safe. Elias holds up his hands.

"I know, I know. I just wanted to give you a warning that it's coming." He swirls his drink, staring at it thoughtfully before cutting his eyes to me. "Speaking of *coming*..."

I roll my eyes, knowing all too well where this is going. "No."

"Oh come on! No one will know. We'll sneak in wearing disguises. You can have a mustache, or perhaps an eye patch. It will be very cunning and dramatic. And *fun*. Did I mention fun?" He purses his lips, thoughtfully. "Do I need to explain what fun is to you?"

I punch him in the arm, but Elias merely chuckles. He's constantly trying to get me to go to the blood house in the village a few hours to the west. He knows that no one would think much of it. I'm the High General stuck in a war camp in the Northlands—no one would blame me for lowering myself to standards unbefitting a Montclare prince. But I've never agreed. I've had women, of course, but never in the blood house and never humans. Elias tends to forget the reason princes don't take humans, and though I remind him constantly how disastrous it would be if I lost control, he always waves it away as if that detail doesn't much matter.

Elias isn't one to give up though. He gives me a knowing look, his stormy-blue eyes sparkling.

"You can't tell me being around that Consort of yours hasn't... stoked the fire, so to speak." He wings his light brows upward suggestively and I'm torn between being exasperated and amused. I run a hand through my hair, letting my mind drift to thoughts of Dahlia, to the sharp stab of desire I'd felt when I'd seen her in the field...

"No blood houses," I say, firmly shutting the thoughts away.

"Have you ever heard the phrase 'stick in the mud'?"

"Have you ever heard the phrase 'pain in my ass'?" Elias laughs easily, holding a hand over his heart.

"I live to be the pain in your ass, your highness."

I narrow my eyes at him. I hate being called *highness*, and Elias damn well knows it. He does it just to goad me.

"She *is* exceedingly attractive, you have to admit that," Elias says more seriously, running his finger along the rim of his glass.

"I'm not blind," I grate, sounding peevish.

"Well, if you aren't going to fuck her, then am *I* allowed—"

A growl rumbles in my chest and I snap my fangs in Elias' direction before I even realize what I'm doing. I blink in surprise, confused at my reaction. My *over*reaction. *What in the fuck is happening to me?* Elias merely smirks, one brow winging upward in response.

"How *interesting*..." he croons as he takes another sip from his glass. He can't suspect the truth...can he?

"Fuck off," I mutter half-heartedly, embarrassed and confused by what had just happened. But the thought of Elias fucking Dahlia had sent utter rage boiling through my veins, instincts rearing up to tear him limb from limb for taking what was mine.

After a few moments, Elias adds nonchalantly, "This friend in Third Quadrant may be fucking her, though. Just a thought."

CHAPTER 12

DAHLIA

I sit around a roaring fire with Wesley and a raucous group of soldiers. It had started as a small group from Third Quadrant but had quickly grown into a full-blown celebration, soldiers from all over the camp joining in. Some of the group had been out with Alaric and are regaling us with tales of battle and blood. It all sounds terrifying to me, but the excitement and energy running around the fire is palpable, and maybe even a little contagious. They clearly live for this and I have a strange longing in my chest to feel something like this, to feel so a part of something like they do.

"You're ready to run screaming for the hills, aren't you?" Nova, a female vampire and one of Wesley's best friends, leans in to ask. Her silvery-white hair is twisted into intricate braids along the crown of her head, the rest of the locks flowing down her back like a river, and her eyes are a beautiful sky blue. She has golden rings lining the shell of her left ear and another in her nose, and tattoos covering both arms. She smiles widely at me, flashing her fangs. She looks entirely terrifying and unfairly beautiful all at once. She had gushed for almost an hour about one of my father's daggers that she'd won off of one of the lieutenants in a knife-throwing contest, and I'd imme-diately liked her. The three of us have spent almost every day together since I first saw Wesley in the training ring.

"Oh, I wouldn't underestimate our Dahlia," Wesley says, bumping my shoulder with his, lips curled up in a sexy half-grin. I nearly sigh at the sight. Nothing physical has happened between us yet, just a rekindling of an old friendship and the beginning of a foundation of a new one, but there's definite possibility there, I think. He's certainly attractive enough, anyone can see that, and though I don't feel that spark between us that we'd had when we were younger, I think maybe we just need to stop skirting around it and dive in. Maybe the spark will come back if we just give ourselves the chance. I'd be lying if I said I haven't *thought* about touching him a hundred different times, relearning the shape of his body and the feel of his lips, but each time it's seemed that something was building and we were *finally* going to give in, another face flashed across my mind. One with dark hair and golden eyes that seemed to look right to the heart of me. Alaric and the cursed bond between us has effectively ruined the moment each and every time. I've told myself that next time, no matter what, I'm going to fall into the moment with Wesley. I think I owe myself the chance of happiness —or at the very least, some fun between the sheets of Wesley's bed.

I glance at Wesley again now, at his easy smile and sparkling eyes, the way his arm muscles move and flex in his sleeveless tunic. He's so much bigger than he used to be, muscles in spades where he'd hardly had any before. *Perhaps tonight is the night. Perhaps tonight we see if the flame can be coaxed back to life between us...*

But even without anything sexual happening, I've been so happy to have him here with me. To have a friend who truly knows me— not as the High General's Consort, but as Dahlia Clayburn, just a blacksmith's daughter with soot on her nose and a penchant for breaking rules. The last two weeks with Wesley and Nova and the other soldiers have made me feel like maybe I can be happy here after all. It's not the life I envisioned or would have ever wanted, but it can be a good life nonetheless, I think.

I take another drink of my ale. It's crisp and sweet, and I'm already feeling delightfully fuzzy because of it.

"There was a time, I think we were, what, twelve maybe?" Wesley begins.

"Oh no," I groan, hiding my face in my hands, knowing what story he's about to tell. My guard sits around us—except for Malcom, who had slipped off into the darkness with Takara hours ago—and they all lean in closer.

"Well now we have to hear it," Viktor says, Isaiah nodding emphatically beside him.

Wesley laughs and continues on, clearly enjoying the spotlight

"We had to be about twelve and there was this utter little prick, Lowell Harkner. He was bigger than most of us—I hadn't hit my growth spurt yet and turned into the fine slab of muscle you see before you," he winks, making Nova and I both snort, "—and he liked to bully the rest of us. Until one day, little Dahlia Clayburn said no more. So, one afternoon when we were all by the pond, she put a *live snake* down his trousers. He screeched like babe and pissed himself!"

"You didn't!" Nova exclaims, a glint of respect in her eyes. My guard roars with laughter and I can't stop the smile that pulls my lips. I hike a shoulder and hide behind my tankard, taking another long sip.

"Then she told him that if he ever laid a hand on any of us again, she'd put snakes in his bed every single night for the rest of his life. Needless to say, there was no more bullying after that. I bet the bastard still crosses the street when he sees you coming, doesn't he?"

I wrinkle my nose but admit, "Perhaps..."

Descartes lifts his tankard in my direction.

"To our Lady Dahlia, wielder of serpents and punisher of pricks!"

Cheers ring out around us. I laugh, rolling my eyes, but I raise my cup in return. Everyone converges, slamming cups together, ale and blood sloshing all over. I squeal just a bit, but laugh, feeling like I'm really part of things here for a moment. Just then, something flashes through my mind.

Not just my mind, my entire body.

Alaric. I know without a doubt that he's near, every inch of me singing with electricity and tension. I'd thought the bond had faded over these weeks, but now it feels as strong and solid as ever. I yank my gaze from the others as cheers erupt around the fire. My eyes land directly on Alaric, as if drawn there by an invisible force. The moon shines down directly on him like a beacon and I can't drag my eyes away, no matter how hard I try. Seeing him again after all these weeks is like being struck by a bolt of lightning.

The men all raise their glasses and clap their fists over their chests. My heart thuds as I realize that perhaps he'll be angry that I'm here, drinking and carrying on with his men. I shrink back, trying to hide behind the hulking bodies around me. Which is stupid, of course. I know he can sense me here.

But he doesn't storm over and demand that I leave. In fact, he doesn't even pay me any attention at all, merely weaving through the crowd, accepting handshakes and slaps on the shoulder and a cup of something with a nod of thanks. He doesn't so much as look my direction. I'd been worried moments ago that he'd be angry that I was here, but now I realize he doesn't give two shits about me or what I do. The thought sours my mood. Which is utterly ridiculous. It shouldn't matter what Alaric thinks of me. Or doesn't think, apparently. I'm his Consort, a glorified blood dispensary, nothing more. If we were in this situation under normal circumstances, I would never see him at all. I remind myself that he isn't being cruel, it's just the way things are. I try not to take it personally, but the ale is making that hard.

I try to shake the thoughts away...and ignore the way my blood heats at his nearness. Regardless of anything else, I can't pretend I don't notice the way my stomach flutters as I study him, heat pooling in my belly. He's all in black, the leathers molding to his muscular body in a way that should be a crime. Embarrassingly, I actually bite my lip as my gaze skates down his body, from his broad shoulders to the smooth skin of his chest, visible where his shirt gapes open, and lower still, to his narrow hips, the way his weapons belt hangs there in a way that's inexplicably sexy. His dark hair tumbles over his forehead and I have the sudden, intense urge to brush it away, to dig my fingers into it and pull his face to mine...

As if he can feel me staring or sense my thoughts, his eyes snap to mine.

My lips part as I inhale softly, and he holds my gaze as he responds to someone to his right. I'm frozen, locked in a strange trance with Alaric that I can't explain and can't break free from. His eyes are dark amber in the firelight, and I wish so badly that I could read the thoughts clearly racing behind them. Is he surprised to find me here? Does he care? Had it been hard for him to be away because of the bond? Is he...thirsty? I swallow hard at that, and Alaric's eyes dip to my throat. His jaw clenches before he turns away to speak to someone else, though it looks as if pulling his gaze away had been an effort. Or maybe I'm just seeing things because of all the ale.

I let out a slow, shaky breath and then throw back what's left in my cup. Though I tell myself not to, I glance back at Alaric, and Elias catches my eye instead. He winks, as if we're in on some secret together that I don't quite understand, and grins widely. I blush and give him a small, awkward wave because I'm honestly not sure what else to do and the ale says a wave is a good idea. I turn back to Wesley.

"Is this...normal?" I ask, gesturing towards Alaric as he continues to mingle with the soldiers. He actually seems to genuinely care about what they're saying. He doesn't look my way again but I know without a doubt that he's well aware of me watching him. He'd told me that he'd be able to feel my moods and emotions, and my cheeks flame, remembering the way my body had reacted when I'd been watching him a moment ago. Would he have felt that? Would he have understood what the feelings meant? *Gods.* I rub the back of my neck.

"What?" Wesley asks, taking a sip of his own ale.

"Alaric...visiting with the soldiers like this?"

"Oh, yeah," he says easily, and then laughs at my incredulous expression. "I know, you wouldn't think it, but it's true. He fights beside us, bleeds beside us, mourns beside us, celebrates beside us. He thinks of himself as one of us, despite being the High General, despite being a fucking *prince.*" Wesley sounds as if he worships the vampire, as if he were almost a god. Seven hells, almost every soldier around the fire is looking at Alaric like that. Do they truly see him that way? I assumed they were all just terrified of him, that he was a rough and strict leader who demanded obedience and loyalty, settling for nothing less, but now I think that I may have been very wrong about Alaric Montclare.

Braddock brings me another tankard of ale and though I probably should stop drinking at this point, I smile in thanks, raising the glass to the big blacksmith before taking another deep drink. I start to relax a bit more with every sip and soon I'm laughing with the men, cringing when some of them begin to sing horribly off-key, and leaning in as more stories begin—now all of them about Alaric. Battles won and lost (though those were few and far between), great heroics and daring rescues. He's like a character in one of Enid's novels for gods' sake, the ones she pretends are all about adventure and chivalry, when *really* they're about a devastatingly handsome almost-villain who does unspeakably arousing things to the heroine in their bed chamber that make your toes curl and your blood heat just reading the words on the page.

I may or may not have sneaked several from her collection and read them myself on occasion...

"And so the bastard has the tip of his sword resting just over the High General's heart," a vampire with russet-colored hair says, talking animatedly, "armor gone, wounded and covered in blood, the rest of us with our backs against the wall—literally. We were backed up against the edge of a cliff with snarling hounds keeping us at bay." Alaric isn't smiling, exactly, but his lips quirk up on one side in an amused half-smirk. "And the Revenant says, 'kneel, High General. Kneel before me and surrender and I might spare your men.'" He pauses dramatically before adding, "And then the High General smiles at him. Fucking *grins.*"

A chorus of cheers rings out. The vampire tamps his hands in the air, telling them to quiet down, but he's grinning, obviously getting the exact reaction that he wanted.

"So, the High General is there, grinning with a sword aimed at his heart, and he says," the vampire looked around for a minute, adding to the drama, and pitches his voice low, "'I kneel before *no one,*' and lunges forward, impaling himself on the fucking sword and putting his fist straight through the Revenant's chest. Ripped out the bastard's spine. He fucking *ran himself through* just to get close enough to end the prick!" Cheers erupt, even louder than before. Elias slaps Alaric on the shoulder, shaking him lightly, and he looks at the ground—hiding his smile?

He's sitting across from me now and when he looks up again, our gazes meet through the flames. My pulse races and his eyes are glowing in the firelight, burning, his body tensing. Fire seems to flick through my veins, my pulse racing and *thoughts* rising in my mind again. Crazy thoughts. Impossible thoughts. Thoughts I need to force away as soon as possible. His eyes dip briefly to my lips and I feel like I'm going to combust. I unconsciously wet them and I would swear that Alaric leans forward, as if he's going to leap across the fire to me. *No, I'm imagining things. It's the ale and the binding and I need to stop staring at him.* But I don't. I can't. He scrubs his hand over his jaw, dragging a finger slowly over his lips and my stomach flips.

"What about the time he used a Revenant's entrails as a rope to climb up the side of a cliff?" someone calls out, and cheers and laughter break out around us, shattering the strange moment. Alaric shifts his gaze to the man who'd spoken, all evidence of the intense tension from a moment ago erased as if it had never existed at all.

Gods, maybe it hadn't. Maybe it was all in my head. Maybe I just really need a good fuck.

"Are you alright?" Wesley asks. I blink and shake myself.

"Of course, why?"

"You look flustered. And mouthwatering, if I'm being honest," he adds with a smirk. "Your blood is pounding in your veins right now."

"Oh, uh, must just be the ale," I say, forcing myself to relax and forget the moment with Alaric. I give Wesley an easy smile and swat him in the shoulder. "And I can't believe you just said I looked *mouthwatering*." I roll my eyes and he snaps his fangs playfully in my direction, making me giggle and squeal.

The night continues with more stories, more songs, more laughter, entirely too much more ale, and thankfully, no more odd moments with Alaric, though I can't shake the feeling that he's watching me like a hawk, despite the fact that he never seems to actually look at me. It's unnerving.

I'm surprised by the comradery, the obvious love among the warriors. I must have said something out loud without realizing it, because Wesley nods.

"There is something between brothers in arms—or sisters—that can't be explained, a bond that is unlike any other. It's love and honor and a willingness to kill and die for the person next to you." I mull that over, realizing I still have much to learn about the vampires and the army.

Eventually, things begin to wind down, soldiers breaking off into small groups or retiring with partners on their arms, making it very clear what they have on their minds. Others have leave for several days and talk of making their way to the village and visiting the blood house there. I rise from my seat, tottering a bit. I laugh loudly, steadying myself on Wesley's arm while Nova grins at me.

"Easy, there," Wesley says, amused. Our gazes lock and his lips curl into a crooked smile, making my stomach flutter. He runs a hand through his shaggy hair. "Did you, uh, want to come back to my—"

"I'll escort you back to our cabin," a cool voice interrupts from behind us. I whirl to find Alaric standing a few feet away. I gasp quietly. Or I *think* it's quietly. I can't be completely sure at this point. If I didn't know any better, I would say there's a note of possessiveness in his tone, a little extra emphasis on the word *our*. But that's obviously ridiculous, so I push the thought away.

Wesley and Nova both incline their heads and put their fists to their chests. Wesley cuts his eyes to me, a clear question, and I nod.

"Of course, sir. I'll see you tomorrow, Dahlia."

"See you," I say, keeping my eyes on Alaric. I'd been completely ready to go back to Wesley's cabin only a heartbeat ago, to see if we could find a way to rekindle things, but one sentence from Alaric and Wesley is all but forgotten. One look at him, and the spark that had been missing between me and Wesley flares so hot I think I might burn to ash. Why is this happening? I shouldn't want him like this. I *can't* want him like this.

And yet...

He gestures towards the path that leads through the camp to the cabin. *Our* cabin.

It's full night now, but the paths throughout the camp are lit with tall torches. The vampires can all see perfectly well in the dark, of course, but the rest of us need a little help. The wide path is mostly empty, a stray soldier or servant here and there. It's much quieter here, especially after the raucous around the fire.

"Did you enjoy your evening?" he asks, startling me. I blink in surprise, not having expected him to talk to me, but I recover quickly.

"Yes, I did. The ale was *delicious*," I say with a grin, my thoughts delightfully fuzzy around the edges. I shouldn't speak so freely, I definitely shouldn't *grin* at him for gods' sake. He seems to relax a bit now that it's just the two of us.

"I'm glad of it. Before I left you seemed...unhappy."

"I was, but I'm doing better now." I toy with a curl, winding and unwinding it around my finger, and he watches intently, as if my hair fascinates him. "I, uh, wasn't expecting to see you there. I didn't know that you mingled with the commoners." I wave a hand airily and he *almost* laughs. Maybe. I turn and walk backwards, eyeing him critically. Or as critically as I can with everything slightly pear-shaped. "Was that story true? The," I pitch my voice low in an attempt to mimic his timber, "I do not kneel. I thrust myself upon yer sword so I can rip yer heart out with ma bare hands because I am a big, sexy vampire warlord."

"Sexy vampire warlord, am I?" he muses, and his lips definitely curl upward this time. I'm...eighty percent sure of it.

I roll my eyes and wave his comment away, the ale making me entirely too forward and informal, but I can't seem to care. It's not as if he's unaware of how attractive he is, after all. I've heard plenty of rumors about the women who practically throw themselves at his feet everywhere he goes, just begging to be in his bed. A flare of jealousy leaps in my chest, a desire to claw those nameless, faceless women's eyes out of their heads. *What in the seven hells is wrong with me?*

I tamp the jealousy away and push on, feeling chatty and wanting to take advantage of him actually conversing with me like two normal people. I frown. Being chatty isn't necessarily a good thing. I have a habit of getting very chatty and very...handsy when I drink too much. I quickly tuck my arms behind my back as I walk, gripping my elbows just to be sure my hands don't get minds of their own and somehow wind up on Alaric's chest or shoulders or...other places.

"So, is it true then?"

He exhales and runs a hand through his hair, making the strands even more unruly. I'm momentarily distracted by the movement, the way the strands fall across his forehead, the way I want to tangle my fingers through it. I try desperately to focus my thoughts, but he isn't making it easy.

"No...it was his spine I ripped out, not his heart." A very small smirk tilts his lips, no doubt this time, and I stop walking and stare at him in shock.

"Did you...did you just make a joke?"

He hikes a shoulder and I grin stupidly, huffing out a laugh. Alaric studies me and I quickly look away from his intense stare before I do the very stupid things the ale thrumming through my veins is telling me to do.

"Your accent," he says, surprising me as I turn forward again and we fall into step beside each other, though I know he's slowing his pace so that I can keep up. I wrinkle my nose, knowing what he's about to say.

"Aye, my da comes out a bit more when I've had too much to drink, I'll admit. Or when I'm spitting mad."

"Good to know," he says, amused. I smile and hike a shoulder. We settle into silence as we walk. I glance sidelong at him though, studying his profile in the moonlight. His golden eyes seem to glow in the darkness, like a wolf's. When he catches me, I yank my gaze away, but can't stop the laugh that bubbles up. The entire situation is just so damned comical, isn't it? A blacksmith's daughter now a Consort to the High General of the vampire army, a Montclare prince for fuck's sake, and here I am, stealing glances at him like a lovesick teenager. I laugh again, harder.

"Have I missed some jest?" he asks.

"It's nothing," I assure him trying to stop my laughter. He gives me a dubious look but lets the matter rest.

"I'm glad you're back," I say as we enter the cabin, standing in the large entrance room. He turns to look at me, arching one dark brow, and I want to kick myself. "I mean, when you were gone, it was...difficult. Because of the binding. I felt your absence, in here." I place my hand over my chest. I don't think I'm explaining it right at all, but he nods.

"I was also...affected." His voice is gruff, as if he's admitting some kind of weakness and is loath to be doing so. Of course he would have felt the distance far more than I did. Though it hasn't faded nearly as much as I thought it would at this point, he's taken far more of my blood since the binding. Speaking of my blood makes me wonder...

"If I'm drunk, and you drink my blood, will you get drunk too?" His brow furrows.

"I...don't know," he answers slowly, sounding surprised and maybe a little intrigued. I smile and meet his gaze, feeling bold and flirtatious and reckless.

"Care to find out?"

CHAPTER 13
ALARIC

Is she...flirting with me? I know she's quite drunk and that's the reason she's acting this way, but I can't deny that I like it. She'd swayed as we'd walked through the camp, almost as if she were dancing to music that only she could hear. The movement of her hips made my cock and fangs both throb. I'd felt her gaze on me throughout the evening, and some ridiculous, ego-driven part of me had been delighted by that fact, by the fact that she'd been watching *me* all night, not the *friend* she'd been spending time with, the one she'd been sitting awfully close to by the fire and touching so casually. The jealousy that had speared through me at the sight had been sharp and jagged, but I'd prepared myself before we'd gone to the fire, knowing what I might see. Even still, keeping my temper reined in while keeping the calm façade had taken every ounce of my training and control.

But she'd been staring at me, a voice whispers through my mind. *Me.* Not Ravenswood. And the way she'd been staring, the way her heart had raced and her breath had shallowed as our eyes met through those flames...

I stare at her now as we stand near the fireplace. She gives me a look that's half flirtatious, half challenging, and I almost smile, my lips quirking up ever so slightly on one side. Feeling lighter than I have in too long to recall, simply being near her easing my soul in ways I never expected, I decide to play along.

"Let's find out." I beckon her to follow me and her heartbeat speeds up, thundering and mocking in my ears. "Your heart, Keeva," I groan.

"As if I can control it," she retorts from behind my back and I can all but hear her rolling her eyes. I do smile now, listening to her stumbling a bit to keep up with my long strides. "Fucking vampires," she grumbles, and I'm fairly certain she doesn't realize that she's said it out loud. I stifle a laugh as we enter her dining room.

I point to one of the chairs.

"Sit," I command. She gives me a crooked grin and a mock salute before waltzing to the table, humming quietly. I rummage around in the large cabinet for a cup and turn to find her perched on top of the table instead of sitting in the chair, swinging her legs and leaning back on her hands. She's running her fingers through her hair as it tumbles down her back in crimson waves. I don't know why her hair is so attractive to me, but I can't keep my eyes off it, constantly imagining what it might feel like to tangle my fingers through the strands. Her cheeks are flushed from the ale and the color does little to help thwart my desires.

She seems so at ease and comfortable now, more so than I've ever seen her. It's...nice. I like seeing her this way, all tension and pretenses and expectations gone. Is this how she was before all of this Consort business, when she was home and happy with her family? Part of my mind wonders if she could ever be this way here— without the help of copious amounts of ale, that is. Could she ever be truly happy here, with me? *No,* I remind myself. Not *with* me. That's impossible. But here, as my Consort. I want her to be. I need her to be. But I honestly don't know how to make that happen. I have no experience keeping the company of women for anything other than a night or two in my bed, let alone with dealing with a human.

I push the thoughts away and approach with a crystal goblet. She gives me a sly grin.

"Ach, yer in for a treat, High General. I am good and sloshed." My lips twitch and damn if her brogue isn't adorable. Drunk or angry, she said, but I can't help but wonder if it comes out any other time, perhaps when she's screaming in pleasure...

She holds out her wrist, pulling me from my thoughts, and I take it. I watch the blood pumping through her delicate veins, my fangs lengthening and throbbing. It's been almost a full month since I've had her blood fresh from her body and the anticipation of it now makes a small shudder run up my spine. I gently rub my thumb across her skin, slow, soft circles that make something begin to shift in the air around us. I know I'm playing a very dangerous game, but I can't seem to stop. I use my nail to slice a quick gash in her skin and she gasps quietly.

"Did it hurt?" I ask softly.

"No," she says, a little breathless. "I..." She holds my gaze for a moment more and then looks away. "No, I barely felt it." I quirk a brow, knowing she'd intended to say something else. Was she gasping at my touch *before* I cut her? I can tell she's feeling...something but the bond isn't strong enough yet for me to decipher her emotions clearly, just a faint impression of *something*. Her pulse is racing, her blood pumping into the cup, but that could be for myriad reasons. Fear. Disgust. Hatred.

But...I don't think it's for any of those reasons. I think it's for something else entirely. *Not that it fucking matters*, I remind myself.

The urge to dip my head and take her wrist between my lips is nearly overwhelming. I swallow hard and inhale deeply, the scent of her blood hitting me like Revenant's cudgel to the chest. *Gods*.

I sit the goblet aside and examine the wound. As I'd suspected, the accelerated healing from our blood exchange at the Choosing has faded. *Yet the binding affected her while I was gone, made her uncomfortable. Interesting.* I pierce the pad of my thumb with a fang, a small bead of blood welling.

"What are you doing?" she asks as I swipe my thumb over the cut.

"The quick healing you've been experiencing from the binding during the Choosing has faded. A bit of my blood over the wound will have the same effect and will keep you from walking around with bandages on your arms constantly."

"Oh," she whispers and when I raise my eyes from her arm, I realize how close I've somehow moved to her. Our bodies are nearly touching, her thigh only a hairsbreadth away from mine, our faces so close that I can see every fleck of gold in her eyes, every nearly invisible freckle on her nose. She holds my gaze and I can feel the danger in the air around us, like a prowling beast circling us, just waiting to pounce. But I don't look away and neither does she.

Slowly, ever so slowly, she raises her other hand and presses it softly to my chest. I shudder, my eyes sliding closed. That simple touch is enough to make my body burn and my soul ache. She slides it upwards, my breaths making my chest heave beneath her fingers. When they reach the place where my shirt gaps and she touches my bare skin, I nearly lose control. Even so, I don't move when she leans forward, her lips so close to mine that I can feel her soft exhales skating over my skin.

"Alaric," she whispers, and the sound is enough to send me to my knees. My fangs sharpen, my body tensing—to strike? *Fuck.* It's enough to break the trance I've been in, fear for her suddenly coursing through my body at the thought of hurting her. My eyes flash open and I step away so quickly she nearly tumbles off of the table.

She blinks as if coming out of a dream and quickly drops her hand into her lap. Her cheeks heat and I can tell she's embarrassed. I don't know what to say or do, so I clear my throat and turn away, snatching the goblet from the table.

"Let's test your theory, shall we?" I say, hoping my voice is as even as I'm willing it to be. I drink, her blood coating my tongue and sending fire through my veins. I keep my back to her as I wander around the room, running my fingers over the carved cabinetry. I hear her yawn behind me, her heart rate slowing from the wild drumming a few moments ago. I force my body to calm as well, to forget what had just happened. Or what had *almost* happened, rather.

I take another sip from the goblet and I almost laugh—I can indeed taste the ale in her blood, and it sends a pleasurable hum through my body. I turn to tell her the results of our little experiment, but she's curled on top of the table like a cat, fast asleep. I huff out a small laugh and shake my head at how quickly she could be pulled under. Then again, I know great amounts of alcohol have that effect on humans.

I move closer and watch her for a few moments. She has her hands pillowed beneath her cheek, almost like a child, and her lips are parted as her breaths grow slow and even. I'm not sure how long I watch her, simply enjoying being near her, the soft sounds of her breathing soothing an ache in my chest that I never even knew was there until now, until she eased it. I give myself these few moments to lean into the mating bond, to feel the connection between us, the power and joy and feeling of rightness washing through me. I can see all too clearly how easy it would be to become used to this, to let myself fall into her completely and be truly happy, perhaps for the first time in my long life. But I cannot. *Enough.*

I shudder and pull my gaze away, glancing around.

What the fuck am I supposed to do now? Leave her to sleep on a table all night? Track down her Keeper to handle the situation? That seems more trouble than it's worth, knowing damn well that she's off with Malcom. *At least one of us will enjoy this evening with company,* I think sourly. Even the thought of summoning a companion for the night makes me feel sick. So, I'm apparently doomed to be celibate for the rest of my fucking life. I pinch the bridge of my nose, forcing the annoyance away, focusing on one problem at a time. And right now, my problem is that Dahlia is asleep on a fucking table and I can't leave her here all night.

I sigh and steel myself before I hook one arm beneath her knees, the other across her back, and lift her easily from the table. Gods, it's as if she's made of feathers, perhaps even air. *So damned fragile, so easily breakable.* I clench my jaw, remembering how close I'd come earlier to doing something reprehensible, something that could have killed her so fucking easily.

She doesn't wake, but stirs a bit, turning to lean her cheek against my chest. I freeze for a heartbeat, not daring to move or breathe or think. The feeling of her in my arms, of her leaning into me so trustingly, it's nearly too much, but not nearly enough at the same time.

"Fuck me," I grate quietly. Why are the gods punishing me so? I've given my entire life to protecting others, to keeping the continent safe from those monsters, and this is how I'm repaid? With a mate I can never touch or claim? To be so close to her and yet never close enough, always having to keep myself away. It's fucking bullshit.

I move swiftly down the hall to her bed chamber. I settle her atop the mattress and quickly unlace and remove her boots. I refuse to let myself even *think* about removing anything else and instead maneuver her beneath the thick blankets fully clothed. I'm just pulling away when her hand brushes mine.

"Alaric," she whispers. The word hits me just as hard now as it had earlier.

"Yes, Keeva?" I say, voice low and embarrassingly rough.

She doesn't answer, just gives a small "*mmm*" and sighs contentedly, a soft smile playing on her lips. Still asleep, I realize. Is she dreaming of me?

It. Doesn't. Fucking. Matter. I step away and quickly retreat to my wing.

Retreat.

The High Fucking General of the vampiric army, the most feared warlord in all of history, *retreated* from a drunk human muttering in her sleep. I slam my door shut so hard the wood creaks and the hinges shake. I lean against it heavily, rubbing the heels of my hands against my eyes.

"I am good and fucked," I whisper to no one.

I wake with my head heavy and throbbing, and mouth parched after a long night in the cups. I groan and stumble to my bathing chamber to splash water on my face and clean my teeth. Snippets from the night before flash behind my eyes: stories and laughter around the fire, Alaric walking me back to the cabin, having an almost normal conversation...running my hand up his chest as I leaned forward...

"Shite," I whisper, putting my head in my hands beside my water basin. He hadn't seemed angry, exactly, but he'd moved away in a hurry. I'm so embarrassed. He must think I'm so foolish, the stupid human thinking she could kiss a prince. But...he hadn't looked repulsed by the idea in the moment...had he? I rub my temples. I can't be sure. My memories are fuzzy to be honest. I hope he isn't angry with me, though. I hope he just pretends it never happened and we can go back to being...whatever we are. I'm honestly not sure. He'd left almost as soon as we'd arrived after the Choosing, and had been gone almost a month, so I'm not really sure how our relation- ship is supposed to work with him back at the camp.

I wander to my dining room and find Takara perched in a chair, the table covered in plates and serving dishes and my mouth waters as my stomach gives an obscenely loud grumble.

"Hungry are we?"

"Starved," I admit. Takara watches in almost fascination as I devour my breakfast of eggs, cheese, fruit, and bacon, taking more than enough for three grown men.

"So, how was your evening?" I ask over the rim of my glass of winterberry juice. Takara grins a fangy grin.

"It was lovely. As was this morning—three times." She tucks her hair behind her ear, practically preening. I huff out a laugh, unable to stop myself. I wonder about a vampire's stamina, but then flashes of Alaric immediately fill my mind. His lips so close to mine, the spicy, woodsy scent of him cocooning me like a warm blanket, the air thick and heavy around us with the promise of something dangerous and exhilarating. I shake myself and force my ridiculous thoughts into line. I'm sure I'm misremembering, just wishful thinking and ale-fueled fantasies getting jumbled in my head.

"And how was your night?" she asks.

"Not as...fulfilling as yours," I say pointedly, making Takara snort, "but it was wonderful. I enjoyed being around the soldiers, drinking and laughing. It reminded me of being home, of spending nights in the square or in the pub." I take another bite of my eggs. "Do you think all of those stories about Alaric are true?"

Takara looks thoughtful. "I know how men like to embellish things...but Alaric is the High General for a reason." She shrugs.

I try to imagine all of the things I'd heard the night before, the battles and the brutality and the heroics. I can see it all clearly, can see Alaric riding headlong into danger all in the name of saving and protecting others. I'm not sure if I'll ever be truly happy here, in this life that was forced upon me that will never be a full life, but I can admit that I'm coming to respect Alaric far more than I could have imagined, and that makes being here far more bearable. I may not find happiness, but I can find contentment, I think, and that might be enough.

"I thought today we might visit the village."

"Village?" I perk up at that, despite my aching head.

THE VILLAGE ISN'T LARGE, but I wouldn't care if it only consisted of a tavern and an inn and maybe a bakery. Living at the camp isn't nearly as bad as I'd originally imagined it would be, but it still feels nice to be away from it all for a bit. Though there are other humans in the camp, squires and laundrywomen and the like, I've only caught glimpses of them here and there. Every time I try to approach, they scatter like birds, almost as if they're afraid to be seen speaking to me. But being in the village, surrounded by people who are just doing normal things that don't involve blood and fighting and preparing for war, feels like being home again, like the camp is just some strange dream.

Word quickly spreads of who and what I am, and I'm soon being waited on hand and foot at each shop. I know it's just the way of things, but I wish no one knew. I wish I could have just spent the day being a normal girl, shopping and eating sweets, wandering the streets and enjoying the very human world around me.

I suppose even if Takara hadn't made it known that I was the High General's Consort, my vampiric guards would have given it away. It's the full group of them since we're outside the walls of the camp, and they're impossible to miss. They're completely different here than they are, all amusement and laughter gone from them. They're all stoic and alert, as if just waiting for a threat from every shadowy alleyway, every rooftop, every wagon that rolls past.

"Am I in danger here?" I ask Takara quietly. I know that though the majority of the Revenant forces are beyond the Sisters, held back by Alaric's army, there are still nests hidden within Braxhelm and attacks still happen from time to time. Plus, humans are just as capable of being monsters.

"You are perfectly safe," Takara assures me. "Your guard are simply doing their jobs."

I cast a glance over my shoulder. Descartes looks like he would tear someone in half without a second's hesitation if they so much as breathed threateningly in my direction. A young boy's eyes widen when the vampire's eyes narrow at him, sending him scurrying away so quickly he almost falls twice. Malcom, Viktor, Isaiah, Cyrus, and Kane all look equally as lethal, equally as ready for a fight. I'd almost forgotten how terrifying they really are. I've grown so used to them and their jesting and easy smiles around the camp. To my relief, Viktor throws me a very quick wink before schooling his features into a hard mask again. I smile and turn to continue on with Takara beside me, pointing out the different shops down the main thoroughfare of the town. I spy the infamous blood house that most soldiers from the camp come here to visit and my mind whirls with curiosity. I don't go in, of course, but...maybe one day...

After a long day and many, many purchases—pastries and writing supplies, a few new garments, gifts for my father and sister, and even a broach in the shape of a wolf that I thought perhaps Alaric might like, though as soon as we left the shop I chided myself for being so ridiculous and decided to give it to Wesley or Nova instead—we finally arrive back at the camp. To my utter surprise, I'm happy to be back. It still doesn't feel like home, exactly, but it's becoming a close approximation. I feel safe here and I like the familiarity of it even after only a few weeks.

I eat a quick dinner and let the night before play through my mind over and over again. I'd been exceptionally drunk, sure, but did I really imagine the moments with Alaric? He'd been more relaxed with me, for sure, but it was more than that. I swear he'd looked at me like...well, like maybe he wanted me the way I wanted him. Had he been able to tell what I was thinking? To know exactly how badly I'd wanted to move those few precious inches when he was taking my blood, our bodies so achingly close, but not touching the way I desperately needed? Had he known that I wanted him to lift my wrist to his lips, to feel his tongue and teeth against my skin?

Even now just thinking about it, my pulse begins to speed, my chest rising and falling quickly as my imagination begins to spin out of control. What would it feel like to have Alaric's fangs pierce my skin? For him to do...other things while he drank? I shiver and then put my head in my hands, groaning.

"What in the seven hells is wrong with me?" I sigh and head to my room, deciding to write to Enid to distract myself.

> *Enid,*
>
> *I got to visit the nearby village today. Well, nearby is a bit of an overstatement—it took us hours to get there, but it was so nice to be around people again. I felt almost normal (and don't even say that I've never been normal). I got you and da a few gifts that I'll send along with this letter. I hope you like the journal. The snow lilies engraved on the front reminded me of the dress you used to wear every day when you were six or seven. Do you remember? Mum could scarcely get you out of it long enough to wash it.*

I smile at the memory, the bittersweetness of it making my chest ache. I honestly don't even know if it's a real memory or if I just heard the stories so many times, mum and da telling them beside the fireplace and smiling fondly down at Enid and me, that it's branded into my mind.

> *Last night there was a small revel with some of the soldiers. I went with Wesley and Nova, of course, but you'll never guess who showed up—the High General himself. I couldn't believe it, but Wesley said he often spends time with*

the men, celebrating and sharing a laugh over drinks. Well, he doesn't really laugh very much, but you get my meaning. Who would have thought? The stories they told of him were crazy. If even half of them are true...well, it's no wonder he's the High General and the greatest warlord Braxhelm has ever known.

I chew on my lip, the need to talk to my sister about my ridiculous growing...what? Infatuation? Desire? *Feelings?* for Alaric nearly overwhelming.

I think there's something wrong with me, Enid. I'm having...thoughts about Alaric. Thoughts that no Consort should be having for her prince. I thought it was just because of the binding during the Choosing, but I don't think that's all it is. I know it's ridiculous, but I can't stop myself, can't stop my imagination from running wild whenever I think of him, can't stop this...wanting. I almost kissed him when I was drunk last night (speaking of which, I'm having a cask of the ale sent with this letter as well—it's absolutely delicious, but dangerous when it comes to decision-making it seems. Use it wisely). What do I do? This has to stop, but I don't know how. I wish you were here.

I scrub tears from my eyes.

I'll write again soon. Give da my love and give him the sketches enclosed so he can make a pair of swords for Wesley and Nova.
   -Dahlia

I seal the letter and lay it on the table with the gifts and sketches so I can give them to the squire tomorrow morning. I crawl into bed and try to sleep, but it's no use. My mind is too busy, my thoughts too tumultuous, my body too on edge. Maybe I should go to Wesley's cabin and slack these desires, take the edge off of these needs that are driving me mad. Maybe that's the whole problem. I just need *someone*, not necessarily Alaric. The bond just has my thoughts confused. Even without the spark between us, Wesley and I can surely find our way to pleasure together.

But even after convincing myself that this is the perfect plan, I don't move to dress or leave the cabin. I remain in my bed, staring at the ceiling but seeing dark curls tumbling over golden eyes. I close my eyes, but the image remains. I sigh and give in to the inevitable, skating my fingers over my breasts and down my stomach, my skin so sensitive that goosebumps erupt over every inch. Eventually, my hand slips beneath the blanket. I let the picture of Alaric in my mind change and move as my fingers delve, making my hips arch and a gasp escape my lips. I cast my mind back to last night, when he'd been standing so close to me.

In my mind, he doesn't pull away when I lean forward. Instead, he cradles my face as I press my lips to his, as I grab the front of his shirt and tug him forward. In my mind, he shifts so that his hips are wedged between my thighs, and I swear I can feel him against me now, hard as steel. In my mind, he whispers my name. I move my hand faster as the vision in my mind grows frantic. I imagine him running a hand down my side before gripping my hip and wrenching me hard against him; his lips hard and urgent on mine, demanding his due, dominating my mouth; him kissing across my jaw and down my neck; him flicking his tongue across the soft skin of my neck before sinking his fangs deep into my flesh—

I cry out as I come in a rush on my own fingers, my hips bucking and writhing. My climax rips through me like wildfire, setting every nerve aflame and leaving me in ashes on the bed. It feels like hours before I come down from it, my breaths finally slowing and my heart quieting inside my chest.

"*Seven hells*," I croak into the darkness before turning to bury my face in my pillow.

CHAPTER 15
ALARIC

I pace in my chambers, trying and failing to keep Dahlia from my mind. I distracted myself with training a new group of soldiers fresh from the academy most of the day, punishing my body and theirs in an effort to keep my mind away from things that had almost happened last night. Things that *can't ever* happen. It hadn't worked of course, just as pacing a hole through my rug isn't helping now. Her soft touch on my chest, the way her lips had parted in what looked like invitation...or demand. The way she'd leaned forward...

A growl rumbles through my chest remembering what came next: the way my body had reacted to her touch, the things it had craved, the way my mind was completely consumed with wants and needs. I'd never felt so animalistic in all my years, never more like the monsters vampires used to be called. The absolute fear I'd felt at the idea of hurting her—or worse—had been the only thing to clear my mind and help me regain control of the primal instincts screaming inside my body.

I run a hand roughly through my hair and toss back my drink, enjoying the sharp burn and closing my eyes. I'll master this, I'll figure it out. I'll—

My eyes snap open and I stare towards her wing, as if I can see through the walls straight to her chambers. My heart races inside my chest, my body tensing as my fangs slide long, sharpening. I thought I'd heard...yes, there again—a gasp...and a soft moan?

"Oh fucking hells," I groan. She's in the throes of something, there's no doubt, but *what* exactly? Is she alone? The thought of her pleasuring herself has my cock as hard as the mountains surrounding us in a heartbeat. But then another thought rises: what if she *isn't* alone? What if she'd brought another man—or woman— to her chambers? A swift and hot rage floods my chest like lava. I strain to hear a second heartbeat, to sense another, but find nothing. The relief that washes through me is absolutely staggering, nearly making my knees buckle.

"Get a fucking grip on yourself," I command, taking deep, settling breaths.

Which is a terrible mistake. A glorious, spellbinding, terrible mistake. Every muscle in my body goes rigid as her scent hits me like a battering ram. Her arousal is even sweeter than her blood, like honey, and I can barely breathe from the force of it, the pull of it.

"Oh *gods*," I whisper as my fangs shoot even longer, nicking my bottom lip. I taste blood and my body shudders, the sudden need for *her* blood and her body nearly shattering my willpower completely. I barely keep control, but I don't know if I can maintain it for long. Eventually, I'll have to learn to deal with this, but tonight...it's too much. I stab my feet into my boots and storm from the cabin, running out into the night as fast as my legs will carry me. I run and run and run until I'm high up in the mountains, crouched on a peak near the top of one of the Sisters.

I'm nearly hyperventilating, my breaths sawing in and out of my chest like razor blades. I close my eyes and force my body to obey my mind. Eventually, my breathing and frantic heart both slow.

"Fucking hells," I say on a shaky exhale as I collapse onto the freezing rock beneath me, sprawling and staring up into the night's sky. I've never felt this way before, this loss of control, this all-encompassing need and desire that nearly made me forget all sense and reason and storm right into her room and do...*gods* the things I wanted to do. I close my eyes and lay there for hours more, forcing myself to remember her scent, force myself to learn to think around it, to accept it and master my body. I make sure I'm entirely under control before I move a single inch back towards the camp.

Having a Consort is an annoyance.

Having a mate is torture.

My solution to the situation with Dahlia is to avoid her entirely. I don't know if it's the best solution, but it's the only one I've got that is guaranteed to keep her safe. Though I worked for days on end to master myself, forcing her to consume my thoughts, forcing her scent into my memory so that I can be completely sure I'll be able to control myself, I still stay away. The fear of what would happen to her if my control slips outweighs the pain of not seeing her. Vampires are meant to be near their mates, their mate's presence soothing in the way no other can be. But if it keeps her safe, and more importantly, alive, I'll gladly take the pain.

So, I stay away. I send a squire to collect her blood as I did when I was away from the camp, though I'm only on the other side of the cabin. I make sure that I won't run into her when coming or going. Part of me feels guilty, knowing she probably thinks she did something wrong or feels as if this is a punishment, but I try to remind myself that if we were in a normal situation, this is how it would be. I wouldn't see her. We wouldn't be near each other. We'd be separated by an entire castle instead of this small cabin.

"The arrowhead is obsidian—veined with *basilisk venom*," Elias says dramatically. "It's how it pierced through your armor." He studies the arrow that had recently been embedded deep in my flesh.

My shoulder twinges slightly at the sight, a phantom pain from that unexpected injury.

"That's impossible," I say, eyeing him and the arrow warily. He shrugs.

"That's what the masters say." I run a hand down my face.

"Where in the fucking hells did they find basilisk venom?? They're supposed to be extinct!"

"There have long been rumors that some remain in caves deep within the ice giants on Zantos Island."

I frown. I know the stories, of course, but to think that Kilgren actually believed in them enough to send his men that far north, through the treacherous Slyndrian Sea to that frozen island, and then into the caves of those icy mountains...all for something that could pierce my armor? That seems extreme, even for him. Though of course basilisk venom has other uses, I can't help but think that this was for me, specifically. But why? Even an arrow straight to my heart wouldn't be enough to end me. I don't understand and I don't like the feeling.

A knock at the door pulls my attention away.

"Enter."

Highspear steps through the door and Elias flashes me a quick, sympathetic smile.

"Sir, I'd like to speak with you, if you have a moment?" the young vampire says. I can tell he's trying not to sound nervous, but his voice shakes ever so slightly. I sigh, knowing what he wants and knowing how this conversation will end. Elias drops his boots from my desk and stands.

"I'll just be going then." He mouths *good luck* before leaving the war room, clapping Highspear on the shoulder as he passes.

"Have a seat," I say, straightening in my high-backed chair. He sits in the one Elias had just vacated, though doesn't dare prop his boots up. He bows his head before speaking.

"Sir, I want to petition for promotion...again." A flash of anger flares in his brown eyes but it disappears quickly. He clears his throat gently before continuing. "I feel I'm ready, that I deserve it."

I study the boy. He's young, by immortal and mortal standards alike, only thirty or so when he was turned, and that only happened ten years ago. He looks young, as well, his features soft and child-like, eyes a bit too big for his face, the brown as dark as chocolate.

"Why do you want to be a sergeant, Highspear?" He blinks at that.

"I...well, doesn't everyone want to be promoted?"

"No, actually. Many are happy to follow rather than lead. So, why do you want to lead?" I watch him intently as his brow furrows, clearly having given this question no thought before this moment. That tells me enough. But I wait, giving him a chance to explore it. Perhaps he'll surprise me. It isn't likely, but there are times when it happens...my mind drifts to a certain firebrand who surprises me at nearly every turn, but I close the thoughts away.

"I...I want people to listen to me," he finally says. "To take me seriously. To do what I say and know that I'm right." I sigh. I am *not* surprised. This is exactly why I've denied his promotion petition twice already. Though I've never asked him before, I've learned to read people very well in all my years, especially soldiers, and I've always known that he wants power for all the wrong reasons. He's a decent enough soldier, seems like a decent enough man, I suppose, though I don't know too much about him other than that he came from very poor, remote village in the far west.

"I have to deny your request, Highspear. I'm sorry." He looks bewildered, his big eyes wide and full of surprise.

"But sir, I—"

"You are not ready to lead, for you want to lead for the wrong reasons."

"But—"

"It's my final word on the matter." I cut him off firmly, though not cruelly. Then, the bewilderment fades and something close to rage simmers in his eyes. His lips press into a thin line and his fingers curl into fists on his thighs. "You are a good soldier and I value you in this army, but you will not be a sergeant."

He stares for a moment longer, disbelief and fury warring in his expression, but then he takes a deep breath and the emotions disappear completely. I narrow my eyes a fraction, the complete wipe of his expression a little unsettling. He gives me one sharp nod.

"Yes, sir. Thank you, High General." He rises from the chair and quickly leaves the room, his shoulders and back rigid with tension. I put my forehead in my hands, rubbing my temples, when I hear the door open again. I snap my head up, annoyed at the lack of a knock, but then blink in surprise.

"Bastian?" My brother smiles widely and holds his arms out as he strides across the room.

"Hello, baby brother." I round the desk and he wraps his arms around me, slapping me hard on the back.

"What the fuck are you doing here? Why didn't you tell me you were coming?"

"I just wanted to check in on you, see how you were settling in with the whole Consort business." He eyes me. "It seems to suit you. You look...different. Better. The fresh blood does that, I suppose." *Or finding your fucking mate.*

I cross to my sideboard and pour us two glasses of whisky. Handing one to him, I lean back against my war table.

"It's taken some getting used to, but I'm figuring things out."

"I knew you would," Bastian says, beaming. One thing I have never had to wonder about is Bastian's love or his pride in me. "And she's adjusting to life here in the camp? Her Keeper has sent no complaints to the Magister."

"Yes, as far as I know, she's fine. She's found...friends, among some of my soldiers. I think that has helped her transition to this new life."

"Good, good. Most Consorts have entire courts at their disposal. It's important for humans to have that, I think. To not feel alone." I mull that over and take a long sip.

"So, you really came all the way here just to check in on me?" I ask, brow arched suspiciously. Sebastian smiles and toys with one of the figurines on the map.

"I did. The first Consort can be overwhelming for any of us, but your situation is quite unique." After a few moments he adds, "And I'm avoiding going through the tithe and tax reports with Gerard."

"Ahh, there it is. You came to escape your responsibilities," I say grinning.

"Ok, ok, fine," he says, throwing up his hands. "The main reason was skirting my responsibilities—some of them are so damned boring," he says, sounding downright whiny. "But also to check on you," he adds, pointing a finger accusingly. "Mostly to check on my favorite brother whom I love so dearly and want to see succeed in every way."

"Oh fuck off," I say rolling my eyes, but grinning. We decide to take a stroll through the camp. The men always enjoy getting a visit from the leader of the Clan and Sebastian is a gracious one, speaking and smiling and shaking hands.

"Have you ever heard of a mate...being human?" I ask, trying my best to sound casual.

He frowns. "Why would you ask?"

"One of the soldiers," I lie easily. "He was absolutely convinced one of the humans at the blood house was his. Just blood drunk, I'm sure." Bastian laughs.

"Probably right. The young ones can get quite infatuated with the donors, it's true." He looks thoughtful and adds, "I suppose it *could* be possible. I read in the old histories of mates that were shifters from the wildlands of Melkane, before the Great Flood, of course. So, I suppose a human isn't *completely* impossible, but I can't imagine something much worse than that."

My chest tightens. "Why's that?"

"Well, you either don't turn them, which means you only have a very finite amount of time with them. You'll watch them grow old and die—and that's only assuming they aren't killed by something else before age takes them. And then you'd be lost. Or you attempt to change them and pray to all the gods it works and that when they die, it isn't for good. I can't imagine being able to bear it."

The exact same thoughts I've had since the moment I realized Dahlia was mine. There is no easy answer. There is no right answer. There is no answer at all, I remind myself, seeing as how I can never actually claim her as mine. I can only stay away and watch her from afar, make sure she is as safe as happy as possible without truly being in her life, and do everything in my power to make that life a long one. It's agony to even think of it, but it's the reality of my life for the foreseeable future.

I think about telling Bastian about the arrow, but I don't want to alarm him yet, not until I understand what it really means. So, I try to push all other thoughts away and just enjoy the time I have with my brother.

"Again," I say in between ragged breaths.

Elias groans from across the ring, his chest slicked with sweat and heaving.

"You can't be serious," he protests, wiping sweat and blood and dirt from his brow. I give him a look that says that I'm, in fact, very serious. "We've been at it for hours, Alaric."

It's true. My plan to stay away from Dahlia is not going well. I've stayed away, that part has worked out fine, but it's torture. Each day that passes, I'm finding it harder and harder to keep myself from going to her. My instincts rebel at the idea of *choosing* to remain away from my mate. When she's in the same camp, in the same fucking house, and I still make the conscious decision to keep us apart—it feels like my chest might collapse under the strain. And not to mention the cravings that wrack my body day and night, the need to touch her, to taste her, to please her until her voice is raw from screams of ecstasy. My body is in an eternal state of torture, never being able to find satisfaction without Dahlia no matter how many times I may find release on my own.

It's fucking agony.

So, I've done the only thing I know to do and that's to throw myself into training with all my might, doing drills until my hands and feet bleed, until my muscles scream in protest. And still, it only helps to occupy my mind for a time. Still, I long to go to her, to do all manner of unspeakable things to and with her, but also just to *be* with her. To sit beside her, to have her mere presence act as a balm on this scorching ache encompassing my entire soul.

Elias gives me a knowing look.

"This wouldn't have anything to do with you avoiding a certain Consort, would it?" I growl low in my chest.

"I'm not avoiding her," I snap.

"Uh huh. Sure. Whatever you say, your highness."

"Pick up your sword or you're losing a limb, Elias. Either way, we're going again."

"Seven fucking hells," he grumbles, grabbing his sword and shaking his head at me as we meet again in the middle of the ring.

CHAPTER 16

DAHLIA

Alaric is definitely avoiding me. I thought maybe I'd been imagining it at first, that he'd just been busy with training and the never-ending duties of the High General, but when a squire came to take my blood a few days after the night when I'd almost kissed him, I knew without a doubt. He wasn't gone from the camp or busy, he simply didn't want to see me. And so it's been for weeks now. I never see him within the cabin, we never pass in the hallway or run into each other outside. He sends a squire for my blood, and even when I catch a glimpse of him across the camp, I swear he makes a point to disappear into the crowd so quickly it's as if I've imagined him there at all.

I know it should mean nothing to me. I know I shouldn't care whether I see him or whether he's avoiding me because I did something stupid. I know that I'm reading too much into a drunken night. I know that I can't have these fucking *feelings* for him—it's ridiculous. And the fact that I know how ridiculous it is and yet can't stop the feelings, is making me want to pull my hair out! What the fuck is it about this vampire? It has to be the binding. It was supposed to have disappeared but maybe something went wrong. Maybe I was given too much, or maybe his blood is special or different than the other princes. Maybe I'm just cursed.

"Fuck," I grate, kicking out at a rock on the hill behind the cabin and sending it sailing through the air before hitting a tree.

"That was quite impressive, my Lady," Kane calls from behind us, and I shoot him a quelling look—which only makes him smile in return.

I walk to one of the boulders strewn around the hill and climb up, lying back and staring up at the overcast sky. The wind blows around me, bringing the scent of dahlias of all things. They grow here in the Northlands. Mum had been born here and had always loved the flowers. They wouldn't grow in the south, so she'd settled for naming a daughter after her beloved blooms instead. I miss her suddenly, a sharp stab of pain through my heart. We didn't always get along—she didn't love my stubborn or reckless streaks by any stretch of the imagination—but she was a good mother and always made sure that at the end of the day, I knew how much she loved me. I wonder what she would think of all of this. Me, a Consort to a prince and living in a war camp in her beloved Northlands. That part she might like, I think. She'd always dreamed of taking us here, of moving us all to the mountains and trying to instill in us her love of snow and ice. The thought makes me actually long for true winter to come, so I can see what she loved, to maybe feel a little closer to her.

"A letter came for you, my Lady," Takara says from just beside me.

I scream and bolt upright, nearly toppling off of the boulder. Kane is there so quickly it's as if he'd appeared out of thin air, catching me easily and settling me back atop the rock.

"Thank you," I say, breathless, my heart racing.

"Of course, my Lady." He steps away and I turn to glare at Takara.

"You scared the piss out of me!"

Takara arches a black brow. "I made sure to make noise as I approached to avoid startling you. I cannot help if you weren't paying attention."

I roll my eyes but hold out my hand out for the letter and gesture for Takara to join me. The vampire leaps on top of the rock as easily as if she were stepping up on a stair, graceful and elegant. She settles in beside me and leans back on her hands as I open the envelope.

Lia,

You must come home at once. Leland Dunlevee will not leave me alone. I made the mistake of kissing him—don't judge me. I'm blaming the ale you sent!—and now he follows me around everywhere I go like a little lovesick puppy. Da thinks it's hilarious and does nothing at all to help my cause or deter the boy. In fact, he invites him over to dinner! The entire house is overflowing with flowers because Leland brings by at least one bouquet a day, sometimes two! We're running out of space and the flower merchants are running out of stock! I can barely breathe past the cloying scent of roses and lilies and orchids. He doesn't even get the flowers that I like for fuck's sake. Trust me when I say that kiss was not worth all of this follow-up torture.

I laugh lightly, and Takara arches a brow.

"My sister has an unwanted suitor, apparently. One who is very enthusiastic." The vampire smiles, revealing her fangs, and laughs.

"My husband was much the same," she says. "I played hard to get, as they say, but he didn't give up. He came by every single day, even when I refused to open the door for him." Her smile turns a little bittersweet, and I can't stop myself from reaching over and placing a hand on Takara's arm, squeezing gently. The vampire shakes herself. "He was a damned fool, really," she adds, the sadness lifting. I huff out a laugh and continue reading.

I suspect I'll be suffocated by them all before you write again. Mourn me, dear sister. And perhaps send one of your vampire guard to scare Leland off? I would consider it a great favor...

Moving on to less flower-related topics, I wish I could offer help when it comes to your feelings for the High General.

I cut my eyes quickly to Takara, hoping that the vampire isn't reading the letter, but she's staring off into the distance, maybe lost in memories of her husband, the family that was taken from her.

But...would it really be so bad if something did happen? I know it isn't how these things usually go, but, well, nothing about your situation is usual, is it? Just be careful, no matter what you decide.

Give Wesley my love. Ask him if he remembers the time I hid from Sally Crenshaw in his father's shop for a whole afternoon while he snuck me candies beneath the counter. He was truly an angel that day. I think I even loved him for at least a week afterward.

I love you.

-Enid

P.S.

If something does happen, you must tell me every single detail! Every single one, I mean it.

I shake my head, half amused, half disappointed. It didn't matter anymore. I'd been wrong about what I'd thought might be between me and Alaric, and now he's avoiding me completely. There will be nothing to tell. I ball my hands into fists, annoyed for reasons I can't even explain. Annoyed and hurt and embarrassed and pissed off and so on edge I could scream.

I suddenly need to do *something* to shove Alaric firmly from my thoughts and get over this strange infatuation. Anything.

And I know exactly what it is.

I STORM THROUGH THE CAMP, dodging vampires and humans as I go, barely offering smiles or nods of acknowledgment as I pass. I know Kane is somewhere behind me, probably thinking I'm insane, but I don't care—and at least he's giving me some space. The sun is setting and the sky is streaked with gold and pink, but I barely notice the beauty. I'm on a mission. I'm going to force a spark to life if it kills me. My old friend, Shreya used to say that the best way to get over one man, was to get beneath another. So, that's what I'm going to fucking do. I'll be beneath Wesley all night if I have to. I'll let his glorious body chase all thoughts of Alaric from my mind.

I make my way past the meeting hall and bath houses, past First and Second Quadrant and through the training rings—but slow as I near the smallest ring, the one reserved for one-on-one combat drills. My lips part on a soft inhale as I watch, unable to pull my gaze away, all thoughts of Wesley and my plan vanishing.

Alaric is there, fighting with Elias, their blades crashing together again and again as they whirl and spin and seem to blur around the ring. They're both shirtless and while Elias has one of the most beautiful bodies I've ever seen, I can barely spare it a glance. Seeing Alaric's bare torso is enough to steal the breath from my lungs, to make my muscles tremble and belly tighten. His shoulders and back are broad, tapering to a trim waist, the muscles at the base of his spine forming a "v" that is intensely sexy. He's all corded muscle and taut skin, ridges and planes that I long to explore. His skin is covered in scars, some large and jagged, others fine white lines that are barely noticeable, but they all make him even more attractive to me, all show that he's fought to be where he is, that he's fought for all of us, to keep us safe.

The way he moves was like lightning and smoke, streaking effortlessly around the ring in a fluid, graceful way that doesn't seem to be possible for someone so big. Elias is good, but Alaric is clearly better, moving as if he and his sword are one being, the blade just an extension of his arm. Every movement is practiced and perfect, as if he's done them a thousand times.

He turns as Elias lunges at him, giving me a full view of his front and *dear gods*. His chest looks as if it's been carved from stone, and even slicked with sweat and smeared with blood and dirt, it makes my mouth water and my blood heat. No, not heat, *boil*. His stomach is lean, row upon row of chiseled muscles across his abdomen that I want to touch and taste. His leather pants hang low on his hips, deep indentions marking either side and seeming to point directly to...

"*Gods*," I whisper.

His head snaps up and turns my direction, and when our gazes collide, his eyes blaze, like the gold has been melted down in the forge. Elias takes advantage of Alaric's distraction—or tries to, anyway. He drives his sword forward, but Alaric deflects it without even taking his eyes off me, twisting his wrist in a way that sends Elias' blade flying across the ring. I barely hear his muttered *fuck* over the ringing in my ears.

Seeing him now, after so many weeks, hits me like the lash of a whip. I can barely breathe, barely think. He stands stock still, chest heaving and staring. Staring like he's just seen a sunrise for the first time...or possibly a ghost. His lips part, but before he can say a word, I take a step back, then another, somehow a third, before I turn and run from the practice rings as fast as my legs will carry me.

I'm not going to let the sight of Alaric's perfect body distract me from, well, my distraction. Seeing him again has only made me want to push him away even more, to forget him completely. Or at least that's the lie I'm telling myself. Either way, I don't dare slow. I run for all that I'm worth to Third Quadrant.

I bang on Wesley's door, out of breath and heart hammering loudly in my ears, so loudly it sounds like thunder. He opens it a moment later, brow furrowing as he takes me in.

"Dahlia? Are you al—"

I cut him off, throwing myself at him and slamming my lips to his. Literally. My teeth clash painfully against his, and I wince, hoping I didn't break anything.

"Ow!" he cries.

"Sorry! Sorry," I pant, and we both laugh. His lips pull into an easy smile, the one I remember from all those years ago—minus the fangs, of course. "Wesley, I just...I need a distraction," I tell him honestly. "*Please.*"

"I am *very* distracting..." he murmurs as he draws me back to him, closing the door behind us.

He leans in and kisses me again, softer this time, and it's...nice. *No. No, no, no. I need the spark. I need fire. I need Alaric erased from my mind.* I wrap my hands around his neck and tilt my head, deepening the kiss...at the same time Wesley tilts *his* head the same way. We both laugh again and try to correct, only to move in the same direction again.

"Ok, ok, you go left, I'll go right," Wesley says, a grin in his voice. We manage to get it right this time, but when I move my hands up the back of his neck and into his hair, my ring gets caught.

"Oh! Oh, shit, don't move. Hang on...there." I manage to free myself and let out a shaky breath. I lean forward again, running my hands over Wesley's stomach and up his chest. He makes a low, appreciative rumble in his chest, and I kiss him again, more successfully this time around. We begin to move backwards towards his bed in the corner when—

"Ow!" I yell when he steps on my foot.

"What—" Wesley trips then, stumbling backwards over his boots and tumbling to the floor, bringing me with him. We collapse in a heap, my elbow cracking painfully on the wooden floor. I wince but a moment later we break into an insane fit of laughter.

"What is wrong with us?" I groan, still laughing, and turn to bury my face in his chest. He chuckles. "We used to be good at this. Well, after that first time anyway. That was a little rough, I'll admit, but we got much better after that. So, what the seven hells is wrong with us now?"

He sighs and wraps an arm around me. There's nothing but friendship in the embrace, and I know then that that's all there is between us: friendship. I'm glad for it, but it won't exactly help me with my little problem.

"I think it's just not meant to be. The same thing happened to me and Nova. We tried a handful of times but it was just awful and awkward every time. We're better as friends and we both know it. That's not to say that friends can't have *great* sex, but sometimes it just doesn't work out that way. Plus, she dabbles with males, but really has much more fun with females."

I sigh. "I had a feeling that was the case—about us being non-sexual friends, I mean, not about Nova's sexual preferences—but I thought maybe if we tried it would, I don't know, force the fire again."

"Sorry to disappoint. You seemed...desperate for a distraction, like you said. Want to tell me from what?"

I exhale roughly and sit up, wrapping my arms around my legs and resting my chin on my knees.

"It's nothing. Just...trying to adjust to everything, I guess. It's all so much and I just needed to not think about it for a while." It's partly true.

"Well, there are approximately two thousand other vampires who might serve as a distraction for you, if you want to give it another go. I have a few in mind right now I could call, or we can hold auditions if you'd like." I smack him in the chest and he laughs lightly, easing up to his feet and reaching down a hand to help me up.

"Do you want a drink? We can get sloshed and go mess with First Quadrant's armory. Or steal all the laundry from Fourth Quadrant's wash house." I grin, a different kind of spark lighting between us. The old mischief, the reckless fun of the young and stupid. I wonder just how much Kane will let us get away with…but knowing that he himself is a notorious prankster, my grin grows wider. Not only will he let it happen, I bet that he'll actually *help* us.

"That sounds like an excellent plan."

ALARIC CONTINUES TO AVOID ME, obviously completely unaffected by seeing me that day at the practice rings, but I've gotten over the initial sting of it. Hardly think of it at all really. I gladly give my blood to the squire—a shy young vampire named Milo who has adorable dimples—not wishing at all that the High General was the one taking it himself. I don't mind not seeing him, and I don't feel the pull to him like I did before, and I don't think about him at all.

Some of those things may be lies, but I'm going to continue to say them until they become truth. Eventually, they have to…don't they?

Though I haven't tried to force Alaric from my mind by sleeping with anyone else, I've thankfully found distraction in other places. I've spent time with Braddock at the forge, made several more trips to the village, and gotten to know some of the other humans here. I've started learning old Nakish, Takara's native language, and though she says my accent is atrocious, she's very encouraging and patient with my lessons. I've also taken to reading late into the night in Alaric's—or, technically, *our*—study. It's got hundreds, maybe even thousands of volumes lining the floor to ceiling shelves, and though many are in languages I don't even have names for, I'm making my way slowly through the collection as best I can.

"Gods, have you ever seen a blade so beautiful?" Nova gushes as we walk through one of the old practice fields behind Fifth Quadrant that's no longer used. It's bordered by a thick expanse of trees on two sides, a steep hill dropping off on the right down to a wide stream, and a small pond at the edge of the far end. The three of us have started lounging around the pond in the mornings after the vampires finish their training exercises and other duties, the area quickly becoming "our" spot.

Nova twirls the sword as we walk, slashing it through the air and looking so graceful and deadly that I don't know whether to be impressed or afraid. Probably both.

"Yes," Wesley says, "mine." He grins and taps the hilt of his own Clayburn sword resting at his hip. Da had done beautiful work, taking my sketches and adding his own remarkable touches, to make twin blades for the vampires. Each has the Wolf Coven's sigil on the pommel, but Nova's has a pattern of vines along the cross guard, while Wesley's has ravens in flight. They're both truly pieces of art and my heart swells with pride at my father's skill.

Nova scoffs. "Widow Maker can't hold a candle to Reaper's Lady."

I laugh and roll my eyes. "With the exception of the vines versus the ravens, they're *identical*. You are aware of what identical means—"

"Stop," Wesley hisses, cutting me off, his body suddenly tense and alert, all joking gone. Cyrus and Viktor are in front of me in an instant, swords drawn and fangs bared, and Wesley and Nova move to put me safely behind them as well. All of them move in a strange, coordinated dance that's both impressive and terrifying. I don't know what's going on, but I've never seen them react this way, have never seen them look so...scary, like a true threat is near. *Revenants?* My heart thunders in my chest and my eyes dart around the field, trying to find the danger.

"There," Cryus says in his low, rough timber, jerking his head towards the tree line in the distance. I squint and a moment later, a small group of hellcats bolt from the forest, sprinting across the field and disappearing quickly into the thick woods on the other side.

"Gods," I breathe in awe. I've read about hellcats, but I've never actually seen one before. They don't typically venture south of Elshrire, preferring the cooler temperatures and the mountain terrain of the Northlands, so I certainly never encountered them back home. They're black and sleek, fur shining like oil, and absolutely huge, nearly as large as horses. Dagger-like claws tip their massive paws, and tails with spiked-balls on the end swish behind them as they run. They're terrifying but beyond beautiful...the smaller ones are even kind of adorable. And, I'll admit, I have the most ridiculous urge to pet one. Surely something so cute can't be *that* dangerous...right?

"Are the herds usually that small?" I ask after everyone finally relaxes, determining that the danger has passed.

"That was no herd, my Lady, not by a long shot," Viktor responds, sheathing his sword at his belt. I decide my next order of business is to get swords made for all of my guard. I laugh inwardly imagining da's indulgent smile when he receives my next request. I can just see him shaking his head. *Supplying the whole of the army, now am I?*

"That was just a small family. A herd can run forty, even fifty deep, and can kill even an immortal if one was to find themselves caught in the middle of a stampede."

"Not to worry, my Lady, they don't usually cross this close to the camp," Cyrus assures me, his islander accent thick and melodic. I nod and the guard shifts back, allowing me, Nova, and Wesley to continue towards the pond, though they stay a bit closer than before. Though he'd sheathed Widow Maker back at his belt, Wesley's hand rests on the hilt, obviously on alert as well. It's easy for me to forget sometimes that he's much more than just my easy-going, mischievous friend. He's a highly skilled, highly trained, killing machine.

"You know," Nova says after a few moments, "I'm so glad you don't make me call you *my Lady*."

"Oh fuck off," I say. "I've asked them not to either, but they won't listen."

"What was that, *my Lady*?" Viktor calls from behind us and I can't help but laugh.

We finally make our way to the edge of the pond and Wesley flops down into the grass while Nova hops up on a fallen tree. She walks along it like an acrobat, twirling Reaper's Lady as she moves. I laugh, thinking that Nova might just be in love with the damned sword, and kick off my boots. I make my way tentatively into the edge of the water. It's chilly, but not so cold that I can't enjoy soaking my feet.

"So, you're going on a mission with Alaric?" I ask Nova.

"It's no big deal," she says, shrugging a shoulder and trying to act nonchalant.

"Oh come off it," Wesley says, tossing a stick at her. She dodges it easily, flipping her body backwards across the log like it's nothing and smirking at Wesley after she lands. "First Lieutenant Kovach hand-picked her." Wesley smiles, and I love that he isn't jealous or disgruntled that Nova had been selected and he hadn't. He's merely happy for his friend. Wesley really is just a good person, a great man. *Gods, why can't I have feelings for him? It would be so easy, so nice.* I sigh inwardly, but then frown.

"Kovach?"

"Elias," Wesley clarifies. *Oh, right.* I'd forgotten that most of the soldiers are referred to by the surnames here, at least the higher-ranking ones.

"It's not dangerous, is it?" I ask, chewing my lip. They're set to leave the next morning but already an icy ball of worry is settling in my stomach. For Nova, of course. No other reason.

"It's only a scouting mission, so it should be fine…but I wouldn't be mad if Reaper's Lady got her first taste of Revenant blood." The vampire's fangs glint in the morning sun as she smiles a dark, hungry smile, and I'm reminded of how deadly she can be.

"I will never understand you vampires, I swear," I say with a laugh, and both Nova and Wesley grin. We spend the next few hours lounging by the pond, the two vampires gloating over their swords some more, going through some exercises while I watch on in fasci-nation. How can something so lethal also be so graceful and beauti-ful? Wesley and I try to teach Nova one of the games we used to play as children, but neither of us can quite remember the rules and we all end up in laughing heaps on the ground before we get very far into the game.

It's a truly lovely day.

And I barely think of Alaric at all.

~

Enid,

You'll be glad to know that I have completely recovered from my strange...feelings for the High General. It was just from the binding, his blood more potent than I could have realized, that's all. I haven't seen him in almost two months now, and I've barely even noticed.

How are things faring with Leland? Has he purchased every flower on the continent by now? Have you already suffocated beneath them all and this letter will remain unread forever!? I kid, I kid, I'm sorry. But I do want to hear more about whether his efforts are gaining any ground with you.

Nova is going on a mission with Alaric tomorrow and though I know it's a great thing for her to be selected and that she's fully capable of taking care of herself (it's literally her job), I can't pretend I'm not worried.

IN TRUTH, I'm worried about more than just Nova, but I refuse to acknowledge the other worry slowly chilling my blood and making my chest feel tight. That worry shouldn't fucking be there anymore. The binding should be long faded, so why am I still feeling so uneasy about him going? Why am I still feeling anything for him at all? I grit my teeth and nearly tear straight through the parchment when I begin writing again. I take a deep breath and then start again, more gently this time.

> *I have more requests for da, so pass these along if you please, with a big hug. I miss him so much that sometimes it feels like my heart is splintering. I've been working in the smithy here with Braddock though, which helps ease the ache a bit, but still—no one and nothing can compare with being with da at his forge. I miss you too, Enid, just as much, especially when I can't sleep at night. Even after all these months, my room is still far too quiet without you here. I'm not sure if I'll ever get used to it.*
>
> *With love,*
> *~Dahlia*

CHAPTER 17
ALARIC

The Revenant army is acting...strange. There have been seemingly random engagements, small, half-hearted attacks all along the borders of the Sisters, in places where there is no hope of breaking through. It makes no sense. It's almost as if they're testing our forces, but they are as strong as ever, coming out victorious and sending the Revenant forces scurrying away within days of each battle. Something feels wrong, but I can't see it yet, and that's driving me mad.

We've seen no more signs of the armor-piercing arrows and while I would like to believe they only had the one, I fear that's not the case. I feel deep in my bones that they're just waiting for another chance to do...something but, again, I have no idea what.

"What the fuck are you up to, Kilgren?" I mutter to myself as I pour over the maps in my war room.

"You know, talking to yourself is a sign of lunacy in many places." Elias strolls into the room as if he hasn't a care in the world. It's one of the things I love most about him. He always appears at ease and totally unflappable, but beneath that, he's sharp as a razor, always seeing and analyzing, always ready to unleash the utterly terrifying warrior within.

"Is the group ready to leave in the morning?"

"Ready and rearing. I reminded them it's just a scouting mission and that we likely wouldn't be seeing battle, but they can hope." He smiles and shrugs, leaning on the edge of the table and narrowing his eyes slightly as he studies the figurines marking the locations of the most recent skirmishes. I can hardly even call them battles, really. *It doesn't make any fucking sense.*

"It's almost like a distraction."

I frown. "What do you mean?"

He waves a hand at the table. "All these fights, up and down the borders, usually several at once at different locations with no clear purpose, only for them to retreat soon after the battle begins. It just seems like some kind of distraction, something to keep us busy while they're doing other things. Misdirection."

I exhale roughly and run a hand through my hair. I'm exhausted. I haven't been sleeping well, not since…well, not since Dahlia arrived, really. Not since the moment I knew she was mine and made the decision to forsake the mating bond, but it's gotten worse these last months while I've done everything in my power to stay away from her. It's like razors being scraped against the inside of my skull, a constant, sharp pain that only gets worse with each day that passes. But I know it's the right decision. It's the only decision that will keep her safe.

When I'd seen her that day outside the training rings, my entire body had responded, needs and desires and urges surfacing like beasts from the darkest depths of the ocean, all sharp teeth and hungry eyes. I'd barely stopped myself from going to her, barely stopped myself from giving chase as she fled. Because that's what she'd been doing as she backed away and ran: *fleeing*. She'd run from me, some baser instincts deep in her bones telling her what I was thinking, screaming at her that I was a danger. That knowledge had held me in place, watching her as she ran away.

So, yes, staying away is the only choice.

But it still fucking hurts.

WE LEAVE AT FIRST LIGHT. It will take our small cadre at least four days to reach the remote village deep in the northwest. It's a small fishing village, but their elder wrote to me personally to tell me of Revenant sightings nearby. We've never heard of them going that far out into the wilds before, so I felt I needed to come myself. Yet more Revenant activity not making any fucking sense. If Kilgren's goal is to drive me insane, he might just succeed at this rate.

The journey goes by in a blur, my mind too full and my body too tense to care much about the trip. The temperatures are much lower here, true winter already creeping in. We still have two months, maybe three, before it hits the camp. I wonder what Dahlia will think of it, having only ever lived in the south of Braxhelm. Has she ever even seen snow?

I push the thoughts away and focus on the task at hand.

"There have been no attacks on the village?" I ask the elder, though I already know the answer.

"None, High General," the man replies. He's at least eighty, with deeply tanned, wrinkled skin and eyes so dark brown, they look nearly black. There's endless wisdom in them, and kindness.

"But you say you've seen Revenants?"

"Yes, sir. More than one crew has reported seeing them near the Great Bear." The Great Bear, we have been told, is a cave on the far edge of the large lake. The mouth is lined with jagged rocks that look like giant fangs, and the formation of rocks above resembles a nose, eyes, and even ears—all together, it looks like a giant bear, jaws gaping menacingly. "But they've never made any move to attack, and have never come across the lake as far as we're aware."

"How close to the cave were the crews who made the reports?"

The elder rubs his chin. "We do not go near the Great Bear, it is a cursed place, but the crews were close enough to know what they were seeing. Black claws and fangs, red eyes, gray skin." I tense, knowing deep down that they had indeed seen Revenants. But what in the seven hells were they doing here? I suppose the Great Bear might be a good place for a nest to hide, but no attacks in the area at all doesn't make sense. And choosing somewhere so remote isn't really the typical behavior of the Revenants. They're bloodthirsty, always hunting and tormenting humans. It's their nature, so to be this close to prey and not hunt? It makes no sense.

"Have there been any disappearances? Not outright attacks, but any members of the village going missing? Any news of those who live in the wilderness beyond the village's borders having issues or being taken?"

"Accidents happen on the boats and out in the wilderness, High General," the elder says pragmatically, "but nothing like what you're thinking. We have no reason to believe the Revenants have been living in the Great Bear for any great amount of time, nor that they ever came near our lands."

"Is there anything special about the cave?" Elias asks, and I can practically see the gears working inside his mind.

"Nothing that we would know of. The oldest tales of our people say that there were dark magics inside that cave, that people who went there were never heard from again. We do not go to the Great Bear." His voice is firm and final. I nod and share a look with Elias, both of us knowing that whatever is going on here, it can't be good.

"We will go to the Great Bear," I say simply. "We leave as soon as possible."

"We'll prepare the boats," the elder says, beckoning towards a young girl.

I incline my head in thanks. The girl is young, his grand-daughter most likely, and her heart is beating wildly as she steps closer to her grandfather, Elias, and myself. She risks a glance at me and her eyes widen, her pulse thundering. My chest clenches painfully. Her eyes are nearly the same shade of green as Dahlia's, though this girl's don't have the beautiful gold flecks that make Dahlia's eyes sparkle.

I clench my jaw and force the thoughts away. We thank the elder again and we ready to depart.

"What the fuck do you think they're doing out there?" Elias asks as he eyes the lake warily. It seems to go on for ages and ages, and while those old myths about vampires being unable to cross large bodies of water are rubbish, Elias hates boats. He loves the sea, but hates being out *on* it. It's always amused me.

"I don't know," I admit. "More distractions?" I shake my head in frustration, not really believing it even as the words pass my lips. I can just make out the shape of the Great Bear far in the distance, a dark mass against the burning orange light of the setting sun. I have no idea what we might find, and the elder seems to think that the Revenants have gone, but I prepare for battle all the same and instruct my men to do the same. They're all busy strapping on armor and checking their weapons when a sword catches my eye.

"Thaylin." The vampire quickly snaps to attention.

"Yes, High general?" she asks, bowing her head, her silvery-blonde warrior braids slipping over one shoulder.

"Is that a Clayburn blade?"

"Yes, sir. Dah—*Lady* Dahlia," she quickly corrects and my lips almost quirk—of course Dahlia would refuse to allow her friends to call her by her rightful title—"asked her father to do me the great honor of forging one of his legendary swords for my use."

Of course she did. Though I'm avoiding her, it doesn't mean that I'm not learning about my mate. One thing that I know above all else is how fiercely she loves. To be counted in that number would be a great honor, indeed.

"What is her name?"

"Reaper's Lady," she says, smiling reverently at the blade, but she quickly clears her throat and adds a quick, "sir."

"A good name for a great blade. Do it the justice it deserves," I say and she bows her head again.

"Of course, High General." I nod and stride away, disquieted by the warmth Dahlia's gesture to this vampire spreads through my chest. *My mate is kind. She is kind and good and loyal, and I can't even acknowledge that she's mine.* My hands curl into fists at my sides, and I join Elias on one of the three small boats setting out to take us all across the lake.

"The only thing out there is water. And fish. And more fucking water," Elias grumbles, eyes darting around like he's preparing for an attack. "Gods, how big is this fucking lake??"

"There has to be something more than that."

"Maybe you're right about the distraction," Elias says, gripping the edge of the boat so tightly the wood groans beneath his fingers. "Drawing you away from the pass? From the camp?"

I don't like the thought and quickly tamp down the wild flare of terror at the idea of Revenants attacking the camp while I'm gone, of Dahlia there alone...

"They wouldn't have known I would personally come to investigate this," I point out, "not with so many other points of attack happening up and down the borders. But even so, the pass is safe. The camp is safe," I say firmly, more firmly than I mean to, almost as if I'm commanding it to be so, as if I'm trying to assure myself.

Elias misses nothing, as always, and arches a brow. I ignore him and turn my gaze back towards the Great Bear. *She's fine. The camp is fine.* I find myself repeating the words over and over in my mind, like a calming mantra. The boats anchor on the bank a mile or so from the cave and we make our way swiftly and silently the rest of the way on foot, leaving the villagers behind with the boats to wait for our return. I strain my senses, reaching out to hear or smell or see any signs of Revenants.

"I don't hear anything," Elias says quietly as we move silent as death through the trees. As we finally approach the cave, I can smell them, Elias meeting my gaze and nodding.

"I don't either, but the villagers were right: they *were* here." The scent is old, not fresh, but it's unmistakable.

"Ten, maybe fifteen," Elias says as we step into the jaws of the Great Bear. "You four, first tunnel. You three, next. You five the next. Thaylin, you and the others take the fourth tunnel," he directs the groups, sending them down various tunnels branching off from the main chamber. "Be alert, all of you."

The soldiers draw their weapons and silently set off on their directed courses.

"Shall we?" I ask, a hint of a smile on my lips. Elias and I take the final tunnel together, as always.

"You know, if you keep luring me into dark tunnels alone with you, I'm going to start expecting things of a salacious and hedonistic nature, your highness."

I do grin at that. "As if you could possibly handle me."

"Please," Elias scoffs. "You and I both know I am capable of handling far more than you could possibly give. Do you not remember the famed four-day orgy? *Four. Day. Orgy*, Alaric. Of which I was the star."

"I recall," I say, shaking my head. I hadn't been a part of those particular festivities, but I'd heard enough stories from the week. We laugh quietly as we make our way farther and farther into the tunnel. It slopes down slightly, so we're moving farther into the earth as we walk, the temperature dropping drastically the deeper we go. I have a sudden, searing memory of being buried beneath those layers of snow and ice, surrounded by a bone-deep cold that I'm not sure ever really leaves me, and scowl. *Fucking Ahmed.*

"Is she yours?" Elias asks after a few moments of silence.

I freeze. "I haven't a clue what you might be talking about."

"Oh fuck off, I know you better than anyone, Alaric. I know that mates are all but myths these days, but...I think she's yours."

I run my tongue over my teeth, not wanting to confirm the terrible truth, but a part of me sighs in relief, at finally having someone I can talk to about all of this.

"It doesn't matter," I finally say.

"Bullshit it doesn't matter. You know as well as I do that mates are revered above all else, more than Consorts, more than honor or family or blood. If she's yours then—"

"She's a human," I snap. "My mate could not possibly be human." No matter how many times I say it, it doesn't seem to make the words true. Elias waves that a way as if it's nothing.

"So, she *is* your mate. I fucking knew it! I knew it had to be more than just having fresh blood making you seem so different." He purses his lips. "...but you've been spending every possible moment *away* from her?"

I glare.

"I don't understand, Alaric. Why—"

"I have to," I say quietly, all fight gone, my shoulder slumping in utter defeat. "I can't acknowledge the mating bond, can't do the things my instincts are clawing inside of me to do, can't feel the peace I feel only when I'm near her."

"But why?" Elias pushes. I stop and stare at my friend incredulously.

"You cannot possibly be asking that. I could *kill* her, Elias. As easy as breathing, I could destroy her. The things that I want to do when she's near, the way my instincts take over and I can't even think straight...it's terrifying," I admit. "I've never felt so out of a control as I do when I'm near her. And if I did something to hurt her, if I..." I swallow hard and force myself to say the words, the ones I've been thinking of constantly, the ones that send cold terror down my spine. "If I *killed* her, I couldn't bear it, Elias. I couldn't live with myself."

Elias studies me for a long moment, taking everything in and rolling it through his mind. I know he has to see the truth of my words, to understand my reasons for staying away, the reasons why I must suffer in silence and keep her safe.

"You wouldn't," he finally says simply. "I know you wouldn't, Alaric."

"You don't," I snap. "You don't know how close I've come, the way my body tensed to strike, the way my fangs ached to sink deep into her flesh. It was like some demon overtaking my body, and I could barely hold the beast back." I shudder and gnash my teeth. "I don't trust myself around her," I admit. "So, I have to stay away. It's the way of all other Consorts and princes. It will be the same for us."

"But—"

"Leave it," I all but whisper, practically begging. I can't bear to think of it, to imagine this torment for as long as she lives, and then trying to live without her afterwards, though I already know I won't be able to.

Elias sighs. "I will—for now. But we *will* be revisiting this, your highness."

I snort, grateful to Elias for finding a way to ease the pain, even for a short time, and the two of us continue deeper into the tunnel.

"They were...digging?" Elias asks as the tunnel finally levels off. He frowns as he runs a hand over the side of the cave wall where chunks of rock had been gouged away, rubble littering the dirt floor.

"For what?"

Elias straightens, brow furrowed. "You don't think...a doorway?"

There are legends of ancient magics, deep, powerful ones that haven't been seen in thousands of years. Magics that could turn day into night with the wave of a hand, magics that could raze entire armies to dust...and magics that could create doorways from one place to another across unimaginable distances. I've never put much belief into any of it...but perhaps *Kilgren* does. Maybe he believed they could find a doorway that would take them into the heart of the continent. The elder said that these caves were cursed with dark magics, that people went inside and were never seen again...because they went through a doorway?

"Impossible," I whisper, but a feeling of unease skitters up my spine. I don't see any signs of anything that could be considered a doorway, don't feel any sense of anything other or dark or magical, but maybe it is something that must be activated somehow. Maybe it wasn't a part of the cave, but rather something that could be transported *from* the cave and taken back to the Revenant stronghold...*Fuck.*

"Let's find the others."

Signs of digging into the earth and the stone were seen in all of the tunnels, but no signs of any recent Revenant activity, the fading scents all two weeks old, at least. It appears that they either found what they wanted or had given up completely. We will remain for another week to observe the Great Bear and do sweeps of the surrounding lands, but I already know that we won't find anything. I send one of the men back with messages for the generals at the other camps, telling them to send groups to remote villages with histories of magic and see if there have been any similar activities there.

We set up camp on the far side of the lake, and as I lie awake in my tent, my thoughts drift to the only thing that fills my mind and heart with any kind of peace:

Dahlia.

CHAPTER 18

DAHLIA

"Bloody hells, that's clever, that is," Braddock says as he studies another pair of the gauntlets I've made. I've improved a bit upon the design from the set Alaric had admired the day of the Choosing, and I plan to give this set to Wesley, another pair on the way for Nova. I smile at the big man and wipe a dirty hand across my brow.

"Thank you."

"You've got your father's eye for the craft, that's for sure. I'm honored to have you work at my forge, my Lady," he says with a bow of his head. I giggle but bow in return, unable to hide my joy at his compliment.

"Thank you. And thank you for letting me mess about here. It helps with the homesickness."

"Well, you are welcome here anytime. It's nice to have someone around who knows what they're doing." He says the last a bit louder, directing the words to his apprentice in the other room, Singh.

"I'm from a fucking *fishing* village," Singh replies indignantly, poking his head through the doorway. "I've never done this shite before!" His dark hair is falling out of the knot on the top of his head, the strands not quite long enough to stay put, but too long to remain down while he works. He blows a lock away from his face in an annoyed huff. "I'm bluidy trying."

"You're doing just fine," I say, trying to sound encouraging without sounding patronizing. "I set my trousers on fire on three separate occasions while I was learning."

"Well, I haven't done *that*," Singh says, smiling pointedly at Braddock, looking a little smug.

The blacksmith rolls his eyes. "Give it time, lad." He winks at me and I can see that he has affection for the new recruit. I think the young vampire will get the hang of things quickly, but Braddock is putting him through his paces to be sure, making him do all the dirty work that's no fun for anyone. Despite being his daughter, da had never spared me that either, so I feel Singh's pain.

Takara clears her throat from the doorway.

"My Lady, if you are quite done with your...work," she says, glancing around the shop and wrinkling her nose slightly, making Braddock and I both laugh, "I thought we might be due for a visit to the village? One of the soldiers just came back and said that Madam La Cruz's dog has had her puppies!" I swear the vampire barely stops herself from jumping up and down like a giddy schoolgirl. Though, I can't fault her. Who doesn't love puppies?

I tell Braddock and Singh a quick goodbye and head out the door.

"We are...friends now, are we not?" Takara asks as we walk quickly towards the cabin, both clearly eager to get on the road to the village.

"Well, you do keep calling me *my Lady*, which is not something a friend would really do..." Takara rolls her eyes.

"That is a very hard habit to break after so many years," she says defensively, and I can't help but laugh.

"But yes, I would consider us friends, why?"

"Good. Because as a friend: I *must* insist that you bathe before we go to the village."

I throw my head back and laugh, and hear chortles behind me from Malcom and Cyrus. I stick my tongue out at them.

"I suppose I can accommodate that request."

"Oh thank the gods," Takara says with a dramatic sigh of relief.

AFTER A BATH and a change of clothes, we set off for the village. I'm excited for an afternoon away from the camp. Nova is still off with Alaric, though Takara says they should be back this evening or tomorrow, and Wesley is out on watch, so I've been a bit lonely. Plus, I've become very fond of the village and its inhabitants, knowing almost everyone by name by now.

We make our way towards the jewelry shop. I've never cared much about jewelry, but Enid *loves* it and the owner, Rayner, is one of my favorite people here.

"Lady Dahlia!" Rayner exclaims, grinning widely and showing off his gold-capped teeth. He begins to make his way towards me, but I quickly cross the space to him instead. The man is almost ninety—if I can save him a bit of walking, I'm happy to do it.

"How are you, Master Rayner?"

"You are too kind to an old man, my Lady," he says, taking my hand in his and patting it gently with the other. "I am well, as I hope that you are." I incline my head in answer and the man beams. "Good, good." He holds up a finger, telling me to wait a moment. I arch a brow but obey as he shuffles behind the swinging doors that lead into the back room of the shop. He emerges a few moments later carrying a small case.

"I think you may like some of my newest pieces. I have several amethyst and blue topaz—your sister's favorite, yes?"

I smile widely. "You remembered!" I'm touched by the old man's kindness. He proffers the case, opening it so that I can see its contents and I gasp.

"These are *beautiful*," I breathe. Rings and necklaces and

bracelets lay within the velvet lining of the case, all of them expertly crafted, the delicate details surrounding the stones making them truly stunning.

"You are again too kind, my Lady," Rayner says, bowing his head. He breaks out into a coughing fit and I reach out to place a hand on his shoulder to steady him.

"Are you alright?" I ask, worriedly. I know that he has problems with his lungs, but he has medicine for it. Is it not working? The coughing subsides and he pats my hand gently.

"I'm fine, I'm fine. I've had to cut back on the amount of medicine I take. The coughing is a bit worse now because of it, but it's alright." He smiles warmly at me, gray eyes shining with kindness.

"Why have you cut back?"

"It is not something you need to worry yourself with, my Lady."

I give him a pointed look and cross my arms over my chest, letting him know that I won't be leaving without an answer. He looks somewhere between exasperated and touched, and exhales roughly, admitting defeat.

"You remind me much of my youngest granddaughter, Rosalind." He gives me a soft smile. "She is as stubborn and immovable as the mountains, just like you. The medicine has become quite expensive, my Lady. I cannot afford to pay the apothecary for the amount I used to take."

A rush of shame spills through me. Here I am, spending the abundance of wealth belonging to the Montclares freely on whatever frivolous thing I wish, while Rayner has to go without medicine he desperately needs.

"I'm sorry," I say quietly and he waves the words away.

"It is no worry, my Lady. I promise, I am fit as a fiddle. A ninety-six-year-old fiddle, true, but I can still carry a tune." He winks and I huff out a laugh.

"Well, I will take this lot, please."

"Of course, my Lady." He bows his head and closes the case, eyes crinkling at the edges when he smiles. I thank him and promise to visit again soon. Once outside, I walk purposefully towards the apothecary shop. He's more than happy to help me in my mission of making sure Rayner never pays for medicine again. I pay the man *double* what a year's supply of the medicine would cost.

"This is quite generous of you, my Lady," Fredrich says as he makes a note in his ledger.

"Are there many others like Rayner? Who cannot afford the things they might need?"

"At times, yes, my Lady." I nod, mind made up.

"If someone cannot pay, you will give them what they need—you may take whatever they can give or nothing at all, I'll leave that to you—but send word to the camp and I will make sure you are paid for your wares and services."

Fredrich's brows arch so high that they're hidden in his black-and-gray hair. "Truly, my Lady?"

"Yes, of course." He blinks, tilting his head to study me.

"You are...very unlike the last Consort I met."

"I will take that as a most esteemed compliment," I say with a smile. His lips curl upward as well.

"It was meant as one, my Lady." He inclines his head and then adds, "I will take whatever people can give. The village is small, but proud. I will take payment in whatever form someone can offer, I promise on my honor, my Lady."

My eyes prick with tears, and I'm not even sure why.

"We have a deal then." I smile and offer my hand. He laughs lightly and takes it, shaking it gently.

"A deal, Lady Dahlia."

My heart feels lighter as we head to Madam La Cruz's, feeling as if I'm finally doing something good with the wealth and privilege given to me because of the Choosing. I finally feel as if I...matter.

"That was truly wonderful," Takara says quietly. "I am...I am very proud to be your Keeper and friend, Dahlia."

I smile widely and she does the same, bumping my shoulder

softly with hers. I open my mouth to say something sweet and profound back, but I don't get the chance.

"Puppies!!" Takara squeals, streaking up the path to Madam La Cruz's cottage where a small pen in the front garden holds squirming, rolling, balls of golden fluff. Seeing a vampire overcome by the cuteness of puppies is something to behold, and I can't help but join in. We *ooh* and *ahh* and cuddle the puppies for well over an hour, and even the guard are not immune.

"You are a very good boy, yes. The best boy even. You will be called Muffin. Would you like that?" We all turn to gape at Descartes as he coos to the puppy in his hands, holding the little face up to his own, pressing their noses together. He sees us and clears his throat, putting the pup back down with his siblings. "Not a word," he says to all of us, sternly. "Not one fucking word." We all try to hide our smiles and laughter, but it doesn't work very well.

I promise the old woman that I'll be back to spoil the puppies soon and she assures me that I'm welcome any time. I eye Descartes and I think he might just come back and buy Muffin for himself.

WE LEAVE the village a few hours later, full of puppy cuddles and pie (me) and blood (everyone else).

"Today was a very good day," Takara says, smiling and resting her head on the velvet-lined cushion behind her.

"It was," I agree. The day was wonderful, with good deeds done and relationships strengthened, and knowing that Nova will be back soon, safely within the camp, makes everything just that much better. And, alright, yes, Alaric being back is a relief as well. Despite everything, I still feel ill at ease with him gone. I wish I could explain it or even understand it.

Takara and I both frown, brows furrowing as the carriage lurches to a stop. We're still at least two hours from the camp, I'm sure.

"What's going on?"

"Stay here, I'll check." Takara slips quickly out of the carriage. I obey for sixty-seven seconds before climbing out and joining Takara and the guard farther up on the road. Takara exhales in exasperation. "You cannot follow the simplest of instructions, can you?"

"Not at all," I say, not even the tiniest bit sorry. Descartes' lips quirk before he winks at me and trots off.

"How did that happen?" I ask, nodding to the giant tree lying across the road.

"Old tree, that's all. Not to worry, we'll have it moved in short order," Malcom says, walking past us to join Descartes, Viktor, and Cyrus beside the trunk, discussing the best way to go about moving it, judging by their hand gestures. Isaiah and Kane pace along the edge of the road, scanning the tree line.

"Go wait inside the carriage. It will be taken care of soon," Takara says before moving closer to the tree. To bark orders at the men, most likely, I think with a grin. I sigh, but agree that I'm not much help when it comes to moving behemoth tree trunks from the road. I walk down the line of horses, stopping to stroke noses and necks as I pass, taking my time to get back to the carriage. The forest is thick on either side of the road here, mountains in the near distance rising up like giants standing watch over the travelers. The leaves have changed from green to beautiful shades of red and orange and yellow, resembling a tapestry of multicolor flames against the dark stone of the mountains.

I reach out to pet Kane's horse, a chocolate brown brute that I named Coco. He leans into my touch and I laugh, scratching his neck and up behind his ears. He noses at my stomach, searching for the treats I often have in my pockets when I come to visit the stables.

"I don't have any carrots today, greedy boy." He huffs indignantly and raises his head again, staring straight ahead as if he's cross with me. I can't help but laugh, but then a strange feeling settles over me, making the fine hairs on the back of my neck stand on end.

A heartbeat later, an arrow buries itself in Coco's eye before bursting out of the back of his skull, hot blood spraying and coating my face and neck.

CHAPTER 19
DAHLIA

I can't even scream. I just stand there, staring in horror as the slain horse's body collapses in a heap, shaking the ground beneath my feet. Time itself seems to slow around me, everything looking and feeling almost like a dream. Sounds are distant, as if they're coming from the bottom of a deep well, but then all at once, they come crashing in upon me again, so loud my ears feel like they're going to bleed.

Chaos erupts all around me as dark figures burst onto the road, seemingly from everywhere all at once. At least a dozen, maybe more. Arrows seem to rain from the sky, exploding like chemical bombs when they strike the ground. Soon, everything around me is fire and smoke and blood. Battle rages as the vampires engage with our attackers. Who on earth would be attacking us? And why? My mind seems sluggish, like it's stumbling trying to reach thoughts that should be obvious. And still, I can't move. I can only stare at the poor animal on the ground, the blood turning the dirt beneath him into crimson mud. I turn my head, trying to see the others, but everything is half hidden in the smoke.

I hear Takara yell my name, someone else—*Malcom, I think?*—

bellowing orders, and the unmistakable cries of pain echoing in my ears. The clash of metal against metal rings out all around me, so loudly it feels like each blow is vibrating my very bones. I hear Takara yell for me again, but this time, the word is cut in a scream of pain. My heart clenches and I'm finally able to move again, fear for my friend unlocking my muscles. I run blindly towards the sound, coughing and choking on the smoke, dodging small fires and the throng of bodies and—

A dark shape rears up in front of me, seeming to materialize out of the smoke itself. This time I do scream as I skid to a stop, slipping in the wet, churned earth, a scream of terror so cold it seems to turn my very blood to ice. This can't be real. This can't be happening.

I can't be looking at...a Revenant.

But that's exactly what it is. I've seen them in books and paintings and tapestries depicting the glorious victories of the vampiric army, driving the beasts from our lands. But as I look into its cold, crimson eyes, I realize the images hadn't even come close to capturing the true horror. The thing before me is a monster, something pulled from the darkest nightmare. Evil radiates off of the creature in waves, the menace and inhumanity etched into every line of its gray skin. He grins at me, black fangs dripping with blood, and my stomach roils.

"Pretty little Consort," it hisses in a voice that sounds like iron dragged over gravel as it stalks towards me. I take a step backward, head whipping around, terrified that more are lurking inches away. The Revenant pulls twin curved blades out of his belt and spins them expertly. He takes another step but halts abruptly when the end of a giant battle axe bursts through the front of his chest, black blood dripping down the blade. He doesn't even cry out in pain, simply looks down at his chest, as if surprised to see the blade, and then collapses in a heap. The ground is soaked in blood within seconds, a black stain like tar spreading across the packed earth, mixing with the red.

Another figure rushes towards me through the smoke and I

scream again, stumbling backwards, but I slap a hand over my mouth as I realize who it is.

"My Lady!" Viktor cries, eyes blazing with fury and battle-lust, fangs sharp as razors and bared in rage. He's covered in blood, both black and red, and I wince at the large gash across his chest and the smaller one on his cheek. Kane is on Viktor's heels, sword out and bloody. Viktor yanks his axe from the fallen Revenant with a sickening wet sound that makes me want to vomit. Three more Revenants emerge from the smoke and Kane and Viktor put themselves in front of me protectively. How many Revenants are here? My guard must be outnumbered. Fear and panic claw at my chest, making it hard to breathe.

"Stay back!" Viktor bellows at me over his shoulder. I cower behind the two hulking vampires, edging backwards as the Revenants attack. This fighting is nothing like the sparring and drills I'd seen at the camp. The movements are similar, of course, but there's a brutal ferocity now that I never could have imagined. There is no mercy to be had, each fighter baring their fangs and landing blows hard enough to make me shake with terror. My heart feels like it's in my throat as I watch my protectors, my *friends*, fight for their lives—and mine.

A Revenant blade barely misses Kane's neck, but he ducks and spins beneath the blow, thrusting his own sword upward and through the Revenant's gut. When he pulls the blade free, blood and entrails spill to the ground and I can't help but gag. Kane turns to help Viktor as he battles the two remaining Revenants, but he's too late.

One of them drives its sword into Viktor's side, the other slamming a war hammer into his temple. He topples to the ground, his body unmoving, and I scream in terror—and rage. Fury overtakes the fear for a brief moment, and all I want is to fight these creatures, to defend my friends, to make the beasts pay for harming them. I let the fire in my blood carry me forward without thought. Kane bellows my name, but I'm already flying between Viktor's prone form and one of the Revenants, just as its blade arcs downward towards the big vampire.

Blinding pain erupts through my arm, just below my shoulder. I scream in agony, an agony I've never known, an agony I never could have even imagined. I fall heavily to the mud, my vision completely white for what feels like an eternity. My arm feels as if it's on fire, the flames spreading through my entire body. Blood pours down my arm like a river, my fingers already slick with it. I feel like the entire earth lurches to the side and I turn my head to vomit violently into the mud.

"Her *head*, Halston," one of the Revenants grates. "We're to take her head back to Kilgren."

"I'm getting there," the other one snaps back.

I blink hard trying to clear my head as terror closes my throat. They're here to kill me. *Oh gods. Please, please, please...*I have to get out of this. I don't want to die. I'm not *ready* to die. There's so much I haven't done, so much life I haven't lived! I try to focus on the monsters coming towards me, but the pain somehow doubles, making me see stars. I will myself to stay conscious. I don't know anything about battle, but I do know that lying unconscious in the middle of it can't be a good idea, especially when these monsters are trying to...I swallow hard...*take my head.*

Kane throws himself into the two Revenants, knocking them to the ground.

"RUN!" he roars to me as the three of them roll and fight.

Despite the pain, and despite part of my heart demanding that I help him, survival instincts take over and I obey, turning and running as fast as I can—which is not very. I stumble more than once, coughing and gagging on the smoke still filling the air and the pain radiating through every inch of my body. It seems as if I'm headed away from the fighting, the sounds growing a bit dimer. I see the carriage ahead and rush towards it, falling to my knees and crawling beneath it.

I bite my lip and glance down at my arm. A whimpering sob

escapes my lips at the sight: my upper arm is mangled, cut clear to the bone, and I can't move the fingers on my left hand at all. My breaths saw in and out raggedly, and blood gushes from the wound with every beat of my heart. A distant part of my mind knows that I need to try to stop the bleeding, but I can't focus, can't make my body move or cooperate the way I need it to.

The sounds of fighting still echo all around: clangs of metal, cries of agony, bellows of rage, the wet, sickening sounds of metal cutting through flesh. I know that everything has only taken a few minutes, but it feels as if it's been hours. The ground beneath me trembles, as if the earth itself is quaking in fear. I don't know what to do. I can barely keep my eyes open, barely stay upright. I can't possibly run in this state, and even if I could, where would I go? The village is an hour back, the camp two hours forward. The only option would be off into the woods and that isn't a very good option at all.

So, no, my only real choice is to stay here and hope someone comes. My guard will save me...won't they? They'd been hand-selected by Alaric, they're some of the strongest vampires in his army. But images of the Revenants flash in my mind: the vicious way they fought, the feral brutality in their burning red eyes. And Viktor, lying lifeless on the ground.

"Oh gods," I whisper. Was he dead? My eyes burn with tears and a fresh wave of agony shoots up my arm.

I suck in a harsh breath when I see a pair of legs emerge from the dust and smoke, walking casually towards the carriage. I clamp my good hand over my mouth, though I know it won't do much good, not with these creatures: their senses are almost as keen as vampires. I'm utterly frozen in fear, my body paralyzed though I desperately want to escape. I need to move. I need to run. I need to do *something*. But I can't.

The booted feet move closer and closer, and my terror grows with every step. What feels like an eternity later, the figure squats down to peer into my hiding place. His crimson eyes are practically dancing with triumph, his black fangs menacing as he grins. He draws a dagger, his black claws coated in blood, and I flinch backwards, the movement sending a fresh wave of blinding pain through my arm. My world tilts for an endless moment, my vision going completely white before the Revenant's menacing face comes back into view.

"Well, well, well, what do we have here?" he almost purrs, and my stomach twists at the gleeful malice in his eyes. "The killing of the great High General's first Consort will be quite a blow, indeed..."

I understand then, despite the clamor in my mind, and the pain and fear making everything a jumbled mess. This is about striking a blow at the heart of Alaric's army, taking something that belongs to him right from under his nose, and destroying it—and him not being able to do a thing to stop it.

"Ah, you understand now, yes?" he asks, red eyes gleaming. "That pretty little head of yours will look quite lovely on a pike. We'll bring it to every battle as a reminder to your great warlord..."

I squeeze my eyes closed. *Please don't let my family know what happened here. Please tell them I fell ill. Please burn my body and send them my ashes. Don't tell them I wasn't...whole when I burned. Gods...*

A bellow of rage unlike anything I've ever heard rings out so loudly that my eyes snap open and I clamp a hand over one ear, my other hand hanging uselessly by my side. Before the Revenant can so much as flinch, a blade slices through his neck—a blade black as night with silver stars flashing brightly as it buries itself in the Revenant's flesh. Black blood sprays, soaking my chest and throat and face, hot and viscous. The Revenant blinks once, twice, and then his head slides off of his neck, landing with a wet, sickening *thunk* before his body topples beside it.

Too much. It's too much. I feel myself slipping away, sliding down a deep, dark hole and I can't do a thing to stop it.

I stare, unblinking.

I'd once seen a man in the village that had been traveling from the east with his family. They'd been attacked by bears, and he had been the only survivor. He'd seen his wife and children torn apart by the beasts, watched them die right in front of him. He'd had a vacant look in his eyes, as if he were staring at something too far for anyone to see, yet seeing nothing at the same time. They'd said that he was in shock, his mind shutting down from the experience to protect itself.

That's what I think is happening to me now. I'm in shock, my body growing so cold with it that I begin shaking, that dark hole closing in closer around me, squeezing...squeezing...

"Dahlia?" a low, gruff voice says urgently. "Dahlia, look at me." Gloved hands gently cradle my face. My mind whispers *Alaric*, and something inside of me leaps with utter joy, but I can't react, can't say his name aloud, can't even breathe a sigh of relief at seeing him or feeling his hands on me. *I'm too far gone. I can't fight out of the darkness. I can't...I can't...*

"*Keeva?*" he says in an almost broken whisper. He sounds anguished and terrified and I can't understand why. I try to speak, try to reach out to him, try to do *anything*, but I'm tumbling, tumbling, tumbling...

A moment later, the blackness engulfs me completely, and I'm gone.

CHAPTER 20
ALARIC

I've never known fear or fury like this. In all of the centuries, in all of the battles, in all of the life-or-death situations I've found myself in—nothing has ever compared to this.

We arrived back at the camp to find that Dahlia and her Keeper had gone to the village. I had already been on the verge of breaking and giving up on the notion of staying away from her before the conversation with Elias out in the wilds, but it had admittedly pushed me over the edge. I'd decided while lying in my tent that first night by the lake that even though I can't claim her as my mate in the ways I want most, this self-imposed torture of keeping my distance was wearing thin. I am a prince. I am the High General of the most fearsome army in the history of the world. I can damn well control myself around my fucking mate.

So, instead of waiting for her to return, Elias and I had ridden out to meet them on their journey back from the village. Elias had given me a knowing look, a self-satisfied smile on his lips as if he were the sole reason behind my choice, but had miraculously refrained from gloating. We'd been laughing about nothing in particular when a stab of terror had nearly felled me. Even Xerxes had stutter stepped, stomping the ground and shaking his head in confusion. But it hadn't been *my* terror I'd felt—it was Dahlia's. I'd taken enough of her blood to truly feel her emotions now, at least strong ones, and the fear and panic and confusion she was feeling were so strong that my chest nearly split.

"What? What is it?" Elias asked, instantly on alert when he saw me tense.

"Dahlia," I managed to grit out. "She's in danger." I spurred Xerxes into a gallop so fast that we were a blur across the road, my fangs and claws sharpening in rage. We pulled ahead of Elias, but he gave chase, his own fangs glinting as he snarled his own fury. Elias loves me like a brother and I know that he will protect my mate with all his power now that he knows the truth. My heart had swelled at the love for my closest friend, even as that iron fist of fear and rage clenched it tight.

Now we ride like the devil himself is on our backs, desperate to find her, desperate to figure out what could possibly be going on. I can feel Dahlia's fear pulsing with every beat of my heart, a dagger of ice slipping deeper and deeper into my chest. What in seven hells could be happening to make her so afraid? To make her panic this way? Then I smell the blood and fire and smoke on the wind, hear the clash of blades and cries of battle in the distance, and my heart stops beating entirely.

No.

"Fuck," Elias grates behind me.

"Come on, boy. Ride. *Fly*," I beg, desperately spurring Xerxes to go faster, pushing the warhorse to the limit of his power, but he can feel everything I'm feeling, and he seems to find some strength in himself, a fierce need to protect Dahlia as well, and he puts on a burst of speed that makes me gasp. *Magnificent bastard*. After what feels like an eternity, I can make out shapes in the distance, the familiar dance of battle through the thick smoke covering the road ahead. I don't dare slow as I approach, but take in every detail of the utterly unbelievable scene before me as I barrel towards the chaos:

twelve Revenants fighting four of Dahlia's guard; bodies littering the earth, the dirt road wet and sticky with blood; no sign of Dahlia. *Where the fuck is she?* I know she's near, can feel her and sense her, but can't scent her over the stench of Revenant blood and smoke and fire.

Xerxes snorts and huffs, the cold and thrill of battle settling into every inch of the horse. He knows exactly what I want to do and where I want to go without me making a single move or command. We careen towards two Revenants fighting Malcom. The big vampire is covered in blood, both red and black. I unsheathe Night's Fury from my back in an easy, practiced motion that's as familiar to me as breathing. I swing the great sword and take the heads of both Revenants in one strike. Their bodies fall and Malcom inclines his head briefly before sprinting through the smoke to aid Cyrus. Isaiah lays in pieces beside him and my chest clenches. *Vale, brother.*

I slide from my horse as Elias hurtles into the fray just behind me and leaps from Orion's back, landing easily and sprinting to engage another pair of Revenants with his twin short swords. He's one of the greatest swordsmen in all the world, second only to myself, and watching him set to work on the two creatures is truly a thing of beauty. Later, I'll recall it and marvel at my friend's skill. Later, I'll commend him for his bravery and valor. Later, I'll even stroke his ego a bit and tell him how glorious he cut through the fray, like an avenging angel, all gold and fire.

But now, all I can think of is Dahlia, the need to find her like jagged claws tearing me apart from the inside. Another bastard charges towards me, but Xerxes throws himself between me and the Revenant. He rears back and kicks out with his hooves, and they crush right through the Revenant's chest. Blood and bone spray through the air. The horse stomps on the Revenant's body, just to be safe, his head popping like a grape, and soon nothing remains of the creature but thick, black pulp and shards of milk-white bone. I scan the area, trying to see through the smoke and bodies. The cool calm of battle is still upon me, as it always is during a fight, but there's a frantic edge to my thoughts now that I've never had before. *Where the fuck is she??*

Descartes lay bleeding a few feet away, a Revenant looming over him. I speed towards them, fangs bared. The Revenant whirls, dark braids spinning wide around her head and her eyes going wide in shock.

"Not supposed to be here," she hisses just before I plunge my blade into her chest, slicing through flesh and muscle, grating against bone. The Revenant howls in agony as the silver stars burn her, and I yank the blade free, kicking out and dislocating her knee caps with a loud snap that echoes off of the trees. She screeches and falls, black blood oozing from her chest and running down her chin. She bares her fangs and raises a dagger, but I lop of her hand at the wrist with a flick of mine, sending her dagger sailing through the mud, still clutched in her fingers. She howls and holds up the other hand to ward me off, fear in her eyes. I take that hand too, just for good measure. I leave her for someone else to finish off, or to be questioned later, if she survives, and rush to Descartes' side.

"Where is she?!" I demand, only realizing a moment too late that the vampire's eyes are wide and unseeing. He's gone. "Fuck," I growl, another swift stab of sorrow slicing my chest. *Vale.*

I feel a pulse of fear, but immediately followed by an even stronger pulse of rage. Dahlia. I stand and whip my head around, trying to find her, trying to—Pain laces through me, a white-hot agony that makes me stumble for a moment. I whirl, trying to find my attacker, but I see no one. My hand flies to my arm, where the pain still lances my body, but I frown—there's no wound. I don't understand...but then realization turns my blood to ice, spiky shards of it piercing every inch of me. It's *her* pain I'm feeling. Dahlia is hurt.

Every instinct roars in my head to find her, to protect my fucking mate. My vision goes red, my mind nearly feral. My fangs and claws sharpen with the need to rip the bastard who had dared harm what's mine to bloody ribbons. I grip Night's Fury so tightly that my knuckles creak beneath my skin.

I let the instincts that I've been fighting all this time lead me now, fully opening myself up to them for the first time, and it's like coming up for air after an eternity under water. I can feel her now, like a beacon in the darkest of night calling me home. I sprint through the melee, squinting through the smoke.

I finally see the outline of her carriage and crouched in front of it, a Revenant. Dahlia's beneath it, cowering and bloody and rage and terror explode in my head. I move so fast that I swear I've somehow teleported. One second, I'm watching the Revenant reach towards my mate, and the next, I'm standing over his headless body, breathing hard and furious that his death had been so quick and painless. I wanted to make him suffer for days, weeks, *years* for daring to try to touch my Dahlia.

The fear is still pulsing from my mate, but something is off now, like the fear is becoming muted. It's difficult to explain, but I know that something isn't right. I drop to my knees and clench my jaw at the sight of her wound. Her arm is nearly severed completely, white bone standing out starkly against the crimson coating most of her body. I can tell within seconds that she's lost entirely too much blood, her skin pale as death. Her eyes are wide, her pupils nearly overtaking the green completely, but they're unfocused. She's staring at me, but not seeing me, I know. This is why her fear seemed muted. Her mind is slipping, everything becoming too much for her to handle.

"Dahlia," I say as gently as I can around the rage and fear and agony coursing through me. "Dahlia, look at me." She doesn't move, doesn't speak, doesn't blink. *Shock. She's in shock.* Panic begins to claw at my throat. Human minds are fragile things. They can be broken beyond repair. But I have no idea how the fuck to help, how to pull her back. But I have to. I *have* to.

I somehow maneuver my big body beneath the carriage in front of her, knees sinking into the bloody earth. *Her blood. My mate's blood.* I gnash my teeth and take a settling breath, forcing myself to be gentle as I reach forward. I cradle her face between my hands and there's the tiniest flicker of something in her eyes.

"*Keeva*," I say, the word a choked, broken whisper. Though she doesn't say a word, I feel relief rush through her a moment before her eyes roll back and she slumps forward into my arms.

"Alaric!" Elias calls.

"Here! I'm here!" I reach above me, gripping the bottom of the carriage and shove it away. It flies into the air, landing on its side a hundred yards away. I hear Elias mutter *holy shit* as I gather Dahlia's limp body in my arms, careful of her injury. It looks even more gruesome up close, and I take in her pale skin again. My heart races as real fear pumps through me. No, not fear. Utter *terror*.

She's lost so much blood...

"Ah gods," Elias says as he skids to a stop before us. "What the fuck happened?"

"She needs blood. Help me, Elias. Gods, please help me..." I've never felt so helpless or so afraid. I can't lose her. I can't. I won't. *Please, please, please.*

Elias nods and puts a hand on my shoulder, squeezing reassuringly. I slide to my knees, careful to keep Dahlia steady in my arms. Elias tilts Dahlia's head back and opens her mouth. I bring my right hand to my mouth, slicing my wrist open with my fangs, and hold it over her lips. Blood pours down her throat and she coughs quietly, still unconscious.

"Come on, beauty. Drink," I urge. I can feel death coming for her and know it will arrive soon if we don't get enough of my blood in her to heal this injury, to replenish the blood she's lost. Finally, even unconscious, her body responds as all humans instinctively do: she begins to drink. They know, on some deep, primal level, that a vampire's blood is life itself, life eternal, and they crave it. Her throat works as she swallows mouthful after mouthful.

"That's it," I whisper. "That's it, love. Come back to me." I can feel Elias' eyes on me, but I don't care. She finally falls limp once more, head lolling to the side, but the blood has stopped flowing from her arm at least. Even vampire blood can only do so much with grievous injuries. She will heal, but it will take time, and she will not escape this day without a scar to remind her.

"Thank the gods," Elias breathes. I whistle but realize that Xerxes is already trotting to me, worry for Dahlia pulsing from the horse as well. I manage to climb onto the saddle with Dahlia in my arms. I cradle her to my chest, the feeling of it so *right* that my whole body seems to glow with it, before turning to Elias. Without having to ask the question, my lieutenant gives me the answers I need.

"Three dead. Seventeen Revenants dispatched. Two fled the fray when you arrived, but Cyrus is in pursuit. One left alive for questioning." That's all I need to know for now. I'll speak to the others later to get to the bottom of what in the fuck had happened here, but for now, I need to get my mate safely back to our home.

"Get things settled, gather the dead, and have everyone report to the war room in three hours."

"Of course," Elias nods. He gives me a long, knowing look, but says nothing else. He simply steps back, slaps Xerxes on the rump, and watches as I carry Dahlia away.

It's been days and Dahlia still sleeps. I know that she's not in any danger from her injury—that is nearly completely healed—but I worry about her mind. What she experienced...well, it would be enough to break any human. I know Dahlia is strong, but there is only so much a person can handle. I've checked in regularly, though I would have much preferred to stand a constant vigil at her bedside, and her Keeper assures me she is doing well, that she just needs time. The healer from the village says much the same. I know they are right, but every minute she remains asleep, alone in the darkness, a part of me dies.

I have put off the funeral rites for Isaiah, Kane, and Descartes for now. I believe that Dahlia would want to be there. She counted the men as more than just her guardians—they were her friends. Something about that catches at my heart. Any other Consort in her position would have seen them as nothing more than servants, vampires there to do her bidding. They would have been little more than objects to her. But Dahlia took the time to know them, to joke with them and drink with them and laugh with them. I think that speaks volumes about the kind of person she is and the kind of heart she has. It makes me...feel things for her. More than just mating instincts, but actual feelings that I don't quite know how to express or explain. Fuck if I have any idea what that means.

I spoke with the remaining members of the guard, and their stories were all the same: the trip to the village was uneventful, no signs of anything amiss; no problems within the village; and then half way back to the camp, they came upon the tree across the road. I hardly even remembered Xerxes leaping over it in our haste to get to Dahlia, but I recalled it once the men spoke of it.

"We were sorting out how to move it from the road, sir, and they came upon us," Viktor said as they sat around the war table the evening of the attack.

"There were no signs of them, no scent either, not until they stormed the road," Malcom added.

"Perhaps they found a lesser wielder to do their bidding? To hide their scent?" Elias suggested.

"Perhaps," I agreed, rubbing two fingers across my chin absentmindedly as I thought through everything. Full magic wielders had been gone for centuries, but there were those with fading bloodlines that gave them some magical abilities. They could do small things, like help your crops grow or give you luck at the dice tables—or, potentially, hide you in plain sight.

"Did any of them say anything?" I'd asked the group.

"Nothing, sir. Other than the usual 'I'll eat your heart' or 'fuck you, your rotting whoreson' that comes with any battle."

I remembered the female Revenant hissing that I wasn't supposed to be there. So this attack had been planned for when I would be gone—they hadn't counted on me riding to find Dahlia. I shuddered at the thought of what would have happened if I hadn't. But why? The only obvious reason was for Dahlia, but no one knows how important she is to me except Elias...But it is no secret that she is my Consort. A Consort is a sacred title among the vampires in Braxhelm. To have one attacked and killed, especially the Consort of the High General himself...well, it would be a blemish to be sure. It would say to the entire continent and the whole of the Revenant army that I cannot protect what's mine.

"Rest. Mourn your brothers. We will have rites once Dahlia awakens," I'd told them.

They all inclined their heads. "Yes, sir," Viktor said, and then added quietly, "How does she fare? Our Lady Dahlia?"

"She heals," I'd told him, and he nodded, relief clear in his eyes. *They care for her as well*, I realized. *The friendship extends both ways.* Leave it to my mate to charm some of the most fearsome vampires in all of Braxhelm.

They'd all exited the room, leaving Elias and me alone.

"There's no way...I mean, no one could know..."

"No," I cut him off. "No one could possibly. I think Kilgren only meant to hurt my Consort, not my...mate," I said quietly, still unused to saying the word out loud.

"That's something at least," he huffed out. "The prisoner is ready for questioning."

I'd nodded and the two of us journeyed to a cave deep in the east Sister. The Revenant was shackled to the wall, the silver cuffs around her throat and upper arms filling the space with the stench of burning flesh—her missing hands made it hard to shackle her wrists, of course. Those chains were some of the last remaining bits of silver in the entire continent. One day, I hoped to wrap the damned things around Kilgren's throat myself, to smile as they burned his flesh and rejoice in his screams of agony.

The Revenant lifted her head as we'd entered, baring her black fangs before spitting at my feet.

"I'll tell you nothing, you leech! Torture me all you wish," she'd said, defiance written in every line of her dirty, blood-stained face.

I'd bent down so that we were eye to eye. She met my gaze, but flinched backwards ever so slightly when she beheld the absolute lethal fury in my eyes. They had planned to take what was mine. They killed my men. They nearly killed my fucking mate.

They would pay.

"Thank you for the invitation," I'd said in a deadly cold voice. "I accept." The defiance faltered, fear flashing in her red eyes.

The interrogation did not last long.

IN THE END, the Revenant confirmed what I'd suspected: that Kilgren's plan was to kill my Consort, knowing that would be a blow to not only my ego, but to the faith put in me by everyone in Braxhelm. She died before she could tell me how they'd managed it, unfortunately.

Now, I stare at the map on the massive table in the war room. I haven't been able to figure out where the Revenants had come from. There are still nests of Revenants throughout Braxhlem, of course, but never in the Northlands, at least not this near the camp. My army constantly sweeps the area for leagues upon leagues in training exercises. There's no possible way there have been any Revenants in this area before the attack.

So, where the fuck had these been hiding? Or had they somehow gotten through the pass undetected? The thought unsettles me more than any other option. I've worked so hard these years to keep that from happening. I set up my camp here for that sole fucking purpose. They've never found their way through before, so how had they possibly managed it now? The idea of a doorway is still in the back of my mind, but I can't quite make myself fully accept it as a real option. It could explain it though...

Then there's the question of how, exactly, they'd known when Dahlia would be on that road, away from me...

I rub my temples and clench my jaw. An obvious answer surfaces but I refuse to accept it. There is not a spy within my camp. Perhaps someone in the village...A low growl of annoyance rumbles through my chest. Not knowing is driving me mad. I'm going to attend the funerals for three of my men in just a few hours, and every time I think about how much worse it could have gone, what I could have lost...

"No," I command myself. "Don't think of it."

"Don't think of what? How much you love me?" Elias asks breezily from the doorway in his customary unflappable swagger. "That's actually a physical impossibility."

"Not in the mood, Elias," I grind out. To my utter surprise, Elias sighs, a bit of the cocky ease draining out of him.

"I know. I know we are no strangers to death on the battlefield, but this feels different. And I can't even imagine what you must have felt, what you must still be feeling. To have your mate in danger like that, *hurt* like that..." He shakes his head, paling slightly. "I'm glad she's alright."

I sit heavily in one of the high-backed chairs surrounding the table and put my head in my hands, running my fingers roughly through my hair. Elias comes around beside me, leaning back against the table.

"Is she though? How could she possibly be?" I ask. Sure, she'd healed *physically* because of my blood, but *mentally*? I have no idea. Her Keeper informed me that she woke again several hours ago and seems... alright so far (she didn't wake screaming this time, at least), but not knowing if she's *truly* ok is killing me. I could feel her terror when she woke the first few times, memories probably clawing at her like a rabid beast, and there was nothing I could do to help her. Fucking *nothing*.

"She'll come through this just fine, brother, I know it."

"I hope you're right."

"And when she does?" Elias asks pointedly after a moment. "What are you going to do?"

"I..." I inhale deeply, letting it out slowly before answering. "I can't stay away from her any longer. It's...too hard," I admit quietly, feeling weak and not appreciating the experience in the slightest. I drop my head into my hands. Elias smacks the back of my head, and I raise my chin slowly, staring at my oldest friend.

"Did you just *smack* your High General?" I ask slowly.

"I did. And I'll do it again if you don't stop being so stupid." I arch a brow and Elias rolls his eyes. "She's your *mate*. You were literally made for each other by the hand of fate itself. Of course being apart from her is difficult. Painful even, I'd bet. It's because you aren't *meant* to be away from her now that you've found her, you horse's ass. You're meant to be together, to complete and balance each other in every way."

I think through his words, knowing that he's right. I feel...whole when I'm near Dahlia. I feel right in a way I never have before. Only with her do I ever feel truly at ease and...happy. Yes, that's the feeling I've had in the few brief moments I've allowed myself to be with her. *True happiness.*

"And you're suddenly the mate expert?" I grumble.

"Ah you forget my parents. I've seen firsthand what mates mean to each other, what they can do for each other and be for each other." His gaze shifts, looking across the room but I know he's seeing far into the past, to a childhood surrounded by love and happiness. I'd known his parents as well—they were part of my father's court and Elias had grown up in one of the manors on the Montclare property in Astoria's Keep—and I still remember the waves of affection and loyalty and devotion that seemed to radiate from both of them, though of course I didn't truly understand it at the time.

Elias focuses back on me again.

"So, yes, I'm a bit of an expert," he says with a grin.

"Well, you're partly right, I'll admit. The draw to her is too much, so I won't be keeping myself from her anymore. But..." I rub the back of my neck, "the urges that arise when she's near are...strong. Too fucking strong."

"So give into them," Elias says with a shrug.

"I could fucking kill her! Easily. It would take one tiny mistake, one second of letting my control slip, and she'd be gone forever. She's a *human*. There's a reason that princes don't bite or fuck humans! There's a reason that mates are never humans." I slam a fist down on the table, nearly splintering the great slab of oak.

"Yes, you could kill her, as easy as breathing," he agrees easily, and I sputter.

"Not helpful," I growl.

"But you *won't*." I might just throttle him and he must see it in my eyes because he cuts me off with a raised hand. "I don't think you'd be physically able to hurt your mate. Your entire being would rebel against the idea, and the mating instincts would take over in the event your mind was...otherwise occupied. They are far stronger than our primal vampiric instincts to fuck and drink."

I open my mouth, but snap it shut again, frowning. That...actually makes a bit of sense, I suppose. But is it worth the risk? Could I possibly put it to the test? I think to the attack, to seeing Dahlia coated in blood with her arm nearly severed, so near death that I could smell it on the air. I shudder and shove the images away. No, I couldn't risk hurting her—or worse.

"For arguments sake, say I believe that. Say I believe I can give in to these urges and not hurt her...it doesn't mean she'll *want* me to. That's the other reason mates are never human, Elias: humans don't have mates. The mating bond can't go both fucking ways if my mate isn't a vampire." It was something I've been thinking about all these months, from the moment I knew she was mine. In the deepest, darkest part of my mind where I allowed myself to think about claiming her as my mate, entertaining the idea of us being together, this fear slept: she might be mine, but I couldn't be hers, not in the same way.

Elias gives me a secretive, knowing smile. "I don't think you need to worry about that. Though, to be fair, you may have to work a bit to bring her around after ignoring her for months after you dragged her from her warm, loving home to a war camp in the Northlands surrounded by bloodthirsty vampires..." I punch him in the arm and he winces, but laughs. He rubs the spot and then, a bit more seriously, he adds, "Listen, just because she might not have the same instincts to call you her mate doesn't mean that she can't come to love you, Alaric."

Love me.

Gods the warmth that those words send through my body and soul, like a low, soothing fire after too much time in the cold. Could she truly? I don't know if it's possible or if she would even want that, but I refuse to stay away from her any longer. I can control myself. I fucking *will* control myself. I won't allow anything to happen between us other than...friendship, perhaps? Is such a thing possible? I think that it...is, actually. She's smart and strong and cunning, with a sharp tongue and a quick wit that makes my lips quirk more often than not. She doesn't act like a Consort or a noble, and I enjoy her all the more for it. She's kind and generous—her Keeper told me of her arrangement with the apothecary in the village to pay for any medications or supplies that the villagers couldn't afford—and is fiercely loyal to those she cares about.

Friendship? Gods I might be falling in love with her already.

I groan and put my head in my hands. Elias laughs and claps me on the shoulder.

"All will be well, my friend. All will be well."

CHAPTER 21

DAHLIA

I dream of blood and fire and agony, of crimson eyes and dripping fangs. I flinch away, as if I can outrun the nightmares. *No. Not nightmares. Memories.*

I gasp and shoot upright, a scream caught in my throat. Warm, firm hands clasp my shoulders.

"My Lady. *Dahlia*," Takara corrects. "You're alright. You're safe."

I meet the vampire's gaze, but I can't really see her. All I can see are the bodies, the blood soaking the earth, the menacing glee in those crimson eyes.

"You need to breathe, Dahlia."

I try, but I can't find a way to get the air into my lungs. I claw at my chest, gasping. It feels as if my ribs are closing in, squeezing my insides, stabbing me and crushing me as they shrink smaller and smaller...

Something pricks my arm and a moment later, blissful darkness swallows me again.

~

"Keeva, you must wake. You *must*..."

I hear Alaric's voice drifting soft as the wind through my mind. Or, I think I do. It's probably just a dream, but I cling to his voice, wrapping my arms around it and holding on as strongly as I can, letting it buoy me in the dark waves trying to drag me beneath the sea, down into the memories again. I push against them, clutching at the soft sound of Alaric whispering *Keeva* over and over and over...

I'm more prepared this time as I slowly rise out of unconsciousness. The memories are still there, but they aren't so sharp and intense now, not enough to overwhelm me completely. Even now, I still cling to Alaric's soft whispers. The ones I most surely concocted in my mind, but I cling to them all the same.

I blink my eyes open slowly. The room is dim, only a fire burning low in the hearth lighting the space, but everything looks clear and sharp.

Takara sighs in relief.

"There you are." I try to push myself up, but Takara reaches forward. "Here, let me help you." I try to protest that I'm fine, but I'll admit that I'm exhausted and weary down to my bones, and decide to take the vampire's assistance. She helps to ease me up into a sitting position, my back against the smooth wooden headboard, and a second later, a cup of water is being pressed to my lips, a touch too forcefully. I take in Takara's worried dark eyes, the strain clear on her beautiful face, and I take the cup from her, drinking deep.

Takara watches worriedly as I drain the cup and take a deep, settling breath before speaking.

"What...how..." I rub my face, trying to organize the hundreds of questions trying to escape my mouth all at once. I settle on the most important: "Is everyone ok?" The memory of Victor's body lying limply in the dirt, blood soaking the ground around him, of Kane roaring at me to run while he fought two of those creatures, rears up behind my eyes and my chest twists painfully. I rub the heel of my hand there while I wait for the answer, dread hanging over me like the hangman's noose.

"Isaiah, Kane, and Descartes were slain," Takara says, bowing her head. Grief floods through me, my eyes burning with tears. I know that those in the army view a death in battle as a great honor, but I can't help the spears of guilt stabbing my heart. They had died because of *me*. They'd only been on that road because I'd wanted to go to the village. Kane had tried to fight two of those things off alone so that I could run. It's a long moment before I can push past the lump in my throat and speak again.

"And everyone else? Viktor...I saw him fall..." I swallow hard as memories rise but I try to push them away.

"He's alright. He was injured and knocked unconscious, but he's already healed." I nod. *Healed.* That reminds me...

I look down and gasp.

"How...?" I run a finger over the thick pink scar on my bicep, the spot where there had been a gruesome wound not long ago. I move and flex my fingers, turning my arm this way and that. I'm a bit sore, just a dull ache, but I'm truly healed.

"Alaric gave you his blood. Your injury was grievous and you'd lost nearly too much blood. It was the only thing to do to save your life."

More memories rise then, ones I wasn't sure were real until this moment. Alaric had saved me. He'd taken the Revenant's head and then he'd cradled my face so gently, spoken my name so tenderly... No. That couldn't be right. I had to have imagined that part. He *did* save me, though. I know that much for certain.

"How did he even know to come?"

"You'll have to ask him that," Takara says, sounding nearly as tired as I feel. "You need to eat something before you sleep again. No arguments," she adds sternly, and my lips curl into a small smile as I bob my head in obedience. Takara grabs a tray off of the table across the room and brings it over, watching me like a hawk as I eat the cheese and fruit and cold chicken. I don't taste much of anything, really. I'm still so…numb, so raw.

I'd been attacked by Revenants. I'd seen people die all around me. I can still smell their blood and hear their cries of agony. I'd nearly had my arm taken clean off by a sword and apparently nearly died as a result. The food almost comes back up, but I force it to stay down, taking slow, deep breaths in and out through my nose. Takara hands me more water and it helps. Eventually, I calm down enough to speak again.

"How long was I asleep? How long as it been since…since it happened?"

"Nearly three days."

"Three days??" I repeat, incredulous.

"Despite Alaric's blood, your body needed time and rest to heal. Your mind, as well," she adds softly. "It was no small thing that happened to you." Takara squeezes my hand and I squeeze it back, holding on to it for dear life. I wonder if she still remembers her attack after all these years. Had she been as afraid as I'd been? As…helpless?

"I heard you scream," I say softly, tears stinging my eyes again. "After the fighting started. Everything was chaos and I didn't know what to do but I heard you yell my name and then you screamed in pain and I tried to get to you and—"

Takara places her hand on my cheek, eyes shining.

"I was worried for you too, Dahlia." She leans forward and places a soft kiss on my forehead. When she pulls back, she tries to look stern. "Do not do that to me again."

I huff out a small laugh, though the sound is a bit hollow.

"I'll try my best." She nods and clears her throat, clearly forcing the emotion away.

"Your friends came to see you. Wesley and Nova. They came the minute word began to spread through the camp." That made the strange, hollow feeling in my chest ease a bit. I lost friends, but I still have others here who care about me. I'll go see them as soon as I can.

"There will be funeral rites for those slain at dusk. The High General thought that you might want to attend, so he held the ceremony off until you woke. I was fairly certain it would be today that you finally pushed through the darkness."

My eyes prick again, both at the thought of laying those who gave their lives protecting me to rest, but also at Alaric's kindness. I wonder again how he knew to come—the bond because of the blood he's taken from me, perhaps? But...no, he must have already been on the way before he realized something was wrong to get there so quickly—we were still at least an hour from the camp when we were attacked, probably closer to two. Why would he be riding towards the town? An unpleasant thought regarding the blood house drifts into my mind and I forcefully cut the thought off at the knees.

Either way, he was kind in holding the funerals until I could attend, somehow knowing that I would want to be there to say goodbye.

"Yes, I'd like to attend." I glance towards the window but the curtains are closed tightly and I have no idea what time it might be. "How long do I have to get ready?" I start to throw my feet over the edge but Takara stops me, gently pressing me back into the pillow.

"Hours yet. Rest, Dahlia. I'll wake you when it's time." I start to protest—I've been sleeping for three days already, apparently—but a wide yawn splits my face and my argument is lost before it's begun. "Rest," Takara says again, pointedly. I nod and settle back into bed. Takara tucks the covers around me and I'm already nearly asleep, my lids feeling heavy as lead.

"Tell Alaric I said thank you...for...for everything..." I whisper before the darkness welcomes me once more.

THE FUNERALS ARE SIMPLE, but beautiful. Alaric's gaze slips to mine as Takara and I approach the gathering and my pulse races even as my entire body seems to sigh in relief, practically melting with it, with each step that I take closer to him. *All the blood*, I realize. I'm even more connected to him now than ever before because of the blood he'd given to heal me. His eyes burn with too many things for me to name, but eventually he simply inclines his head in greeting as I take my place in the first row of soldiers beside him. A place of honor.

Takara slips in beside me, clasping my hand and squeezing gently. Three wooden pyres have been constructed, and atop each one is a body of one of my guards—of one of my friends. My throat feels thick and acid churns in my belly, my eyes already pricking with tears, but I try to hold them back. I need to be strong, like the thousands of soldiers behind me.

On some signal I don't see, Elias steps forward, a torch of rowan wood in his hands.

"A death in battle is a death well given. Descartes Moreau, we mourn you and honor you by battling another day. Vale, brother."

A seemingly endless echo of *vale, brother* rumbles through the lines of soldiers. Tears slide silently down my face and I grip Takara's hand tightly as Elias touches the end of his torch to Descartes' pyre. The flames dance up the wood, sparking and jumping until they're so high they seem to touch the clouds above. He moves to the next pyre and repeats the words.

"Isaiah Burrowleaf…"

Vale, brother.

"Kane Aurelius…"

Vale, brother.

The tears continue, though I manage not to sob. I feel empty and hollow as I say my silent goodbyes, thanking them for what they gave to protect me. Telling them that I'll miss them. Telling them I'm sorry.

After the last pyre is lit, the soldiers all bow their heads and thump their fists over their chests three times in perfect synchrony. That's apparently all there is to it. They begin to leave their formation in quiet, practiced precision, but I don't move. I stare at the flames for what feels like forever, and, to my surprise, Alaric stays beside me. He doesn't speak, but his presence beside me is a comfort that I can't help but cling to.

"I'm sorry," I say quietly as the flames finally begin to die, smoke and ashes sifting on the wind towards the mountains.

Alaric turns to me, but before he can say anything, one of the men calls his name. He turns towards the voice and before he can turn back again, I walk away. He doesn't come after me but I don't expect him to. I find Wesley and Nova waiting on me near the path back to the cabin and Takara tells me she'll see me in a while, letting me have my time with my friends and, I suspect, going to spend time with Malcom. I squeeze her hand before she walks away, silently thanking her for too many things all at once.

I throw my arms around Wesley's neck, a fresh wave of tears scalding my eyes.

"Gods, Dahlia, I can't believe...When I heard what happened... Fuck, I was *terrified*," Wesley confesses, squeezing me almost too tightly. I bury my face in his neck for a long moment and when I pull back, he chucks me under the chin lightly. "I just found you again. Don't you dare try to leave me already."

I laugh a little bit through tears before Nova yanks me into a bear hug.

"We were so worried," she says quietly. She pulls back and holds me at arm's length. "You're alright? We heard you almost lost your whole damn arm, that you almost..." She trails off, beautiful face pinched with worry.

I nod. "I am." Mostly. "My arm is all healed thanks to Alaric's blood." I sigh. "It was...scary. Terrifying, actually. I don't know how you do it, day in and day out."

"It's alright to be scared. I still am some days. If you aren't afraid, you aren't alive," Nova assures me.

"But I just...I *stood* there. I was completely frozen by the fear for far too long." I shake my head in frustration, remembering how I'd done nothing while the chaos and fighting erupted around me, while the others bled and, in three awful cases, died for me.

"That's nothing to be ashamed of," Nova says. "Truly. The first time I came face-to-face with a Revenant, I nearly wet myself—well, I would have if I was still human, I mean. I froze, couldn't even lift my blade. Someone else cut the bastard down before he could gut me like a fish, thankfully. And that was after a *year* of training at the academy and another here at the camp. So, you shouldn't feel anything but proud that you even made it out of there alive."

They ask if I want to go back to Third Quadrant with them, drink until I can't remember my own name, but I decide to hold on to that offer for another night. I just want to be alone for a bit. We say our goodbyes and make my way to the field behind the cabin, collecting stones as I go.

CHAPTER 22

DAHLIA

"What are you doing?" Alaric asks softly from behind me. I don't gasp or start in surprise—I'd *felt* him approaching, like a warmth spreading through my veins from the center of my chest.

I'm on my knees beneath a towering scarlet oak on the far end of the field. It's night now, but there are no clouds and the moon is full and bright, giving me plenty of light to see by. Plus, with all of Alaric's blood, my senses are keener than usual—I can see pretty damn well in the dark for the time being. I place another smooth stone on the stack. Two others stand beside it, already completed.

"I'm saying goodbye in my own way," I tell him.

"May I?"

I glace up at him. Though I wasn't surprised by his *arrival*, I'm surprised by his *presence*—why is he here? He's been avoiding me at all costs for months. Now he's out here with me...and he seems almost nervous? Regardless of the reason, I remind myself that he is my prince and I'm his Consort and he can do whatever he damn well pleases, so I nod. He sinks to his knees beside me and eyes the rocks with interest.

"My father's people, they build cairns like these in memory of the dead, a way to honor them. The funeral rites were beautiful, but I just...I wanted to do this for me, to honor them in the way of my family."

"I think that's...lovely." I glance up at him in confusion, but he's staring down at the rock in his hand as he twirls it between his long, deft fingers. "Are you alright?" His voice is low and rough, and I know he isn't talking about my state of mourning.

"I am." I would swear a small shudder runs through his body at that, like he's been holding on to all the tension in the world, waiting for my confirmation that I'm ok. I don't understand what's going on, to be honest. Not at all. But I don't have the energy to fight against it, not today, and I'd be lying if I said that I *wanted* to. Because of the blood he gave me, being near him is like a compulsion, like we're magnets and I can only be whole if I'm with him. Right now, I'll take this comfort, forced and false as it may be, and use it to cushion myself against the sorrow and pain.

"I'm sorry," he says. "I'm sorry that you went through that. I'm sorry that you were hurt and that you were afraid." He says the next through gritted teeth, fangs sharp and extending before my eyes. "I'm sorry that those bastards somehow attacked what's mine in what equates to my own home."

"What's yours...?" I say quietly, the words sending a strange shiver up my spine. He blinks as if he hadn't realized he'd even spoken the words out loud.

"My Consort. My men," he clarifies, and I nod. Of course.

"Thank you," I say after a few moments of silence. "For saving me." He's silent for so long that I finally glance up at him and he looks taken aback, truly at a loss for words, but something burns behind his eyes, something I can't decipher...but something that makes me want to lean into him, to spend the rest of my life trying to figure out.

"You're welcome," he says finally, though it doesn't seem to be what he really wanted to say. I sigh and turn back to the cairn, placing my last stone on top.

"Kane, Cyrus, and Descartes. May the suns find your face. May the winds find your sails. May the gods welcome you home. May we always remember. And may we one day meet again." My throat feels thick. The last time I said these words was at my mother's funeral.

Alaric reaches forward and adds his stone.

"Vale, brothers," he says quietly. I turn and our gazes meet, and I wish so badly I could read what's churning beneath his golden depths. Again, that longing to lean forward, that desire to climb into his arms and never leave, rushes over me, covering me like a blanket as soft as a whisper.

"My Lady," Takara calls hesitantly from a few feet away. I jerk my gaze from Alaric to my Keeper. "Your dinner is served in your quarters. I...I think you need to eat a proper meal," she adds a little sternly, giving me a pointed look. As if in answer, my stomach chooses that moment to make an obscenely loud grumbling sound, demanding its due. I pull in my lips to keep from laughing and when I look back at Alaric, he looks to be doing the same.

"You better go," Alaric says. "That sounded...dire." His tone is dry but I do believe he's trying at humor. I scramble to my feet, inclining my head to him before I turn and join Takara.

"And what was going on out there?" she asks quietly in my ear as we walk back across the field and into my wing of the cabin.

"He was...making sure I was alright, I think."

"Hmm," is all she says in return as she escorts me to my dining room where a feast large enough for ten people waits.

"Takara!" I gasp.

"You need to eat!" she says defensively. "And I didn't know what you might be wanting after...after everything, so I had Reginald make some of everything. There's pheasant and elk and chicken, and the foul-smelling stew that you seem to love for unknown reasons. Cheese and fruit and freshly baked bread. Potatoes with extra cheese...Oh and the pudding! Four different kinds of pudding. I know how much you love pudding..." She trails off as I wrap my arms around her middle. After a moment, she embraces me back and lets out a long, shuddering breath.

"Thank you," I say, my eyes stinging yet again with tears. Will they ever cease?

Takara sniffles and when I pull away and look at her, there are crimson-tinged tears in her eyes. She quickly wipes them away and shifts her shoulders back.

"Well get on with it then. The sounds your stomach is making are truly horrendous. Humans are so awful sometimes. I can't believe I used to be one." I roll my eyes and she smiles, settling into the chair across from me as I admittedly gorge myself on a little bit of everything.

Somehow, after everything of the past few days, I go to sleep tonight with a smile on my lips.

I pace in my room, working up the nerve to go see Alaric. I'm going to ask for—no, *demand*—what I want. I'm his Consort. My wish is supposed to be his command, but...I know for certain no Consort has ever wished for this. I bite my lip and fiddle with the ring my father gave me the day of the Choosing. It has become a habit over these months, to rub the stone for comfort or when I'm feeling nervous. It makes me feel closer to him, as if he's in my ear, encouraging me or comforting me.

"Just fucking do it, you coward," I tell myself in the mirror. On a whim I can't even quite explain, I pull the pins from my hair, letting my curls fall loosely down my back. I march determinedly to Alaric's wing, but just outside the door to the war room, I pause. He's speaking with someone inside. I don't mean to eavesdrop but with my senses a bit sharper because of Alaric's blood, it's much easier to do. I can't help but lean in a bit closer when I hear my name.

"Sir, I would like to put in my name for consideration as a replacement on Lady Dahlia's guard."

"Highspear, I am not making any decisions on that front at this time," Alaric says, not unkindly, but there's a slight tremor of annoyance in his voice.

"I would take the position very seriously, sir, I promise you. I know you did not...trust me," he sounds as if he's saying the words with a barely hidden sneer, "to be a sergeant yet, but you can trust me in this."

"Highspear—"

"Please sir. I want...I want to matter! I deserve to matter!" the soldier explodes, startling me. "I am *ready*."

"You aren't," Alaric snaps, cool authority in his voice. "I am sorry, Highspear, but you are not ready. You are not ready to be a sergeant, you are not ready to lead others, and you are sure as fuck not ready to protect what's *mine*." I blink at the fire in Alaric's words, the vehemence and...possessiveness.

There's a long, uncomfortable silence before the soldier says in a deadly quiet voice, "you have no idea what I'm capable of." The words sound like a threat and I hastily retreat down the hallway, trying desperately not to get caught listening in on conversations I'm obviously not meant to hear.

I make it back to the entrance room of the cabin when I hear the doors to the war room open. I think about trying to hide, but decide against it just as the vampire's quick footsteps draw near. He freezes when he sees me. He looks young, maybe only nineteen or so when he was turned. His face is round and boyish, his eyes a bit too big for his face and a deep, muddy brown. His hair is the same color, short, but with a bit that stands up awkwardly in the back.

He inclines his head quickly. "Lady Dahlia."

"Hello." I smile at him, knowing he's upset by the meeting with Alaric. The one that clearly went badly. His hands are opening and closing into fists at his sides, the muscle in his jaw clenching and unclenching. My da always says that sometimes what someone needs on their worst day is just a kind smile—and a pint. I can at least offer this man—Highspear—the first. "I don't believe we've been properly introduced, but I've seen you about the camp."

He relaxes a bit at that, blinking in surprise, but then his lips tilt up ever so slightly at the corners. He's clearly happy to have been recognized among all of the soldiers by the High General's Consort.

"I'm Luca. Luca Highspear, my Lady."

"It's an honor to make your acquaintance, Luca."

"The honor is mine." He studies me for a long moment, suddenly looking a little uneasy and pale. "I...I heard you were injured in the attack on the road. Are you quite alright?"

"I am," I assure him. "I've got a very tough-looking scar to show off now. I fancy it will get me lots of free drinks around the tavern back home." I smile widely and he smiles hesitantly back, still look-ing...off. Probably still upset about how Alaric had dismissed him so harshly.

"I'm very sorry that happened. That...that you were hurt. The Revenants never should have gotten within the borders. We should have stopped them, my Lady." He looks upset and I wonder if perhaps he was one of the men on duty that day at one of the many guard stations along the road and surrounding the camp. Does he feel guilty for not seeing the Revenants, like the attack was his fault somehow?

"It's no one's fault," I tell him gently, stepping forward and laying a hand on his shoulder. He meets my gaze, his big eyes making him seem so, so young. He nods his head and says a quick goodbye before retreating from the cabin.

I make my way back down the hallway to Alaric's door and this time, I knock.

"Come in," he calls, sounding tired and annoyed. I take a quick, settling breath and push the door open. Alaric sits behind his massive desk, a stack of letters beside him. I let out a low, soft breath as I take him in. He looks more handsome than I'd ever seen him. He's in a simple black shirt, the top few buttons undone to reveal the smooth, tempting skin of his chest and throat. His hair is its usual mess, but now I can see that some of the strands are so black they look almost blue. He meets my gaze, the gold burning and beautiful and...I've suddenly forgotten how to speak. I was still so out of sorts at the funerals that I hadn't truly *seen* him, but now, he is all I can see.

Are my keener senses making him more attractive, letting my weak, human eyes see him more clearly? Dear gods, is this how he looks to other vampires? No wonder there are rumors of him fighting females off with a stick, of him entertaining too many companions to name...there's even one that claims he made a female vampire come so hard her knees gave out just by *winking* at her across the room. That...that couldn't be true...could it? I swallow hard as a shiver skates over my skin and my stomach dips at the mere thought.

"Dahlia," he says in greeting, voice low. His eyes drop to my lips and then lower. A sharp stab of desire flares through my core, but... I'm not completely sure it's *my* desire. My eyes fly wide. Could I be feeling *Alaric's* emotions? No, surely not...but he'd said that I might be able to after the binding ceremony, and that had only been a tiny sip of blood. This time he'd given me *mouthfuls*...

But there's no way he's feeling...desirous of me. Perhaps it's just the lust for *blood* that I'm feeling, not anything else. His gaze meets mine again and I force all other thoughts away. I have things I need to say and I won't be deterred. *My little firebrand*, my father's voice echoes in my mind as I run a finger over the ring on my right hand. I push my shoulders back.

"I want to learn to fight," I say without preamble. His brow furrows, clearly surprised by this outburst.

"What?"

"I want to learn to fight," I repeat. "I've always thought that I was strong, that I could take care of myself. But I realized on that road how wrong I was. I...I just *stood* there," I say closing my eyes, remembering. "I stood there, completely frozen and useless. I couldn't protect myself—or anyone else—even the tiniest bit." Fury pulses hot and jagged in my chest. *Not all my own?* I open my eyes to find Alaric's blazing, though he keeps his expression passive. "I didn't like feeling helpless. I know I have a guard and I appreciate the protection they give me, but I just..." I trail off, exhaling roughly, not knowing how to explain to someone who is so damned strong and brave and resilient, what it feels like *not* to be.

"Alright," he says and I blink in surprise.

"Alright?"

He nods. "It is a general rule that everyone who enters this camp knows the basics of self-defense and swordplay. Every human member of the staff here could raise arms against a threat, should they need to. I did not realize you might want to be afforded the same opportunity."

"Yes. Yes, I do. Thank you." I add hastily, "I know you're far too busy to do it yourself, but Wesley and Nova have offered to teach me. I promise it won't interfere with their training schedules or any of their duties. We'll only do lessons when they don't have other obligations."

He stares at me for a long moment and then inclines his head.

"I think that's...an excellent plan," he says, though his voice is a little stiff. Perhaps he doesn't actually want me to learn, but knows it's a good idea anyway. Either way, he's said yes, and that's all that matters.

"Oh. Uh, thank you." I hesitate, not sure that I need to remain, but not quite wanting to leave. "Do you need blood?" He inhales quietly but shakes his head.

"Not yet. You need more time to recover from your loss before I take again." After a moment he adds, "I'll send for you when I am in need, though." So, he doesn't plan to go back to ignoring me then? What on earth had happened up in the wilds that had caused this change? Whatever it is, I'm happy for it, even knowing how foolish that is. I smile and his own features soften slightly in return.

"Alright then," I say, inclining my head and turning to leave.

"Dahlia," he calls and I turn at the door. I would swear there's amusement dancing in his golden eyes now, a quirk of his lips ever so slightly as he says, "enjoy your training."

CHAPTER 23
DAHLIA

"How...in all the gods' fucking names...does running around the entire damned camp...help me protect myself?" I demand as I fight to breathe, my side feeling as if it's being stabbed repeatedly by a very sharp stick. I lean over, hands on my knees, and curse when sweat drips into my eyes, stinging like the devil. Even with Alaric's blood giving me increased strength and speed and everything else, I'm still all but dying with these "exercises" Nova and Wesley are putting me through. I'm not wholly convinced that they aren't actually torture tactics or just plain practical jokes.

"We need to build up your strength and endurance before you can learn the rest," Nova says matter-of-factly. "You're not as bad off as I thought you might be though, being a noble from your high castle on a hill and all," she mocks with a wink. I glare at her and Wesley laughs, the sound echoing oddly through the low fog all around us. Autumn has officially arrived at the camp, with crisp, cool mornings usually accompanied by heavy fog that gives the mountains and surrounding forests a sinister air. Other than these early morning runs, the Northlands are truly stunning and I find myself falling more in love with them each day.

But *not* before the sun rises every fucking day.

The morning after Alaric had agreed to my training, the two vampires who were formerly my closest friends, but have now turned traitors, woke me before dawn, making me scream in my bed like a banshee.

"Rise and shine, my Lady," Wesley had said with a crooked grin as he lit the chemical lamps. I winced at the sudden flare of light, pulling my blanket over my head

"What in the fuck are you doing?" I'd yelled from below my toasty warm fortress.

The blanket was yanked away and thrown across the room, and I'd yelped before scowling. Nova only grinned.

"Training you, of course."

"What?" It was entirely too early and my brain wasn't functioning properly.

"We received word last night from the High General that we were to begin your training immediately. We have been officially reassigned to your training sessions every morning until..." Wesley frowned. "Well, until he says otherwise, I suppose."

"Now—up, up, up. We need to beat the sun." Nova had tossed a bundle of clothing at me, smacking me in the face. I held them up, trying to force my vision to focus after being so rudely and abruptly awoken—before the fucking sun was even up.

"What are these?"

"Training clothes," Wesley said, giving me a pitying look. "You are not the brightest flower in the garden in the mornings, are you, my love?"

"Out. Now," I'd demanded, throwing my legs over the edge of the bed to go clean my teeth, wash my face to try to help me wake up, and apparently put on training clothes—whatever those were, exactly. Nova and Wesley had laughed and headed for the door.

"Wait," I'd called. They'd turned at the door. "What if I had been sleeping naked?"

"Then we would have had a most excellent morning indeed," Wesley had said, waggling his eyebrows. "Maybe try that tomorrow?" Nova shoved him out the door at that and though I was intensely annoyed, I laughed.

Now, I struggle to breathe and glare at the two vampires.

"I hate you both."

"You are many things, Dahlia Clayburn, but a liar is not one of them," Wesley says, grinning. "Possibly the slowest human on the planet, yes. But a liar? No."

"I'm not *that* slow," I grumble. I am, in fact, extremely slow. "Fine. Maybe not *hate,* but I definitely dislike you right now."

"Well, you're going to *really* dislike us now—it's time for abdominal work," Nova says with a wicked gleam in her eyes that makes me think that this is the worst decision I've ever made.

After two grueling weeks of running around the camp, pulling myself onto things or over things or under things, lifting heavy objects, and doing Nova's favored abdominal exercises, I'm starting to get the hang of things and am actually seeing improvements— probably mostly thanks to Alaric's blood still running through my veins. Without it, I imagine it would take me much longer for my body to grow accustomed to these changes. Even so, the first week I was so exhausted, irritable, and sore in spots I didn't even know existed, that I'd nearly fallen asleep while eating dinner every night. Takara thought it was all very funny, but liked the idea of me learning to defend myself, though she insists that I'll never have the need.

"Over my dead fucking rotting corpse will you ever be in danger like that again," were actually her exact words on the matter, but still, she approves of my training.

Alaric had to leave for an expected trip to one of the other camps, but had a squire bring me a note explaining his absence and telling me he would be back soon. It was...nice of him. I really want to know what changed on that trip to the wilds, but I'm not sure if I'll ever get the chance to ask—or if he would actually tell me, truth be told.

I can't sleep, so I decide to finally write to Enid. I haven't in weeks, not since the attack. A package from her had arrived the day after, while I was still sleeping—with the swords for the guard. I had barely been able to speak around the lump in my throat, realizing that three of them would never meet their new owners. The swords belonging to Descartes, Isaiah, and Kane remain in my trunk. I know I should give them to someone else, to the replacements Alaric has yet to appoint I suppose, but I just can't stomach the thought of it. They weren't just my guards, they were my friends. I can't just give their swords away to someone else. I feel like if I do that, I'm saying they didn't matter, that they are interchangeable with anyone else, their gifts easily passed on to anyone else.

I know I can't put off writing to Enid any longer—she's probably already worried—but I just don't know what to say. I don't want her and da to be worried about me, but not telling them what happened feels like a lie, and we've never lied to each other. Skirted the truth on silly things like staying out past curfew or who broke the ugly-assin vase that used to sit on the mantle, sure, but never on anything important. I take a deep breath and put pen to parchment.

Enid,

I'm sorry I haven't written in a while. Things have been a bit...crazy here. Before I write these next words I need to you know that I am alright. Read that again. I am perfectly fine, I promise you. But...there was an attack on our way back from the village several weeks ago. A Revenant attack, if you can believe it. Alaric and his men are doing all they can to try to figure out how they got through the pass and why they attacked, but no answers yet that I know of. Three of my guards were killed and…

My hand shakes and I have to stop for a moment before I can continue.

I was injured. I know you're having a fit, but remember what I said before: I. AM. FINE. Alaric saved my life in more ways than one, and now I have a very bonny scar that I think makes me seem very mysterious and maybe even a bit of a rugged-arse, as da would say.

But guess what's happening now? You'll never guess, so I'll just tell you: I'm being trained, almost like a real soldier! You know I've always wanted to learn to wield the weapons I make and now I am—and I'm being taught by Wesley and Nova, so it's perfect. Though, to be fair, I haven't gotten to start learning actual weapons yet, but I'm to start tomorrow. Soon your sister will not only have the sharpest tongue in all of Astoria's Keep, but the greatest hand with a blade. Ok, that's probably a bit farfetched, but I'll be able to look quite tough I imagine.

I miss you so much. Even after all these months, my room still feels too big and quiet without you at night. Have you had any luck deterring Leland in these weeks? Or, in the alternative, has he won you over? He's not entirely horrible looking…

Also, to make up for my lack of letters and the worry I know you are feeling now, I'm sending you some gifts I got from the village that day. Don't worry, I've cleaned the

*blood from them...Is it too soon to joke about this? Again —
I really am fine now. It was scary, I won't lie about that.
Terrifying really, but I'm alright. Anyway, back to the gifts.
I'll give you a hint: they are very shiny and sparkly...I hope
you love them.*
   Give da a hug for me.
   I love you both so much.
   -Dahlia
   P.S.
   I AM FINE. I just thought I'd remind you again.

I re-read the letter, hoping that I've said I'm fine enough to convince them both, though I know they'll still be worried. I'm debating crumpling up the entire thing and starting over when I feel the tightness in my chest ease. *Alaric.* With all the blood he gave me, I'm back to feeling the strain when he's gone like a fist around my heart—and the utter relief when he's back. I breathe the first easy breath I have in two weeks and decide the letter is fine. I seal the envelope and rummage in the trunk to find the necklace and ring I want to send, trying to ignore the swords as I do. They're like giant accusatory fingers pointing at me, blaming me. I know that no one else sees it that way, but I can't help but feel responsible for the deaths.

When I'd plucked up the courage to finally see the others, the first words from my lips had been an apology, but Viktor had stopped me.

"My Lady, please. None of this was your fault, you must know that. This is the world we live in, the world we chose to be a part of because each of us answered a call in our blood to fight and to protect. We all knew what the outcome may be for us on any given day when we joined this army. You cannot blame yourself."

The others had agreed and though I would forever feel guilt, it did make me feel a bit better. I'd sniffled and nodded, pushing my shoulders back and forcing the tears away.

"That's our Lady of the Serpents," Malcom said softly with a grin and I'd huffed out a laugh, surprising myself.

"I...I asked my father to make these for you all...before...before that day." I swallowed hard, but forced myself on. "I wanted you all to have something special, something that—I hope—shows how much I appreciate and care about each of you."

I'd presented the swords and Cyrus and Viktor let out low whistles of awe. Malcom was silent, but I would have sworn I saw him wipe a tear as he took up his blade, turning it this way and that so the sun glinted off of the dark gray metal, only a few shades lighter than Night's Fury. The snarling wolf's head was set in each of the cross guards, ruby eyes gleaming, an elegant *CG* beneath it in gold. *Consort's Guard.* My protectors. My friends.

"These gifts are too much, Lady Dahlia," Cyrus said, shaking his head. "We couldn't possibly accept them." He looked to the others, a mix of longing and uncertainty and confusion in his eyes.

"Oh don't be daft," I said, making them all laugh, "of course you can accept them. It's my wish and I don't know if you're aware, but a Consort is supposed to get almost anything she wishes." They'd grinned at that, excitement bubbling up within them like children once they accepted that these were truly their blades now.

Later that night, Takara told me how much the blades truly meant to them.

"Malcom told me that he'd grown up in the gutter, starving most of his life, hardly a night spent with a roof over his head. To have a Clayburn blade now, made specially for him on the request of a prince's Consort, the High General's at that...Well, it means more than you can imagine, Dahlia." She eyed me in that way of hers that made me feel as if she were looking into my very soul and taking my measure. "You really are the kindest person I've ever met. It's a pure sort of kindness that I don't see often. Many people are kind, but in hopes of getting something in return for it. Your kindness is simply for the sake of being kind. It is...beautiful."

I hadn't known what to say to that, so I'd snatched her cup away and thrown it across the room, spilling the blood across the wall. She'd stared at me wide-eyed, mouth gaping.

"But I can still be a little shit." We'd both laughed so hard we had tears streaming down our faces, Takara's pink from the faint tinge of blood.

I clean up the desk a bit now and try to decide what to do. Despite feeling more relaxed than I have since Alaric left, I'm not ready to climb into bed. Now that the utter exhaustion from training has eased, I'm back to having nightmares and I put off sleep as long as possible most nights. So, I throw a robe over my nightgown and pad quietly from my room. I pause in the entry, staring down the hallway to Alaric's wing, straining to hear him, but all is silent.

I quickly slip through the room and down the other hallway towards the study, silent as can be. I don't know why, exactly. It isn't as if I'm not allowed to be out of my wing or barred from the study, but I still slink through the cabin like a thief. I think part of me is nervous to see Alaric. I know I'll see him tomorrow, but I need the night to prepare myself, to ease these nerves flaring through my body like fireworks in my veins.

I ease the door to the study open and quickly slide inside, keeping an eye down the hallway outside. Nothing at all. I ease the door closed, exhaling quietly as I lean my forehead against the cool wood.

CHAPTER 24

ALARIC

I stand before the fire in the study, one arm propped on the mantle as I stare into the flames. I tilt my head when I hear footsteps in the house, catch Dahlia's scent and hear the beating of her heart. Every nerve in my body stands at attention. I turn towards the door and see her open it just enough to slip inside, glancing back out into the hallway...as if she's sneaking into the room? Is she trying to avoid me? *Well, too late for that*, I think as I brace myself for being so near her again. My body tenses even as it seems to sigh in utter contentment at the sight of her. Her hair spills down her back in loose waves of fire, and the thin robe and gown beneath do little to hide the shapely curve of her ass. I swallow hard and call on my control. I've been training myself, shoring up my defenses at it were, every day that I was gone, preparing for this new...relationship I'm going to attempt to cultivate with her.

No more avoidance. No more denying the bond. I may not be able to have my mate the way that I want, the way I need and crave, but I will have her in the only way I can, and that will have to be enough.

After she appears to be sure she hasn't been followed or found out, she quietly pushes the door closed and exhales in relief, leaning her forehead against the wood. I arch a brow and wait, honestly curious what she'll do when she realizes I'm here. *Might as well find out.*

"Good evening," I say in a low, even tone.

She whirls, screaming and grabbing a small statue from the shelf next to the door. She hurls it towards my head with all her might. I move to the side easily and it slams into the stone of the fireplace with a loud crack, the pieces of marble flying in every direction. I blink and brush one from my shoulder.

"Fucking hells!" Her heart gallops in her chest, so loud I think the whole camp can probably hear it. She holds one hand to her chest and runs the other through her hair, pushing the strands away from her forehead.

"I didn't mean to alarm you." I realize now that I should have let her know I was here. The fear that flashed in her eyes for a moment before she processed who was standing across the room reminded me with a visceral punch what she'd been through so recently. She didn't need to be startled. I want to kick myself for being so stupid.

"Ye scared the living shite out of me," she says, breathless. My lips twitch as her brogue slips through more than usual.

"As opposed to the dead shite out of you?" I say, and to my surprise, after a moment, her lips curl up at the corners.

"I didn't know you were in here."

I study her for a moment, and realize that she's surprised to see me *in this room*, not in general.

"But you knew I was back at the camp." A statement, not a question. She nods.

"I felt it when you were close again. I guess with all the blood you gave me when you saved my life...well, the bond is stronger than it was after the Choosing. I could feel you gone like a bow string pulled too tightly, and I felt it when the tension eased."

I assumed as much, but wasn't sure quite how strong the bond had gotten on her end. She could sense my presence, it appeared, but could she sense my emotions? *Gods I hope not.*

We simply stare for a long moment, and too many things seem to be passing between us. Tension, fear, uncertainty...desire. I clear my throat, knowing I'll have to get used to this and find a way to put it from my mind if this is going to work. She seems a bit unsure on what to do now, fiddling with the ring she always wears on her right index finger.

"I'll...go. I didn't mean to disturb you."

"No, that's alright." I take a deep breath. "Stay." I deliberately try to make sure the word isn't a command. I want it to be an *invitation*. She blinks in surprise and her pulse beats wildly at her throat. She studies me for a long minute and I realize I'm holding my fucking breath waiting for her to decide, but she finally nods.

"Alright then." She makes her way towards the couch and I try to keep my eyes from dipping to her throat and lower. I fail, of course, and nearly growl at the sight of her nightgown. It's thin silk, the color of a cloudless sky, with delicate lace lining the material that dips in a low V between her breasts. Again, the silk leaves so little to the imagination that I clench my fists at my sides, my nails digging deep furrows in my palms, blood pooling. I cross the room to pour a drink and wipe the blood away before she notices.

"Would you like a drink?" I turn and she quirks a brow, staring pointedly at the glass in my hand.

"I think I've had quite enough blood, thank you very much."

My lips quirk ever so slightly.

"I have plain whisky. *Sans* blood."

"Oh, then yes, please." I pour another glass for her and cross back to the sofa. I hand her drink over and we both stand there awkwardly for a moment before she seems to shrug off the strange situation and settles onto the couch, pulling her feet up beneath her and pulling her robe closed. I can't decide if that's a good thing or not.

"It is quite late, are you not tired?"

"I...haven't been sleeping well." After a moment she adds softly, "Nightmares."

I want to kick myself. Of course she's having trouble sleeping. She was attacked by creatures that strike fear into the hearts of even some of my most hardened soldiers. I should have foreseen the nightmares and done...something. I haven't a fuck all idea of what, but I should have found a way to help her. Instead, I left. Again. *Fuck.* I know this is my job, my *duty*, but leaving her is becoming harder and harder to bear. How the fuck am I supposed to be the High General when I can barely stand to leave my mate behind? I take a long drink, knowing that I'll have no answers tonight, so I try to push the thoughts away. I want to focus on this moment, this hopeful start to something real with Dahlia.

"I'm sorry," I say, wishing she could possibly understand how much I mean the words. My duty might be to protect Braxhlem, but it's also to protect my mate from anything and everything, even from things as intangible as nightmares.

"It isn't your fault," she says, taking another sip of her drink. *But it is*, I think. *All of it.*

"And how is your training going then?"

"The last two weeks have been...what is the opposite of fun? They've been whatever that is." I hide my smile behind my glass as I take another sip of my drink. "But I'm going to start learning actual weapons and fighting tomorrow. I was hoping that meant no more early morning exercise sessions, but I've been assured those will continue and weapons and fighting will be in the afternoon." She rolls her eyes.

I laugh lightly and she smiles.

"You don't enjoy rising before the sun, I take it?"

"I believe *loathe entirely* is a more accurate statement of my feelings on the matter...but I'll admit that I already feel stronger for it." She takes another drink and we slip into another somewhat awkward silence.

"You come here to read then? To distract yourself from sleeping?"

"How did you know...?" Her brow furrows.

"Your scent is all over the room," I say lightly, though it had hit me like a battering ram when I'd first entered. It was everywhere, surrounding me, and it was like coming home and the most exquisite torture all rolled up together.

"Oh. Right, of course," she says, shaking her head. "I, uh, hope that's alright?"

"This is as much your study as it is mine now." She holds my gaze and I get the feeling that she's trying to stare right to the heart of me, to break down every wall and defense I have and strip me bare before her.

"Something's changed," she finally says and my heart stutters in my chest. She can't possibly know the truth...can she?

"What do you mean?"

"I mean," she says, twisting on the couch so that she's facing me. I don't even notice how the movement makes her robe and night-gown ride up, baring her thigh, the soft, smooth skin...No. I don't notice it at fucking all. *Control, control, control,* I chant, calming myself. "That you avoided me for months and months, and now you aren't. Something had to have changed."

"I..." How the fuck to answer this? I don't want to lie. I can't tell her the truth. Not the whole truth anyway, but perhaps a portion of it. "I tried to handle the situation as other princes would have, keeping our lives separated, but as I told you before—I'm not like other princes. So, I don't want to handle this situation as they would."

"And that means...?"

I take a long, slow breath, bracing myself before I answer. *Here it goes then.*

"It means...that I don't want to avoid you any longer."

She inhales softly and my eyes dart to her lips, the way they part slightly as she breathes, the way the top one forms a perfect bow, the way the bottom is full and practically begging to be pulled between my teeth...I force my eyes back up to meet hers and wait. What will she think? What will she say? I'm equally excited and terrified to find out.

"Alright then." Such a simple answer, but as her lips curl upward, my chest warms.

"Alright then," I echo.

She nods her head once and then rises from the couch, going to the bookcase beside the fire and running her fingers gently along the spines until she finds one that sparks her interest. She pulls the volume and glides back to the sofa, that easy sway in her hips that makes it hard to breathe—and keep my hands to myself. She curls up again and begins to read without another word. I blink but decide this is a much better start to this new situation than I could have hoped for, so I simply pick my own book up off of the low table before us and begin to read as well.

It's...nice. Calming. We read for what feels like hours, the only sounds the fire popping and crackling, our soft breathing, and her heart beat lulling me into utter contentment like a babe. I steal a glance at her from the corner of my eye and find her completely engrossed in her book. The firelight dances across her face, the flames' reflections sparking in her green eyes. She absently toys with a lock of hair, twirling it around her finger again and again. *Gods, she's beautiful.*

"Do you need blood?" she asks after a while, startling me.

"No, no, you're still healing, you—"

"Alaric," she says, and the sound of my name on her lips makes my blood heat, my chest clench. She closes her book and holds my gaze. There's a fierce determination there that calls to me. "I am fine. I am perfectly healed. And I am also your Consort and it's my duty to give you blood. Let me do it." I hold her gaze and I see no fear, no trepidation, only stone-hard resolve.

"Alright," I finally say, moving closer to her across the sofa. She holds out her wrist and I take it gently, barely suppressing a shudder at the feel of her soft skin beneath my fingertips. Her pulse beats quickly, thrumming against my thumb like a hummingbird's wings. I slice a quick gash and she barely even flinches, her gaze still locked with mine. *Fuck, fuck, fuck. This isn't good. She looks like...like she wants...No.* I clench my jaw and force control through every inch of me. I add her blood to my glass but don't release her wrist...and she doesn't pull away. Again, I keep my gaze on hers as I lift the glass to my lips and drink. Only then do my eyes slide closed, the taste of her blood on my tongue like fucking heaven. Fire licks through my veins, Dahlia filling every fiber of my being.

She's my lifeline. She's my heartsblood. She's mine.

"I knew an old drunkard in the village where we lived before we took the title," she says quietly. I crack open my eyes and meet her gaze, having no idea where she might be going with this. "There was a beat of time when he swore off the stuff, though. Didn't touch a drop for months and months. But I saw him the day he broke, the moment the alcohol hit his lips after all that time. It was like agony and ecstasy all at once, like he was stepping foot into heaven and hell at the same time." Her eyes flick to my lips for a quick moment before she lifts them to mine once more. "That's what you look like right now. You have that same look on your face."

I exhale roughly. "Fresh, true blood is quite different than the replicated version. It's...intense."

I realize I still have her hand, am still tracing slow circles on her wrist with my thumb, and something heavy and hot suddenly surrounds us. My fangs are still out, my heart thundering in my chest and my blood thundering in my ears.

"I think..." Her eyes dip to my lips again and she wets her own before yanking her gaze back up. She clears her throat softly. "I think I should go to bed."

I force myself to release her hand and shove that heavy heat away.

"Of course. I can walk you—"

She stands quickly and backs away from the sofa, towards the door. I narrow my eyes ever so slightly. There's desire coming through the bond between us in waves strong enough to swallow even the most stalwart of ships. Is it just because of the blood I gave her? Does that cause her to...feel things for me that she wouldn't normally feel? Or...

"No, that's ok. Really. I'll, uh, see you...tomorrow?" There's a hope in her voice that sets my chest aflame again. She wants to see me again like this.

I nod. "Tomorrow."

"Good night, Alaric," she says as she opens the door.

"Goodnight, Keeva," I say quietly just before she slips into the hallway.

I scrub a hand across my face and run my fingers through my hair. How the fuck could sitting in the study, reading beside Dahlia be one of the best nights I've had in centuries?

"And I'm doing it again tomorrow," I say to the flames, a slow smile spreading across my lips.

CHAPTER 25
DAHLIA

"Alright, same drills as last time," Nova says a week later. We'd started my real training sessions and though I'd honestly been hoping for a sword or a dagger or one of those deadly-looking balls with the spikes on the end of a chain things I'd seen some of the soldiers training with, it made sense to start with the basics of hand-to-hand combat before moving to weapons. It was the same when learning at the forge with da. I couldn't just start with a hammer and anvil without breaking my fingers or knocking myself unconscious. I had to learn the craft of it first, how to move, how to work the instruments, to *understand* them.

And according to Wesley, my body is my most important instrument. It's my first weapon, and I need to understand how to wield it before I can learn to wield anything else.

"There you go...shift your weight a bit...there, that's better... strike...spin...good!"

Though I convinced Alaric that my guard doesn't need to be on duty while I'm training (I'd argued that if he trusted Wesley and Nova enough to train me, then he had to trust them enough to be able to defend me if need be, and he couldn't really argue with that logic), they liked to watch my sessions anyway. I don't actually mind. It's kind of nice having them all here supporting me, acting like I can really do this, not like this is just an indulgence for a spoiled Consort's ridiculous request. They're helpful as well, giving pointers and advice and good-natured jeers, and Malcom graciously agrees to act as a punching bag most days. Even Takara participates, deciding she could stand to learn a bit of fighting as well, so I'm not always alone in my lessons either, which is nice.

It's...exhilarating. I never thought of fighting as something I'd ever *want* to do, but now that I'm learning and can see the beauty and art in it, something in me stirs. I never want to be a soldier or anything like that, of course, but the idea of being able to defend myself—or, more accurately, someone else—sends a tingling excitement through my veins, a sense of...purpose, of doing something good and noble. The way Alaric and every soldier in this camp do every day. I'm sure it's just a silly dream to think I'll ever be in a position to truly help someone in this way, but the dream is enough to make me want to work harder...maybe even enough to make me not loathe the early morning workouts quite so much.

Maybe.

After a couple of hours, I'm a sweaty, dirty mess, but I can't stop grinning.

"You're doing quite well, my Lady," Viktor says as I take a long drink of water by the edge of the practice ring.

"You have to say that."

"I most certainly do not. If you did poorly or looked ridiculous, I would simply say nothing at all." He winks and I smile at him. Nova, Wesley and I decide to head to the pond to lounge and relax after what, in my opinion, was a very hard day's work. To them, it was nothing, but they indulge me anyway.

We pass Luca on the way and I make a point to stop and speak with him. I've seen him a few times since that first day in the cabin after Alaric denied him a spot on my guard and I always try to at least acknowledge him. He seems a little uncertain at first, but relaxes and smiles tentatively at me after we exchange pleasantries. That flash of guilt flares in his eyes again and I know he still blames himself for the attack, though all of the guards on duty near the pass were cleared of any wrong-doing or lapses in duty. They believe the group of Revenants had been in hiding within the boundaries long before that day, somehow managing to stay undetected.

I tell him goodbye and jog to catch up to Nova and Wesley.

"And what was that about?" Wesley asks with a quirk of his brow, looking back towards Highspear over his shoulder.

I shrug. "I ran into him in the cabin once after he was speaking with Alaric and he seemed...dejected. Sad. A little awkward. I get the feeling he doesn't fit in as well here as the two of you."

"That's true," Nova says, a considering look on her face. "He's a good enough soldier—obviously good enough to be chosen as one of the High General's own—but he just doesn't...fit, as you say. He's the butt of a lot of good-natured jibes, gets put on less-than-desirable duties, is never on the front lines—that sort of thing. I heard he's petitioned for promotion a few times but he's always turned down. I think he wants to be a sergeant mostly just so he can talk down to the rest of us, finally feel...I don't know, important?"

I think about that as we walk. I feel bad for him, maybe even a bit protective? He has a vulnerability to him that reminds me a bit of Enid when she was young. When she was first diagnosed with the blood disease, before they found the medications to help her, she was so sick and weak. Some of the other children teased her or called her names and though I'd always loved my sister fiercely, that brought out a whole new side of my love. A raw, primal need to protect that honestly horrified mum and delighted da. I may have pulled hair and kicked shins of anyone who dared tease my big sister...there was also an incident with a leech-infested pond. I don't think that Luca and I will be great friends or anything, there isn't much of a connection there, but I do feel a bit of that protectiveness and compassion for him.

And maybe I see a bit of myself in him as well. Always underestimated and dismissed by people. Maybe we'll both prove everyone wrong one day. I push the thoughts away and we make our way to the pond. The temperature is cool, but not cold, and the water looks entirely too inviting after my training.

I strip down to my undershorts and chemise and Nova *whoops* while Wesley pretends to be scandalized.

"My delicate sensibilities!" he cries, shielding his eyes. I put my hands on my hips and narrow my eyes at him.

"I do believe I took those from you *years* ago." I buff my nails on my shirt. "The first one to take them, might I add."

"Fair point," he says with a fangy grin.

"I need all the details of that fateful day," Nova says, taking off her own gear.

"Well, first, he couldn't figure out how to unlace my corset. All thumbs, I swear. Then—"

Wesley interrupts the story by picking me up bodily and tossing me into the chilly water before I can divulge the rest of the embarrassing tidbits. I squeal and sputter but laugh as I surface, finding him yanking off his shirt and striding into the water behind me.

"That's a long enough stroll down memory lane, if you please." He crosses his arms over his chest and smirks. "I've *much* improved, thank you very much."

I splash him and Nova tackles him from behind, making me squeal again as the water sloshes all over me. We all play around a bit, acting like children, really, but none of us seem to care.

"You really are good," Nova says to me a while later, floating in the water with her braids fanning out around her head like a silver halo. "With all the training, I mean. You have a natural ability to move your body that's almost impossible to learn, and even harder to teach."

"Really?"

"Really," Wesley confirms. "I've been in charge of training exercises for plenty of new soldiers fresh out of the academy and you're better than many of them."

"Just wait until I have a blade in my hands," I say, "you might be singing a different tune—or missing fingers."

They both laugh. "We'll start with wooden swords, don't worry, but you'll be there sooner than you think. You'll be a verified rugged-arse as your da would say," Wesley says with a wink.

Eventually I decide it's time to lounge on a blanket like a bump on a log, and stride out of the water, pushing wet hair off of my face. A flash of heat sears through me like a wildfire, nearly making me stumble. I gasp, confused and almost dizzy from...desire? I blink and look around, trying to figure out what's happening, only for my gaze to lock with Alaric's. He's standing a few yards away, a basket in his hand—the handle completely pulverized in his grip. He looks as if he's been carved from granite, not moving a muscle save his eyes as they skate slowly down my face and throat, over the swells of my breasts and my pebbled nipples that are very much visible through the thin chemise, down further still over my stomach and hips and legs. My chest rises and falls rapidly as my pulse races. The way he's looking at me...well, no one has ever looked at me like this before. Like nothing else in the world exists, like no one has ever looked so beautiful, like he's...ravenous.

I swallow hard, unable to move or think or speak. He's in his typical black gear, the leather hugging his muscular body in ways that are nearly criminal, and the gold of his eyes is a dark, piercing amber as he takes me in.

"Holy shit," Nova breathes behind me and then I hear splashing as she and Wesley apparently bolt out of the water.

"High General," Wesley says.

"Do you need us, sir?" Nova asks, voice laced with respect and reverence, slightly at odds with the fact that she's standing there in her underwear.

I'm still frozen, staring like a buffoon. Alaric seems to pull himself out of whatever trance he'd been in—with some effort, I note—and strides forward. It takes me a bit longer to shake this intense moment off. My entire being yearns to step closer to him, to wrap my arms around him and pull him against me until there's no way to tell where his body ends and mine begins. It's more than just physical, it's an ache in my soul, a strange hollowness that I somehow know can only be filled by him. *What in the actual fuck?*

"At ease," he says to Nova and Wesley, but his eyes don't leave me, and I feel both of their stances shift subtly beside me. "Your chef prepared something for you—your Keeper thought you might be hungry after your training—and I offered to bring it to you on my way to check the southwest watch tower." He says it so casually, as if it's the most normal thing in the world for the High General, a Montclare fucking *prince*, to deliver food to a human.

"Oh," I say, my voice coming out hoarse and breathy. I clear my throat. "Thank you." I step forward to take the basket from him, still feeling a little dazed from the force of feeling I felt from him, from the force of my own feelings.

We've spent every night together for the last week reading in the study, and by the end of each night, I feel a little closer to him. I know it's just the blood, the bond between us now because of it, but it doesn't seem to matter. I feel utterly content with him in a way I can't quite explain. It's almost like a piece of myself has been carved away and I only feel whole when Alaric is with me, like he's the perfect shape to fill that carved away bit. The strangest part is that it feels as if that has *always* been the case, like I've never been complete without him. It doesn't feel like something that's only just happened because of the blood he gave me after the attack. I wonder what he feels from me now that I know he's taken enough of my blood to feel my emotions. I haven't asked him directly how clear those emotions are, but I know he has to have some kind of idea what I'm feeling, the strange intensity of these confusing thoughts.

"I did not mean to interrupt. Enjoy your afternoon." He holds my gaze for another second longer before he looks to Nova and Wesley in turn, nodding to them when they place their fists over their hearts. He turns and strides off, his broad shoulders stiff with tension.

I turn to face my friends, hoping my cheeks aren't as red as they feel.

"Was it just me, or was the High General fucking you with his eyes just now?" Wesley asks, a look on his face somewhere between incredulity, amusement, intrigue, and respect.

"Fuck off," I say, settling down on the blanket and wrapping one of the towels that Takara had shoved in Wesley's arms before we'd made our way to the pond earlier around my shoulders.

"No. Seriously. I am an expert in the art of eye-fucking. And that, my friend, was some of the most intense—and might I add *sexy*—eye-fucking I've ever seen."

"Shut up, shut up, shut up."

"Dahlia Clayburn," Nova says, settling beside me on the blanket, toweling her hair dry. "Are you sleeping with your prince?"

"Of course not!" I snap, cheeks heating even more. Nova laughs and lays back, tucking her arms behind her head.

"You know, I've heard rumors that *all* the princes fuck humans, they just pretend that they don't. None of them are actually above it or still adhere to Etienne's rules, at least not in private."

"Well, Alaric isn't like any of the other princes, is he?" I say again, half exasperated and half...hopeful. Which is stupid. He's made it clear he would never—*could* never—do such things...no matter how badly he might want to.

And despite everything, I know he wants...

CHAPTER 26

ALARIC

I am in a great deal of trouble.

I've spent every night over the past two weeks with Dahlia and it is becoming harder and harder to keep my hands off of her. I'd nearly combusted when I'd seen her coming out of the pond that day last week, the silk undergarments she wore hiding absolutely *nothing*.

I've had to find release alone in my bed with her name on my lips more times than I can count simply to stay sane. It's too much. It's not enough. It's torture. It's bliss.

Every minute that we're together in that study, in that room that has become my heaven on this earth, makes me long for more, makes my feelings for her deepen and strengthen in ways I never thought possible. The mating bond draws me to her, makes me want to be with her and protect her and see her happy, but it doesn't make me *feel* for her, it doesn't make me...love her. She's doing that all on her own.

And the feeling is glorious. I want to know everything about her and her life, about her family and her friends and her weapons designs. We talk well into the night most evenings and I could listen to her for the rest of eternity. She's funny and kind and smart—and a damned con woman.

I'd spied her studying the chess set near the fireplace one evening that first week, her book long abandoned.

"I can teach you," I'd offered, "if you like." She turned her gaze on me, a sparkle in her eyes that I hadn't recognized at the time for what it was—cunning. She'd smiled demurely.

"To be taught by the High General would be an honor indeed."

I'd explained each piece, the movements they could make, the keys to the game. She'd watched intently, a most studious pupil. She'd tentatively made moves, reaching towards pieces and then changing her mind again.

"And the steed—" she'd said.

"The Knight," I'd corrected.

"Ah, yes, the *Knight*, he can move...here?" she'd questioned, biting her lip as she moved the piece in question across the board. I'd tried very hard to ignore how attractive that was. I'd failed miserably.

"Yes, very good."

We'd played several games, with me beating her rather easily each time, of course.

"Ok, ok, I'm starting to really understand, I think. Let's play again."

"Alright," I'd agreed, enjoying the time we were spending.

"Would you allow me to ride Xerxes?" she'd asked casually as she made her initial move.

"Absolutely not. I know he allows you to pet him, but being near him and being atop him are very different things. He could kill you in seconds." She'd pressed her lips into a line, that calculating look in her eyes.

"How about a wager then? If I beat you, you allow me to try—with you close by to intervene if necessary—to ride him."

I'd all but scoffed, knowing how ridiculous the wager was, but deciding to humor her since she wanted to make it for whatever reason.

"Alright then." Her eyes had lit at my agreement and it had warmed my chest. "And if I win?"

"Anything you want, Alaric," she'd said and I don't know that she meant for the words to come out quite so sensually. I'd had to clear my throat before answering.

"A debt to be named at a later time then, agreed." She nodded and we began playing. I'd found myself focusing less on the game and more on my opponent. On the way the firelight brought out the gold flecks in her green eyes; on the way she twirled a curl around her finger when she was concentrating on the board or ran her finger over the ring on her right hand; on the way she absently ran her tongue along her bottom lip sometimes when she glanced up to my own. It had been all I could do not to throw the chess board and table between us aside and pull her into my lap, to slam my lips to hers until we were breathless.

But then I'd straightened, too late realizing what had happened. I'd narrowed my eyes at her, but she only grinned: I was already beaten and she knew it.

"Check mate," Dahlia said before leaning back and crossing her arms over her chest, an extremely self-satisfied grin on her face.

"You...you little *wench*," I'd said in genuine astonishment, looking at the board in disbelief. And then, I'd laughed. Lightly at first, and then a deep, full laugh that shook my shoulders and warmed my chest. Dahlia had blinked, her lips parting on a soft exhale.

"What?" I'd asked eventually.

"I've never seen you smile," she'd said, sounding a little dazed. "*Really* smile."

"Oh," I'd said, clearing my throat. "Well, it doesn't happen often, I suppose."

"It should," she'd said simply. She'd held my gaze and I thought that if it made her happy, I would smile like a lunatic for the rest of my days.

"And where, pray tell, did you learn to play chess like that?" I'd demanded.

"Lord Burren taught me when I was ten. We used to play every week. I got quite good," she said with a modest shrug, but there was a proud, cocky glint in her eye that made me fall even more in love with her right then and there.

"Though you are a cheating, conning harlot," I'd said with a smile and she'd laughed out loud, grinning back, "you can attempt to mount Xerxes tomorrow afternoon, but I make no promises past that."

Of course, the damned horse had not only let her ride him without so much as a huff of annoyance, the two of them seemed to have some strange connection I can't even comprehend. It was as if she had been made for the horse, and he for her. They were perfect together, moving as if they were one creature without a shred of shared blood between them. Of course, they were connected in a round-about way with her being my mate, but it was more than that. This was simply something of the divine that couldn't be explained, a connection between souls.

We've ridden several times together through the rolling hills and thick forests surrounding the camp and they've been some of the best times of my life. I don't know if that's pathetic or not, but it's true. The feel of my horse beneath me, the air and beauty of my home surrounding me, the sight of Dahlia beside me, taking it all in and seeming to love it as much as I do—it's damn near perfect. When we rode just last night the thought hit me like a lightning bolt as I watched her gaze in wonder at a hidden waterfall I'd found years ago.

I love her. I really fucking love her.

Things have most definitely changed between us. I don't know that she could possibly feel the same as I do, but she seems to genuinely enjoy our time together and that's enough for me. It has to be enough. There are very few people in this world that I let see my true self: Elias, of course, Sebastian, and Fiona. Even my other siblings are more like acquaintances than family or friends and though I'm less rigid with them than I am with most others, my inner circle as it were consists of only three. Four now, I suppose.

So, needless to say, I have no real fucking clue how to navigate this new...relationship with Dahlia.

She, on the other hand, seems to have no trouble at all in adapting to our new circumstances. I'm not surprised, of course. Everyone that crosses her path seems to fall in love with her. I am nothing special in that regard. But there have been moments. *Heavy* moments. Moments where it took every ounce of strength I possess not to give in to what I so badly wanted. Moments that I knew without a doubt that she wanted almost as badly as I did. I know the blood I gave her is somewhat responsible for that, but...I don't think it's only that. It may be wishful thinking, but I believe that she might want me all on her own. She's slowly moved closer each night on the couch, inching ever closer, testing...and I've only craved having her closer. I should stop this, should make her keep her distance, but I *can't.* I physically can't force her away. It's too hard, it hurts too much.

Now, I make my way towards the ring where Dahlia is working on weapons training. I've been getting regular reports on her progress, but I can't help but want to see it for myself. They've been using one of the older training areas, not used by most of the soldiers, so the area is nearly deserted as I approach. She convinced me that her guard doesn't need to follow her around every moment within the camp, and I grudgingly agreed that she was safe within the walls and that they only need to escort her outside. They are also to watch her any time I'm away from the camp, though discreetly, but she doesn't need to know that.

My entire body reacts the moment I see her. She's in training gear, the pants and top cut close to her body so as not to interfere, but a softer material than leather to allow for easier movements. They hug her in all the right places, and make me wonder why I haven't been watching every session before now.

They're working on throwing knives at a dummy stuffed with straw, and based on the number of blades scattered on the ground—and the lack of ones actually sticking into the target—this may not be my mate's forte. I stay in the shadow of the nearby shed, watching as she pulls her arm back to let another blade fly. It sails almost a whole yard wide of the dummy.

"Fucking hells," she yells in frustration, kicking out at a nearby bucket of water. The bucket flies a few feet, water sloshing over the sides and splashing on Nova's legs. She watches the water and then looks up pointedly at Dahlia with a quirk of her brow. "I'm not sorry," Dahlia says a bit peevishly, making me grin in my shadowed hiding place.

"You need to release later," the female vampire says, clearly amused by Dahlia's response.

"Really? Because five minutes ago I needed to release earlier. And five minutes before that I needed to move my arm more this way, and before *that*—"

"Ok, ok, calm down, Clayburn." Ravenswood—Wesley. I'm trying to remember to use their given names since they are friends of Dahlia's and she speaks of them often—collects the fallen blades and strides towards Dahlia.

"Don't tell me to calm down, you mule's arse," she snaps. "I can't do this."

Wesley rolls his eyes. "Yes, you can. Look, fix your feet. With your balance off, you can hardly expect to throw straight. There you go, that's better. Now," he says as he sidles up behind her, placing his body far too close to hers. He places his arm behind hers, guiding her body with his in the movements. Though I know that there is nothing between the two of them—Dahlia seemed to make a point of telling me that fact more than once—it doesn't matter: instincts flare and I suddenly want to tear Wesley's head from his body and use his spine as a candle holder on my mantle. My claws and fangs flash out and rage boils in my chest, melting my bones. I have just enough wherewithal to think logically and not murder one of my most promising young soldiers.

But I can't stay in the shadows and watch any longer. In a heartbeat I'm beside the two of them, trying desperately to keep my temper in check. It would be disastrous if someone guessed what Dahlia truly means to me.

"High General," Nova gasps, quickly snapping to attention. Wesley wisely steps away from Dahlia, standing at attention as well.

"High General," he says, inclining his head. "An honor to have you here, sir. We're working on throwing knives."

Dahlia stares, a soft heat warming her cheeks. Her hair is in a thick plait on the side of her head, but a few strands have escaped and curl against her temples. She's got a smudge of dirt across her cheek and my fingers twitch. I barely resist the urge to wipe it away and grind my teeth at how ridiculous that is. I hold Dahlia's gaze, but direct my question to Wesley.

"And how are we faring?"

"She's shit, if I'm being honest," he says, a hint of a smile on his lips. My own curl up slightly as her mouth pops open in utter outrage. She whirls on him, every bit the firebrand I know she can be.

"You traitorous little weasel!" She pummels him in the arm and he lets her, laughing. He dances around, evading her but letting her get a few licks in. Their comradery is palpable and I'm happy that she's found something like it here at the camp. Nova chuckles and steps towards me.

"She's not really, sir" she says. "Just needs a bit more practice and needs to mind her balance. She's done very well with hand-to-hand."

"May I?" I ask, loud enough to interrupt the fight, and Dahlia finally stops hitting Wesley, turning to slowly stare at me.

Wesley bows to me and offers one of the knives to Dahlia, hilt first. She takes it, seemingly having forgotten all about his traitorous words from a moment ago. She swallows hard but steps up to her spot.

"Go ahead," I tell her. She eyes me for a moment and I nod, and she finally sighs and turns back towards the target. She steps and throws, the knife bouncing off the ground at the dummy's feet.

"Fuck, fuck, *fuck*," she grits out, running her hand over her hair, tossing her braid angrily off her shoulder. I hold my hand out to Wesley who places another blade in it. I take a deep breath and step forward, putting my body behind Dahlia's as Wesley had done moments ago. I grit my teeth as my eyes slide closed for a long, blissfully agonizing moment. To have her so close, to feel the heat of her against my chest, to have only to lean down a few precious inches to run my tongue or fangs along her throat. She inhales sharply, her heart racing, and my mouth waters and my cock pulses.

I clear my throat quietly and force every thought from my mind except what I know best: battle. I place the knife in her hand and reach down, settling my hands on her hips. Her heart stutters for a second and then slams against her chest so violently I think it might just burst through her body. I bite the inside of my cheek, the pain and blood grounding me for the moment. I use my grip to shift her hips and use one of my feet to shuffle hers farther apart.

"There. Shift your weight...that's better." I leave my left hand on her hip and guide her right arm back with my own. In a low voice, I say, "Now, you need to relax."

"That's...much easier said than done," she says, voice breathy but amused, and I can't help but huff out a small laugh.

"Try your best. Now, when you release, don't flick your wrist, just release the blade as your hand moves downward. You aren't throwing the knife, you're guiding it to its target."

"Is that not the same thing?"

"No, Keeva, it is not," I say, fighting a smile. This is...fun. I've always enjoyed training my men, sharing knowledge and skill and watching them learn and improve, but sharing it with Dahlia is an unexpected thrill. I slowly move our arms in tandem, showing her the way her body should move and stopping where she should release her grip. "There. That's where I want you to ease your grip on the blade and let it fly towards the target. Are you ready?" She nods and, through great effort and personal loss, I step away. She takes a deep breath and then throws the knife.

It sticks in the dummy's right shoulder and she whirls, grinning.

"She can be taught!" Wesley shouts, looking to the heavens with arms spread wide in prayer and gratitude.

"Give me another knife," Dahlia says, eyes narrowed at her friend. *Friend*, I remind myself again as the image of him pressed against her flashes, that terrible rage clawing at my chest once more. *They are just friends.* "I found a new target I want to hit."

"Big talk from the girl who hit one out of thirty-seven attempts," he mocks.

"You two are as bad as children, do you know that?" Nova says, stepping between the two, hands out to try to keep the peace.

"Well, I beat you when we were children and I'll do it again!" Dahlia calls, trying to duck around Nova.

Wesley scoffs. "That was *one* time! And I was sick, if I might remind you." He dances away and Dahlia chases him.

"Are they always like this?" I ask Nova.

"More often than not, sir," she confirms, lips curling up slightly, and I find my own doing the same.

CHAPTER 27
DAHLIA

Lia,

YOU WERE ATTACKED AND YOU TOOK WEEKS TO TELL ME!?! I am so mad at you I could spit!! But I am also so glad you're ok that I'm going to overlook my anger. I never thought you'd be in danger there in Alaric's camp. How did this happen? How could the Revenants possibly have gotten through the pass so near the camp?

I'm shaking I'm so irritated with you. Da spent hours locked away in the shop after he read your letter, but seems to be ok now that he's processed everything and knows you're alright. You are alright, aren't you? Do you swear?

I'll admit that it's a bit exciting that you're getting to train now. Maybe you can teach me someday as well.

The thought would probably scandalize Leland, but that's alright. No, he hasn't given up. I think...no, I know, I'm going to accept his official courtship request soon. He's very sweet and gentle, and gods knows he enjoys showering me with gifts. There are worse matches to be had, so I should be grateful for it.

I frown. She's most certainly *not* in love with Leland, that's clear to see. I get the distinct feeling that she's settling and if that's what she wants, I will of course support her, but...Enid has always been the dreamer of the two of us, the one who reads those secret novels and believes in the *love story* of it all (whereas I mostly believed in the naughty bits where the dark prince took the princess up against a cave wall...). She's always wanted the knight in shining armor to fight for her, to live in a world where great love conquers all. My heart twists a little at the idea of her settling for less than what she's always dreamed of.

Moving on from my love life – Yes, it is too soon to joke about your blood being spilled...but I do love the jewelry, so I will forgive you. I love you so much, Dahlia. I don't know what I would do if something had happened to you. But you're stronger than even you know. Something as silly as a Revenant couldn't take our firebrand from this world.

We're hosting Leland's family for dinner, so I better go and make sure da looks presentable and doesn't have soot on his face or blood under his nails. He already scares the poor folks being so big and brawny. The entire Dunlevee family is very...gentle and easily spooked, I'm afraid. The mere mention of the fact that my sister is the High General's Consort makes them all turn the color of milk. It's a bit ridiculous...but a tad funny, truth be told. I think da now tries to see just how far he can push them before they faint as a new favorite pastime.

He sends his love and told me to remind you of his gift to you, whatever that means. What gift? You two and your secrets, I swear...

Love,

Enid

I run my finger over the black stone on my finger. Of course, I'd completely forgotten about it when I needed to remember it most. I shake my head in frustration, but have decided I am not going to dwell on the past. I am looking forward from now on. I am doing well with my training and I've found that it isn't only physical training, but mental as well. I think (after far more sessions, of course), that I wouldn't freeze if the time came. I would be able to move past that fear that kept me in place during the Revenant attack. I suppose I hope it's never put to the test, but it is still comforting knowledge to have.

While my days have become filled to the brim with training, working at the smithy with Braddock, and spending time with my friends, the nights in the study have gotten...*heavy*. That's the best way I can describe them. There's a thickness in the air around Alaric and me now, like a summer storm cloud that's just waiting to burst —and gods am I ready for the storm. Ever since the day he came to training, when he stood behind me and guided my body with his own, I can barely control the need to be near him again, to feel him so close. We haven't touched again, save when I'm giving him blood, but we're only inches away from each other on the couch now while we read or talk, each of us seemingly unable to keep the distance there once was. He's showing me sides of himself that I'm not sure he's ever shown anyone before and if I didn't know any better, if I didn't know that it was an impossibility...I might think that I was... his. There's something about the way he looks at me, the way he seems to move and watch instinctively without even realizing he's doing it. Even if that can't be the case, I know that he cares about me now, more than just as a Consort or a friend.

And fuck me, I think I'm falling in love with him too. Not that I know he loves me, but...maybe he does?

But either way, I have no idea what in the seven hells to do about it. He can't be with me. Or won't, I suppose. Nova swears that all the princes fuck humans, but Alaric seems adamant that that's not the case. Not that we've actually discussed it since that very first time at the inn, but he always stops himself from touching me, from doing anything that might lead us down a road we can't come back from, no matter how much I know he wants to do otherwise. I wonder what would happen if I just threw myself at him, if I didn't give him a choice. He could stop me, of course, but...maybe he wouldn't. Maybe he would finally just give in.

We may just be finding out for sure one way or another soon. I'm going to lose this battle within myself soon enough, I just know it. I can feel it bubbling up within my chest, like a volcano waiting to erupt.

"Is there a reason you haven't appointed new members of my guard?" I ask, taking a bite of chocolate as we walk. I received a letter from the apothecary in town, letting me know what is needed to be paid on our arrangement, and I realize how much I've missed going to the village over the last few months. It's part of the reason I'm bringing up the guard question: I have no idea if Alaric will let me go back there again, especially with only half a guard.

We took a ride near the river tonight and seeing Alaric atop

Xanthus, the two of them moving as if they were one soul in two bodies, left me speechless. When we ride, it's like every bit of worry and stress leaves Alaric and, if only for a short time, he's truly free and happy in ways he won't allow himself to be when we're back at the camp. I understand why, and don't fault him for it. He's the High General, for fuck's sake. He's responsible for countless lives, for the safety of the *entire* continent. He has to be focused and stoic and determined. And honestly, it makes me love our time together that much more. It's like a secret between the two of us, a private world that no one else is privy to, something special shared only with each other.

Xerxes bumps my shoulder roughly with his big nose now, demanding his share of the chocolate. I laugh and give him a nibble, breaking another bit off and handing it to Alaric for Xanthus without a word. He shoots me a half smirk, one of my favorites, and gives the treat to the horse.

His shirt gapes just over his chest and his hair is windswept after the ride, leaving him looking too handsome for words and making my mouth practically water. I clench my thighs and my teeth and try to keep a rein on those particular emotions.

He contemplates my question for a long minute before answering.

"Mostly because I didn't think you would *want* me to." My brow furrows. "I know that they were not just your guardians, they were your friends, Dahlia. I..." He runs a hand through his hair and sighs. "I didn't want you to think I was being callous simply replacing them, as if I didn't know what they meant to you. You are completely safe within the camp, I have no doubts of this, despite what happened on the road. You haven't needed the extra protection of three more swords watching over you."

I stop walking and blink in surprise. He'd actually thought about how this would make me feel? My chest twists and I feel myself slip that much further towards the edge. Soon, I'll be over it completely, free falling into the unknown of loving Alaric Montclare. The sun is starting to set in the distance and for this moment, the two of us on the grassy rise behind our cabin, alone in a world no one else can touch, loving him seems like the most logical thing in the world, like the one thing I was born to do.

"Thank you," I say softly, looking up to meet his gaze. He holds mine for a long minute, too many things flashing in that molten gold to keep track. Slowly, he reaches towards my face and I barely stop a gasp. My heart seems to stop beating completely for an endless moment before it slams into my chest double time as he lightly brushes his thumb across my cheek. He's closer than I realized, so close that I can reach out and touch him. Without thought, I drop Xerxes' reins and place my hand on Alaric's stomach instead, steadying myself. He inhales sharply, a low, rumbling sound echoing through his chest. Something hot and powerful slams through me, through the connection between us, but I can't find the words to explain what it is. *Mine*, it seems to say. *Mine, mine, mine.*

"You had...chocolate just there," he says, voice low and rough, like saying the words takes great effort. His body is almost vibrating with tension, that same tension echoing through the bond and sending shivers up my spine. His throat works as if it's hard to swallow, and he softly and ever so slowly grazes his fingers along my cheek until he's cupping my face gently. I can't breathe. I can't move. I can't ever let him stop touching me.

I curl my fingers into his shirt, holding on for dear life as he moves his thumb in lazy strokes across my cheekbone, seeming to revel in the contact, eyes sliding closed in what appears to be pure bliss. He holds himself completely still save the movement of his thumb. I don't even think he's breathing. All of his vast stores of focus trained on that one, small motion.

"Alaric," I whisper. It sounds like a prayer, like a plea.

He exhales slowly. "When you say my name like that, it makes everything else in the world fade away," he says quietly. He opens his eyes and as his gaze falls to my lips, I wonder if he's finally going to kiss me the way I've been dreaming of for weeks. Well, since the Choosing, if I'm being honest with myself. He starts to move his face towards mine, again with that slow, practiced deliberation that I know comes from his centuries of training, of learning to master every inch of his body, and now I stop breathing.

"Keeva," he whispers as he moves closer...closer...

"Sir," a voice calls from the other side of the rise and we spring apart. I grab Xerxes' reins again and run a hand over my braid, though I'm not sure why. Alaric didn't even touch my hair. *But he* did *touch me*...I shudder at the thought but try to put a mask of normalcy on before whoever is coming crests the hill. Alaric must have far more practice than me at masking his emotions because he looks completely fine, as if we hadn't been about to kiss, as if that moment between us hadn't meant something far more than a simple touch.

"What is it, Caldwell?"

"Captain LaRouche has just arrived, sir. He awaits you in the war room."

Alaric's lips thin. "He's early," he nearly growls. The young squire, Caldwell, looks terrified, as if this Captain arriving early is his fault and Alaric is going to take it out on him.

"I-I'm sorry, sir. I didn't realize—"

Alaric holds up his hand. "It isn't your fault. The bastard likes to make an entrance," Alric says with a roll of his eyes. "Either early or late, never on time, and usually in ridiculous finery that has no place in a war camp." Caldwell seems to relax, even smiling a bit.

"He is indeed in...finery, of a sort, sir, though I don't know what region uses quite so many feathers in their formal dress..."

Alaric's lips quirk and I huff out a laugh.

"Take Xanthus to the barn, please, Caldwell. I'll go greet Captain LaRouche." The lad takes the horse, bowing to Alaric. He turns to me in question, clearly wondering if he should take Xerxes as well, but the horse answers the question by stomping angrily in the squire's direction, flaring his nostrils and generally acting like an ass.

"I've got him, it's alright," I assure the man. He bows to me, looking more than a little relieved, and heads off with Xanthus in tow. Alaric turns to me.

"I have to go. I'm not sure how long I'll be stuck entertaining the Captain..."

"It's alright. I'll see you...when I see you."

It looks as if he wants to say more, as if he wants nothing more than to fall right back into the moment from before, but he quickly pulls his gaze from mine and stalks off towards the cabin.

Xerxes noses me again and I give him a pat before heading in the other direction towards the barn. I can't stop replaying that moment in my mind, the feel of Alaric's fingers on my cheek, the feelings rushing through my chest as he leaned down...

I puff out my cheeks and let out a long, shaky breath. Xerxes looks at me, a question in those too-intelligent eyes.

"I am in need of something strong to drink and a very, very cold shower," I tell the horse.

～

Captain LaRouche, who I have nicknamed La Roach because he has bug eyes and irks me, remains for three days. Though of course Alaric and I have been parted for longer when he leaves the camp, we've never been parted after *almost kissing*. Not having been able to be alone with him since then, to make sure that he isn't having some internal crisis and pulling away from me again, is driving me mad.

To make matters worse, Nova and Wesley have both been put on a training exercise for the week to the south. So, I don't even have training or time with them to take my mind off of things. I couldn't seem to concentrate in the shop this morning, nearly setting Braddock's beard on fire, and Takara is spending a much-deserved afternoon doing ungodly things with Malcom. So, I'd decided to come spend the afternoon soaking up what might be the last bit of warmth of the season before winter arrives in the field beside the pond. I brought a blanket and a few books and Reginald packed me a small picnic as well.

I try to read, but find that I'm scanning the same page over and over without actually absorbing anything at all. I groan and toss the book aside, flopping onto my back and staring up at the clouds. The breeze blows in and though it's cool enough to make bumps erupt across my skin, it feels good. I start making shapes from the clouds, the way Enid and I did when we were young: a rabbit, a crocodile, a sword. My lids get heavy and I let them slide closed, the gentle sound of the breeze through the grass around me quickly lulling me to sleep.

I dream of fields of flowers and gently swaying oceans, of snow-covered mountains and babbling brooks. Everything bends and changes every few minutes, never fully settling into one specific dream. I'm alone in the dream, but I can feel Alaric nearby and I feel safe and whole. The dream shifts again and I'm standing on top of what appears to be a giant beehive. I laugh at the absurdity. The buzzing sends shudders up through my feet, small shivers through my entire body. The buzzing gets louder and louder, the vibrations rumbling beneath me now, making me lose my footing. I nearly stumble and then—

KEEVA!

I jolt awake, groggy and confused, but with my heart hammering against my chest, panic churning like acid through my veins. I blink, trying to clear the fog of dreams from my mind...and frown. I still feel the buzzing, still feel the shudders beneath my body.

"KEEVA!!" Alaric's voice thunders in my ears and I realize that the voice isn't an echo from the dream. He's speeding towards me across the field, so fast he's nearly a blur. There's panic in his eyes and when I glance over my shoulder, I see why: there's an entire herd of hellcats stampeding towards me. *Oh gods, that's what the buzzing was.* My heart leaps into my throat, but somehow, I flip my body and push myself to my feet, the training I've been doing all these weeks paying off in unexpected ways. But my blood turns cold as I watch the enormous creatures barrel towards me, their spiked tails flicking behind them, their claws digging into the ground and shaking the very earth beneath my feet. I know that no amount of training will let me outrun these beasts. I whirl back and meet Alaric's eyes.

He's still too far away.

He's never going to make it in time.

I'm going to die.

N o. No. NO!

A roar tears from my throat, a primal, deranged sound that I've never heard before. My thoughts are a maelstrom of panic and fear and fury. My mate is in danger. *My mate. My mate. My mate.*

I'd come to find her once LaRouche finally left the camp, practically coming out of my skin with the need to see her. Her chef had told me she'd come to the pond she usually frequents with Nova and Wesley some hours ago, and when I'd come into the edge of the clearing, I'd smiled. She'd fallen asleep on a blanket in the middle of the field, near a crimson oak that overlooks the water. She'd looked beautiful, face soft and relaxed in slumber, lips slightly parted. I'd come so, so close to kissing those lips not three days ago. I knew how foolish it was, how irresponsible, but I couldn't stop myself. If Caldwell hadn't interrupted, I don't know that I would have stopped at a kiss. I don't know that I could ever be satisfied with a mere brush of my lips to hers.

I'd watched her for a minute, so lost in memories and fantasies that I hadn't caught their scent or heard their approach until it was too late. The herd of hellcats burst through the trees, barreling directly for Dahlia. My heart had clenched in my chest, twisting painfully as terror choked me into near immobility.

"KEEVA!" I'd roared, willing her to hear me, putting everything I had into the bond between us, hoping she could feel my fear and panic, praying it would wake her in time. She jolted upright, looking a little dazed, but she turned and met my gaze immediately, as if she'd known I was here. I'd taken off towards her, running as fast as I could, everything around me blurring around the edges as I sped across the field. She pushed herself up to her feet, turning to see what was coming for her, and I could feel the terror seize her, the cold realization: there isn't enough time.

She whirls back to me now, gaze meeting mine, pleading for me to save her when we both know I won't make it.

"Alaric," she whispers, and even across the distance, I hear her voice as if she's whispered it directly into my ear.

"NO!" I roar. I almost lost her once, and here I am, about to lose her forever. I think the Goddess of Fate must be punishing me for refusing the gift she bestowed me in Dahlia, in giving me not only a mate, but someone I love more than my own life. *No. I will not lose her*. I refuse. I snarl a curse at the goddess, telling her to fuck right off. Something within me cracks then, splintering and opening, but not *breaking*. No, it's as if new, raw power I never could have imagined is pouring through the cracks, filling every fiber of my being. *Purpose*. That's what's filling me now, erasing everything else. Purpose. My purpose is to protect this woman, to protect what is mine, in all ways, forever.

I have no idea how it happens, but somehow, between one heartbeat and the next, I'm beside her, pulling her against me and diving to the side just as the first hellcats race by. A spiked tail catches me across the back and I grit my teeth against the swift flash of pain, but I'll take it gladly if it means that Dahlia is safe and out of harm's way.

We tumble together down the hill. I try my best to tuck my body around hers, to use my own as a shield as we fall, slamming into rocks and sticks until we finally come to rest in the small hollow beside the stream. The stampede continues on above, running parallel to us atop the hill, but still, I don't move, continuing to cradle her body beneath mine. The ground shakes all around us from the force of the herd and she grips the front of my shirt, pulling me even harder against her, shrinking into my body.

Finally, the shaking eases and I know the herd has moved on. I slowly push myself up so I can see her. She's wide-eyed and breathing hard, pulse racing, but looks to be mostly unharmed.

"Keeva. Keeva, are you alright?"

She takes a shuddering breath but nods.

"I'm ok."

I brush the hair from her face, pushing myself up onto one arm so I can inspect her more thoroughly.

"You're certain?"

"Yes, I'm alright, I promise. You saved me—again," she says, breathless.

"Gods, Dahlia, I thought—" I bite back the words, unable to give them life. I squeeze my eyes shut, trying to calm the storm raging inside me. Panic, terror, need, fury. It's too much. Suddenly, her hand is on my cheek, her soft skin burning me where she touches my face. My eyes fly wide and lock with hers.

"I'm alright," she says again. "Breathe, Alaric." I let out a long, shuddering breath and put my own hand over hers, holding it to my cheek and leaning into her touch, needing it so badly that I'm positive that I'll die without it. I almost laugh—she almost dies, and here she is comforting *me*. Whatever filled me before, whatever gave me the power to get to her, isn't subsiding. Every fiber of my being is calling out to her in ways I can't comprehend.

My eyes skate down her throat.

"You're bleeding," I say, voice thick and rough, and I finally release her hand.

She blinks and moves her fingers to her neck, finding the small cut. It isn't a deep wound, but enough that the blood is flowing easily. She holds her hand before her eyes, examining the crimson painting her fingers. Then she lowers them, holds my gaze, and very deliberately tilts her head, exposing her throat to me.

"Take it," she whispers.

"Dahlia," I warn, even as my mouth waters, my fangs sliding out.

"It's yours, Alaric. Everything...all of it...it's yours." A shudder runs through my body at her words. Is she saying...no, it can't be... but I feel it in the bond between us, feel the dangerous truth in what she's saying: she's telling me that she's mine. Not a bond, not an instinct, but she, herself, is telling me. I swallow hard as I eye the blood flowing from her neck, her offer echoing in my head...

I will not bite her. I will not...

But I do lean down, unable to stop myself, and slowly run my tongue along the gash. She gasps and shudders as a tremor works its way through my body, the taste of her blood like a chemical shock to my entire system. I pull back ever so slightly, but she grips my shirt and pulls me back towards her, arching her body upward. I keep my fangs firmly in check but I do lean down again, burying my face in her neck and latching my lips around the wound, sucking gently.

A moan slips past her lips and the sound has a direct line to my cock. I'm hard as steel in seconds, desperate for her, barely holding onto the tiny shreds of my self-control that are left. She slides one hand into my hair, clutching me to her neck while she maneuvers the other beneath my shirt. I hiss in a startled breath when her fingers graze my skin, my muscles jumping at the contact. Her touch is like fire, consuming me, branding me, forging me into something new. *Hers. I'm hers.*

I know I need to stop. I know I need to pull myself away from her, because if I stay, I'm going to do something that's impossible...but I can't *think* when she touches me like this, when she moans and grinds her hips against mine, begging and needy. The smell of her is enough to make my muscles quake, my fangs sharpen, my cock throb. She moves her hand around my hip and up my back, seeming not to know where she wants to touch me and settling for every-where. She writhes beneath me and I don't have the strength to stop myself from arching my hips forward, my aching cock pressing hard against her.

She gasps, nails digging into my lower back.

"*Alaric,*" she breathes.

All I can think about is sinking my cock and fangs into her delicate flesh, of feeling the heat of her body and her blood, of claiming my mate. I claw my fingers into the dirt on either side of her head, seconds away from sliding my fangs into her throat, but the sounds of approaching soldiers give me just enough clarity in my lust-addled mind to stop this insanity.

I quickly pull away, practically leaping off of her. She gasps and presses herself up on her arms to stare at me where I stand a few feet away, breathing hard and clenching my jaw to regain my composure. Her pupils are wide, her pulse racing, her cheeks flushed. Her hair is a tangle of fire and grass and sticks, but my gods, she's never looked more beautiful.

Before she can say a word, a handful of soldiers pour down the hill towards us, a chaotic chorus of voices filling the air.

"Sir! Are you alright?"

"Oh gods, Lady Dahlia! I didn't know she was here."

"Fucking biggest herd I've seen pass through in years."

I move forward again and help Dahlia to stand as the men converge on us.

"We're both alright," I say over the din, causing them all to quiet immediately. "Harkness, escort my Consort back to our cabin if you will—"

"I'll do it, your highness," a voice rings out. I glance up to find Takara, Dahlia's Keeper, bolting down the hillside. She's a bit disheveled and I can smell Malcom all over her. From what I hear, the two of them are all but betrothed at this point. She reaches us and pulls Dahlia into her arms.

"Are you doing this on purpose? Trying to get yourself killed or maybe just to scare the life out of me?" she demands. My lips twitch in amusement. Takara is not to be trifled with—it's one of the reasons I selected her as Dahlia's Keeper—and I appreciate her fierce love of my mate.

"Definitely just to fuck with ye, of course," Dahlia says with a roll of her eyes, her brogue slipping a bit with the stress of the situation, I imagine.

"I figured as much, you little wench," Takara says in response, cupping Dahlia's cheeks affectionately. "Come on, let's get you home and in the bath. You're a mess." The vampire plucks a twig from Dahlia's hair and she huffs out a laugh. She meets my gaze for a moment, so many unspoken things passing between us before Takara pulls her up the hill.

"I want patrols of these woods added to the rotation immediately to keep an eye on the hellcat migration. They don't usually use this path through camp, but if this herd did, another might as well."

"Yes, sir," they all say in unison.

Now that the danger has passed and I'm coming down from the ecstasy of having Dahlia in my arms, the enormity of what had happened here comes crashing down. It threatens to swallow me, but I manage to keep everything at bay until I give a few more orders to the men and make my way to my chambers.

I hit my knees as the panic and fear and desire and love and need and protectiveness and anger all attack me at once, like wild beasts caged inside me now freed from their prisons. I claw my fingers into the floor as everything comes for me again and again, an enemy that won't relent.

I could have lost her. I somehow saved her. I have to protect her. I was almost too late. I need to be better. I have to be more. I can never be parted from her. I need her. I want her. I love her.

The last thought silences the rest and allows a cool, calm to settle over me. It's the most important one after all, the only one that matters anymore. I let it echo in my mind like a mantra, a lullaby to keep the nightmares at bay.

I love her.
I love her.
I love her.

~

I HAVE no idea what to do. I know that we cannot continue down the path we did in that field today...but, whatever shifted inside me and gave me the power to save her will not recede. It will not answer to my will. It will not be controlled. It wants one thing only...and that thing, is my mate. I'd tried to talk to Elias about it earlier, but it hadn't been at all helpful.

"Elias, I...fuck, I almost..." I leaned over my desk, palms on the smooth, wooden surface. I tried to slow my breathing, to force my body to heel and stop reacting to what had happened earlier, to what had *almost* happened.

"Kissed her? Bit her? Fucked her?" he asked, clearly not worried about my panicked state. In fact, the bastard was smirking like a very clever cat and I wanted very much to put him through the wall.

"All three," I said with a growl, "right in the middle of a fucking field." His smirk turned into a full-on grin.

"Gods that's *sexy*. Come on, you have to admit it's sexy!"

"Would you be serious! I almost bit and fucked my Consort in a field in the middle of my war camp where the gods and every soldier in my army could have seen. That is not sexy, that is unacceptable."

Elias pondered that for a few minutes, running his fingers along his jaw thoughtfully.

"Ok, I take your point...but it's still a *little* sexy..." I turned a killing look on him and he held up his hands in surrender. "Ok, ok, I'm sorry. Yes, I understand that may not have been the best situation all things considered, but...well, what if the situation were different? Say, like in the privacy of your cabin?..."

"I can't...but," I sighed heavily, "but something is different now. I don't think I can hold these feelings and desires and needs at bay."

"Different?" he asked, blonde brow quirking upward.

"When I knew I wouldn't make it to her in time, when I knew without a doubt that I was about to lose her forever, something inside me burst to the surface, filling me with a strange power that I've never felt before. I think...I think I teleported."

"Teleported?" he echoed, incredulous. Special gifts like teleporting, telepathy, the power to thrall or entrance, used to be more common among vampires millennia ago, but for whatever reason, the abilities faded over the years. "I haven't heard of anyone having that power in...fuck, a thousand years, at least."

"I know, but it was like something long ago buried inside me came to life, calling upon those long-dormant gifts in order to save my mate. One second I was running to her, but still too far across the field, and the next, she was in my arms and I was pulling her out of the way."

"Holy shit," Elias breathed. "This is...fuck, this is insane." He looked at me in awe and then his lips curled into a smile. "But can you imagine battles with the Revenants if you can learn to control it?" I couldn't help but smile at that, imagining the looks on their faces if I were able to move across the entire battlefield between one breath and the next. *If Kilgren ever shows his face, I can end him finally.*

I shook myself, focusing on the problem at hand.

"But with this power came something even more primal and demanding than ever before. It's like the mating instincts have been multiplied by a thousand and are taking complete control over my entire being, every inch of my body and soul screaming out for Dahlia. I don't think I can physically deny it for much longer."

"My advice on this matter has not changed, my friend. You say you can't deny these desires much longer. I say stop denying them then." I shot him a look that must have told him easily how close to the edge I was. He tilted his head as he studied me, and added, "but maybe, uh, take things slow?"

Slow, slow, slow.

I keep repeating the words now as she opens the door and steps inside the study.

And I realize then that I might just be good and fucked.

CHAPTER 29

DAHLIA

I'm tired of denying what I want. I've practically been on fire all afternoon after the incident with the hellcats. The feel of Alaric's body on top of mine, of his lips against my neck and his skin beneath my fingers—it was too much and not nearly enough.

I need more. I need *him*, in every way you can need a person. It isn't just the physical, though that's so intense that I can hardly breathe at the thought of it, but it's the connection I feel to him, the love coursing through every cell of my body and soul. I love him. Gods, I love him so much it almost hurts. I tried to tell myself over these months that it was just the bonding, the blood exchanged between us forcing me to feel this way, but the blood only tethered us together, it didn't create this connection between us, these feelings.

I know it isn't allowed, that there are so many barriers between us, but I don't care about any of them. Somehow today we defeated death itself—*again*. Everything else seems so small in comparison now. I'm a Consort and he's my prince—who cares? He's a vampire and I'm human—so what? But I need to know what he feels. I know he wants me physically, that much was so deliciously obvious this afternoon when he was on top of me. I nearly shudder at the memory, the feel of him hard and ready against me...

But I need to know if he feels more, if he *wants* more. I need to know if he's willing to travel this dangerous path with me or if I'm traversing it alone.

I bathe, taking extra care to scrub and shave and buff every surface I can think of, just in case...and put my hair into a loose knot at my nape with an emerald-studded clip that Takara gave me. I wonder if I should wear something special, but decide against it. It's just a normal night in the study, like we've had so many of in these past months. I'm determined to talk about things tonight, but I don't want to put pressure on the situation. So, I put on a short, midnight-blue silk nightgown, pull a matching robe over it, and set out for the study.

I know he's already inside before I open the door, and I can't stop my heart from thundering at the thought. The way he'd reacted in the field today, the way he'd somehow gotten to me in time, to save me—again—the way he'd murmured my name and *Keeva* over and over without seeming to even realize he was doing it, the way he'd shuddered as he'd licked the blood from my neck, his body hard against my own...

I swallow hard and open the door, striding inside. He's standing in front of the fireplace, his gray shirt unbuttoned at his throat and leather pants riding low on his hips. His eyes travel down my body, the gold darkening and burning as his gaze skates over every curve.

"Are you well, then?" he asks, voice a bit husky.

"Yes, I'm fine. All healed," I say, tilting my head so he can see my throat easily. We both stand for an endless moment. "How did you get to me?" I ask. It hadn't actually been what I meant to say, but blurting out *I'm in love with you* didn't seem like a good plan. "In the clearing. You were too far, I know you were. But then...you were there."

I've drifted closer to him without even realizing it, now standing just before him by the fire. The warmth seeps into my skin through the thin silk.

"I'm not entirely sure, honestly, but it seems as though I some-how...teleported."

I blink. There were legends of vampires having special gifts long ago—the ability to travel from one place to another in the blink of an eye, the ability to move objects with their minds, the power to control someone's thoughts, that sort of thing—but they're just legends now. Vampires didn't have those kinds of gifts anymore. *So how in the seven hells...*

"And this is, um, the first time that's happened?" I ask, though I know it is. He nods. "But how...why..." I shake my head. "I don't understand."

"I...I don't either," he says, though I get the feeling he's not being entirely truthful. I tilt my head back to meet his eyes, trying to read the truth there. That heavy feeling settles over us as it so often does, but this time it's different. It's volatile now, combustible. Dangerous. Like we're standing on the very edge of a cliff. Once we step off the edge, there will be no coming back.

I can see what happened between us earlier running through his mind, the same way it's running through mine. I know my heart is probably loud in his ears, pounding like warhorse hooves against stone. He moves as if to touch my face, but drops his hand, taking a half step away.

"Dahlia, we can't...what happened earlier..." He runs his hand through his hair, making the curls stand out like a tangled halo. I take a step towards him and he retreats again, slowly. "We...can't," he says again, though it's only half-hearted, sounding almost as if it pains him to say it, like he's trying so hard to say what he's *supposed* to. I lay my palms against his stomach and his eyes slide closed, his body shuddering beneath my touch.

"Alaric," I whisper. I can't stop myself. It's like I'm not even in control of my body anymore, some bone-deep force compelling me forward, crying out for Alaric in ways I can't even understand. And it will not be denied.

He steps back again, but I move with him this time, my hands never leaving his body.

"Shouldn't…" he croaks, barely even half-hearted this time. He's breathing hard and a jolt of surprise and feminine delight sings through my veins. I'm making a Montclare prince, the High General of the entire vampiric army, lose his grip on his centuries-honed control. Me. A powerless, little human.

Another step back, another step forward. He hits the edge of the couch and sits heavily. I don't hesitate, immediately climbing into his lap, my knees on either side of his hips. His hands fly to my waist, fingers clenching gently, his touch burning me through the thin silk of my nightgown. I need it gone. I need his hands on me, I need our bodies touching skin-to-skin. I slide my robe from my arms and let it fall to the ground behind me.

I drape my arms over his shoulders and he inhales sharply. I can see how hard he's working to keep himself still, to hold himself back, to find the strength to stop this. But there is no stopping it now and I think we both know it.

I brush my fingers along his nape, gently sifting them through his hair and lean forward. His eyes are squeezed shut, his lips parted but his muscles tight, as if he's in pain. *He's fighting*. Still fighting so damned hard. I know deep in my bones that he isn't fighting because he doesn't want this. He's fighting because he's afraid of what he might do because of the things he wants.

But I trust him. More than anyone else in the world, I trust this man with my life.

I lean closer, putting our lips so close that his harsh breaths warm my skin, but not quite touching. Not yet. He has to make the decision. I understand his reservations, not just for my safety but for his honor as a prince and the High General. So, *he* has to be the one to make this choice, in the end. I respect him enough to leave this to him, but my gods I hope he makes the decision I need him so badly to make...

"Alaric," I whisper again, almost against his lips. He lets out a shuddering breath.

"You play with fire, Keeva," he warns, hands gripping my hips tightly, fingers bunching the silk.

"Then let me *burn*."

He groans and suddenly, his lips are on mine. I gasp in surprise, but it quickly transforms into a moan. It's pure fire the moment our lips meet, unlike anything I've ever felt. He moves one hand to the back of my head, removing the clip and tossing it across the room. My hair tumbles down my back, tickling my bare shoulders. His lips are warm and soft, demanding and sure. He takes my bottom lip between his, sucking ever so slightly, and I melt. I open my mouth to him and he tilts his head, deepening the kiss. Each roll of his tongue against mine sends jolts of pleasure through my entire body, making my toes curl. He tunnels his fingers into my hair, holding me hard to him. As if I'd possibly pull away now, as if I possibly *could*.

One touch of his lips and I'm done for. One kiss and I'm his, forever.

I spread my knees wider, sinking down fully on his lap and we both moan loudly into the kiss. I roll my hips, grinding my core against him. He's hard as granite beneath me, and I nearly whimper.

"*Keeva*," he growls, fingers clenching on my waist. "You must be still..." He kisses across my jaw. "I'm doing everything in my power not to hurt you..." He grazes my earlobe with his teeth and I shiver.

"You won't," I pant, rolling my hips again despite his warning, digging my hands into his hair, urging him on. He kisses down my neck, pausing when he gets to the pulse point at the base of my throat. I gasp, wondering if he'll bite me...perhaps more than wondering. Perhaps hoping. Perhaps praying. Perhaps wanting it almost as badly as I want the rest of him.

He licks my throat, groaning, but doesn't bite. He pulls away and kisses me again, harder this time, more fevered. My blood is fire in my veins, every inch of me screaming out for more. He thrusts his tongue against mine, dominating, commanding. I drag my hands from his hair to the front of his shirt, yanking at the buttons. I need my hands on him, need to feel him beneath my fingertips. I push the fabric apart, exposing his chest. I run my hands over the sculpted muscles, the hard planes and enticing hollows. I can feel the faint raised lines of scars and one day, I'll take hours exploring every inch of him, memorizing every single scar and hearing every story of how they got there, how these badges of honor were pinned to my vampire's skin. *My vampire. My prince. My love. Mine.*

I dip my hands lower and his stomach clenches in response, the muscles rigid beneath my touch.

"Gods, the feel of your hands on me...it's like heaven." His voice is low and husky, almost pained. I grind my hips harder, needing more. "Dahlia, you must *stop*..."

"No," I say simply, ignoring his command. It was only half-hearted anyway. I think. I'm becoming so out of my mind with need that I feel almost drunk, not able to focus on much of anything except the feel of Alaric beneath me, the heat of his body against mine and how badly I need him. "I can't stop, Alaric. *Please*," I beg in whispered breaths against his mouth. I bite lightly on his lower lip, eliciting a sexy half-groan, half-moan, and he seems to release a fraction of his control as he uses his grip on my waist to pull me harder atop him while he bucks his hips upward. I gasp at the contact, and then cry out when he does it again, and again.

"You're soaked, Keeva," he pants between gritted teeth. "Can feel you through my leathers. *Fucking hells*..." His entire body shudders and tenses and I can tell how hard it's becoming for him to hold himself back. But I don't want him to. As stupid as that may be—he's warned me how easily he could kill me if things were to go awry here —I want him, all of him, and deep down, I somehow know that he won't hurt me, even if he gives himself up fully to the lust roiling inside him.

Lust.

That gives me an idea, and I'm past caring if it's a good one or a bad one. I kiss him again, delving my tongue against his—and then running it along one of his fangs, drawing blood.

CHAPTER 30
ALARIC

This is reprehensible. This is dishonorable. This is fucking ecstasy.

Feeling Dahlia's lips on mine after all of these months, of finally having her in my arms the way I've dreamed about almost every night since the Choosing, is like having a missing part of my soul back where it belongs. The mating instincts inside me are singing, everything about this moment feeling so completely *right* that I don't care about anything else.

Her lips are warm and soft beneath mine, open and wanting and begging. Her tongue is hot and greedy, the taste of her like heaven. Her scent is driving me near mad and I can feel how wet and needy she is for me even through my leathers. I'm barely holding onto my control. I know I have to stop this before it goes any further. I know that I can't possibly do the things every fiber of my being is screaming out for me to do. To bite. To fuck. To claim my mate from this day forward.

And then I taste it: her blood hot and wet against my tongue. I freeze as instincts flare and I nearly lose all sense of time and space around me. I don't dare move. I don't dare breathe. I should have known that kissing was too dangerous that this might happen...but then I realize that she *deliberately* ran her tongue along my fang. The little minx did this on purpose.

"Please, Alaric," she begs quietly against my lips, gently rolling her tongue against mine, her blood setting my entire body on fire. She...wants this. She wants me to feed while I touch her...she...fuck, she wants me to *bite* her. I can feel it through our bond, that desire pounding like a drum. I'd thought as much in the field, when she'd offered her throat, digging her fingers into my skin and urging me forward, but I'd thought it had just been wishful thinking. But now...

I growl and kiss her harder, winding her silky hair around my fist and using my grip to tilt her head back, commanding her to let me deepen the kiss. I take the blood from her tongue as I kiss her, wrenching her hips against my aching cock as I do. It's agony. It's bliss. I need more. I release her hips and rip her nightgown away as if it were nothing but smoke on the wind. She gasps in surprise, but doesn't seem to mind my destruction of her garment. I pull away and let my gaze fall upon my mate, bare before me save a small scrap of silk masquerading as panties.

Gods. Almighty.

The sight of Dahlia's breasts steals my breath and makes my cock and fangs both pulse painfully. She pants quietly as I stare, her chest heaving, her peaked nipples begging to be licked and sucked. She's unabashed, letting me look my fill while she lazily continues to rock her hips over my lap, the friction making me grind my teeth. I kiss along her jaw and quickly down her throat, forcing myself to ignore her pulse hammering at the base. *Later*, I tell that insistent voice screaming at me to sink my fangs there, to drink and drink...

I kiss over her collar bone, over the top swell of her breast before twirling my tongue around one hardened peak.

"*Ah gods!* Ahhh don't stop," she begs, digging one hand into my hair, holding me tightly to her breast. I chuckle darkly at my demanding little mate, and obediently continue to lave her nipple with my tongue before closing my lips around it and sucking gently.

The sound she makes is so intoxicating that I swear I could come just like this. I make sure that my claws retract before snaking a hand between our bodies, lifting her up slightly from my lap and ripping her panties to shreds, the silk practically disintegrating in my grasp. I don't hesitate, quickly delving my fingers between her thighs. I groan as my fingertips skate over smooth, creamy skin. I know that many females rid themselves of hair all over their bodies, but knowing that Dahlia has done so sends a jolt of desire through me, my fangs snapping long and practically throbbing. I can't stop myself, though I do try to be gentle at least, and press a finger inside her. She gasps into my mouth, nails digging into the back of my head.

Hot. Wet. Tight. *Fuck me.*

"Fuck, Alaric," she gasps as I pump my finger, in and out, moving it deeper and curling it in just the right spot. Over and over. "That feels so good..."

I groan around her nipple, licking and sucking and biting ever so gently, before I add another finger. She groans loudly, grinding her hips in time with my thrusts, and I don't think I've ever been so aroused in my life. I move to her other breast, continuing my slow torture with my fingers and flicking my tongue across the sensitive peak.

"So wet, Keeva. So wet for me," I growl, forcing her lips to mine once more. She rides my hand, chasing her release, but it isn't time yet. I need more. I need to taste my mate.

I remove my hand making her whine and my lips curl upward.

"Up," I demand.

"Wh-what?" she stutters, looking more than a little dazed, her hair a tangled mess and her lips red and swollen. I grip her hips and lift her up gently until she understands, realization making her green eyes blaze.

"Up, beauty. I need my mouth on that pretty quim." She gasps and bites her lip, but rises above me, looking a little unsure but wholly intrigued and aroused. She stands before me and I lean forward to kiss her stomach, her skin taut and hot beneath my lips. Her body trembles and she rests one hand on my shoulder, the other lightly running through my hair. I wrap my hands around to grip her magnificent ass, squeezing and kneading, trying so desperately to be gentle, not to lose control of my strength. I have to trust that Elias is right and that I won't hurt her, no matter how lost in desire I might become.

And when my gaze dips down between her legs, I know that I'm about to be very, very lost.

A low, desperate growl rumbles in my chest and my fingers clench on her ass.

"Put your knee up on the back of the couch," I tell her, shifting down ever so slightly so that her body aligns right where I need it to. She's practically panting, entire body trembling, but she does as I ask, leaning forward and resting one knee beside my head on the back of the couch. "That's a good girl," I whisper, and she gasps quietly, a quick shudder running down her spine. *Hmm, does my mate like to be praised?* I'll worship and praise her until the sun comes up, then. Until the end of fucking time. I take a moment to appreciate the view before me.

"*Gods,*" I groan as I see her, open and dripping before me. I've dreamt of this for months, imagined what she might look like, what she might feel like, what she might taste like. And now that she's here, I can scarcely believe this is real. Perhaps I perished in the stampede this day. Perhaps none of this is real and this is simply the heaven that was promised me. I will gladly spend my eternity here.

I lean forward and use my grip on her ass to guide her to my mouth. I hold my breath and lock my muscles, trying to prepare for the first taste of ecstasy, but nothing could ever prepare me for this. I run my tongue along her pussy, bucking my hips and shuddering at the feel and taste of her on my tongue. She cries out, rocking her own hips against my mouth, and I lick again, a long, slow lap of my tongue that makes her moan and writhe. I lose myself in her, licking and sucking and delving my tongue deep inside her until she's cursing and praying and panting.

"*Gods, gods, gods,*" she rasps, legs trembling and nails digging into my skull.

"They aren't the ones making you quiver, Keeva," I say quietly against her skin before flicking my tongue across her clit. "They aren't the ones making you shudder and scream." Another lap of my tongue that makes her cry out. "They aren't the ones who are going to make you come so hard that the earth shakes." I take the bud between my lips, sucking, making her buck wildly against my mouth. I pull away and blow gently across her sensitive skin. I look up her body and wait for her to meet my gaze. Her pupils are blown wide, burning, and my gods looking at her from this angle is something that will forever be seared into my memory, even if I live for another thousand years, this moment will never fade from my mind.

"So, try again, Keeva," I whisper, moving my hand quickly and pressing two fingers inside her again. She gasps but then her lips curl up ever so slightly, and I grin wickedly back at her, loving that she understands the game. Not just understands it, but *enjoys* it.

"Alaric," she breathes, holding my gaze. "*Alaric, Alaric, Alaric,*" she moans, each repetition of my name punctuated by a thrust of her hips and my fingers.

"That's better," I rasp, before leaning in to suck on her clit while I pump my fingers.

"Oh gods, right there...don't stop...I'm going to...ALARIC!" she screams as she comes hard, her inner walls clenching my fingers in tight pulses as her climax rocks through her body. I groan against her flesh and remove my fingers, replacing them with my tongue. The taste of her pleasure is enough to make my own hips buck upward, my cock so hard it's painful, desperate to be buried so deep inside my mate that I can barely think.

No. *Slow,* I remind myself. *Slow, slow, slow.*

I rip at the laces of my pants with one hand, quickly gripping my aching cock. I dig my heels into the floor, hips arching upward as I stroke, licking every last drop Dahlia has to offer. Her heart is thundering so loudly I can barely hear her panting my name, over and over. Her legs shake, but I don't stop. She continues to ride my tongue, rocking her hips and digging her fingers into my hair. I'm already close, my spine tightening, and I can't stop myself: I turn my head and sink my fangs deep into her inner thigh.

"Fuck!" she cries as another orgasm rips through her. She screams as I suck, her blood setting me on fire, hot and wet and perfection on my tongue. Her entire body convulses, shuddering all around me. My toes curl and I cry out against her skin as I come in a rush, bucking my hips, hot lashes of cum coating my stomach.

Her body finally gives out, melting to collapse on top of me. I catch her and quickly maneuver her so that she's beside me, tucked against my side with her legs thrown over my thighs. I use what's left of her nightgown to wipe up the mess on my skin and we both sit tangled together trying to catch our breath and wrap our minds around what just happened. Her heart eventually slows, that steady beating that's become the most important sound in my entire world.

"I'm not broken," she finally says, voice a little husky from all the screams. I wince slightly, knowing that her Keeper at the very least would have heard if she was in her own cabin...perhaps even the entire camp with the way Dahlia was crying out. Even so, I can't help my smirk, my male ego preening at the thought of the pleasure I've given my mate this night, at the idea of all the other pleasures I can bring her in the future...but I shake myself, focusing on the present. This is a...delicate situation, one that should probably remain as private as possible until I can figure things out fully.

"What do you mean?" I ask, frowning. I run a finger along her thigh, not seeming to be able to stop touching her, even for a moment. Gods, this is going to be problematic. I'm going to have to learn to handle this.

"You were worried about hurting me. But here I am, completely intact. Not a scratch on me." I shift her leg to show the two puncture marks on her thigh and arch a brow. She laughs lightly. "Ok, maybe a few scratches, but *dear gods* are they worth it." She reaches over and runs her fingertip across my stomach, drawing idle shapes it seems. "Does that always happen? When you bite people...do they always, uh..."

"Come instantly and so hard that their legs shake and the gods themselves hide from the force of their screams?" I supply helpfully.

She throws her head back and laughs and the sound warms my heart. I've never had this...what is it Elias always calls it? Afterglow? He says that you must always bask in the afterglow with your women, but I've never done such a thing. I enjoy my time with them, we both find our pleasure, and then I leave—or ask them to leave— almost immediately. None of them have ever seemed to mind, but I can't imagine not having this time with Dahlia. To just be with her after we've just shared something so intense and profound, to...bask in the afterglow of it all, I suppose. *Gods, I sound so ridiculous. Elias will never let me hear the end of this.*

"Aye, that sounds about right," she says, "ye right arse," she adds quietly, though of course she knows I can hear her. I smile at her brogue, at the fact that we're here together like this, touching so effortlessly and joking about orgasms. I never would have dreamed...

"Yes, I understand that it can be very pleasurable."

"You understand...?"

"I've never taken blood from the flesh before you, Dahlia." I hold her gaze and she swallows hard.

"Oh," she says quietly. She starts to say something else but yawns widely instead, her eyes becoming glazed with exhaustion. *Oh, little mate, we'll have to build up your stamina...*My pulse speeds up at the thought of what's to come. Because I know that it is inevitable now. I will take Dahlia. I will claim her fully as my own in time. It is not a matter of *if*, it is a matter of *when*, and my gods when that day comes...

"To bed," I say, scooping her up into my arms and rising from the couch. She doesn't argue, only wraps her arms around my neck and rests her head in the crook of my neck. I stride from the study but instead of turning towards Dahlia's chambers, I go towards my own. It's foolish, of course, but I cannot be parted from her, not yet. I know I must learn to be, but I do not need to learn tonight. She doesn't seem to notice where we've gone, eyes closed and her breathing becoming soft and even.

I settle her into my bed and stoke the fire before sliding in behind her. I pull her tightly against my chest and wrap my arms around her. I sigh in contentment, never having felt so completely whole in all of my long years. This is where I'm meant to be. This is where I belong.

"Stay with me?" she whispers, her words slow and slurring as sleep takes her in its clutches.

"Always," I promise.

CHAPTER 31
DAHLIA

The nightmares don't find me in Alaric's arms, and when I wake the next morning—*in Alaric's room?*—I feel better rested than I have in months. My heart falls when I realize that I'm alone in the giant, unfamiliar bed, but then I see a note on the pillow beside me, along with a flower. A dahlia. I smile and pull the flower to my nose, inhaling deeply while I read the note.

DAHLIA,
I'M SORRY I MUST LEAVE BEFORE YOU WAKE, BUT I AM
EVER THE HIGH GENERAL AND DUTY CALLS. I WAS SORELY
TEMPTED TO TELL DUTY TO FUCK OFF, BUT ALAS, SHE IS A
DEMANDING BITCH. I WILL FIND YOU LATER.
  -A
  P.S.
YOU LOOK BEAUTIFUL.

I grin like an idiot as I read the note twice more. This has to mean that he doesn't regret what happened between us, right? I sigh and decide I should go back to my own room, only to realize that I have no clothes. My nightgown is in tatters somewhere in the study and I smile and blush as the memories of the night before come flooding back. Alaric's fingers, his tongue, his fangs…A shiver runs through me and I suddenly want my hands on him so badly I have to curl my fingers into fists. I rummage in Alaric's closet and put on one of his tunics. It's long enough that it covers everything that should be covered, though if Alaric isn't here, I don't anticipate running into any of his men in the halls. I slip from his chambers, padding quickly down the hall and across the expanse of the cabin to my own wing.

I nearly scream when I come into my room and find Takara sitting in front of the fireplace. She looks somewhere between impressed, astonished, worried, and amused.

"And where might we have been, Lady Dahlia?" she asks with a knowing arch of her brow and I cross my arms defiantly.

"Just out for a morning stroll."

"A morning stroll in the High General's tunic without your panties?" I gape at her and she laughs, lips curling up into an affectionate smile. I stride over and collapse into the chair across from her, tucking my feet up beneath me and pulling Alaric's tunic around my knees.

"Tell. Me. Everything," she demands, holding out a plate of bacon and eggs and fruit to me while sipping on a cup of blood.

And I do. I don't know if I should since I get the feeling this thing between Alaric and myself should probably be a bit of a secret, but I know that Takara won't tell a soul, both as my Keeper, duty bound to me and me alone, but more importantly as my friend.

"Gods, I knew it," she says, shaking her head. "I just knew it! The way he acted after the attack…"

"Knew what?" I ask, polishing off the last bite of fruit.

She hesitates ever so slightly, and then says "I knew that he cared for you, more than a prince usually cares for his Consort I mean." I'm not sure that this is actually what she meant, but I let it go.

"I don't know what happens now. I know this isn't exactly…normal."

Takara snorts. "Nothing about this Choosing or any moment since has been normal, Dahlia. But I'm thankful for it. I wouldn't have it any other way." I smile at her. "But as far as what happens with you and Alaric now, that I'm not sure either. I think it's best that this remain...private for the time being, at least until Alaric has a chance to decide how he wants to handle it. I know for a fact of at least five other princes who have fucked their Consorts in the past, so it isn't as if this *never* happens, but...it is supposed to remain secret when it does. So," she shrugs, "secret it is for now."

I nod in agreement, figuring as much as well. She grins a wicked grin, her fangs glinting in the morning light streaming in through the windows.

"But that doesn't mean you can't have as many orgasms in private as that puny little mortal body of yours can handle."

I bark out a laugh and soon we're both clutching our sides, and while I'm so glad I have someone to share this with here, a part of my heart aches at it not being Enid. Takara says she has things to take care of, a mischievous glint in her eye that sparks my interest, and once she leaves, I fly to the desk. I pen a quick letter to Enid, one simple sentence that means more than anything else I've ever written.

Enid,
I'm in love with Alaric Montclare.
-Dahlia

I DISTRACT myself at the forge with Braddock for most of the day, getting lost in the familiar rhythms and sounds and smells. I've perfected the gauntlet design after some input from Alaric and have now made sets for Alaric, Elias, Wesley, Nova, and, after I finish this pair, every member of my guard.

I spy Alaric walking through the camp with a group of his men in the afternoon, and even across the distance, his eyes find mine. He inclines his head, his lips curling up ever so slightly. His golden eyes spark with the mischief of this shared secret between us and seem to burn with the memories of last night. I try to hide my smile and obviously fail miserably if even Braddock notices.

"And what has our Lady Dahlia in such a good mood today?"

I shake myself and hold up the gauntlet.

"Finished," I say with a smile.

He takes it from me, turning it over in his big hands.

"Very impressive, my Lady. Very impressive, indeed." I incline my head in thanks and say my goodbyes for the day, hanging up my apron on the peg by the door on my way out. I stop mid-motion when I hear Singh cry out from the back room just before a loud crash echoes through the place. Braddock rolls his eyes.

"That boy, I swear the gods..." he mutters quietly.

"I'm alright!" Singh calls "It's fine! Fire is out...Oh shit!!" Braddock and I look at each other and he holds up one finger, a smile playing on his lips. A moment later Singh calls again. "Ok, *now* it's out!"

We both chuckle lightly and I wave as I head out the door. I do some training exercises that Wesley and Nova had left for me to practice while they're gone, counting down the minutes until the day is over and I can see Alaric. Finally, the light begins to fade and I practically sprint back to the cabin. There's a sharp bite to the air now that winter is creeping in and my lungs don't care for it yet. I sigh in relief when I enter the cabin and find a giant fire roaring in the hearth in the entrance hall. I rush to Alaric's wing, heedless of who might be there or if he might have other business to deal with. I know that he's in the war room, sensing him there through the bond that I still don't quite understand, and jog down the hallway. I raise my hand to knock but the door flies open to reveal Alaric, eyes burning and fangs extended. Without a word, I jump into his arms, wrapping my legs around his waist. He kicks the door closed and presses me against the wood, his body pinning me as his lips crash to mine.

I melt against him, feeling as if it's been days without him instead of only hours. His tongue thrusts against mine, hot and demanding.

"Missed you," he pants between kisses. "How is that possible?" He turns and walks us across the room and I tunnel my fingers into his hair, rolling my tongue against his, biting and sucking on his lower lip until he groans huskily, making me grin and shiver with desire.

"Me too," I say as he sets me on the giant table, scattering the figurines in all directions. I widen my legs and he shoves his hips between them, making me gasp. I yank his shirt upward and he obliges me, helping to pull it over his head and tossing it to the floor. I give an appreciative *mmm*, running my hands over his stomach and chest, as he presses himself more firmly between my thighs.

He kisses along my jaw and whispers in my ear, "I've been hard nearly all day, Keeva. Couldn't stop thinking about you, about how good you taste..." He runs my ear lobe between his teeth and I make an obscene sound, bucking my hips against him. I can feel him grin against my skin as he kisses my throat. "Been dying to have my tongue on you again."

Before I even realize he's moved his hand, my tunic is open, the buttons scattering across the floor with soft *tinking* sounds. He slices my corset away, my breasts springing free, and immediately they're in his palms. I moan and arch my back, pressing them more firmly into his grasp, begging—for what, exactly, I don't know. Anything. Everything. He massages my flesh, running the pads of his thumbs over my nipples before pinching them lightly. I grip the edge of the table and kick off my boots before wrapping my legs around his thighs, holding him close to me as he continues his delicious torture. He kisses me again, tugging at the laces of my pants and stepping back long enough to lift my ass off the table and yank them down my thighs. He licks his lips as he stares between my legs and my entire body shudders in anticipation, but no. As much as I want that again, I want something else more.

Before he can move forward again, I slide off of the table to stand before him. He arches a dark brow, eyeing me hungrily as I go up on my tiptoes to kiss him again. My hands drift downward, untying the laces of his pants. I shove the leather down and tunnel my hand inside, and he hisses in a sharp breath as I wrap my hand around his length. I stroke as I kiss him, my tongue rolling in time with the movement of my hand. The sounds he makes send shivers down my spine, little groans and growls and pleas that I don't even think he realizes he's making. I break away from the kiss, leaning in to kiss his chest, trailing kisses lower across his stomach as I sink to my knees before him. He seems to stop breathing. He meets my gaze, his eyes churning like molten gold.

"Dahlia…" I can't tell if it's a warning or a prayer, but I don't dare stop. I lean in and run my tongue from his right hip bone, along the indention leading downward. I take the guttural sound he makes as approval, and shove his leathers down his thighs, his cock springing completely free.

Dear. Gods.

I knew Alaric was big, of course. I just had my hand wrapped him and I caught a glimpse of him after his release last night, but neither of these things could have prepared me to see him in his full glory. Long. Hard. Straining. I gulp, but not in fear. Oh no, it's absolute desire coursing through my veins, making me wet and needy. I grip his shaft and take the head between my lips. He makes an unintelligible sound that I believe means *please keep going*, and take him deeper into my mouth, swirling my tongue along the swollen crown as he slides deep into my throat.

"*FUCK,*" he hisses out as I slide back, sucking on the tip before taking him deep again. Over and over, bopping my head and gripping his hip with one hand, splaying my other hand over his stomach and dragging my nails over the muscles. I moan around his cock and he tunnels his hand in my hair, brushing the strands back from my face. I pull back, running my fist up and down his slick shaft as I meet his gaze. He licks his lips, his eyes dark and burning.

I hold his gaze and lean forward again, licking the bottom of his shaft from hilt to tip, and his entire body shudders. I pull the head between my lips again, never taking my eyes from his. He groans and wraps my hair around his fist, keeping it from obstructing his view.

"Fuck, Keeva. That's it, keep your eyes on me, beauty. Watch me while I watch you take my cock between those beautiful lips." I moan, and obey, keeping my eyes locked with his while I take him deep into my mouth again, sending his length down my throat. I love it when he talks, the dirty things he says and commands. I dig my fingers into his hip as I keep going, watching him watch me while I suck his cock and *dear gods* it's too much. I reach down between my legs, delving my own fingers between my thighs. I whimper at the touch and he moans loudly. "Gods..."

I pump my fingers as I take his shaft over and over, twirling my tongue and sucking hard and I can feel it the moment his body shifts and I know he's close.

"You're going to make me...come...Keeva...you must stop..."

I don't.

Instead, I release his hip and use that hand to stroke his length in time with the movement of my mouth. Up and down, up and down. So hard. So slick. I move down and palm his sac, sucking hard, and he roars my name as he comes in my mouth, hot spend lashes down my throat as his hips buck forward with every pump. I moan at the taste of him, of how I've somehow made this strong, centuries old vampire prince come undone. I pump my fingers harder, plummeting over the edge and crying out around his cock.

Suddenly, he's gone from my mouth and his hands are around my upper arms and he's lifting me to the table once more. He brings my fingers to his mouth, sucking hard and gods it's so erotic I can barely stand it. His eyes slide closed as he licks them clean, pushing his own fingers inside me in one quick thrust. I cry out in sudden pleasure. He releases my fingers and holds my gaze before bending his head to my neck and sinking his fangs into my throat. I scream as an orgasm rips through me out of nowhere. His fingers pumping, his fangs in my flesh, the pull as he sucks my blood—it's indescribable. Stars explode behind my eyes and I have no idea how long it is before the tremors subside and Alaric is holding me tight against him, both of us breathing as if we've just run across the entire continent.

"Fucking hells, Dahlia," he says against my hair. I bury my face in his chest, trying to breathe normally.

"Is it always like this for you?" I ask before rising my head to meet his eyes. He cradles my face, brushing his thumbs along my cheeks and I rest my hands on his hips. "Because it isn't for me, this is...this is something else entirely. I can't explain it, Alaric. It's like...I *crave* you. Not just physically, but on every level, like every bit of me needs every bit of you." I shake my head in frustration. "I can't think straight to explain this right. You've addled my brain with orgasms." He huffs out a quiet laugh.

"I understand," he says softly. "And no, it isn't like this. It's never been like this." He stares deeply into my eyes, trying to look to the very heart of me it feels like. My chest heats. He seems to steel himself, like he's about to deliver important news. His throat bobs as he swallows hard and then he exhales roughly. "It's because—"

A knock on the door interrupts whatever he's about to say and he curses under his breath as we spring apart.

"One moment," he calls. I scramble to try to put things to rights —which is impossible since my top won't close without buttons, and if the person at the door is a vampire, they'll be able to smell...*Oh gods*. My cheeks heat and I freeze, meeting Alaric's eyes. He seems to know exactly what I'm thinking because he laughs, his shoulders shaking as he finishes lacing his pants.

"It isn't funny," I hiss, snatching a figurine from the table and throwing it at him. He catches it easily and strides across the room, grabbing a sweater from a hook beside the fireplace. He holds it up in front of me, giving me a commanding look and I sigh, holding up my arms obediently. He slides the soft fabric over my head, and I inhale deeply, sighing. It smells like him. He tugs the hem down and kisses me softly.

"This looks ridiculous," I pout, but it's only half-hearted. He smiles playfully and taps the tip of my nose with his finger. It's... adorable. I can't deny that this side of him, this gentle, playful, adorable side, makes me love him even more.

"Come in," he calls and I blanch. Elias opens the door and waltzes inside, a huge grin on his face and not looking at all surprised to see me in this...predicament.

"Lady Dahlia, looking lovely as ever," he says breezily, and I see Alaric roll his eyes, though he's smiling.

"Hello," I respond, because I don't know what the hells else I could possibly say. He looks between me and Alaric, his smile hiking up a notch.

"Have I interrupted something?" Elias asks, all feigned innocence. He glances around and puts a hand to his mouth in mock-surprise. "Oh dear, are those *buttons* on the floor? Has someone's garment malfunctioned? Goodness me..."

"Enough, Elias," Alaric says and I pull in my lips to hide my smile. For some reason, the fact that Elias knows and doesn't seem to be fazed at all, or at the very least, isn't judging Alaric for what's happening between us, makes me ridiculously happy. I know that Elias and Alaric are as close as brothers and that his approval means more than Alaric would ever admit. Elias winks at me and then turns to Alaric.

"I really am sorry to interrupt, but I have..." he cuts a quick glance my way before turning back to Alaric, "news of a somewhat concerning nature."

Alaric's entire posture changes, his muscles tensing and pulling himself to his full height. His smile fades and the playful, flirty Alaric is gone. He's all High General now and a knot forms in the pit of my stomach.

"What's going on?"

"Scouting reports say that the Revenant army is marching

towards the Obsidian Plain with the largest contingent we've seen in months—even Kilgren is rumored to be with them."

Alaric had explained that Kilgren was the leader of the Revenants, hellbent on the destruction of Braxhelm, but even more so, of Alaric. But he *never* comes to battle with his men. I personally think that cowardly, but when memories of the Revenant attack flash behind my eyes, memories of me frozen in fear and hiding while others fought and died around me...well, who am I to judge cowardice?

"How long?" Alaric asks and I can see the calculations running through his mind, the strategies and plans and back-up plans, the entire war a giant chess board and Alaric anticipating moves and countermoves. Something about this feels wrong, an uneasy feeling skittering up my spine, but I think it's just the idea of Alaric leaving to go into an apparently huge battle, which I know without a doubt he's about to do.

"Three days."

Alaric nods. "Gather the men. Three battalions, plus archers, and call back the groups on patrol and the ones doing training exercises and have them join us." My stomach twists: that's the group that Wesley and Nova are with. So they'll be joining the fight as well.

"Already done. They're preparing now and Braddock and Singh are packing the weapons cache."

"Good. I'll meet you at the gates in twenty minutes."

"Yes, sir." Elias turns to me, looking more serious this time. "I'll watch over him, my Lady."

I nod, trying to keep the panic from rising in my chest and the tears from springing to my eyes. I know that Alaric must do this. I know that he wouldn't have it any other way, and really, I wouldn't either. I know how much he loves what he does, this calling he answered so long ago. It makes him happy to put himself between evil and the safety of everyone within the kingdom.

But even so, I can't stop the fear from turning my blood to ice and making it nearly impossible to breathe. As soon as Elias closes the door, Alaric is there, wrapping me in his arms.

"I'm sorry, I must go."

"I know," I assure him. He kisses me softly and I rest my palms on his cheek when he pulls back. "I know," I tell him again making sure he knows that I understand.

"I hate to leave you."

"Make sure you come back then," I whisper, leaning in to kiss him again.

"I swear to you," he says sternly, almost as if he's not just saying it to me but daring the gods themselves to try to stop him. He kisses me fiercely, and I try not to think of it as a gallows kiss. He picks me up and carries me to his bed chamber, tossing me on the bed and making me laugh. I wrap my arms around my knees and rest my chin there and watch as he dons his fighting leathers and a thick coat lined with fur, and straps Night's Fury to his back.

"No armor?" I ask. I know his armor is specially made and nearly impenetrable.

"Not on the journey to our temporary camp. A squire will pack it for me though, not to worry." I nod and all too soon, there isn't anything left for him to do. We walk hand-in-hand from his room, and I marvel at how nice something so mundane is. Simply walking with the man I love, his hand in mine, is something I never imagined I'd get to do. I want so badly to go with him, though I know how ridiculous that is.

"Oh! Wait here." His brows fly upward but I hold up one finger and he nods, silently promising to obey. I sprint down the hall to my room and rummage through my wardrobe.

"Where the hells...ah there!" I hold up my prize, smiling widely. I decide to take an extra minute to put on a new shirt and tame my wild hair before running back to Alaric. He looks me up and down when I arrive.

"Was my sweater not good enough for you?"

"I thought that was sure to get the soldier gossip mill running full steam ahead, your highness," I say with a roll of my eyes and he laughs. "Here, this is for you." I reach up and pin the wolf's head broach I bought all those months ago at the market to the lapel of his coat. He studies it and then looks back to me.

"When did you get this?"

"An embarrassingly long time ago, actually, but that isn't important." His lips curl. "Wear it for me." I can't find the words to explain that I want something of me there with him (other than my blood that he's going to take), to protect him. My father's people used to wear strips of their lover's family clan colors woven in their braids when they rode off to battle, like a talisman to keep them protected when they were far from home. This will have to do.

"I will," he says solemnly before pulling me into another slow, deep kiss. He's trying to tell me things with this kiss that he can't say in words, at least not yet. I kiss him back, echoing his feelings. I could tell him that I'm in love with him now, but I don't want to do that. I don't want it to be a declaration as he rides off to face death. I want it to be something that's said without a blade hanging over either of our heads—hopefully a metaphorical blade, of course. Again, fear crawls through my veins, but I try to push it away and put on a brave face as da would say.

Alaric pulls away and sighs. "I must go."

I nod and walk him to the door. Takara walks up as soon as Alaric walks away, taking Xanthus' reins from a squire and pulling himself easily atop the giant horse. I would swear that the animal meets my eyes and bows his head, promising me that he'll protect his master, the man we both love. Alaric meets my gaze once more, inclines his head, and then rides towards the gates to meet the gathering cadre.

I exhale roughly and Takara reaches down to grip my hand. I squeeze it back and the two of us stand on the steps of the cabin for what feels like hours, until the very last of the soldiers ride through the gates and disappears from sight.

CHAPTER 32

ALARIC

Riding away from camp has never been harder. It feels as if a piece of me is being ripped away, like I'm leaving a vital piece of myself behind. My heart. That's what I'm leaving back at camp as I ride to battle, to possible death. My fucking heart.

But I know it must be done. I will return from this battle as I've always returned. I have something far too precious to return to now and I will not lose that when we haven't even started yet. I haven't even told her how I feel, I haven't even told her that she's mine.

Elias rides beside me, giving me the rundown on our men, where the advanced group has made camp, and the latest update from the scouts.

"So..." he says after we've taken care of business for the time being. I quirk a brow and he rolls his eyes in annoyance. "Come on, Alaric. Did you tell her?"

"Not yet," I admit, glancing around to be sure no one is listening. "We were rudely interrupted, if you do recall," I remind him when he looks about to berate me. He is of the mind that I should tell Dahlia that she's my mate immediately, and while I do want her to know, I want us to explore this thing between us more before I tell her. I don't want there to be any pressures or questions as to my feelings or hers. I want her to understand that I love her, regardless of the mating bond.

"Did you at least tell her you love her then?" I rub the back of my neck and he shakes his head. "I wish I had something to throw at you right now. Why not, you daft idiot!?"

"I don't know if you are aware, but I *am* your High General and a prince to boot...maybe you shouldn't insult me?" He waves that away, scoffing, and I laugh. Then I sigh. "I didn't want to tell her when I was riding off to battle, like I was only saying it because I might die."

"Gods, you're bad at this, you know that?"

"I am not!...Ok, maybe I'm not the *best*," I admit, realizing that this is my first...relationship? Is that what I'd call this? It seems like such a simple word for something so profound and all-encompassing. But yes, this is the first relationship I've been in and perhaps I do not know the best way to navigate the roads of the heart. "Is that not the right way to look at this?"

"No, you moron. If you love someone, you tell them. As soon as you feel it and as often as possible. Time isn't guaranteed, Alaric, especially for us." I blink, taking his words in, rolling them around.

"Fuck," I grate.

"Fuck, indeed," he agrees. "Speaking of fucking..."

"No," I say firmly. "No, not yet." He exhales dramatically in exasperation and I whip Night's Fury from my back quick as lightning and smack him in the back with the flat of the blade.

"Oy! Don't make me beat you senseless in front of all of your men, High General..."

We laugh and pass the rest of the journey swapping conjectures about Kilgren's motives and what he's planning, and talking about random things. We ride through the night and make it to camp before first light.

"Highspear!" Elias calls, sliding from Orion's back while I dismount Xanthus, patting the horse affectionately before handing him off to a squire. Elias passes Orion off to the lad as well and we stride off towards our tents.

The young vampire sprints over.

"Yes, sir," he says, bowing his head and putting his fist to his chest.

"At ease," I tell him and he relaxes slightly, but still seems tense. He won't meet my gaze directly and I know he's still feeling stung by my refusal of his promotion and to be appointed to Dahlia's guard. I recall snapping at him, which I rarely do, and feel a twinge of guilt. I was in a frantic state after Dahlia's attack and might have taken out frustrations on the boy.

"Latest report," Elias demands.

"Yes, sir. The Revenant contingent is still moving towards the Obsidian Plain, five hundred in the first group at our last count."

"Good work," I tell him and he glances towards me, surprise flitting across his boyish features, but he quickly averts his eyes again. "Rest up and relieve your partner in four hours."

"Yes, sir." He bows his head again and scurries off.

"Was it just me, or was he more squirrely than usual?" Elias asks.

I run a hand through my hair as we step inside my tent. It's a monstrous thing, far larger than I need, but it's customary for the commanding officer to have larger quarters. There's a pallet of furs atop several crates, giving the illusion of an actual bed, a wash basin, a desk and several trunks of weapons and clothing on one side of the space. My armor rests on a mannequin in the corner, a smaller version of the table from my war room just beside it, already set up and ready for me to strategize over, and a fire pit near the bed, the smoke escaping through a slit in the top of the tent. Almost all of it is unnecessary, but I stopped arguing with my squires over it long ago. It makes them happy to see to my needs, as they see them at any rate, and I appreciate the care they take.

I unbuckle my sword and place it in its stand beside the bed, stretching my muscles this way and that after the long ride.

"I might have yelled at him the last time I saw him," I admit.

Elias looks at me questioningly as he takes a sip of blood from his flask. I can still taste Dahlia's blood on my tongue and I barely stop a shudder at the memory of taking it straight from her body, of feeling her soft flesh glove my fangs...I clear my throat and continue, "It was just after the attack on the road and I was...quite harsh."

"Out of your fucking mind with rage, you mean."

"Also that," I agree. "Highspear caught me at a bad time and I snapped at him. I think it rattled him."

"Ah, he'll be fine. You aren't as scary as you think you are, you know." He grins and I can't help but laugh.

"Alright, we have less than two days. Let's start planning."

Elias nods and we head to the war table, my mind already working, envisioning the map like a chess board and calculating the probability of the moves and the motives behind them, how I'll combat them, how we should attack or defend.

THE BATTLE RAGES all around me, brutal and frenzied and making my blood sing in my veins. Despite the chaos, I'm calm, that cold detachment covering me like a blanket as it always does. I'm covered in blood—most of it not my own—and I bring Night's Fury down in a vengeful arc, cutting another Revenant down. I keep searching for Kilgren, wanting the chance to finally end the bastard. There's been no sign of him yet, and I fear that the rumors of his presence have been exaggerated. The rumors about the number of Revenants, unfortunately, were under-reported. There are at least seven hundred, maybe more, and a large number of them are holding their lines behind the brunt of the battle, far behind the invisible barrier of safety, as if waiting for something. What, I have no idea, but there's a skittering of unease up my spine. *Something is wrong. Something is happening.*

I've tried teleporting more than once, but to no avail. I guess at this point, it only works if my mate is in danger. It's no matter. I've been battling for over a century without that skill, I'll continue to do it now. I cut through our enemies, twisting and parrying, clashing and dodging, performing the deadly ballet that burns in my blood. I feared that worry for Dahlia, that the pain of being away from her would distract me from my mission here, but it seems to be doing the opposite: it's somehow aiding me, pushing me to move faster, to strike truer, to move like smoke through the battle. Is it my desire to get back to her, to return to her safely? Or simply my feelings for her, and hers for me, I daresay, giving me a new strength that I've never had before?

I see Elias up a small rise, battling three Revenants, and I take off towards him. I slide between him and a Revenant who thought to catch him from the side, Night's Fury clanging loudly against the Revenant's sword. He grunts, but doesn't attack with the usual ferocity I've come to expect from these monsters, no rage burning in his crimson eyes, no snarling or taunting jibes. He's acting almost... robotic, like a clockwork creature. It's strange.

"Took you long enough," Elias says with a grin, spinning to avoid one Revenant's flail and slicing a deep gash in the other's thigh. I laugh and square off against my opponent. His black hair is shaved low on one side, warrior braids hanging down the other. He lunges forward with his thin blade, the kind made for slipping between a man's ribs, but I block and spin, cutting a deep gash to the bone of his upper arm. He howls in pain, but it ends abruptly when I take his head with one swift slash of Night's Fury. His body topples to the ground. I turn to face one of the two remaining beasts, but a small blade slams into my hand. It doesn't pierce through Dahlia's gauntlet, of course, but it knocks Night's Fury from my gasp.

"Fuck," I rasp, as the Revenant across from me grins wickedly.

"You are nothing without that blade," she hisses, looking victorious. She lunges forward and I dart back while Elias fights brutally with the other one, both of them hacking at each other like two bears. The Revenant has abandoned his flail and is now brandishing a giant war hammer. The other Revenant pushes her luck in my moment of distraction, thrusting her sword towards me again. Her blade slices across the front of my armor but doesn't pierce the dragon scales, and I grab her forearm, holding her tight against me as I flick my wrist, releasing the hidden blades from my gauntlet and driving them into her throat. I tear her open from ear to ear with one vicious movement. She gurgles and clutches at her neck before falling to her knees.

"Not completely nothing," I correct her. I turn to Elias and find him standing between the two halves of the Revenant. We grin at each other.

"Nicely done, brother," I tell him.

A heartbeat later, an arrow sails through the air, passing just beside Elias' shoulder, and slams into my chest, just to the right of my heart. Pain laces through me and I stumble backwards from the force of the blow.

"Alaric!" Elias calls. "Fuck, more of the armor-piercing arrows??"

"I'm alri—" I scream in agony as fire seems to explode from the wound, sizzling through my veins and spreading outward through my entire body. I fall to my knees and Elias cries my name, slamming to his knees beside me. I blink past the pain, trying to focus, but I'm burning. I'm fucking burning and I can't...I can't...

"Alaric! Alaric, what's happening?"

"S...silver," I gasp as the pain doubles, the poison spreading through my veins like wildfire.

"A silver arrowhead!?" Elias braces me for the briefest of moments before yanking the arrow free and flinging it away.

"N...no." My body bows under the agony, and I feel blood well in my palms where my claws have sliced to the bone. "...powder...o-on the tip..."

Elias' face goes white as the words sink in. Silver is bad enough, but silver powder spreads through the blood, taking the poison to every inch of the vampire and burning him from the inside out, destroying him slowly and in utter agony.

"No. Ah gods. No, no, no. Help!" he roars, turning towards the melee below the rise. "Help me, NOW!"

I bite through my lip in an effort to keep from screaming out, blood pouring down my chin. The pain is excruciating, unlike anything I've ever experienced and I'm no stranger to pain. More of our men leap atop the rise, taking up defensive positions around me, while others pull me to my feet. Elias throws my arm around his shoulder and half drags me down the hill. I glance back over my shoulder, my gaze zeroing in on a spot far off in the distance, up on a stony overlook, somehow knowing exactly where to look.

There, gray lips pulled back into a snake's smile, is Kilgren.

CHAPTER 33

DAHLIA

"You're going to dig a rut clear to the first circle of hell, my Lady," Viktor muses as I pace back and forth for what must be the hundredth time in the last half hour. I've barely slept in the two nights that Alaric has been gone. I'll admit that I've wrapped myself in his sweater each evening, and that has helped ease a bit of the pain of him being gone, but sleep itself has been elusive. I've dozed a bit here and there in the very early hours of the morning when exhaustion became too much, but fretfully. The first day had been torture, but I'd done my best to act normal. Today has been even worse. Training, the forge, walking with Takara, more training—everything only manages to keep the worst of my stress away for what feels like mere moments.

Now I've taken to pacing in the field behind the cabin while my guard and Takara watch on.

"Do you want to spar?" Cyrus asks cheerfully.

"No, thank you."

"Do you want to watch Cyrus and I spar?" Malcom suggests.

"Oh, I would like to watch that," Takara says, raising her hand. "Perhaps shirtless?"

"I second the shirtless sentiment," Viktor chimes in with a grin, blowing a kiss in Malcom's direction.

I can't help but laugh, pausing my pacing.

"I wouldn't be completely opposed to watching shirtless sparring, I suppose..." I grin and wink at Takara. "Maybe even pantless —" I gasp and double over as pain spears through my body, burning like someone's touched a hot poker directly to my heart.

"Dahlia!" Takara cries, running to my side as I fall to my knees.

"My Lady, what's wrong?" Malcom demands, drawing his blade just as Cyrus and Viktor do the same, placing themselves in a protective loose circle around me. I claw at the ground, fingers curling into the cold earth as I try to breathe around not only the pain, but the *panic*, because this pain—it isn't mine.

"Alaric," I gasp out before pushing myself to my feet and running faster than I've ever run before. I hear them calling after me, giving chase, but I don't dare slow. Something is very wrong with Alaric and something inside of me that I don't understand is screaming at me to go to him. It's more than just worry, it's something much more primal. I run to the stable, Xerxes stomping in his stall, feeling that something is wrong with Alaric the same as I am. I throw open his door and don't even waste time on a saddle.

Malcom makes it to the stable first, Takara just on his heels.

"Don't try to stop me," I warn. "You can follow if you want, but I have to go. *Now*."

Takara studies me, a flash of understanding that I don't even quite comprehend sparking in her eyes, and then she puts a hand on Malcom's arm.

"Help her up, Mal," she says quietly. "Do it now. We'll follow, but she needs to do this. Trust me."

Malcom doesn't question it, simply strides forward and lifts me by the waist, settling me on top of the giant horse.

"Ride swift, my Lady."

With that, I dig my hands into Xerxes' mane and he takes off like a bolt of lightning.

"Come on, boy. Get me to him," I beg. "Please get me to him." The horse runs faster than I've ever seen him run, the camp falling away quickly and the forest blurring around us as we speed towards Alaric. My heart threatens to burst through my chest, terror consuming me and making it almost impossible to breathe. What could have happened? He can't be hurt, not truly. He's...*Alaric.* Nothing can harm him...right?

We run on and on, and though I know the journey takes hours, it flies by so quickly that it seems like mere moments. I ignore the pain in my thighs, the chill seeping into my bones. We speed towards the temporary camp, not slowing as shouts arise from those on patrol, cries of warning and then of recognition. We run through the makeshift camp, passing rows of tents and huddles of men around fires. Somehow Xerxes knows exactly where to go, drawn to his master, I assume, and we pull up to a hard stop just outside the largest tent. The warhorse is frothing with exhaustion and I can only pray that he hasn't pushed himself too far. I slide from his back, hitting the ground hard and falling to my knees, but I ignore the flare of pain. I force myself up and give Xerxes a grateful pat before stumbling towards the opening of the tent. Elias' head snaps up when I enter, quickly crossing to me.

"Dahlia? What are you—"

"Where is he?" I demand. "What happened?!" I stalk past Elias, charging further into the tent—and freezing in absolute horror. Alaric is on a raised pallet of furs, bare from the waist up and writhing in pain. There's a gaping wound in his chest, one that...isn't healing. Why isn't he healing? Dark lines branch out from the wound, like tentacles of some sea beast. His body is slick with sweat and trembling, his skin flushed with what I assume is fever.

There are a few others in the tent, but I can't focus on any of them. All I can see, all I care about is Alaric. Elias steps up beside me.

"Silver, my Lady," he says quietly. "An arrow was tipped with silver powder and it's gotten into his blood stream." He takes a deep breath and my heart stops beating as he says the next words:

"There's…there's nothing we can do to stop it."

The pain is unending, a burning from within that's consuming me inch by inch. I try to fight against it, pushing back with all my might, but it's only a matter of time. I know that I'm back in my tent, having vague flashes of my men dragging me from the battlefield as the agony pulled me in and out of consciousness.

Kilgren planned this. Despite the pain making my thoughts a snarling mess of excruciating pain, I know that Kilgren planned this without a doubt in my mind. It's why he tested the arrow all those months ago. It's why he had such numbers with him, most of them waiting behind the lines until...until I fell. I know my army will not give up until the very last one of them breathes their last breath, but this fight will not be easy, especially without me there.

Another wave of fire burns through me and I grit my teeth, trying to stop another broken scream from tearing past my lips. I've been tortured more than once in my long life. I've been flayed, broken, and burned; I've had limbs cut off and regrown; I was once buried in snow for weeks, the cold slowly killing my extremities while I clawed my way out with bloody, numb fingers (*fucking Ahmed...*). But none of that compares to this pain. This is agony on a level that I didn't think could exist. I tried to fight past it, to remain silent and strong as I suffered, but I lost that battle far sooner than I would like to admit.

Now, I'm nearly delirious with the pain. I don't have the strength to open my eyes any longer, but as I float on the surface of consciousness, I can hear voices around me. Elias, a few other soldiers, and then…Dahlia? I must be on the cusp, the Goddess of Death coming to collect me finally, but giving me this gift of hearing my mate's voice one last time, even if it's a mere hallucination.

"What do you mean nothing can be done?" she snaps.

"It's spread too far, my Lady. There's no way we can stop it," Hawthorn answers.

"Bullshit!" Dahlia screams. "Bloodletting! Or…or…leeches! That's what human healers do! Use fucking leeches to suck the poisoned blood away!"

"It's too late," someone else whispers, but I don't know who.

"No. No! Don't touch me!" she screams at someone. "There *has* to be something. He's the High General. He's a fucking *prince*! You have to do something!" I want to tell her that it's ok, that I'm sorry and that I love her, but I can't make my body obey even the smallest of commands.

"Elias, *please*," Dahlia begs, voice breaking. What must my other men be thinking to see her like this. Consorts are not known for being this…protective over their princes. I can't spare much effort to worry about what they're thinking as the pain spikes again, making my body nearly give out. My heart stutters and even I wonder for an endless moment if it will start again.

"Everyone out," Elias suddenly demands. "Now! Lady Dahlia needs time to say goodbye in private."

"No. No, gods damn you! I'm not giving up, there has to be something! I won't say goodbye, I won't fucking do it, Elias, I—" Her voice cuts off abruptly. *I wonder why…* "Out!" Dahlia demands a moment later, the full authority of a noble Consort echoing in her voice. I want to smile as a twinge of pride swells in my chest. *This really is the strangest death dream though...*

I can hear retreating steps and then I sense her beside me. Her scent fills me, her presence somehow easing a bit of the pain. She's really here? How?? No, she's too close to the battle! She must go, she must get as far from here as she can. Should the lines fall and the Revenants break through...

"Will this work?" she asks quietly.

"It's the only hope we have," Elias says. I want to ask them what in the hells they're talking about. I want to demand that Elias get my mate away from here. I want to tell Dahlia that I love her more than life itself and kiss her, just one last time. But I can't move. I can't speak. I can't do anything but lie here and fucking burn.

Elias leans close to my ear and whispers, "I'm sorry, brother. I know it wasn't my secret to tell, but...well, your life means more to me than your secrets." *I don't understand...*

"Do it," Dahlia says, steel in her voice. A moment later, the scent of her blood fills the air just before something is pressed to my mouth. "Come on, Alaric," she whispers. "Please."

I want to open my lips, to do fucking *anything*, but I can't. I just can't. My body bows violently as another wave of agony spears through me, completely out of my control.

"Damnit, Alaric, I know you can do this! If anyone can, it's you." Elias is close on my other side and I imagine they're sitting on either side of the furs beside me. "Come *on*..."

The thing against my mouth—Dahlia's wrist, maybe?—presses harder against my lips.

"Fucking drink, Alaric. This is not a request! You will not leave me, do you understand?" Dahlia's voice is hard and I can imagine her green eyes blazing with determination. *My firebrand.* "We've only just gotten started, you and I. We have so much more we need to do. You haven't even fucked me properly yet, gods damn you." I hear Elias huff out a pained laugh and I want to smile. I want to laugh. I want to pull her to me and hold her in my arms and do all manner of unholy things to her.

But I can't. Fucking. Move.

Suddenly, her lips are at my ear, whispering low. "I haven't even gotten to tell you that I love you yet, Alaric. But I do. I love you so much that it hurts, but in the best possible way. It's the kind of love people write terrible sonnets about and minstrels sing awful songs about. It's the kind of love that can move mountains and make the impossible possible. So, it's going to fix you, do you hear me? It's. Going. To. Fix. You. But you've *got* to drink, Alaric. Fucking do it. *NOW.*"

She loves me.

And somehow, I force my lips apart and my teeth to unclench. Her blood drips over my tongue and down my throat and...the pain recedes the tiniest fraction. A drop in the ocean, but still, it recedes.

"Yes, that's it. Keep going, Alaric. Please..."

I swallow as more blood trickles into my mouth. And again, the pain ebbs ever so slightly. Somehow, I push back against it with more force now, Dahlia's blood, her mere presence, giving me more strength to fight. Dahlia presses her wrist harder against my lips.

"Come on, Alaric. Drink!"

My fangs slide out without any actual command from my mind, some baser instincts taking over. I sink them into her flesh, tearing and sucking, blood pouring down my throat now in great mouthfuls. I drink and drink, every drop chasing the pain away little by little. I suck harder, taking more and more. The pain fades as Dahlia's blood battles the poison in my very veins.

"Dahlia, are you alright?" Elias asks quietly.

"I'm fine," she pants. "Don't you dare fucking stop, Alaric. Take everything that you need. Take it all," she whispers, "as long as you make it through this."

I obey, tearing her flesh wider, taking more and more. Part of me knows I should stop. Part of me knows that I'm acting like an animal.

But right now, those parts aren't in charge and I can't stop. So I don't. After an eternity, the pain all but disappears and I release Dahlia's wrist, collapsing back against the furs. I still can't open my eyes. I still can't move or speak, but I can breathe and I somehow know that the poison is gone, that I will be alright.

"There," Dahlia breathes, relief heavy in her voice. "It...worked..." she adds, but it sounds like she's struggling to speak.

I hear Elias gasp her name and then a soft thud, but the darkness drags me under before I can even wonder what's happened.

I come fully awake with a choked gasp, bolting upright atop my furs. Elias is there, hands on my shoulders, holding me steady.

"What..." I croak, my voice rough—from screams, I assume. I clear my throat and try again. "What the fuck happened?" Everything is a jumbled mix of sights and sounds that aren't making much sense.

"The bastards found silver. Coated the arrowhead in powder and shot you straight through the heart with it. Well, *almost* straight through the heart. If it had been a clean shot...well, we got lucky."

I reach up automatically to run my fingers over the spot, remembering the pain of the arrow piercing my flesh, of the silver burning me from within. The wound is completely healed and I shake my head in confusion, trying to force the nonsense in my mind to fall into line, desperate for clarity.

"But how..."

"Dahlia," Elias says simply. "She felt your pain and knew to come. I don't know how, but she did. She rode like the devil himself was on her heels, that bastard horse of yours running faster than any should have been able to. Somehow, they made it in time. She healed you, Alaric." Memories start to solidify in my mind like puzzle pieces clicking together. Hearing Dahlia's voice, her demanding that I drink, her...telling me that she loves me. My heart clenches and I exhale a ragged breath. "A *mate's* blood is the only thing that could have possibly saved you from this, Alaric," Elias adds quietly. I blink and remember him whispering that he was sorry to have spilled my secret...Oh gods, she knows.

"Where is she?? Is she ok?" Ah gods, I'd taken so much. That thud I'd heard, it must have been her collapsing.

"She's fine," he assures me, trying to keep me in the bed. I shove him away and he flies across the room, righting himself at the last minute to remain on his feet. We both freeze, wide-eyed. I've always been strong, but I've never been able to throw Elias around like he's a child's doll.

"Holy shit," he breathes. "All that blood..."

I feel it as he says the words, the nearly limitless strength coursing through my veins now. *Holy fuck, how much had I taken?* A mate's blood is always more potent, but I've never taken more than what was necessary from Dahlia. To have so much of her blood flooding my system right now is having...interesting effects. This is one reason that mated vampires are considered so fearsome—not simply because the instincts to protect their mate are so strong that their brutality is unmatched, but because they are literally *physically* stronger because of the blood shared. I feel like I could take on the entirety of the Revenant army myself...

Fuck. The battle. What had happened after I'd been taken out? Are we holding on? I shake my head, trying to focus on one thing at a time. The most important is Dahlia. I can feel her easily now that I let myself focus for a moment—breathing and whole on another pallet of furs beside the fire. I rush to her side, moving faster than I've ever moved before (save the time that I teleported, of course). I brush the hair back from her face. She looks so pale, light bruises beneath her eyes.

"What's wrong with her?" I ask Elias, though I try to be quiet as not to wake her.

"She's alright, just...recovering. You, ah...well, hells, Alaric, you drained her nearly dry." I clench my jaw, trying to hold back the bile rising in my throat. I'd almost...killed her? "Don't worry," Elias adds quickly, "you didn't. She's completely fine. Ajax was a human healer before he was turned—he's checked her out and we've given her the tonic that her Keeper brought to replenish her blood. Oh, yes, her Keeper and guard arrived an hour or so after she did and Takara brought the tonic with her..." I meet his gaze, the question in my eyes. "She just said she had a feeling it might be needed...so, I think yes, she knows."

"Fuck, I guess everyone will soon enough."

Elias rubs the back of his neck. "I've been trying to spread the rumor that you're just so gods damned unstoppable and amazing that you fought silver powder all on your own, but...there are some who will assume the truth, yes. Perhaps it's time you write to your brother? Before word somehow spreads all the way to Astoria's Keep." I exhale roughly and brush Dahlia's cheek gently.

"The battle?"

"Rages on. We're pushing back as hard as we can but the whole of their forces attacked after you were taken from the field. It's been brutal. Reinforcements from the camp have already arrived and are marching to the Plain now. It's...it's not looking good, Alaric. Between the sheer number of them and the hit your rumored death made on the morale of the men...A retreat may be necessary."

"No," I growl, fury burning hotly in my chest. "My armor," I demand. "NOW." The rage boils inside of me, every muscle tensing and bulging, my fangs and claws already sharpening and craving destruction. Elias eyes me but nods, calling for a squire to come and assist me. The blood has been cleaned away, but a hole remains over my chest, a reminder of how close I'd come to losing everything. Elias dons his own armor quickly and I bend down to place a soft kiss on Dahlia's forehead.

"Sleep, my love. I'll return for you soon."

I give her guard instructions to watch over her and if they receive word from me, they are to take her from this place immediately. If it even looks like the line might fall, I want her as far from this place as possible.

"Of course, sir," Malcom says, inclining his head. The other two are already standing on either side of the entrance to my tent, hands on their sword hilts, ever ready. I nod at them all, give Xerxes a loving pat and a thank you where he rests beside his brother. I mount Xanthus and ride into battle.

I HEAR my name being whispered in reverence…or yelled in terror as I cut a bloody path across the battlefield. I'm stronger and faster than ever before, though I still haven't been able to teleport again, and I slice through the Revenants as if they're nothing but parchment. The sight seems to energize our men, my strength seeming to flow into them as well, and they push themselves into the fray with renewed life. I stab and slice with Night's Fury, the blade completely coated in thick, black blood and begging for more. I punch a hole through one Revenant's chest, and tear another's head from his shoulders with one hand. Those closest balk at the sight and retreat. I grin a bloody, blood-thirsty grin and give chase. I've never felt battle lust like this before, it's like a thick, red haze has settled over my vision and I'm not sure if it will ever fade.

I look for Kilgren among the chaos—I know for a fact I saw him after I was shot—but it seems like the coward has already turned tail as word of my miraculous return spread through the lines. We push them back. Against all odds, we come back from this near defeat and push the bastards back. The Obsidian Plain is littered with bodies now, piles of them. Not only did we push them back, we fucking *decimated* them. Those Revenants left call for retreat, running for their lives, and we roar in victory in the middle of the carnage. Elias claps me on the shoulder and we share a moment between brothers, one that needs no words spoken. *I love you. I am proud to fight beside you. I will always be here.*

Now that the battle is done, there is only one thing I want. One thing I *need*.

My fucking mate.

CHAPTER 35

DAHLIA

I wake, groggy and a little weak, but overall fine. Alaric is alive. The thought fills my chest with an incredible warmth, chasing away the cold terror that had gripped me since the moment I felt his pain in the camp. *It had been so close. I'd almost lost him...*

I push myself up and Takara is there.

"Easy, now. You might be a bit dizzy. Drink this." She hands me a tankard of something sweet-smelling and I don't question her, just down the entire cup. It's crisp and cool and bitingly sweet. I hand it back and wipe my mouth with the back of my hand.

"What was that?"

"Something similar to the tonic you've taken in the past that replenishes your blood, but think of this as a...stronger proof." I huff out a small laugh, but whatever it is, it starts working immediately. The bit of lightheadedness I felt when I sat up disappears and a wave of strength and energy slowly crashes into me, starting in the center of my chest and working its way through every inch of my body.

I glance to the bed and panic grips me. I jump to my feet.

"Where is Alaric?? Is he ok? What happened?" I rub the heel of my hand against my chest, trying to stop the thunderous beating, trying to tell myself that I would know if something had happened, if he'd taken a turn after I'd passed out.

"He's fine, Dahlia. Look at me," she says, putting her hands on my shoulders and making me meet her eyes. "He's fine. More than fine, I'd wager, with that much of your blood in him..." She eyes me for a moment, and then adds quietly, "legends say a mate's blood is exceptionally powerful..." There's a question in the words. My eyes fly wide and I swallow hard. I still can't quite believe that it could be true.

I'd been frantic but also somehow numb when I'd arrived in the tent and found Alaric on the bed, wounded and bleeding and writhing in pain, *screaming* in agony. The sounds of the strongest man I've ever known screaming as he burned alive from the inside is something I will never forget.

"What do you mean nothing can be done?" I'd asked, somehow pushing the words past numb lips.

"It's spread too far, my Lady. There's no way we can stop it," one of Alaric's men had answered. Hastings? Hawkins? Something like that.

"Bullshit!" I'd screamed, something inside me breaking, pounding and clawing against the words like a caged animal fighting to escape. I'd been frantic, my mind desperately clutching at anything it could think of. "Bloodletting! Or...or...leeches! That's what human healers do! Use fucking leeches to suck the poisoned blood away!"

"It's too late," someone had whispered. I think her name was Collins.

"No. No! Don't touch me!" I screamed when Elias laid a gentle hand on my shoulder. "There *has* to be something. He's the High General. He's a fucking *prince*! You have to do something!" Everyone had simply looked away from my pleas, my agony, already having accepted the inevitable.

The High General would die this day.

The thought had stopped my own heart, my world coming to an abrupt halt all around me.

"Elias, *please*," I'd begged of him, my voice breaking as tears streamed down my face. He held my gaze for a long moment and then something lit in his stormy blue eyes, as if an idea had struck.

"Everyone out!" He'd suddenly demanded. "*Now*! Lady Dahlia needs time to say goodbye in private." My mouth had gaped in horror. He couldn't possibly be serious! He wasn't just going to give up hope!

"No. No, gods damn you! I'm not giving up, there has to be something! I won't say goodbye, I won't fucking do it, Elias, I—" He'd gripped my shoulders then and leaned in, lips close to my ear so even the other vampires' hearing wouldn't be able to pick up the words.

"Dahlia, he needs your blood. You can save him...a *mate's* blood is the only thing strong enough to pull him back from this." A mate's blood. Elias had pulled away, looking at me again seriously, showing me the truth of the words. I didn't understand how it was possible, but if there was even a chance it would work, I would give him every last drop from my veins.

"Out!" I'd screamed, putting as much authority as a Consort into my voice as I could, pulling myself up to my full (and relatively unimpressive) height, but the effect was enough. The others had all scurried quickly from the tent and Elias had secured the flap behind them. The word had echoed through my head as we'd coaxed Alaric to drink.

Mate. Mate. Mate.

I try to make sense of it all now. I don't pretend to know just how profound the bonds of matehood between vampires are, but even as a human I know enough to understand that this is no small thing. Mates are exceedingly rare, only a handful documented over the last millennium...and mates are never human. Ever. I don't understand how this could be possible. I've always mocked Enid's steadfast belief in fate and signs and kismet but now...it seems as if the universe brought me to Alaric, brought him to me, as if everything was conspiring to put the two of us together because...because I'm *his*.

I inhale deeply before letting it out slowly.

"It's true," I say softly to Takara. "I didn't know it until I arrived here, but Elias knew. He was the one who realized that I might be able to save Alaric because of it."

Though a part of me is so damned happy at the news that I'm Alaric's, that we belong together on some cosmic level that I can't even properly understand, the other part of me is angry that he kept it from me all this time. Spitting mad, actually.

"I had my suspicions," Takara says leading me to the raised pallet where Alaric had lain...gods, how long had it been? Hours? Days? New furs had replaced the blood and sweat-soaked ones. We sit down and she holds my hands in hers. "Are you alright? I can't imagine what that news might mean to you, especially as a human..."

"I'm...I don't know. Part of me is relieved, part of me is happy, part of me is angry, part of me is afraid...mostly I'm just confused and there are just too many other things clamoring in my mind for me to process it fully right now. I need to know where Alaric is. I need to talk to him."

Takara digs one fang into her bottom lip.

"He's...gone." I blink. Surely I couldn't have heard her correctly.

"Gone?"

"Gone. To battle."

I leap from the bed. "What!? He just nearly died, what in the fucking seven hells is he doing riding off into battle again already!?"

"You know the answer to that," she says pointedly and I scowl at her. She quirks a brow right back and I exhale, throwing my hands up. I do know the answer. It's in his blood. It's his duty. And I can only imagine the wrath boiling within him right now after what happened.

"Alright, fine. But still!"

"We're getting reports that it's turned, that his presence back on the field has shifted everything and they've rallied and beaten the Revenants back. It should be done soon, Dahlia."

Well, that's something, but I'm still...I don't even know what I am. Mad. Worried. Terrified. Tired. Hungry. Happy. Grateful. It's all too much. I storm out of the tent, Cyrus and Viktor glancing at me with looks of concern from their spots flanking the entrance. I don't even know where I'm going or what I'm doing, I only know that I'm beyond frustrated and all of the emotions I've been feeling for the last...

"How long has it been?" I snap, tired of not even knowing if it's been hours or weeks. "Since I left camp."

"A day and a half only, my Lady," Malcom answers as he strolls up, hand resting on the hilt of his sword.

All of the emotions that I've been feeling for the last day and half are all mixed up and threatening to overwhelm me at any moment. I pace furiously, trying desperately to calm my thoughts, but everything is like a cyclone inside my mind.

And then I feel him.

I whirl just as a group of soldiers round the corner into the clearing in front of Alaric's tent. Some are limping, all are bloody and dirty, but they're beaming and cheering. A victory then. And then I see him at last.

Alaric pauses for a moment when he sees me, our gazes locking. Everything else falls completely away then. There is only me and him and nothing else in the world matters, nothing else in the world even exists. He's covered head to toe in blood and gore, his hair hanging in damp tangles around his face, the hilt of Night's Fury gleaming darkly over his shoulder. His golden eyes are blazing with a wild intensity and locked entirely on me. I gasp quietly: he's never looked so fierce...or sexy.

A determined, hungry look settles over his face, making my heart race and my lips part. This isn't a prince looking at his Consort. This isn't a man looking at the woman he might love.

This is a vampire looking at his mate.

And the look is enough to set me on fire.

He crosses the clearing to me in a few long strides and wraps one arm around my waist. A sudden pressure closes in around us, darkness descending like a thick shroud.

"Alaric?" I gasp, clutching at his waist. *What in the hells is happening??*

As quickly as it came on, the pressure ceases and the darkness falls away to reveal one of the grandest entrances I've ever seen. A soaring ceiling, so high that the corners are nearly in shadow, dual staircases curving around to a second-story landing overlooking the entry. Everything is dark wood and brushed metal and deep colored gemstones, not the typical glittering golds you'd typically find in a place like this, but still obviously regal. It's gorgeous—I never cared for gold, honestly—but completely foreign to me.

"Where..."

A female vampire rushes into the space, three humans trailing in her wake. I blink, completely confused and my head swimming.

"Your highness," the vampire says, clearly startled but recovering quickly as she bows deeply, the humans following suit behind her. "We didn't expect you."

"Everything is in order, I presume." His voice is stern and flat, but I can hear the tension beneath, how much it's costing him to speak right now.

"Yes, sir, of course." Four sets of eyes look from Alaric, to me, to the firm, possessive grip of his hand on my waist. Two of them are better at hiding their surprise than the others, but none of them dare say a word.

Alaric nods and turns to stride up the stairs, every line of his body thrumming with tension, and I try my best to keep up.

"Expected? Where the hells are we, Alaric?" I hiss quietly as I practically run to keep up with his long strides. Did we just...*teleport*? I can't wrap my mind around that, so I focus on following Alaric.

We sprint up the main stairs up one...two...*five* floors, then turn down a long, wide corridor lined with dark blue carpet and black marble wainscoting. At the end is another grand staircase, snarling wolves carved into the banister posts. I'm breathing hard, but silently thank Wesley and Takara for all of the morning exercises to build up my endurance. *How big is this fucking place?*

"Alaric, what the hells is going on?" Again, no answer. He just continues to pull me up the stairs beside him. I begin to wonder if he can even hear me. He seems...off. I peek out one of the windows when we finally reach the landing and realize that we must be at the very top of a high tower—and that we've traveled a great distance from the camp: the sea churns below, a dark bluish-gray with white caps erupting as the waves crest and fall. I want to linger and enjoy the view, but Alaric continues on, so I follow.

There are multiple rooms along this corridor, some doors standing open and I try to peer inside as we pass—a study, a lounge of some sort, a library, a training room similar to the one at the cabin but larger. At the end of the hallway are a set of towering double doors, black as night. Alaric's sigil is carved into the center of each, ruby eyes staring at us as we approach. Ornate *M*s to represent the Montclare name are etched into each iron handle.

"Alaric," I say, clutching at his hand. "What is this place?" I ask again. Finally, he finds his voice.

"Our home," he says simply, almost absently, as he throws the doors open and strides inside. *Our home?* The room is absolutely massive, adorned in all black and dark wood, hints of red here and there. There's a large sofa in front of a great stone hearth on one side, a black fur rug covering the stone floor beneath. A huge bed sits on a raised platform on the other side, the headboard carved with wolves and swords, and a large marble pillar stands at each corner. Bookshelves line the walls, another sitting area with a chess set sits in a corner, and of course a wall of weapons. It's all very...*Alaric.*

He stops in the middle of the room and I step before him.

"Alaric?" I whisper, growing a little concerned. His chest is heaving and his eyes are wild, like an animal trapped in a snare. He seems to be seeing me but also...not, like he's somewhere else entirely. Still on the battlefield? I've never seen him like this before, but, well, if what I've been told of a mate's blood is true, then he's never *been* like this before. I can feel the tension roiling through him, the bloodlust and the fear and the elation, all melting together in an intense maelstrom that I can't quite wrap my head around. It's making my own heart beat erratically, and my pulse jump uncomfortably. Despite the blood and gore, I reach out and place my hands on either side of his face. He shudders and leans into the touch, like he's desperate to find something to ground him, to bring him back from whatever this strange trance is.

"Alaric, be at ease..." He squeezes his eyes shut and I can feel him spiraling, losing his grip on everything. I trace my thumbs along his cheeks, his stubble thick and...sticky against my skin. I release his face and grip his hands tightly in mine, leading him to what I hope is the bathing chamber and he follows obediently. The servants downstairs said that everything was in order, so I assume that means that the house—*Manor? Castle??*—is ready for him at all times. I'm hoping that includes soap in the—

"Seven hells," I breathe as we step inside the room. It's almost the size of my entire bed chamber at the cabin, everything carved from black marble with veins of crimson, and it's absolutely beautiful. Masculine but beautiful at the same time, just like Alaric. There's a water basin, a tub that could easily fit ten people, and a...private privy? *Why the hells would that be here?* I put the thought in the back of my mind to focus on later and focus instead on what we need: the shower that's as large as Xanthus' stall in the stable. I turn the lever and hot water pours from the pipes high overhead. I step away as steam begins to fill the space and turn back to Alaric. He's standing in the center of the room, watching me with that wild, almost lost look.

Without a word, I start to unbuckle the straps on his armor, trying to ignore how much thick, black blood coats it. I gently pull it off of his chest and thank all the gods for all of the exercises Nova and Wesley put me through: with Night's Fury still in the sheath attached to the back, the armor weighs a ton and nearly knocks me over when it comes loose. A stab of panic flashes through me worrying for my friends, not knowing what their fate might be after the battle, but I push it aside. There's nothing I can do about that now. In this moment, I can only take care of Alaric, only help to bring him back to me.

I pull his tunic off next, taking a selfish moment to admire his bare chest and run my hands over his sweat-soaked skin. I take a steadying breath when my fingers trace over the spot where the gruesome wound had been when I'd come to him almost two days ago. Now, only smooth, wet skin remains. I lean forward and plant a soft kiss over the spot, unable to stop myself. A low growl rumbles through his chest and I quickly pull away and kneel down to unlace his boots. He kicks them off and I rise. I know he needs to get out of his leathers but...well, honestly, I don't know that I'll focus on what needs to be done if I remove those at this point. So, instead I grip his hand and lead him to the shower stall, stepping inside with him though I'm still fully clothed. The heat is that beautiful pleasure-pain sensation after being out in the freezing Northlands. I hadn't even realized how cold I'd been until it's being chased away by the warmth of the water now.

"What are you doing?" he rasps, sounding like it's still a struggle to speak.

"I'm getting you cleaned up. You're covered in blood and...bits of Revenants," I say, trying not to gag. The worst of it had been on his armor, but his neck and face and hair are all still coated. I silently thank the staff for keeping things at the ready as I reach for a new bar of a soap and a cloth on the shelf set into the marble wall. I work the soap into a thick lather, inhaling deeply the luxurious scent of pine and snow and something spicy that I can't even name.

He lets me wash his chest and arms, scrubbing all of the grime of battle away. With every sweep of my hands, he seems to relax a fraction. Bit by bit, stroke by stroke, he's coming back to me. I clean his neck and face, and maneuver him beneath the stream of water to wash his hair. By the time we rinse the soap from his curls, he seems to be back to himself.

"*Keeva*," he breathes and all of the tension that has been squeezing my chest since I awoke falls away. I sigh in relief.

"There you are," I say quietly. Without warning, his lips are on mine, his hands tangling in my hair. I gasp and groan as he forces my lips apart, his tongue thrusting frantically against mine. The fire engulfs me immediately, and all of the worry and panic from these last hours reach a fever pitch. I need him in a terrifyingly desperate way. I tug at his pants, and he literally rips them off of his body. He quickly gives my clothes the same treatment and heaps of fabric and leather litter the floor of the shower. His big body shudders as he wraps his arms tightly around me, pulling me hard against him. He backs us up until we're against the stone wall and lifts me easily, hands beneath my ass and urging my legs around his waist. I obey, digging my fingers into his shoulders and back. He kisses me as if he'll die any moment if he doesn't. It's desperate. It's hungry. It's devastating. I can feel everything clamoring inside of him, the connection and the love and the fear, the sharp, intense desire that isn't just desire at all, it's *need*. It's a physical, aching need of a vampire for his mate. I moan into his mouth, running a hand through his wet hair, as that same need echoes within me.

Every lap of his tongue stokes the fire burning inside, threatening to leave me in ashes.

"Need you," he croaks against my lips, and the fire flares. He moves away from the wall, fumbling with the levers on the wall to turn off the water as he passes by. He strides back into the bed chamber and we're greeted by blissfully warm air and the smell of burning wood. *The servants here are quick and silent as death*, I think. I can only imagine what they must be thinking after seeing the way Alaric had me clutched in his arms when we arrived, what one of them must have known was happening in the shower. I shake away the thoughts. It doesn't matter. None of it matters. The rules, the expectations, the honor or the dishonor of it all. All that matters is this moment with Alaric. All that matters is that he's alive and whole and here with me.

The memory of how close he'd come to death, to leaving me to navigate this world alone, slams into me and I kiss him harder, desperate to feel him and chase away that nightmare. As if he can feel what I'm thinking—*and hells, at this point maybe he can?*—he kisses along my jaw, murmuring as he goes.

"I'm here, Keeva. I'm here, I'm here, I'm here..." I gasp and moan as his tongue and fangs gently glide over my skin. He makes his way down my throat, never biting, but driving me mad with the anticipation, before coming back to kiss my lips once more as he walks us through the room, up the two steps to the platform where the bed sits. He stops, pinning my back against one of the large pillars, and leans his forehead against mine. Both of us are breathing hard, chests slick and heaving. He slowly lowers me to the floor, steadying me with his big hands on my waist. He kisses me again, slower, though no less desperate. He kisses down the column of my throat before dipping his head to my breasts.

I gasp and buck my hips forward as he swirls his tongue over one hardened nipple, quickly taking it into his mouth and sucking deeply. I dig my fingers into his hair and writhe my hips. He releases me and I nearly whimper as he takes a step back. I watch raptly as he slowly sinks to his knees before me. My eyes go wide. Words said around a campfire all those months ago suddenly echo in my mind:

I kneel for no one.

"But...you don't kneel," I stammer.

"I kneel for no one—*but you*, Dahlia. I kneel *for you*. I am yours, body and soul, forever." Forever. The word sends a hollow sort of shiver through my spine but I ignore it and it drifts away into the distance like smoke on the wind. I stare at this man before me, the High General of the vampiric army, the most fearsome warlord in the history of our world, a Montclare prince...kneeling before me and calling himself mine. I swallow hard, the gravity of what this display truly means almost too heavy to bear. I'm his mate, but he's telling me that *he* belongs to *me*, not the other way around. It's...heady.

He leans forward and places a soft kiss on my stomach, just below my navel.

"Yours," he whispers. He kisses again, an inch lower. "*Yours, yours, yours...*" Each word is accompanied with an achingly tender kiss, trailing across my stomach, over my hip bones, just above the apex of my thighs. I'm trembling by the time he plants a final kiss so close to my quim that I make a strangled groaning sound that's honestly a bit embarrassing. He chuckles lightly against my skin, a dark, sensual laugh that sends shivers through my entire body.

"You might want to hold on to that pillar...soon you won't be able to stand, Dahlia. I promise you that."

"Wh-what?" I stutter, my heart hammering like Xerxes' hoofbeats.

"I said..." He leans in and flicks his tongue over my clit, making me cry out and buck my hips, "that I'm going to lick this pretty little pussy until your legs give out, love."

He holds my gaze and his lips curl up into the most devastating, sensual smirk I've ever seen.

"So, I'm advising you to *hold on tight*, Keeva."

CHAPTER 36
ALARIC

I watch as Dahlia swallows hard but reaches over her head and grips the pillar behind her. I smile, the sight so damned sexy that I can barely stand it.

"Good girl," I rasp and she whimpers quietly as I lean forward again and lift her left leg, resting it over my shoulder. I stare at her for a moment, marveling at the sight of my mate open and ready before me. My mate. I can't quite believe that she finally knows the truth, but it's as if a weight has been lifted from my chest. Of course, the whole of Braxhelm might very well know the truth as well, but that is a problem for another day.

Right now, I need to be with my mate. I need to touch and taste and convince myself that this is real. I'd been on the brink of death before she saved me, and then with her blood roiling in my veins like a great tempest, I'd ridden into battle. It had been a blur of screams and smoke and blood, and I'd felt like something bigger than myself, like a deity of war and death sent to earth to raze our enemies to dust for even daring to put my mate in danger. The battle fog and blood-lust had been almost too much to bear, and I'd been lost in some strange place between battle and life, knowing only that I needed

Dahlia in a way I've never needed anything or anyone in my life. I'd somehow teleported us here to Ashcliff without thought, only knowing that I wanted her far away from the battlefield and safe in my arms.

Even still, once I knew we were safely away, I couldn't quite come back to myself. It's difficult to explain, but it was as if I were being carried away on the waves of bloodlust and the fever of battle. But Dahlia had been my tether, keeping me from losing myself completely and ever so slowly bringing me back.

Now, I want nothing but to worship her for hours upon hours, days upon days; to kiss and lick and touch every last inch of her; to make her feel more pleasure than any human could possibly hope to feel in a lifetime; to claim her as my own in all ways and try to communicate what this all truly means; to show her, by word and deed, how much I love her.

I dip my head and run my tongue along her opening, one long, slow lap that makes her shudder and moan. Over and over, I take my time, savoring every taste, every touch. The noises she makes drive me mad and I'm already hard as stone, desperate to sink so far inside her that our bodies become one. I groan against her pussy at the thought, speeding up the flicks of my tongue. I close my lips around her clit and quickly slide two fingers inside her, pumping as I lick and suck.

"Ah gods, Alaric..." she rasps, grinding her hips against my mouth, holding onto the pillar behind her for dear life as—as I promised—her legs tremble and threaten to give out. She's close, I can tell, on the very cusp. I curl my fingers as I pump and she screams, coming apart beneath my ministrations. I can feel her come, clenching my fingers over and over. The leg not over my shoulder trembles so violently that I pick her up for fear that she'll collapse, and ease her onto the bed. I slide her upward until her head rests on the pillows and I'm thankful that I have such competent staff. I haven't visited Ashcliff in...fuck, it's been decades, I think, but they keep it ready at all times on the chance that I should desire to come home. The sheets are clean and crisp, freshly laundered and smelling faintly of roses.

I follow Dahlia down and she reaches out for me immediately, circling her arms around my neck and kissing me deeply. I'm still aware of how easily I could hurt her, especially now—taking so much of her blood has made me stronger than ever before—but a deep sense of surety that I won't settles over me.

This is right. This is necessary. This is fate.

"Need you, Alaric," she pants against my lips, skating one hand down my chest and stomach. My eyes slide closed for a moment and I simply revel in the feel of her hands on me, her warm skin against mine, her touch burning me in ways I never could have imagined. It's a burn that sears me to my soul, that renders me to ash and rebuilds me as something new, something wholly belonging to this woman alone. She is my reason for living now, my reason for existing. My entire world now centers on this perfect creature that the gods themselves deigned to be mine.

I hiss in a breath and my eyes snap open when her hand circles my cock. She wraps her palm around my shaft and begins to stroke, making me moan loudly, fingers digging into the bed on either side of her head. My claws rip into the sheets and I vaguely realize that Elias had been right about the fact that I'm physically incapable of harming her, that my body knows what to do even if my mind is lost to desire: my claws had retracted completely when I'd fingered Dahlia moments ago, without thought or command from me. The thought gives me solace and I give myself completely over to the needs tearing through me.

"*Fuck.*"

"So hard for me, your Highness," she says, a little breathless, flashing me a sultry half-grin.

I choke out a quiet laugh before leaning down and resting my forehead against hers. She sighs as she continues to stroke and when she swipes her thumb across the head and spreads the bead of moisture already there, I can't take it anymore. I kiss her then, hard and deep, beginning to burn with a frenzy I can't control. I push myself up onto straightened arms and have barely enough control left to ask her. I have to ask her. I need her to choose this, fully.

"Are you sure? This..." I trail off and gnash my teeth as she continues to stroke. I clear my throat. I have to get this out, to explain to her. "This is more than just...Gods, *be still*, Dahlia," I beg and she pouts. I lean down and nip gently at her bottom lip. "Once we do this, once I claim you...this is forever. There is no going back. Do you understand?"

She reaches out with her other hand and cups my cheek, holding my gaze. Before she even speaks, I know that this moment is one that will forever change the course of my eternal life, that will be seared into my memory for all time.

"Alaric, there is already no going back for me. I'm yours. I have been for...what feels like always," she says, brow furrowing a bit. "I know that doesn't make any kind of sense, but it's true. I'm yours. I always have been. I always will be."

I let out a ragged exhale and lean down to kiss her again.

"I'm ready, Alaric," she breathes and positions the head of my cock at her entrance, settling her other hand on my hip. I hiss in a sharp breath as the head kisses her wet heat.

And then, I let go completely, giving myself over to what my body desperately wants. What it *needs*. What the bond between us is demanding.

CHAPTER 37

DAHLIA

Alaric pushes inside and it's fucking glorious. And tight. And maybe a little uncomfortable. He's big. And big is an understatement, but it's a delicious kind of big. The kind that makes you quiver and ache and think about for the rest of your life.

He's been so careful to keep a tight rein on his control, but now, it's like something else has taken over. Something primal and possessive and beyond arousing. I worry for the briefest moment, those words from long ago echoing in my head:

I could kill you easily.

Easily?

Easier than breathing.

But I know, I *know*, that he won't hurt me. Even though his control has snapped, I feel into the depths of my soul that he can't hurt me, no matter what. He slides inside me in one long, measured thrust and I arch my hips upward at the pleasure of it, the fullness. My toes curl and I dig my fingers into his back, crying out in pleasure. He waits a moment, sweat beading on his forehead as he holds himself still.

"Al...right?" he chokes out and I can tell it's taking all of his strength to stop, to make sure I'm ok. I can only imagine what his instincts are screaming at him to do right now.

"Yes. More. *Please*, Alaric," I beg. It's a tight fit, but *my gods* does it feel euphoric. I don't want him to stop. I want him to keep going. I want him to give me everything he has to offer. To claim me. I'll admit, I don't know exactly what that means, but something deep inside my soul somehow understands even if my mind doesn't, and it fucking *yearns* for it.

He shudders all over at the words and then he starts moving, pulling back and slamming forward again. I gasp and moan, digging my nails into his skin and hiking my thigh over his hip. In and out, over and over, the sounds of our bodies coming together, the harsh echoes of our breathing, and the popping of the wood in the fire the only sounds in the room. Our chests slide together, slick with sweat, my hair sticking to my temples with it. He grasps my wrists and moves my hands away from his back, pinning them above my head. My entire body arches up to meet his as he thrusts, both of my wrists locked in one of his big hands. The other grips my thigh, shifting it higher on his hip and allowing him to move even deeper.

"Gods, you feel so good, Keeva. Been waiting centuries for you," he pants before kissing me again. Our lips crashing together as he pounds on and on.

"Alaric, oh gods, right there..." I can feel my orgasm building already, that tight coiling in my belly like a snake preparing to strike. He pushes himself up and holds my gaze, and then I turn my head, exposing my neck. He groans, as if it's the most glorious thing he's ever seen, but like he isn't sure...

"Please," I beg. "Please, Alaric. It's yours. I'm yours. I want you to..."

That snaps whatever was holding him back and he leans down, kissing and licking before sinking his fangs deep into my throat.

I scream something unintelligible, my back bowing at the most intense pleasure I've ever felt. My orgasm rips through my body like an explosion, leaving nothing but ash and smoke in its wake. He sucks and pounds, groaning against my skin, and...and...

"Alaric," I gasp. "It won't stop...I can't stop..."

The orgasm goes on and on, not crashing down as it usually does but somehow building and building, like an enormous wave. My entire body convulses, the pleasure so intense it's nearly painful, but I never want it to stop. The feel of his fangs, the pull as he drinks, the feel of his cock thrusting and filling me—it's all too much.

I scream again as the orgasm intensifies, slamming into me like a battering ram. That tidal wave finally crashes and it shatters me completely, my entire body and soul splintering into a thousand tiny pieces and drifting out into the ether.

"Keeva!" Alaric roars, and I feel him come in a rush, shattering with me. He pounds harder, slamming between my hips as he pumps so deep inside. My climax finally subsides, as Alaric's does, both of us slowly coming back to earth. He collapses atop me, burying his face in my neck, licking the spot where his fangs were just moments ago lazily, his body shuddering every few moments. My body is a bone-less puddle, and all I can do is trace my fingers along his back as I fight to catch my breath and make sense of what the seven hells just happened.

He exhales heavily and rolls to the side, pulling me with him so that we're face to face. He reaches out and strokes my cheek gently, pushing hair away from my face and running a finger along my nose, then my lips, then my cheek bone. It's as if he's trying to convince himself that I'm really here, that this is really happening.

"Did I hurt you?" he asks quietly, a note of real fear in his voice.

"Not at all," I say and he gives me a look. "I will probably be a little sore—I'm not sure if you're aware of this or not, but you have a *giant* cock, High General." He laughs loudly at that, smiling in a way that I've never seen before and I can't help but grin back. "—but no, you didn't hurt me. You didn't grind my bones to dust or drain me dry." He flinches and I reach out and cup his cheek, loving the feel of his scruff beneath my palm. "I'm fine, Alaric. That was...gods, that was amazing."

He studies me for a long minute. "You're...sure?"

I lean forward and kiss him, slow and languid, and he runs his hands over my body leisurely, exploring every curve.

"So...so, it's true then? I'm...your mate?" He'd implied it before, and the truth of it was evident by his survival from the silver poisoning, but I need to hear him say it. I need to hear the words from his lips, no one else's.

"Yes," he says, running his fingers through my hair. "I don't know how—I've never heard of a human mate before—but there is no doubt. These things are...it's difficult to explain, but our kind have instincts that are never wrong and cannot be denied." Takara explained it to me as best she could back at the camp when I awake. "I thought for a time I could deny them, that I could keep myself away from you and not acknowledge what was screaming inside of me, but it was inevitable. You are mine, Dahlia. You have been since the dawn of time, since both of our souls were but specs of stardust in the heavens."

"You believe that?" I ask, propping my head up on one hand.

"I do. I never truly understood until I found you, but now it makes all the sense in the world. My soul and yours were destined to be together, even before we existed on this earth."

I think about that, about how it's felt as if a part of me had been missing until I found him, how I only feel completely whole when Alaric is by my side. I know humans don't have mates, but it's as if somehow the same instincts that reside in him somehow guide me as well.

"Well, that's very sweet and tender and I will be sure to spread the word that the High General is a hopelessly romantic fool."

He laughs again, throwing his head back and pulling me atop him. I balance myself with my hands splayed on his chest and he wraps a hand around my nape, guiding me slowly down to kiss him.

Slower this time, deeper. We take the next few hours to explore and worship and learn every inch of each other properly.

"Wait here," he says after another shaking orgasm has turned me completely immobile.

"I couldn't move even if I wanted to," I grumble. He laughs and kisses my forehead before leaving the bed. I turn my head enough to admire the view of him stalking naked across the room to the closet. *Dear gods is there any bit of this man that isn't sexy?*

He emerges and to my dismay is in low-hanging pants and tugging a sweater over his head.

"Where are you going?"

"To get my mate some food. I need you at full strength for what I have in store for you," he whispers as he ducks down to kiss me again. I shiver at the thought and he chuckles as he pulls away. "I'll be back shortly."

I sigh and somehow manage to muster enough strength to roll onto my back and pull the thick fur blanket over me. I sink into the plush mattress, practically numb with pleasure, and let everything that's happened wash over me. My lids get heavy and I drift off into the most blissful sleep I've had in months.

"Keeva," Alaric whispers and I feel a gentle stroke down the bridge of my nose. I wrinkle it and groan, sinking deeper into the pillows. I hear his deep chuckle and he strokes my nose again. "Wake, Keeva...I brought bacon."

I perk up at that, my stomach taking all control over my actions. I pry my eyes open and find a grinning Alaric above me. I stretch my arms over my head and smile at him.

"There you are. You slept like the dead. I thought perhaps I pleasured you into a coma."

I try to scowl at him, but can't help but laugh. It's nearly true.

"I believe you mentioned bacon?" I say, attempting to remain aloof.

"Over here," he says with a smirk, pulling the covers away. I grumble curses but the smells that reach my nose make them all dissolve away. I leap from the bed and grin when I hear Alaric's low growl of appreciation. I put a little extra roll in my hips as I stride to the table by the fireplace laden with enough food to feed twenty people.

"Dahlia," he says, somewhere between a warning and a prayer. "Behave or you'll be back in this bed in seconds..."

"You say that as if it's a threat, High General," I retort over my shoulder, and suddenly he's at my back, wrapping his arms around me and pulling me against his chest. I can feel him hard against my lower back and my eyes slide closed. He leans down and kisses my neck, making me gasp.

"If I didn't have the innate desire to take care of my mate in all ways," he whispers against my skin, making me shiver, "I'd bend you over this table and fuck you until your screams shake the rafters." I groan and wiggle my ass against him, food suddenly forgotten and wanting nothing but what he's promised. "*But*," he says pointedly, stilling my hips with his big hands, "you must eat. So, again I tell you, *behave*."

"Only if you promise to make good on that threat after I've been sufficiently nourished."

"Anything you wish, Keeva." With that, he releases me and I sigh, but continue on to the table. Before I reach it, Alaric is there again, pulling a robe over my shoulders. "Even my need to keep you healthy is not enough to keep my hands off of you if you sit there unclothed."

I laugh and pull the robe tighter around me. I settle into one of the large chairs and dig into the food. I can't remember the last time that I ate—before I ran to the battle?—and I'm suddenly famished.

"Have you spoken to Elias? Was everything well at the battle after you and I...left? Oh gods, Takara and the guard must be so worried. Are Wesley and Nova ok??"

"All is well, do not worry. Elias made for Ashcliff—that's where we are, by the way. Our home on the Lyranian Sea—as soon as you and I teleported from the battle." I look at him in surprise. "He had a feeling that I would bring you here, to get you as far from there as possible but somewhere I knew was safe. He arrived early this morning while you slept. The Revenant forces were decimated, my miraculous return from the brink of death a severe blow to whatever advantage they thought they had after that arrow—" He cuts off, as if worried that speaking of it will upset me.

"It's ok," I tell him, putting my fork down and pulling my knees up into the chair. "How did it happen?"

"Silver powder on a specially made arrow that can penetrate my armor." I run my finger over the ring that da gave me, a cold pit forming in my stomach. *They have arrows that can pierce Alaric's impenetrable armor—and fucking* silver??

"Where in the hells did they get silver? I thought it was all but gone from the entire continent, the entire world. And that the Mont-clares controlled what little remains?"

"We thought the same, but months ago we found evidence that the Revenants had been digging in some caves far out in the wilds. We had no idea for what, but it turns out that they found a long-buried store of silver there. We have reports that Kilgren was in a rage state when he learned that his attempt had failed—though of course the coward fled the battle before I could find him." His voice shakes with fury and I can feel how badly he wanted to end the Revenant leader, end this entire war once and for all. "So, I can't imagine they have much silver left, if any. The arrows, too, must be in short supply."

"Well thank the fucking gods for that," I say, a little breathless. Images of Alaric, poisoned and dying on that bed, flash behind my eyes and I rub at the sudden ache in my chest. *It had been so close, I'd almost been too late, I'd almost lost him...*

I push myself away from the table and crawl into his lap, suddenly desperate to erase those memories, to prove that he's safe and whole and alive in my arms. He wraps his arms around me, understanding exactly what I need, and rests his chin on the top of my head as I snuggle into his warm chest. He strokes my back lightly.

"Your Keeper and guard are on their way here now. Wesley and Nova as well. They will arrive shortly."

I pull back to look at him, confused. "Are we…staying here?"

"For a time, yes. The Revenants will not be attacking again any time soon after that defeat, and," he brushes hair away from my face, almost reverently, and it makes my chest clench, "I need time with my mate, away from a war camp."

My lips curl into a smile and I shift in his lap to wrap my arms around his neck. I kiss him softly, sucking gently on his bottom lip and I can feel him shoot hard beneath me again.

"Mmmm," I murmur against his lips but then other needs make themselves known. "Ah, hold this thought. I have to be a pesky human with pesky human needs for a few moments." Then I remember. "Speaking of, why oh why, did you already have a privy in your bathing chamber?" I ask with a quirked brow. "I thought princes didn't entertain humans?" I give him a pointed look.

He rolls his eyes. "That was added very, very recently at the discreet request of my most faithful but overzealous First Lieutenant who chaps my ass at every turn…but I suppose is actually very thoughtful and deserves to be thanked." So Elias has known for a while then. Interesting.

"And the staff didn't think anything of such a request?"

"It is not their place to question the requests of a prince—whom I'm sure Elias said the request was actually coming from." I mull that over and he sets me off of his lap. "Go on then, human. Do what thy will." He gives a very haughty wave of his hand and I can't help but laugh. Gods I love this playful side of him. I turn and stroll towards the bathroom, accidentally dropping my robe in the process. I smirk when I hear him growl behind me and shiver a bit at the thought of what he might do when I emerge again.

CHAPTER 38

ALARIC

Elias and I go through some business while Dahlia naps. I was worried that perhaps I'd been a little too...zealous in these first few days, but despite her mortal body's need for rest, my mate is damn near insatiable. I have an errant thought, imagining the possibilities if she were a vampire, her strength and stamina closer to my own, and shudder before I scowl, pushing the thought firmly away. That is an impossibility and I refuse to entertain it, even for the briefest of moments inside my own mind.

"And all of the funeral rites have been performed?"

"Yes, it's all been taken care of. The wounded have all healed, and replacements for those lost are on their way to the camp now. I put Bracken in charge in my absence."

"Good. And scouting reports?"

"No movement from the Revenant stronghold. Looks like Kilgren is sulking with his tail between his legs after the defeat. Once he stopped all his raging of course—reports say he killed fifty of his own men in an incoherent rampage after he saw you appear back on the field. He must have really thought this was to be it, he was going to finally break through and claim a victory against you."

"He would have," I say seriously, absently rubbing the heel of my hand over the spot where the arrow had pierced me, "if not for Dahlia. Everything could have turned out so differently. It could have meant the end of…everything."

"I know," he says somberly, sipping his blood. "I know, Alaric. I think about it far more than I'd like to admit. Don't ever fucking do that to me again, by the way."

I smile at him and incline my head. "I shall do my best."

"Speaking of our fair Dahlia…" He waggles his eyebrows and I roll my eyes. "Come now, you can't deny how different you are since finally claiming your mate, brother. It's…astonishing, really."

I exhale roughly and run my fingers through my hair, remembering Dahlia's fingers pulling at the strands earlier as I feasted on her on the edge of the tub in our bathing chamber. My lips curl at the memory.

"It's…I can't explain it, Elias. It's like I am finally whole after having a piece of me missing my entire life. Not just any piece, the most important one."

"I'm happy for you." He takes another sip, swirling crimson around his goblet. "And what does Sebastian think of all of this?"

My lips press into a hard line. I open my mouth to speak but whirl as the doors to my study fly open and I see Sebastian himself striding into the room as if we'd summoned him by simply speaking his name. My stomach clenches: I hadn't expected him to arrive so soon after receiving my correspondence. I honestly don't know what he'll think about any of this. The laws of matehood are some of our most revered, but Dahlia being human throws quite a kink into things. I have a good idea of what he'll want me to do, but I will refuse and I don't want there to be a fight. It's a fight I will have if need be, but I don't want it.

"Sebastian thinks that this is fucking insane," my brother says in answer to Elias' question, shrugging out of his coat. Alora, the head of my staff, is at his heels, taking his coat and looking at me apologetically.

Elias and I both rise to our feet, inclining our heads to my brother. Sebastian claps Elias on the shoulder first in greeting before turning to me.

"Heard you almost left us forever, brother." His voice is tight with emotion.

"It was closer than I'd like to admit, yes." He nods and I can see the tension at the corners of his mouth, uncomfortable with the thought.

"Well, let's not do that again, shall we?" He pulls me into a bear hug, nearly cracking several ribs, and I squeeze him back fiercely. He pulls back after a few moments and studies me before adding, "Especially now that you have a mate to look after."

Elias clears his throat and sets his glass down on the table before gesturing towards Alora.

"You know, I had a question about the, uh, soap in my room, if I might ask for your assistance, dearest Alora." He flashes her a winning smile, the one that can get any female—and most males—to do exactly what he wants. She flushes slightly and nods, understanding that he's trying to get both of them out of the way as efficiently as possible.

"O-of course, sir."

Elias gives me a look that clearly says *good luck*, inclines his head to Sebastian, and bolts out of the room with Alora, leaving Sebastian and me alone.

"Well, offer me a damned drink, Alaric. Gods almighty, I get a letter saying that you almost died—from *silver poisoning* of all things, from the tip of an arrow that penetrated your impenetrable armor—but that you survived because of your mate—who also happens to be your fucking human *Consort*—and then I rode like the devil straight here. So, a drink, if you please, little brother. A blasted strong one."

My lips quirk and I'm relieved that he isn't entirely irate with me. Not that I have any control over who my mate might be, of course, but he still has every right to be angry. Or at least perturbed. It's a...precarious situation. I pour him a blood whisky and hand it to him as he sinks heavily into the chair before the fire. He takes a deep drink and I wait, easing into the chair opposite him.

"Ok, out with it. How did this happen?"

I snort. "What the devil do you mean how did this happen? Fate is a fickle wench apparently, that's how."

He barks out a laugh. "You knew at the Choosing?" I nod. "Why didn't you say anything then, Alaric?"

I rub the back of my neck. "I...well, I was hoping I was wrong, honestly."

"And after you realized that you weren't?"

"I decided to forsake the bond. I refused to acknowledge it for months." His brows hike up so high they're hidden beneath his light hair.

"That's...impossible, is it not?"

"It was...difficult, yes," I admit. "But having her in the camp at least allowed me to protect her." *Mostly*, I think darkly, remembering the attack on the road. Fury simmers deep in my chest. I will pay Kilgren back for that one day, if it's the last thing I ever do on this earth. "So, it was worth the torture. For a time. But then things began to shift and...fuck, Bastian, it isn't only the mating bond—I'm in love with her."

He blinks, watching me for long moments in that analytical way he has.

"And she saved your life? From the silver?"

"Yes. I nearly drained her fucking dry, honestly, but she was ready to give her life for mine."

"Then I owe her my thanks," he says somberly.

"I owe her my life, in so many different ways."

"So you've claimed her then?" I swallow hard but square my shoulders.

"Yes, I have." *Thirty-seven times, give or take...*

"And you, ah, haven't...hurt her?"

"No," I assure him, "She is well. Sleeping now." He lets his head fall back against the chair and exhales, long and slow.

"This is...quite the situation, indeed. There has never been a human mate at all that I'm aware of, let alone a *prince's* mate. You know we don't partake in those particular desires with humans." I give him a pointed look and he rolls his eyes. "You know what I mean. *Officially* we do not. What happens behind closed doors is another matter and is something for each prince to deal with, but publicly, as the head of the Clan, I say that we do not fuck our Consorts or any other human." I grind my teeth. "But," he adds, "a mate trumps almost everything else in our world, you know this. So...we will adapt." I look at him incredulously. "What? How else do we survive for millennia? We must change as the world does, Alaric."

I let out a breath, feeling the tension inside me ease, but then the inevitable question arises.

"Will you try the turning, then?"

"Absolutely not."

"Alaric—"

"No, Bastian. I will not risk her life—again." He clenches his jaw and I can see the anger simmering in his golden eyes.

"So you will sentence yourself to certain death then?"

I grind my teeth. I've gone over this a thousand times in my mind. There are only two options: leave Dahlia human and spend as much time with her as possible before she dies—hopefully of natural causes many years from now—and follow her after; or attempt the turning and take the chance of her dying in the process now.

"There is a good chance she will survive, Alaric. You could have eternity with her."

"And if she doesn't?" I snap. "If we attempt and she dies tomorrow?? I cannot do it Bastian, I need...gods, I need more time with her."

"You could have forever with her if the turning works," he points out.

"*If.* Are you ready to lose me so soon, brother? Because make no mistake, I will not live without her. Not for a single fucking moment. Where she goes from this day forward, I will follow—even if that is to the grave."

Sebastian exhales roughly and downs his drink.

"There is no easy answer here, is there?"

"No," I sigh. "No, there isn't. Of course I want to spend eternity with her by my side, but the thought of losing her in an attempt to have that chance terrifies me in ways I cannot explain, Bastian."

He sighs and shakes his head a little ruefully. "Leave it to you to find yourself in this mess. You always did have to be different, didn't you, little brother?"

"All will be well, Bastian. Whether I have a year with her or fifty, it will be the best time of my very long life, of that I am sure." He watches me through narrowed eyes.

"You've become quite a romantic sap now that you've found your mate, Alaric."

"Fuck off," I say, smiling.

"Now that you lot are finished with official business, can I please hug my stupidly reckless brother?" I blink in surprise as Fiona storms into the room. I glance at Bastian and he gives me a look that says *as if I can control the little devil.*

I leap to my feet and wrap her in a hug, squeezing her tightly. She hugs me back fiercely and when she pulls away, pink-tinged tears stand in her eyes. She wipes them away and swats me in the chest.

"Don't fucking do that again, damn you!"

"Why does everyone act as if I *wanted* to get shot with a poisoned arrow? As if I thought it sounded like a jolly old time?" She ignores my question and looks around the room, arms crossed.

"And where is your mate then?" I run my hand through my hair and exhale in irritation.

"Does everyone know then?"

Fi pats my cheek indulgently, as if I'm a child. "Only the important ones, dear brother. Not to worry. But where is she? I only got to see her from afar at the Choosing."

"She's resting," I grate, wondering what Dahlia is going to make of having my most headstrong sister here. Fi waggles her light brows at me.

"I'll bet she is, you dog."

"FI," I warn, exasperated already.

"Alright, alright. I promise to be on my best behavior, sir." She gives me a mock salute and I can't help but huff out a laugh.

We talk about this and that for a while, catching up on Clan business and Fiona supplying plenty of gossip from Astoria's Keep. I tell them both all about Dahlia and our...courtship I suppose you could call it.

"Well, I love her already," Fi says, grinning over a glass of blood-laced wine. I inhale sharply when I sense Dahlia begin to wake and Bastian laughs, knowing exactly what's going on, though Fi looks a bit confused.

"Go, brother. Get your mate, we will see you later."

"You're staying?"

"For a few days, yes. I need to meet your Dahlia properly—and shield her from this she-demon," he says, tilting his head towards Fiona. She makes an indignant huffing sound and throws a pillow at him. His eyes sparkle with a mischief that makes my stomach drop. I point an accusatory finger at him.

"No stories about me as a child, Bastian. I mean it."

"I would never," he says, full of feigned innocence.

"I certainly would though," Fi adds with a grin, and the two of them look at each other, falling into a fit of laughter. The three of us have always been closer than any of our other siblings and I can't explain how nice it is to have them both here, to have my whole family here within my home. I feel content in a way I never thought possible.

But now, I need to go wake my mate properly.

CHAPTER 39

DAHLIA

Life is practically perfect. We've been at Ashcliff for a little over a week now and it's feeling more and more like home. I know we can't stay forever, but it's nice to know that this is waiting for us any time Alaric can step away from battle for a time. We've had plenty of company—namely Sebastian Montclare (who thankfully did not seem upset that a human turned out to be his brother's mate), and Alaric's sister, Fiona, who I adore already. She'd hugged me fiercely the moment we walked into the sitting room.

"I just want you to know that I don't care if you're human or a shifter or a mermaid for fuck's sake—though I would have many anatomical questions if that were the case—I've never seen my brother even close to this happy before and you are the reason for it. Some of the others might have more...thoughts on the matter, but fuck them, yeah?" I'd huffed out a nervous laugh, surprised by her acceptance and overall demeanor. She reminded me a bit of Wesley, so I felt instantly at ease. Her mother must have come from the old Selkish Isles, her accent a bit similar to da's, but much more lyrical and lilting. Her hair is a deeper shade of red than my own, her skin pale as ivory and her features delicate.

"Cassandra always has a stick up her ass about everything, so don't let her reactions bother you too much. Plus, one day I'm sure you'll be one of us anyway," she'd said lightly and Alaric growled fiercely behind her, snapping his fangs. I'd narrowed my eyes at his reaction, but Fiona had merely rolled her hers. Fi and Takara had apparently been friends for nearly a century while Takara had served the Montclares at the palace in Astoria's Keep, so the two of them spent lots of time together, laughing and telling old stories.

The rest of the guard had arrived with Takara, with Wesley and Nova arriving not far behind. I'd nearly come out of my skin when they'd gotten here, flying down the stairs so quickly only Nova's quick reflexes had saved me from tumbling and probably breaking a few bones. Alaric had muttered something about fragility, but I'd ignored him, throwing my arms around my friends.

"I was so worried," I breathed, squeezing them both as tightly as I could. When I'd pulled away, they had both stiffened and bowed to Alaric.

"Sir, thank you for granting us liberty and, uh, inviting us to your home," Nova said.

"Home? More like fucking castle," Wesley muttered, eyes roving around the entry. Nova had elbowed him in the ribs and he'd cleared his throat. "I mean, yes, thank you, sir." I glanced to Alaric who looked a little uncomfortable with the gratitude, and smiled at him. I'd mentioned being worried about them since I hadn't seen them since well before the battle and he offered to have them come and stay for a time. Things were entirely quiet on the Revenant front after the great loss when Alaric had—from what Takara had told me— destroyed their forces like some avenging warrior god, so he assured me they could be spared from the front lines of the camp without worry.

"Is it true?" Wesley had whispered as I'd shown them around the...hells, it really is a castle, I must admit. "Are you really...his??"

I'd bitten my lip as I'd eyed them both and Nova had jumped up and down clapping.

"I knew it!!"

"You did not," Wesley had said, rolling his eyes.

"I did too! Or, well, I suspected maybe. I knew there was definite attraction there, at least."

I let out a long, almost ragged exhale. "Attraction is quite the understatement."

"Details. All of them. Now." Nova and I glanced to Wesley, wearing what I was sure were identical expressions of surprise. He held up his hands. "What? You've seen the man! No one is immune. Plus, you know I don't discriminate: man, woman, human, vampire —I love *everyone*." He'd grinned and Nova and I had laughed. She assured me that she was all healed from the injury she'd sustained in the battle—a deep cut through her thigh—and that she was going to receive some kind of award for valor because she saved some captain's life.

Alaric and I have been nearly inseparable save the times he meets with Elias or needs to attend to High General duties, and I've never been so happy in all my life. The question of what happens with us later hangs in the corners of our happiness, but neither of us wants to address it just yet. We just want to live in this beautiful bubble we've found at Ashcliff for a little longer. I know what I want but I know that Alaric is going to have...thoughts on the matter if his reaction to Fiona's words are any indication.

I lie with my head on his chest now, my body still shuddering lightly after the intense string of orgasms this man managed to wring from me just moments ago. He brushes his finger over the puncture marks on my neck where his fangs had sank in so deliciously while he pumped into me from behind. I shiver at the memory and at his touch.

"Your healing is slowing to normal again," he observes. I'd been healing almost immediately after the attack on the road, but the effects of his blood have waned over time. He pricks the pad of his thumb with a fang and swipes the blood over the wounds, and I feel them knit back together.

"Mmm," I say, letting my lids flutter closed. "Good thing you're around to heal me then." He traces shapes along my back.

"So sleepy already, Keeva?" he muses, skating his fingers over the curves of my ass and making me perk up. *Oh that reminds me.*

"I know you lied," I say, opening my eyes and shifting so I can look up at him. His brows furrow. "I heard from...someone," I say vaguely, not wanting to reveal my source, "that *Keeva* doesn't mean my name in the old vampire language."

He sighs, lips curling. "No, it doesn't," he admits, stroking a stray curl from my cheek. "It was Fi, wasn't it?" I make a motion as if I'm locking my lips tightly and throwing away the key. He chuckles lightly. "It means *mine.* It's a...term of endearment, I guess you could call it, for a vampire's mate."

A tingle of excitement and joy shoot through my body every time he reminds me that I'm his, that this is real. Suddenly not tired in the slightest, I roll on top of him and settle my knees on either side of his waist. He's already hard again beneath me and I bite my lip, toes curling in anticipation. I lean down and kiss him lazily, rolling my tongue against his, biting and sucking on his bottom lip.

"Mmmm, *Keeva,*" he rasps, putting extra emphasis on the name he's called me since the beginning, the only way he had to claim me as his for so long. Something about it makes my chest clench and my pulse race. I rise up and quickly maneuver myself above him, sliding down his shaft in one long, slow movement. He throws his head back and groans, hands gripping my hips as I begin to move. Up and down, up and down, riding his cock in a deep, steady rhythm.

"You're mine too, Alaric," I rasp. Not in the way of the vampires of course, but he's mine in all the ways that matter, in all the ways a man can possibly belong to a woman. "*Mine.*" Eventually, I increase the speed, leaning back and bracing my hands on his thighs behind me.

"Yours," he pants. "Yours, Dahlia. Always." He slides one hand from my hip and begins to massage my clit, making me cry out and buck my hips, whipping them in a frenzy as the pleasure builds and builds.

"Ah, just like that, Alaric. Don't stop…"

"Gods the sight of you above me, riding me…" A low growl rumbles in his chest and I dig my nails into his thighs. "You take my cock so well, Dahlia. Look at you…" His words make a fresh wave of wet heat flood through me, soaking him, and pushes me right over the edge.

"Alaric!" I cry as I career over the cliff into another endless pool of ecstasy. He grips my hips and bucks his own up once, twice, three times before roaring my name and coming hard. I collapse onto his chest, panting and blinking the stars away from my vision.

"Gods, will this ever ebb?" I ask. "This…intensity? This constant need?" No matter how many times we're together, no matter how many climaxes rip through my body until I can literally no longer stand or move, it's never enough.

"I don't know," he says between gasping breaths. "I don't think so." He strokes my spine and my heart slowly begins to return to a normal rhythm. "It's a common, ah, trait of matehood."

I laugh lightly, and then harder, shoulders shaking beneath his hands. He pulls me upright so he can look at me in confusion.

"What's so funny?"

"It's just…a trait of matehood is to fuck like rabbits??" His lips curl into a slow, sexy grin.

"I suppose that's one way to put it, yes." And then he's laughing with me, the two of us sprawled across the bed, laughing until my sides hurt. A knock at the door finally pulls us from our hysterics and once we're sufficiently covered in a silk sheet, Alaric calls for whoever it is to enter.

It's Livia, one of the humans who works for Alaric. I smile and wave and she gives me a tentative smile in return. She's young, maybe seventeen, and a little shy, but I've been trying to put her at ease. I think she took this job with the understanding that she would basically never be around the prince, so our arrival sent her into a bit of a spiral. She's coming around though, and I hope that we'll be friends.

She bows her head. "I'm sorry to interrupt you sir, but..." She cuts her eyes quickly to me, lips curling before she looks back to Alaric. "The, uh, *package*, is nearly here. Perhaps thirty minutes or so."

"Excellent, thank you." She ducks her head and scurries from the room.

"Package?" I ask with a quirk of my brow, but Alaric is already off the bed and tugging me with him. "What are you doing?" I exclaim, but erupt into a fit of squeals and giggles when he tosses me over his shoulder and smacks my ass playfully.

"We need to shower and then I have a surprise for you."

My eyes light up. "A surprise??"

"Yes, a surprise, but one you cannot receive naked and smelling of sex, you little harlot."

"Harlot?? Oooh, you'll pay for that one, your highness..."

"I look forward to it," he says sensually as he slowly slides me down his body in front of the shower. "But for now—bathe," he says sternly.

good one. I surely should have thought of it myself, but I've been... distracted, to say the least. Sometimes Dahlia and I spend days at a time in bed, forgetting nearly everything and everyone else in the world. The others have been entirely understanding and have managed to entertain themselves about the castle and the sea below. Nova, Wesley, Takara and Dahlia's guard had taken one of my smaller ships out to the islands not far off the coast a few days ago and they've been very liberal with my stores of wine and whisky. Bastian and Fiona left for Astoria's Keep to work on spreading the news of my new mate to the others and addressing any issues that come up.

"I don't like being patient," she grumbles. I lean down low and plant a soft kiss just below her ear, grinning when she shivers.

In a low whisper I say, "I have ways to teach you patience, Dahlia...they involve you tied to our bed and me bringing you just to the brink over and over and over, but never quite letting you fall..." She inhales sharply and I laugh before nipping at the shell of her ear and straightening.

"You are truly evil," Elias mutters from beside us.

Dahlia swallows hard and smooths her hair, trying to act nonchalant but her pulse is racing. She clears her throat lightly and, without looking at me, says, "I would like to learn, I think..."

I clench my jaw and a low growl rumbles in the back of my throat. The thought is enough to make me hard as stone and I have to shift my stance and adjust myself. Elias barks out a laugh beside me, not even attempting to hide it with a cough.

"Bastard," I grumble but then he and I both straighten when we hear steps outside. Dahlia can't hear them, but notices our shift and watches the door like a hawk.

"I'll go get the others," Elias says quietly, clapping me on the shoulder and heading down one of the hallways leading from the entry. Alora hurries to the door and with a look to me for approval, pulls it open.

Dahlia makes a sound that is somewhere between a gasp and a sob, flying to the door as her sister and father step through.

"Enid!!" she cries, flinging her arms around the girl and hugging her so tightly I fear she might bruise her. I can feel the love and elation pulsing from my mate and it warms me to the core of my soul. I knew she missed her family of course, but I hadn't fathomed the depths of her loss and aching heart until this moment. I will find ways to make these visits more frequent if it makes Dahlia happy.

Arwan Clayburn stands behind his daughters, smiling widely, his green eyes, so like Dahlia's, shining with tears. He catches my eye and inclines his head and I return the gesture. I will never be able to properly thank this man for giving me the most precious thing in my life.

Dahlia finally breaks away from her sister, holding her at arms' length to look her over for a moment before turning to her father. The two share a look before he gathers her up into his arms.

"Ah, I've missed ye, my wee firebrand," he whispers into her hair.

Enid is still grinning but it falters slightly when she glances my way. She dips into a curtsey, bowing her head in respect. When she straightens, I incline my head and smile at her. Blood floods her cheeks, blushing just the way Dahlia does. They don't look very much alike save that blush, but the girl is beautiful to be sure. Her eyes are a deep brown with striations of warm amber, her hair long and almost the same shade of chocolate as her eyes. She's more pixie-like than Dahlia, her features more delicate. She has an overall gentler air about her than her sister, and I don't know if that's just her natural disposition, if it's a residual effect of her bout of illness from her childhood, or if she chose to be more reserved to counteract Dahlia's fiery personality. Perhaps I'll learn during this visit.

The others come into the entry then, and Enid's gaze slides from me to just over my left shoulder, her eyes lighting up in excitement.

"Wesley!?" she exclaims as the vampire sprints over and picks her up, twirling her around and making her laugh. Nova, Takara, Malcom, Viktor, and Cyrus walk over and a flurry of introductions happen all at once, everyone talking over each other.

Elias steps up beside me, having just come back into the room and hands me a glass.

"Thought you could use a—"

He cuts off with a gasp and his glass slips from his fingers. I react far quicker than anyone else in the room could have thanks to all of Dahlia's blood still running through my system, and catch it before it shatters. I straighten, brows furrowed.

"What the hells, Elias?" He's staring as if he's mesmerized, as a blind man might stare at a sunset for the first time after regaining his sight—directly at Enid. I look between him and Dahlia's sister, listening to the thundering of his heart, see the lengthening of his fangs, and realization dawns. "No..." I breathe, incredulous.

Elias swallows hard, blinking rapidly as if trying to clear his vision, as if he thinks that what he's seeing before him must surely be a lie.

"My gods, what is it about this fucking family?..." I mutter. Are human mates becoming common? Is it just *this* particular bloodline? Are the Clayburns special in some way that we don't understand? Halfling children between vampires and humans are said to be impossible but...maybe that's not completely true either. Maybe there was a vampire ancestor somewhere in Dahlia's line.

I have no real answers, but I do know that there is no doubt that my best friend has just found his mate.

"I...I don't..." Elias stammers. Fucking *stammers*. I have never seen this man anything even approaching flustered in all of our almost four hundred years and now he looks down right panicked. He turns to me, wild-eyed. "What the fuck do I do, Alaric??"

Dahlia turns to me then, smiling through tears of happiness and I know she expects me to join in the celebration.

I turn to Elias and say quietly, "for now, we entertain our guests." I squeeze his shoulder. "Focus on your control, brother. All will be well," I say, smirking, repeating his words to me from all those months ago when he so casually insisted everything would turn out alright for Dahlia and me.

"Seven hells..." he says on a rough exhale, but I can see him calling on his training, on the quiet and often underestimated strength he possesses. He runs a hand through his hair and then we stride over to join in the introductions.

"MATE? YOU CANNOT BE SERIOUS!" Dahlia says as she steps into the tub, a soft moan escaping her lips as she slides into the hot water. Steam and the scent of ice lilies fill the air, and I lock my muscles into place as I watch her sink beneath the soft layer of bubbles coating the surface of the bath. With all of the visitors and Dahlia wanting to spend much deserved time with her sister and father after so many months apart, we haven't had much time together in days. It feels like years. Centuries. Eons. I don't mind the time with our friends—because, yes, somehow they've become mine as well—and family, as strange a group as they are, but I've missed my mate desperately.

"Does the news bother you?" I ask, watching her like a hawk as she glides through the water towards me. Her hair is piled high on her head, soft droplets of water beading on her delicate, exposed throat. I clench my jaw and dig my claws into the stone back of the tub where my arms are spread wide.

She purses her lips, considering the question. "No, I suppose it doesn't. I love Elias and I know for a fact that you lot can control yourselves around your mates now," she says with a sultry grin, "but..." Her brow furrows.

"What is it?" I ask as she finally reaches me, settling on to the low submerged bench beside me and throwing her legs over my lap. I stroke her soft skin, and even this small contact sends shocks of plea-sure rippling through my body. She shivers and I know that she hasn't been unaffected by the break from our bed.

"Well, she's practically engaged to another man, for starters, and Enid takes her promises very seriously. If she's made them to Leland, it won't be easy for her to break them..." Her lips curl up. "Though I have a feeling Elias can be *very* convincing when he wants to be."

I laugh lightly. "You have no idea. He once convinced an entire blood house to...actually, you don't want to know."

She grins. "I'll have that story one day." Then she looks thought-ful. "If their bond is anything like ours, Enid must be feeling things towards Elias already as well...and if he makes her happy, then that's all that matters to me. She might have made promises to Leland, but between you and me, I know she was settling and doesn't particu-larly love the man."

"If their bond is anything like ours," I say, reaching out to brush a stray hair from her temple, "then he will stop at nothing to see her happy in all ways." She gives me a soft smile and then purses her lips.

"How will that even work? He can't just run off to Astoria's Keep and be with her, he has lots of responsibilities serving under a tyrannical warlord..." She yelps and giggles when I pull her over my lap, settling her thighs on either side of my hips. She hisses in a breath and wraps her arms around my shoulders.

"*Tyrannical warlord, am I?*" I demand, freeing her hair from its knot and wrapping the long strands around my wrist, using the hold to pull her head back, exposing her throat. I lean in and kiss her neck, licking and grazing my fangs along her skin, slowly teasing her until she's digging her nails into my shoulders and gasping.

"Absolute slave driver, I've heard," she whispers between soft, panting breaths.

"Hmm," I rumble, reaching between us and quickly thrusting two fingers inside her. She moans loudly, bucking her hips against my hand, begging for me.

"Do you...think that...ah gods, *don't stop*," she rasps, "do you think that...Elias will be...as stubborn as you were...?" She slowly rocks her hips in time with the slow, deliberate thrusts of my fingers. A wicked idea has been brewing in my head for days and now it's time to put it into motion.

"I don't want to talk about Elias," I whisper. "I want to teach my mate *patience*..."

She gasps as realization strikes, and before she can blink, she's in our bed. I'm slowly gaining more control over the teleporting, but I'm still only able to use the ability when I'm either holding Dahlia or, like with the stampede, when she's in danger.

"What—Alaric!" she squeals, somewhere between amusement, alarm, and intrigue, as I quickly bind her wrists with a strap of leather and attach the length to the headboard, pulling her arms above her head. Her back bows and her chest rises and falls in rapid bursts. "Oh," she says, breathless, holding my gaze as I finish securing the knot on the headboard. I hover above her, letting my eyes drift down her body. Her skin is flushed and wet from the bath, her breasts practically quivering. She writhes gently under my stare, not having any idea what might be coming. I lean down and kiss her softly and she arches up to meet me, desperate to have me touch her.

"Not yet, Keeva," I whisper against her lips. I move down the bed and she watches me like a hawk, eyes wide and burning. I grip one ankle and attach another strap of leather, running the length around one of the pillars at the end of the bed.

"Fucking hells," she whispers as I repeat the process on her other leg. I go slowly, letting her know that she can stop this at any time, but she looks more aroused than I've ever seen her and I know that my mate is all in on our game. Once she's secured, I step away from the bed to take in the sight fully.

"My gods, Dahlia," I rasp, running my hand over my mouth as I stare at her tied to our bed, legs wide and hiding nothing. She moves as much as she's able, my stare seeming to drive her mad. I crawl back onto the bed, holding myself above her. I lean in and kiss her again, slow but hard, my tongue dominating hers in languid, commanding thrusts. When I pull away, I hold her gaze. "You will tell me if you wish to stop, yes?"

"Yes," she breaths, arching her body towards mine, desperate for contact.

"Until then," I say quietly, "you will not come until I allow it." She swallows hard, her pulse racing, but I can tell that she's excited by the idea, already dripping. My lips curl into a slow, wicked grin.

"Hold on tight, Keeva."

CHAPTER 41

DAHLIA

Holy. *Fucking. Hells.*
It's torture.
It's bliss.
It's agony.

Alaric has brought me to the very edge of climax with his tongue and his fingers and his fangs so many times that I've lost count. It's been hours or maybe days, and I'm covered in sweat and trembling from the need for release, but I have never in all of my life been so aroused, so wholly connected to or dependent on another.

"Do you think you've learned patience, Dahlia?" Alaric's voice rumbles against my inner thigh before he places another soft kiss there.

Part of me wants to say no. Part of me wants this game to never end. But the other part is so desperate to find release that I finally give in.

"Yes," I say, voice low and raspy.

"Hmmm, that's a good girl."

I whimper and then cry out as he licks me again. My body bows, every little touch enough to set me on fire now. He spreads me wide and pushes his tongue deep inside, making me cry out and writhe as much as I'm able being tied up. Not being able to close my legs even a little makes the pleasure that much more intense, makes each lap of his tongue somehow feel better than ever before. I'm already close, having been constantly hovering on the edge, desperately chasing the release that won't come.

"Alaric," I moan as he rolls his tongue expertly. "Please," I beg, pulling against the restraints, more desperate and frenzied than I've ever been, could ever have even imagined being.

"Come, Keeva. Come for me," he growls as he shifts, latching his mouth over my clit and sucking hard, two fingers suddenly thrusting inside and curling in just the right spot

I scream as the strongest climax I've ever experienced rocks through me like an explosion. My body convulses, pulling against the leather straps until they creak and whine, and before I can even begin to come down, before the spasms even begin to slow, Alaric is above me, sliding inside and kissing me deeply. The straps holding my legs fall away and I wrap my thighs around him, desperate to hold him to me, needing him so badly it scares me. My hands are still tied, but he reaches above me and intertwines our fingers as he moves, rocking his hips in long, measured thrusts. I would have thought he'd be in a frenzy, going what I always lovingly refer to as "primal vampire," lost to everything but his basest desires and needs, but as always, my Alaric surprises me.

He pulls back and holds my gaze as he moves, my orgasm never quite stopping completely and already building on itself again.

"I love you, Dahlia," he whispers. My heart swells and cracks finally hearing the words.

"I love you too."

He closes his eyes, his body shuddering. "Say it again," he begs.

I do. I say it over and over as he moves, as I clench his hands so tightly I'm sure I would have broken his fingers had he been a normal man. He growls it once more at my neck before he sinks his fangs into my flesh and another orgasm rocks through me. I cry out and cling to him as I fall, spiraling out into the nothingness. He follows behind, roaring against my throat and collapsing on top of me.

We lay there for what might be hours, both out of breath and slicked with sweat. He eventually moves to the side and reaches above me to untie my hands, bringing my chaffed wrists to his mouth and kissing them gently. I'm sure they must be a bit sore, but the feeling is so distant that I can't even wrap my arms around it. Even so, he pricks his thumb on a fang and smears a bit of his blood over the red marks. He pulls me tightly against his side, kissing the top of my head.

"Are you alright?" he asks in that husky voice I love so much.

"I'm not sure that I can ever move from this bed again," I say honestly with a sleepy grin, "but I'm fantastic." I place a kiss on his chest. "I might just forget everything I learned about patience again soon..."

A rumbling growl of pleasure vibrates through his chest and I chuckle lightly. I let out a long, slow exhale and suddenly, I can barely keep my eyes open.

"...tired," I mutter.

"Sleep, Keeva," he whispers, pulling me even tighter against him.

"Love...you..." I say again as the darkness swallows me up.

DA HANDS over a small bundle after we finished breakfast. It's just the Clayburns this morning, and being alone with my family again is so bittersweet that it makes my chest ache a bit. I miss the days of us all together, of sharing meals and stories by the fire, but I can't imagine my life without Alaric and know that my new life is where I've always been meant to be. Still, I hope that visits like these are not so infrequent now.

"For me?" I ask with a quirk of my brow.

"Aye. I hear yer quite the weapons master these days," he says with a grin.

"I've gotten rather good, I must say." I preen and Enid throws a breakfast roll at me.

"And so humble. Truly your best quality," she says with a roll of her eyes, but she smiles. "Would you open it already?"

I unwrap the silk and find a small, soft leather pouch. A metal clasp holds it closed and when I study it I realize that it's the knot of the Clayburn family surrounding the sigil of Alaric's coven. I run my fingertips over the symbols, the two parts of me coming together as if they were always one, meant to be together from the beginning. Da is a poet when it comes to weapons, but I know that he wouldn't have thought of this detail. I look to Enid.

"You did this?"

"I designed it and had Widow Kline make it."

"It's beautiful, Enid. Truly."

"Well, wait until you see the rest of the gift," she says, gesturing for me to continue. I let my gaze travel from the carvings to the hilts of two knives. Again, the wolf head stares at me, ruby eyes shining. I pull the blades free and gasp.

"Da," I breathe. "They're..."

"Daggers befitting the High General's mate," he finishes for me and I tear my gaze away from the knives to meet his gaze. Had someone told him? "Aye, I know," he says, answering my unasked question. "It isn't hard to see, lass." He smiles, as if the news makes him happy. I guess he knows how fiercely a mated vampire will protect what's his and knows that I will be safer than any other person on this earth, but I think he can also see how happy I am with Alaric, that though humans don't have mates the way vampires do, we do have great loves and Alaric is mine.

I smile widely and look back to the blades in awe. They're miniature versions of Night's Fury, though of course these stars aren't real silver like on Alaric's blade...at least, I don't *think* they are. I glance to the ring on my index finger as I run my finger tip over the blade, knowing that da is full of surprises, so who knows. The daggers are thin, sharp, and absolutely perfect. They aren't just weapons, they're works of art. I hold them in my hands, unsurprised by the absolute perfect balance, the beauty of the craftsmanship.

Enid leans forward and fiddles with the clasp on the pouch, eventually pulling it free. My brow furrows as she takes the daggers and—

"Oh my gods," I say on a soft laugh. The blades slide into the clasp perfectly, looking as if they are all one piece, and that piece is a hair pin. "This was one of my first designs!" I exclaim, looking to da. He beams and nods.

"Aye. It was always one of my favorites and now that ye know how to use the things, I thought you should have one for yourself."

"This is amazing!" I leap from the table and throw my arms around him, hugging him as tightly as I can before finally letting go and pulling Enid into my arms for the same treatment. I turn and make her put it in my hair immediately and da watches on fondly. We settle back into our chairs and talk about town gossip until we hear the sound of metal clashing against metal below. We all make our way to the balcony and glance over the edge to find Alaric, Elias, Wesley, Nova and my guard all broken into pairs or small groups and going through training exercises on the beach below.

"I want a closer look at this," da says, excitement sparking in his green eyes. He turns and strides back though the house and Enid and I laugh. Takara looks up from her perch on the edge of one of the rock formations and winks. I know how much she loves watching the men while they train, especially when they end up—

"Holy *hells*," Enid gasps as Elias strips his shirt off, tossing it to the sand. He jerks his head up, his gaze landing directly on us. No, not on *us*—on *Enid*. She is the only one he has eyes for, it seems. The two stay locked in a strange trance for long moments before Alaric barks at Elias to pay attention, glancing up to shoot me a quick wink before returning to the business at hand. Enid shakes herself, her cheeks flushing, but her eyes never leave Elias as he moves and spins in the beautiful, deadly dance with Alaric. If I didn't know any better, I would say he's showing off a bit. Ok, I do know better and he's showing off *a lot*.

I chew on the inside of my cheek, torn on whether I should tell her the truth or not, but decide against it. It's something that the two of them will have to figure out on their own, as Alaric and I did, but I decide that singing his praises can't hurt either.

"He's Alaric's oldest friend and best lieutenant," I say casually. "He's become a very good friend. Helped save my life when I was attacked on the road, too."

"He's..." She swallows hard. "He's very...*formidable*." The way she says it makes it seem like *formidable* is akin to *sexy as all fuck* and I try and fail to hide my grin. Maybe Elias won't have such a hard time winning Enid over after all. "What's it like?" she whispers. "Being with a vampire? Is it as good as the rumors say?" I can see Elias and Alaric both slow their movements, obviously listening to every word we're saying.

I narrow my eyes at them and say loudly, "it's quite lackluster, honestly. Barely above average." At that Alaric turns to stare at me, mouth gaping in outrage and the rest of the vampires snort and double over with laughter. I smirk at him. "It's rude to eavesdrop!" I call before taking Enid's hand and dragging her back into the house where we can have a proper conversation. We settle into one of the drawing rooms in the south tower where our guests are staying and I tell her truth about sex with a vampire. All the mind-blowing, intoxicating, life-altering details.

She looks pensive, toying with the pendant around her neck that she's had for as long as I can remember.

"What's wrong?"

She chews on her lip. "Do you think...well, do you think it's possible to not feel that kind of passion for someone and still ever be in love with them?" I give her a look that tells her to go ahead and give up the pretenses. She exhales roughly. "I feel nothing like that with Leland. He's sweet and kind and he tries to be funny, though gods bless his heart, he fails miserably, but...there's no fire, Lia. Nothing even *close* to approaching fire. Barely a smoldering ember on the very best of days." She buries her face in her hands and confesses, "but every time I see Elias, I feel as if my entire body is burning with need for him."

"Well, he is obscenely attractive," I agree.

She drops her hands and looks at me. "It's more than that. When I'm around him, I feel...content, in ways I never even knew I could feel. He makes me smile and laugh, and every time he does *he* lights up, as if coaxing joy from me brings him infinitely more of it. He listens when I talk, *really* listens and asks me questions no one else has ever thought to. I feel like I can talk to him for hours and hours and he'll never get bored of it. I can't explain it without sounding crazy. I *feel* like I'm crazy but..." She trails off and shakes her head. "I just think that perhaps I've been trying to force myself to feel things for Leland because...well, I was lonely after you left," she says sheepishly. "I know, I know. That's a terrible reason to agree to marry someone, but here we are." She takes a deep breath and lets it out slowly. "I just feel like I'm connected to Elias, like I've always been connected to him even though I've only known him a few days. It makes no sense."

I know all too well what she means and wonder what the hells it is about the Clayburn blood that seems to defy the laws of matehood as we know them. Whatever it is, I know that I'm thankful for it and while Enid is still free to make her own choice, I know that no one on this earth will protect my sister the way Elias will, the way the whole of the army will protect and accept her as one of their own if she so chooses.

But if she does choose to be with Elias, she'll be faced with the same dilemma as I am: being human with a ticking clock counting down the moments of our mortal lives. I shake myself, not wanting to go down that road in my mind yet again.

"It makes more sense than you might think," I murmur. She eyes me but I wave her off and she thankfully allows it. We spend the next hour talking and I answer the hundreds of questions Enid has about my relationship with Alaric. It's so nice being like this with her again, to have someone that I can talk to in a way I can't with anyone else. I know that my heart will break a little again when we all leave to go back to our real lives.

But for now, I enjoy every moment with my sister.

ALL TOO SOON, we're back at the camp. I miss my family already, but Alaric has promised that he'll arrange for visits to Ashcliff or have Enid and da come to the village near the camp as often as I'd like. Judging by the way Enid couldn't keep her eyes from Elias, I have a feeling that she will be all too happy to visit sooner rather than later. She claims nothing happened between them save a mostly-innocent kiss that last night before we all departed, but with the way she blushed and wouldn't fully meet my eyes, and the way Elias couldn't stop grinning like a lunatic, I know it's complete and utter bullshite. I know that Enid is honorable to her core and wouldn't want to do anything with Elias before breaking things off with Leland, but at the same time, I know just how hard it is to fight those feelings and how easy it is to give into temptation. I'll demand all the details soon enough.

We fall back into the normal rhythms of camp with Alaric being the High General and me being his...whatever I am. I don't believe there's been an official announcement that I'm his mate or anything, but I know that news spreads through the camp faster than wildfire, so I'm sure that anyone who wasn't at the battle must surely know by now. I wonder what they think about it. Is it shameful that their High General's mate is a feeble human? Are they simply just happy that he's found me at all with mates being so rare?

About two weeks after arriving back at camp, Alaric left to go on a scouting mission. Being apart, even for these few days, had been like torture. I know we must both learn to bear it, but my gods I hated every second of it. The only good thing about it was that I was free to go to the village again after all this time—with my guard plus another contingent of fifteen vampires hand-picked by Viktor of course. It was so nice being back, almost like coming home again. I was happy to see that Master Raynor seemed to be doing much better now that he's been able to get his medication regularly without problem. I made sure to put some extra coin in the apothecary's pocket as a thank you and he assured me that everything was going well with our arrangement. No one in the village was going without what they needed now and I couldn't have been happier.

A week later, I came down with a bad cough and could barely get out of bed for days on end. The healers came and everything turned out alright, but it reminded me all over again at the position we're in. I'm human. I'm fragile. I'm dying. Every single day I'm closer to death.

I've tried to bring it up more than once, but Alaric always manages to know what I'm about to say and distracts me in deliciously wicked ways. But now, I stare at the faint pink line on my palm where I'd sliced through it this morning while I was working in the shop with Braddock. Alaric had healed it as soon as he'd heard, of course, but it's yet another reminder.

"What is it, Keeva?" he asks softly, coming up behind me at the window and kissing my neck. I give a mmm of appreciation and reach back to run my fingers through his hair.

"I was just wishing we had a balcony..." I smile when I hear him groan against my throat. Alaric had taken me on the balcony of our tower at Ashcliff more than once, bending me over the railing and pounding into me so hard that my screams were lost to the roar of the sea below, and I still dream about it. So, I'm only half lying.

I turn from the window and wrap my arms around him, reaching up to brush a fleck of snow from his hair with a laugh. True winter is here now and it's just as beautiful as mum always said it was. I feel a connection to her every time I walk through the white fields around the camp, every time I sit in front of the fire and watch the flakes drift down through the window. I can see the beauty the way she did, and feel like I understand her a bit better now somehow.

I settle my hand on his cheek, searching his eyes. I know he doesn't want to discuss it, but I can't wait any longer. I won't let him distract me this time—which is why I'm waiting for him fully dressed instead of naked in our bed like usual. I take a settling breath and he tenses. I can feel the knot in my chest tighten through our bond.

"Alaric, we need to talk about this."

He knows exactly what *this* I mean and his expression immediately turns dark and closed off. He steps away from me and strides across the room, pouring himself some whisky. He seems to know better than to try to distract me with sex this time and I prepare myself to have it out. We've never really fought. Argued here and there but it usually dissolves quickly enough, but I have a feeling this will be different. But I won't back down. This is important.

So, if this means a fight, then I'm ready. Da and Enid are on their way to the village right now for a visit. I can go stay there with them for a few days, *really* storm off and let him know how serious I am about this.

"There is nothing to discuss, Dahlia."

"That's ridiculous. There's plenty to discuss."

He turns and leans against the sideboard. "No, there isn't," he says again, voice carefully calm. "You will not be turned." He takes a long drink, eyeing me over the rim of his glass. I stare at him, incredulous. He's already *decided*? I knew he didn't want to talk about it because there is no easy answer, but to have him not even consider the option? To not even consider what *I* might want? My blood starts to boil, my hackles raising.

"And you get to make this decision on your own then?"

"I do."

"How can you say that?" I sputter. "This affects *both* of us, Alaric. This is *my* life too."

"And you will have a long, mortal one. I will be by your side for every second of it and when it is over, I will join you in whatever comes after this, but I will not risk the turning."

"You don't want a chance at forever with me?? You'll settle for fifty, maybe sixty years as long as I don't get sick or attacked by Revenants, or run over by a carriage?" I shout, trying and failing to keep my temper in check. This has all been building for too long, the what-ifs and the possibilities festering in my mind for months.

"You. Will. Be. Safe," he growls. "And I would rather have that time than risk the turning and lose you tomorrow!"

"But what if it works!? What if I can be with you forever, be as strong as you and even safer than I am now?"

"Of course I would want that but..." He looks both pained and angry. "I will not risk it. I am not ready to possibly lose you, Dahlia. Don't you understand??"

I pace back and forth, understanding completely but also furious that he won't even consider it, that he's made the decision without consulting me...that every day that passes is a day closer to the end of our time together. I understand his fears, and a part of me is terrified of what would happen if the turning failed, if I died in the attempt and he had to deal with that pain alone...of what would happen to the world without him in it if he truly decided to follow after me. I know many mates do, simply unable to survive without their other half, but...not Alaric. He's strong. He could survive it. He would have to survive it, for the good of Braxhelm. This world *needs* him. The army is strong, but they're mostly that way because of him. His strength bolsters them, their shared blood and bond, and the love and respect and trust they have in him making them more formidable than any other in history. Without him...I shudder to think how they might fare. It's the very reason Kilgren's plan had been a good one.

"You've turned hundreds of humans, Alaric, thousands even. But you refuse to even try for me? Even if it's what I want?"

"Because I never loved any of them!" he roars. "I didn't give a fuck if they lived or died except as so far as whether a good soldier was lost to my forces! I. WILL. NOT. LOSE. YOU!!" He bares his fangs in an almost feral snarl, and though it's terrifying to behold, I don't cower.

I stand, seething, torn between love for this man and fury at his insistence and refusal to even consider my point of view. I don't want to grow old with him. I don't want to age before his eyes, to grow frail and feeble while he remains strong and sure, to have my entire life be a short blink of his eye. I cannot stomach it. And he won't even think of these things, or if he does, he doesn't care. But they matter. They count. What I think and feel counts, damn it! I didn't get a choice in becoming his Consort, or his mate, but I get a choice in how I spend the rest of my life with him as his *partner*.

I shove my feet into my boots and stalk across our chambers.

"Where are you going?" he barks.

"For a walk. Doona follow me, *yer highness*," I snap, my glare daring him to try. I fly from the room and through the cabin, grabbing my thick, fur-lined coat from the ornate hook by the door before storming out into the night. I pull the hood up against the chill. The snow is already beginning to coat the ground in a thick, fluffy blanket and I'm glad that I had the wherewithal to at least put on my boots before leaving. I don't know where I'm going exactly, I just know that I need away from Alaric. For the first time in the better half of a year, I don't want to be near him...though of course, that's only half true and part of me is already yearning to go back to him. I clench my jaw and storm through the camp. I'm not in the mood to talk with Wesley or Nova, knowing I really shouldn't be around anyone right now, so I walk towards the pond.

Lanterns had been added to the path and the field around the pond after I first started spending time here, so I can navigate the trip easily enough, even in the dark. I wear a deep trench in the snow as I pace, back and forth, back and forth, a hundred times, a thousand. I can't believe that he won't even consider it. I understand his reservations and I can't say that I don't share them to an extent or that I'm not afraid of the potential...less than favorable outcome, but a potential life together forever is worth it to me. To not have to be protected, to be strong enough to stand beside Alaric and the rest and not be a liability...

No matter how much training I get as a human, I know that I'll never be strong or skilled enough for Alaric to feel as if he doesn't have to protect me. And I appreciate his desire to do so, of course I do, but I want him to look at me as an equal. I want to be able to protect myself.

I stop my furious pacing and lean against the fallen tree, rubbing at my temples. A part of me feels terrible for being so angry at Alaric when his only desire is not to lose me. How can I possibly fault him for that? I take a deep breath and try to think of things from his point of view. If our roles were reversed, would I risk his life? I...don't know. The thought of losing him is enough to make my chest clench painfully and I sigh, the worst of my fury fading.

"My Lady," a voice says from a few feet away.

I jolt to my feet, barely stifling the scream building in my throat. I hadn't even heard him approaching. Highspear looks apologetic, ducking his head and wringing his hands.

"I'm sorry, I didn't mean to frighten you," he says, taking another step forward. "The High General sent me to fetch you. You must come at once." A cold tendril of fear slowly skates up my spine.

"Is everything alright?"

"There's been a threat at the gates." Worry gnaws at my throat. A threat at the gates? Could it have come from the village? Have da and Enid made it there yet? Are they safe?? "The High General wants you back at the cabin just to be safe. I'll escort you."

"Oh," I say, blinking. "What kind of threat?" I ask, wondering vaguely why Alaric would send Luca and not Elias or one of the guard. Something feels wrong, but I don't know what, exactly. I step towards the young vampire and he clasps my arm. I'm shocked by the contact—most of Alaric's soldiers wouldn't touch his Consort so casually, and most vampires wouldn't dare touch another's mate— but I don't have time to question it.

"I'm sorry," he says quietly before twisting quickly and pulling my back hard against his chest, one arm wrapped around my middle like a vice.

"What are you doing!?" I demand as I struggle against his hold, that trickle of fear now growing, spreading ice through my entire body like a deluge. Something is very, very wrong. He squeezes tighter, a clear threat in his embrace now, and panic rises.

"What must be done," he says, sounding half resigned and half… gleeful? My heart gallops in my chest, true fear settling over every inch of me like a suffocating blanket.

"Let me go!" I yell, kicking out at him the way Wesley taught me. He grunts in pain as my boot collides with the inside of his ankle, but he doesn't release me. Surely someone can hear me? How does he expect to get away with this?

A moment later, there's a sharp prick of pain in the side of my neck and my entire body suddenly feels as heavy as lead. My arms drop lifelessly to my sides, my legs giving out completely and only Luca's hold on me keeping me upright. He tosses me over his shoulder like a sack of potatoes.

"I'm really am sorry," he says again, sounding like he means it, and then the darkness drags me into the abyss.

CHAPTER 42
DAHLIA

"It's time to wake, Dahlia."

The voice must be Alaric's—who else would be telling me to wake?—but something feels off, some instinct deep in my bones warning me that something is wrong. I claw my way up from the darkness, not sure why it feels so heavy, almost like I drank too much last night, though I don't remember doing so...in fact, I don't remember much of anything.

"Come on, now," the voice beckons again. And though everything in me is telling me that this is wrong, that I should stay in the darkness as long as I can, I pry open my eyes. I blink several times to clear the spots from my vision. A face slowly comes into focus and I scream, scrambling backwards only to hit something hard behind me.

A *Revenant* squats in front of me, smiling widely. His black fangs are sharp and glinting in the low light. I swallow hard as instincts flare to life, instincts born of months of training. I try to remain as calm as possible, forcing a deep, settling breath in and out of my lungs. My mind works surprisingly quickly, already confirming that the thing must not want me dead, or he would have killed me while I was unconscious. Of course, the reasons he might want me alive send a sickening wave of nausea roiling through my stomach, but I clamp my lips tightly and push the feeling away. As long as I'm alive, I can fight. As long as I'm alive, I have a chance...no matter what he might have planned.

I dart a glance around the space, not wanting to take my eyes off of the monster for too long. I'm on the cold, dirty floor of what looks to be a cell of some sort, but much larger than what I imagined a dungeon room would be. The walls are made of dark, craggy stone, and there's an open door made of iron bars on the other side. Chemical torches burn in a few iron sconces hammered into the stone around the room. I look down to find that I'm shackled to a bar running the length of the back wall, lengths of chain connected to thick metal cuffs that encircle each wrist uncomfortably.

I cringe away from the monster before me, and his crimson eyes dance with amusement and...triumph. My stomach churns violently at that expression but I try to keep my thoughts from running away, to use everything that Nova and Wesley taught me to stay calm and in control.

"I thought perhaps the leech gave you a bit too much," the Revenant muses. *The leech?* I frown and he arches a brow. "Don't you remember?" he asks in a mocking tone. My brow furrows as I try to pull the last memory from the fog in my mind. Alaric and I had argued over my turning...I'd stormed from the cabin in a huff and gone to the pond...and then Highspear—

I gasp as I finally remember: the feigned threat, the sharp pinch at my neck, the heavy feeling settling over my entire body. He'd given me some kind of drug and brought me to a Revenant? But...why? My brain is whirling, trying to fight past the panic to find the right answer, until it finally becomes clear as glass:

Traitor.

The Revenant chuckles, the sound like carriage wheels rolling over gravel.

"Ah, figured it out then, have you?" I don't understand everything, but I know that I've been betrayed and understand enough to know that nothing good is going to come from me being in this place with a Revenant. How long have I been unconscious? Does Alaric know that I've been taken? Does he know where I am? Terror starts to rise, but I press it away. Wesley told me to think of the fear as a physical thing inside my mind, something that I could imagine taking in my hands and putting away in a closet or trunk, and closing it up tight until it's time to deal with it.

So I do as my dear friend instructed and imagine the fear as a large black stone. I imagine putting it inside of a heavy, iron box with an even heavier, iron lock. I imagine turning the key and then burying that box far beneath the earth behind the cabin, near the cairns that still stand in memory of Kane, Descartes, and Isaiah. My friends can guard this fear for me until I'm ready to face it.

And, unbelievably, it works. I feel an almost cold detachment from the fear, as if it isn't mine for the time being, not a part of me at all. I press my shoulders back and rise to my feet. The Revenant watches, unconcerned with my movement, and rises as well. He's not quite as tall as Alaric, and has a rangier build, but I know he'll still be incredibly strong and agile. All Revenants are, as all vampires are. The legends say that the two species were one and the same long, long ago, but at some point, the Revenant line somehow split off and they became what they are now. It's why they're so similar: both supernaturally strong and fast; both have keen senses, fangs, and a thirst for blood; both can be poisoned with silver.

"What do you want with me?" I ask, surprised by the lack of tremble in my voice.

The Revenant studies me for a long moment, and I force myself not to squirm beneath his gaze. I am a Consort. I am the High General's mate. I am Dahlia fucking Clayburn, my father's firebrand. I will not be cowed by this monster, not like before. I jerk my chin up in defiance and something flashes in his crimson eyes. Amusement, a touch of admiration and surprise, and...something else I don't want to name, something that makes my stomach churn.

He ignores my question, and instead says, "You know, I wasn't sure what to make of a leech coming into my territory, claiming to want to betray his own kind all those months ago." Despite knowing the truth, I deny his words, hoping that somehow I'm wrong, that I'm misremembering or that Luca had a reason for what he did and then someone *else* came and took me...

"No. No, I don't believe you. None of Alaric's soldiers would betray Braxhlem like this. They would never work with something as vile as you."

"Hmm, is that so?" He turns and nods towards the door and a few moments later, Luca steps into the cell. The vampire somehow looks proud and ashamed all at once, and something deep inside of me tears free from its cage. It wasn't a mistake. He did this. And he's *proud* of himself for bringing me here? After I was kind to him? And what of the vow he made to Alaric? To break that is beyond incomprehensible.

"You fucking bastard!" I scream. I lunge at him as he steps up beside the Revenant, something primal and animalistic taking over my body and roaring inside of me to tear his fucking throat out. The chains pull taut and yank me backwards before I can get my hands on him. He has the decency to look guilty, but that doesn't do much to assuage my rage. He tenses and averts his gaze.

"How could you?!" I roar, seething and pulling at my chains until the metal bites painfully into my wrists, the sharp metal cutting into my skin and drawing blood, but I don't care. I keep pulling, desperate to tear him to pieces.

"Oh, I quite like this one," the Revenant muses. "She's much changed since the first attack," he says, studying me in a way that makes my skin crawl. "Not at all the meek, worthless creature they described. Hid under a carriage, did she not? Cowered like a dog?"

I grind my teeth, knowing that he's not entirely wrong and being all the angrier for it. I cut my eyes back to Luca, fury spiking as all of the pieces begin to click into place like those wooden puzzles da made when Enid and I were young.

"You were involved in that as well then? That's why you looked so guilty when I first met you??" No answer. "And now you've drugged me and kidnapped me and brought me to this creature? Why? How could you do this?" Again, he doesn't respond. "Fucking answer me!!" I scream.

He finally snaps his gaze up, all guilt gone, his eyes blazing with a fury I wouldn't have thought him capable of.

"Because I am more than a worthless foot soldier!!" he yells, fangs snapping free. All of those boyish, innocent features that made me once feel sympathy for the vampire disappear, transforming into something dark and desperate and feral. "He didn't think I was worthy of being a sergeant, passed me over time and time again! He never picked me for important missions. He didn't even think I was worthy of guarding his precious little Consort! But I AM FUCKING WORTHY!!" I flinch back as he roars. He's breathing hard and the Revenant watches on with a look that's a mix of annoyance and pity and disgust.

"How?" I demand. "How did you orchestrate the attack on the road? How did you get me from the camp with no one noticing you carting my limp body around??"

"I have wielder blood in my family," he says, shoving his shoulders back proudly. "I hid the truth so that I could be turned." Wielders are rare these days and are forbidden from turning. There were many instances years ago where wielders attempted, and when the vampiric magic that made the turning possible bonded with the magic in their blood, their gifts became too strong to be contained. Their bodies were literally ripped apart from the inside, like a dam bursting from all of the raw power. I don't know why Luca was able to withstand the turning. Perhaps his wielder magic was all but dormant until *after* he turned, like the vampiric magic powered his own somehow? I suppose it doesn't really matter either way. He survived and now we're here. No use dwelling on the *whys* and *hows* of it all, at least not in this moment. If I live past tomorrow, maybe I'll think on it more.

"I can shade objects completely and hold a shield for a time."

"Shade..." I frown and then gasp when realization hits. "You were able to hide the Revenants and sneak them through the pass, to hide their scents from the vampires and get them past the guard stations."

Luca grins, a wild gleam in his eyes. "Exactly. And the High General tried to say that I wasn't good enough?! I brought his enemies into his home right under his nose," he adds smugly.

Before, I'd had the urge to protect this vampire, to befriend him and try to ease his feelings of not belonging and disappointment. No longer. Now, I want him to hurt. Now, I want him to fucking bleed and I make the silent vow that one day, I'll make that happen. For now, I'll settle for using the barbed tongue of mine that mum always loathed. I think in this situation, even she would turn a blind eye.

I huff out a mocking laugh. "A mere dozen or so Revenants? If you were truly powerful, truly worth much of anything at all, you'd be able to sneak a whole contingent of Revenant forces into Braxhelm, to overtake the camp and then the entire continent easily. And alas, your plan *failed*. I was right to pity you, you pathetic little worm."

The jibe hits just as I intend, and Luca's face flushes with anger and shame. Despite everything, I smirk at him then, pulling myself up to my full height and looking down my nose at him the way a true Consort should, the way a prince's fucking *mate* should.

The Revenant laughs in earnest then, making Luca flush even more.

"I can see why Alaric so enjoys you, little human. I'm so glad you'll be with us for the foreseeable future." My blood goes cold and the fear pounds on the top of the box beneath the earth. I will it away, beg my fallen guard to keep it under lock and key.

"Chieftain Kilgren," someone says, striding into the cell. I blink at that, barely stifling a gasp when I realize who's standing before me. Not just any Revenant—their fucking *leader*. I'm in much bigger trouble than I thought, and despite my best efforts, my hands begin to tremble.

"The message has been delivered," the other Revenant says, stopping on the other side of Kilgren and tossing a disgusted look at Luca. Whether because he's a vampire or a traitor or both, I can't be sure.

"Good," Kilgren says. "Good. Prepare the men. We'll be heading to the Plain soon enough. I have no doubt of what the answer will be." He grins wickedly and the Revenant nods, looks me over once, and then hurries from the room. Kilgren turns to Luca. "Go prepare yourself, leech. There is a human waiting for you in your chambers. You will need all of the strength you can muster. Do not make me remind you what will befall you if you fail."

Luca pales slightly and nods, cutting his eyes to me for a brief moment, almost looking like he might apologize, before scurrying from the room.

Kilgren casually pulls over a chair from the corner of the room and settles himself into it. He somehow makes it seem as if he's sitting upon a throne instead of a misshapen wooden relic that looks like it's been gnawed on by rats. I swallow bile and can't stop my eyes from darting around, swearing I can feel the rodents staring at me from the shadows.

"Whatever you're planning, it won't work," I say with as much confidence as I can muster.

"Do you know how my kind rise to power?" he asks, catching me completely off guard. I don't answer, but he acts as if I had, continuing the conversation as if we're old friends having a pint at the tavern. "We *take* it. A new leader must challenge the current one—a fight to the death. If one should perish on the battlefield or of some other cause, two potentials must step up and fight. The power must be taken, one way or another. Revenants are all linked, all bound by an ancient magic that came about when the old single species split into two. You see, vampires are not *forced* to serve and obey their leaders. They have free will, the ability to strike out on their own should they wish. They are honor bound to obey, but long ago, there was a vampire who thought it should be more than honor. He believed that whoever lead the clan should have complete power and control over the members. The details are murky as to the exact dark magic that the vampire invoked in order to try to force others to follow him, to magically tie their allegiance to his rule, but whatever it did caused a rift in the entire species. A new one emerged, though a bit disfigured as a consequence of such darkness," he says with a smirk, "one that follows that magic to this day."

I simply stare at him, confused why he's giving me a history lesson. He leans forward and rests his elbows on his knees, red eyes shining like flames in the dim light of the cell.

"Do you know who the last Chieftain of our people was?"

"They don't teach monster politics in the schoolhouses in Braxhelm, in case you weren't aware," I spit. I bite the inside of my cheek, knowing that I need to tread carefully. He kidnapped me for a reason, so I don't think he'll kill me—yet—but that doesn't mean he won't hurt me. Thankfully, he looks more amused than offended.

"My father. I challenged my own bloodkin to a fight to the death to take control of our people. He failed to defeat Alaric and his gods forsaken army. He brought shame to our family time and time again. So, I challenged him, ripped out his entrails with my bare hands, and brought every Revenant to heel under my command. There were some who had been speaking of peace between the species, and my father was actually listening to them! *Peace*," he says, spitting the word as if it were the most vile thing he could imagine. "They did not want to follow me, yet here they are, following like good little dogs." He gestures to two Revenants standing guard outside the door. One clenches his jaw, the other gives no reaction at all, looking sullen.

My mind is reeling. Could this be true? Not all Revenants wanted the war to continue? Not all of them are...evil? I can't even begin to contemplate what that might mean.

"Why are you telling me all of this?" I ask through clenched teeth.

"Because I need you to understand the lengths that I am willing to go to in order to win this war, to finally lead my people to a victory that no other Revenant before me could. I eviscerated my own father, Dahlia. There is nothing I will not do to take Braxhelm. *Nothing.*" I swallow hard, his words leaving a hollow feeling in my chest with their cold truth. I know that he will stop at nothing to win this war. I realize his plan a moment before he speaks again and I nearly collapse.

"Now, I'm going to use you to make Alaric surrender—which he will, of course. You have no idea how elated I was to hear the news that he had a mate, explaining his miraculous recovery from the silver." His lips curl into a snake's smile. "A mate is a vampire's greatest weakness, you see."

I had always thought of mates as a strength, never realizing just how wrong that was until now. I'm a bargaining chip, one that Alaric is physically incapable of leaving in danger.

"And after he does," Kilgren continues, "I'm going to make him watch as I torture you to the very brink of death, over and over and over, using his own blood to heal you so I can start again. It is nothing personal, of course. As I said before, I actually quite enjoy your spirit. This is simply business and vengeance, which are honestly one and the same, are they not?"

Panic rises in my chest at the thought, not for fear of my own pain, but of Alaric's. I can't let him go through that. I would rather die. I know that will hurt him too, but it will be quick at least, a pain he can learn to grieve, I hope. Watching me be tortured will be torture for him, and I can't allow that to happen. I wonder if I can goad Kilgren into lashing out, into ending this before it begins. *Worth a try...*

"You're pathetic," I spit. "How long ago did you kill your father? Hmm? It's been a century at least, has it not? And yet here you are, still hiding out in this frozen wasteland like a scared pup. You failed in your attempt to kill me on the road. You failed in your attempt to kill Alaric with that silver. You. Have. Failed. Over and over and over again. You're just as pathetic as your father w—"

A crack echoes off of the stone around us as his palm connects with my cheek. I tumble sideways from the force of it, the pain taking a moment to register, but when it does, it feels as if someone's put a hot poker to my face. My ears ring, my eyes water as black spots fill my vision, and I taste blood in my mouth. A second later his hand is around my throat, tugging me back upright. He lifts me so that the very tips of my boots scrape frantically on the floor. I pull on the chains, trying to reach his wrist, even though this is what I want. The desire to live is a powerful one, it seems.

He tilts his head, studying me. A small smile tugs his lips upward.

"You will not taunt me into killing you, Dahlia. But make no mistake: I will not allow disrespect from a vile little human. I promised Alaric you would be alive when he arrived—not that you would be *whole*." I swallow hard against his hand, still squeezing ever so slightly, and his smile widens. "I think we've reached an understanding, yes?"

I nod as best as I can and he releases me. I tumble to the floor, gasping for air.

"Now, I must prepare. Alaric should be responding to my invitation shortly—though, we both know what his answer will be." He winks—fucking *winks*—and strides out of the cell. The door slams shut behind him with an echo that sends a shudder deep into my bones.

I let out a strangled sob when I hear his footsteps disappear, doubling over as I try desperately to get air into my lungs. He's going to win. He's right. I know that Alaric will do anything to keep me safe, even knowing that Kilgren will never keep his word about not harming me if Alaric surrenders.

This can't happen. I can't let him forsake all of Braxhelm for me. I have to stop this. I pull my knees up in front of me and wrap my arms around them, sobbing quietly as I realize the truth:

There's not a damn thing I can do. Braxhelm will fall, my friends and family will die, Alaric will suffer a fate worse than death—and it's all my fault.

CHAPTER 43
ALARIC

My mate is in danger.

My mate is in danger.

MY mate is in danger.

The words will not stop echoing in my head, drowning out everything else in the world. I clench the parchment in my fist, seeing Kilgren's words behind my lids as I squeeze my eyes shut and try to breathe:

Oh great High General,

I have your mate, evidenced by the lock of hair and drop of her blood enclosed with this missive. If you want to see her alive again, you will come to the Obsidian Plain and surrender to me. If I do not receive a response within a day, I will send her back to you piece by piece.

Your move, Princeling—though I do believe this is checkmate.

Kilgren Skov, Kinsblood Slayer, Chieftain of the Revenants

I know how this ends. I know that I will go to the Obsidian Plain and surrender to Kilgren's forces. I know that his army will murder mine without mercy. I know that they will sweep through the whole of Braxhelm, leaving devastation in their wake. I know that he will not let Dahlia go. I know he will hurt her to hurt me.

And yet.

I cannot forsake my mate, no matter what the cost, no matter how badly the odds are stacked against us. Perhaps I can find a way to…I clutch at my chest at the mere thought, but force it to life: perhaps I can find a way to kill her before Kilgren can torture her. After that, I will spend my last days on this earth finding a way to tear him apart before joining her on the other side.

Decision made, I meet Elias' eyes. His are bleak, his jaw clenched tightly.

"I will not ask you to follow me in this, brother. Go to Enid. Get your mate and Arwen to safety on the islands," I say, plans and backup plans sifting through my mind. "Evacuate as many as you can there, use the academy grounds and surrounding islands to house them. Any civilians who wish to stay and fight may do so. Make Fiona leave Astoria's Keep. I know she'll try to stay and help, but I need her to go. Gather the rest of the army at the port to make our final stand. I have faith in you to lead them in my absence. I will try to stop this before it starts somehow but…I will surrender to him, Elias. You know I must."

"I know," he says quietly, pain clear in his voice and sending a stab of it through me. He strides over and pulls me into a bone-crushing hug. "I love you, brother. Go save our Lady Dahlia. I know you'll find a way." We both know the odds of that happening aren't good. I can only hope that we give everyone else enough warning that we can save as many as possible. They can survive for years on the islands if they can keep the Revenants from crossing the channel. Sebastian will figure out what to do from there, I have all the faith in the world in my brother. Elias and I pull away and our gazes hold for a long moment, hundreds of years of love and friendship flowing between us. He nods and my throat burns.

I quickly write out a response to Kilgren and send it back with the raven that delivered his message, my heart clenching painfully as I resign myself to the fate I've brought down on us all. I write out several more to Sebastian and the other generals, another quick note to Fiona. Part of me even has half a mind to write one to Ahmed, consisting of only two words of course: *fuck you*, but I refrain. I seal all the letters and send them off with Elias, watching my oldest friend leave me for the last time.

Somehow in the blink of an hour, hours have passed and I know it's time to go. I pin the wolf broach that Dahlia gave me to my chest, put on my armor, strap Night's Fury to my back, and make my way to the stable. Both of the brothers are in a frenzy, feeling the pain and fear and panic of both me and Dahlia. The squire quickly gets Xanthus ready, and I try to calm Xerxes, though I know it's useless. I can practically hear his thoughts as he meets my gaze: *just try to go without me, you fucking bastard.*

"Will that devil let me ride him?" a voice asks from the doorway. I turn to find Takara wearing battle gear, her long black hair tied back in elaborate warrior braids.

"You should have left with Elias."

"She is my Lady," she says, shoving her shoulders back, her voice harder than I've ever heard it. "She is my *friend*," she adds. "I go where she goes, and if that's into the seven hells themselves, so be it." Xerxes stills, seeming to calm a bit and Takara takes that as permission to approach him. She speaks directly to the horse when she says, "will you take me to her?"

The big bastard snorts and stomps at the ground in what appears to be affirmation. Takara turns to me and arches a brow in challenge. I roll my eyes.

"Fucking hells," I mutter, but turn to the squire. "Get me his saddle as well."

"With haste," Takara says, stepping away so that I can get the damned horse ready to go as quickly as possible, "the others are waiting for us."

"Others?" I ask, freezing my movements for a heartbeat.

I told Elias to tell the men they were free to go to their families or fall back to the port. I know there will be no battle, no chance for us to win this at the Plain, so there is no reason to doom any others to immediate death.

Takara grins a smug grin, fangs glinting in the light. I remember when she was first turned, she had aspirations of joining the army to avenge her family—those had quickly disappeared because she didn't particularly like being dirty and bloody, but now I can see that initial fire that had surprised me all those years ago and made me give her a chance to begin with. She has a warrior's heart, despite what she might believe.

We mount the horses and as soon as we start down the hill from the cabin I see a massive group waiting at the edge of camp. My heart twists, love and respect for these soldiers flooding me. I do not wish them to go down this path that leads to nothing but pain and death, but I cannot lie that it touches me that they want to follow me.

I spur Xanthus into a gallop, riding through the camp and to the front of the gathered soldiers. I look at them all, so ready to die beside me this day.

"You're sure?" I ask them all.

Malcom, at the front of the group with his Clayburn sword strapped to his back, nods. "We follow you, High General, no matter where the path leads. We fight for you. We fight for Lady Dahlia." I want to tell them that there will be no fight, that they are riding into surrender and massacre, but I know that they know it already. I shift my gaze down the line, over Cyrus and Viktor, Braddock and Singh and Wesley and Nova, over so many others that I know are there not only out of loyalty to me, but out of love for my mate.

A pounding of hooves draws my attention and I tense when Elias breaks from the group on Orion's back.

"What the fuck are you doing here?" I demand, furious. I know all too well the terror he must be feeling at the potential threat to his mate. He needs to go to her. He needs time with her, no matter how short it may be.

"We save your mate first, then I go claim mine," he says simply, brokering no argument. He reaches up and rests his hand on his chest for a moment, where a chain disappears inside his tunic. I've never seen it before but don't have time to wonder about it right now. "I've already gone to the village and told them what's going on. I've left Milton there with orders to get the Clayburns to safety," he adds and all I can do is nod. He has made up his mind and I can only honor his wishes. I turn back to the small army gathered behind us and whip Night's Fury from my back.

"For the wolf!" I cry and a hundred voices echo the words back to me.

With that, we ride to Dahlia.

We ride to my mate.

We ride to our deaths.

CHAPTER 44

DAHLIA

With every second that passes, terror and despair threaten to swallow me completely. I try to tell myself that Alaric won't come, that he won't bow to Kilgren's demands, but I know that he can't stay away. So, I have to find a way to stop this somehow.

I pace along the cell, the loud scraping of the metal chain along the bar as I walk sharp and grating. I nearly scream when the cell door opens and Kilgren strides in—with a plate of food and a pitcher of water. I eye him warily, backing away towards the wall I'm chained to. He pulls the rickety table from the corner into the center of the room and puts the tray atop it.

"I'm told a side effect of the drug the leech gave you is extreme thirst," he says casually, cordially even, as if he's invited me to high tea. Unfortunately he's right: my throat is raw and scratchy, the thought of water sending a pang through my body, but I won't take anything from this monster. I lift my chin in defiance and he grins, those black fangs sharp and terrifying. A shiver of fear runs through me and his gazes sharpens, as if he can sense it. Fuck, maybe he can... and it looks like he enjoys it.

I swallow hard and take another step backwards as his gaze roves over me in a way that's entirely possessive and vile. My pulse begins to race, my breaths coming short and shallow as fear threatens to paralyze me. *No, no, no. Lock the box. Shove it away.* I imagine my fallen guard taking the box from me, holding it tightly between them and keeping the lid firmly closed. It helps, but I'm still very aware of the way Kilgren is staring at me, red eyes darkening to scarlet so deep it's nearly black. His gaze roves down my body, and I wish I still had my thick coat to pull around myself and hide. They took it from me before I even woke, so I'm only in the leather trousers, thin tunic, and vest I'd been wearing when I'd stormed from the cabin. Thankfully a small fire has been burning in the far corner of the room and keeping me from freezing.

He stands slowly from the table and strides towards me. I try to retreat further, but my back hits the wall and I'm trapped. He continues forward, stopping when he's only a hairsbreadth away. I press my lips into a thin line, turning my face away. He leans down and I shudder in revulsion as he runs his nose along my throat.

"You know that I plan to torture Alaric," he muses against my skin. "Do you know what the worst torture for a mated vampire is, short of their mate's death?" His lips are at my ear when he whispers, "For someone else to *defile* what's theirs."

A violent shudder racks my body, but I don't cry out, I don't whimper or sob or scream, even when his hand tangles in my hair and he yanks my head back to meet his gaze. I've been taught to be strong and I will be fucking strong. I clench my hands into fists and wait for the right moment to fight back—because I *will* be fighting back. I know I can't defeat him, especially not with my hands chained, but I will not simply allow him to do what he pleases.

"He'll be able to smell me all over you," he rasps. "It will be agony for him. Delicious fucking agony." The fear all but vanishes, the box buried so deep in the earth that no one can touch it now. The only thing I feel now is absolute, all-consuming rage. He wants to use me, in the most vile and literal sense of the word, to hurt Alaric, to torture him on a level that most would never be able to even comprehend. How fucking *dare* he. A strange, cold confidence settles over me, an absurd surety that I feel deep in my bones. I make a vow to the Gods of Death and Vengeance and War that I will make good on this promise:

"I'll kill you for this," I hiss at him, and he laughs, low and gravelly. I jut my chin and his eyes darken, as if my defiance is enticing. Just as his other hand goes to the laces of my vest, someone at the door clears their throat. He growls in annoyance but stops what he's doing to turn his head towards the visitor.

"What is it?" he snaps.

"Your raven has returned," the Revenant says. "The High General rides towards the Plain as we speak."

My heart stutters, though I'm not at all surprised. Kilgren turns back to me and smiles a wicked smile that sends ice through my veins.

"Not to worry, pet. We'll continue this later—while your precious vampire is chained in silver and forced to watch." Something flares in the back of my mind, not even an idea, but the mere *idea* of an idea, the barest whisper of one. I grab onto it with all the strength I have, something deep inside me that I don't even understand telling me that this is the key.

Kilgren releases his hold on me and steps away. Without looking from me, he tells the other Revenant, "Ready the men. We leave in two hours. Make sure that leech is prepared." The Revenant scurries off and Kilgren smiles. "This is going to be fun, little human."

He rakes his gaze down my body once more before giving me a disgustingly salacious grin and striding out of the cell. I nearly collapse as the rush of everything falls over me: what he plans to do, what he would have done if we hadn't been interrupted, the thought of Alaric's pain and panic as he rides ever closer to what will be our end. I brace my hands on my knees and take a few ragged breaths before forcing myself to calm, to inhale slowly, hold it, and then exhale. Over and over, until my heart stops hammering inside my chest and my ribs stop feeling as if they might crush my insides at any moment. Finally, I straighten and try to focus on whatever that whisper had been.

I know that Alaric, the glorious, genius, mastermind of battle that he is, will not have a plan to stop this. He wouldn't risk my life by trying to trick Kilgren, the mating bond overtaking everything else.

So, it's up to me.

I think and think, pacing back and forth and rubbing the ring my father had given me that day that seems so far away now, and slowly, oh so slowly, a plan starts to form. It's crazy, pure insanity really, and there's almost a one hundred percent chance that it won't work, but...it *might*.

I go through it again and again, trying to think the way Alaric does, trying to think of it as a game of chess with moves and counter-moves and possibilities and odds. After what seems like forever, I've solidified the plan as much as I possibly can, so I stop my pacing and turn to the door of the cell.

"Is it true?" I ask. Neither of the guards acknowledge that I've spoken. "That not all of you want war? That you've been forced into it all these years?" Again, no answer. I blow out an irritated breath, stirring a curl from my forehead only for it to fall again.

"So, it *isn't* true. You're all monsters, just as we've been taught for the last thousand years," I spit, annoyed. I'm about to be raped and tortured for the rest of my life apparently, the least they could do is answer a simple question.

The one who hadn't reacted to Kilgren's taunt earlier turns to face me and I see that he has a scar on his cheek, a thick *X* with a line bisecting it through the middle. It looks as if it's been burned into his skin—branded. The other Revenant turns just enough to give his companion a wary look.

"Malek," he warns, but Malek ignores him, holding my gaze. I'm shocked to see so much depth in his crimson eyes, so much...pain and sorrow.

"It's true," he says quietly. "There are many of us who did not want war, who wished to seek a peace between our people and the vampires and the humans—or at the very least, the freedom to find a new home and remove ourselves from this fight completely." I blink, surprised to hear the words and even more surprised by how entirely I believe him. There's something different about this Revenant, something more...human. He isn't like the bloodthirsty beasts that attacked me on the road, he's almost *gentle* for fuck's sake.

And broken. So utterly broken.

"Malek," the other one sighs, but gives up and turns to face me as well. He has the same scar as Malek on his cheek and I have a feeling that it's no coincidence. "When Kilgren learned of the talks of peace, he was furious. He challenged his father, took control of our people, and commanded that all of us who wanted peace show ourselves. Of course, we had to obey. The compulsion to do as commanded by our Chieftain is too powerful for even the strongest of us to push against. He branded us as traitors," he says, pointing to the *X* on his cheek and I try to cover my mouth with my hand, horrified, but the chains rattle and the cuff digs into my wrist. I wince at the pain, my skin raw and bloody from trying to pull myself free.

"They killed our families," he continues, "even those with mates—and forbade their other halves from ending their pain and joining their beloveds on the other side of the eternal river." I blink, unable to hide my shock. The Revenants have *mates*?? I'd honestly never even thought of them as having feelings at all, or families or, uh, *relations*, though of course they must for there to be new Revenants created without humans around to turn. But the idea of them having mates the way vampires do never occurred to me as a possibility. It makes sense, I suppose, but my mind is reeling at this revelation.

The Revenant continues, "And now he forces the rest of us to serve him in this war as punishment, to spill blood at his command. If he told me to slit your throat now, I would have no choice but to do it, no matter how much I might want to resist, no matter how much I would recoil inside." He huffs out a humorless laugh. "Punishment is perhaps not a strong enough word for what this is. Torment. Torture. Agony. Perhaps those are closer to the truth."

"We don't want to hurt anyone. We don't want to kill," Malek says, almost pleadingly, as if he's wanted to say these words to someone for so, so long. "I wanted a life of peace and it got my wife and daughter killed, and yet I still want no part of this war. Our ancestors may have all been bloodthirsty, but we have changed. We do not all believe as they did, as many of our brethren still do. As the Montclares changed the way of the vampires, some of us have evolved and found a better way to exist, a better way to live."

Tears well in my eyes. I wonder how many of the Revenants that Alaric has fought have been there against their will, how many of them had families or even mates that were slaughtered and were then forced to fight a battle they had no interest in fighting. How many innocent lives had been taken? How much innocent blood spilled?

"Why do you ask?" the other Revenant asks, studying me.

"I just needed to know the truth," I say vaguely. Malek narrows his eyes at me and then sighs.

"Whatever you are planning, young one, be careful."

"I won't make a promise that I can't keep...but I will do everything I can to make this right."

"You are very brave," the other Revenant says, inclining his head and putting two fingers to his forehead. Malek does the same and when they both straighten, Malek's lips twitch ever so slightly into a ghost of a smile long forgotten. "It is a sign of respect among our people," he explains. They both tense, heads jerking towards the end of the hallway. "They come," he says quietly.

"What's your name," I ask the other one quickly.

"Xavier," he says in a whisper. "Be strong, Dahlia."

They both straighten and face forward, as if the conversation never happened, and I shrink back against the wall. A few moments later, steps echo down the corridor and then Kilgren steps up to the bars.

"It's time," he says with a twisted smile, something between vicious and elated.

I take a deep breath, send up a quick prayer to every god I can think of, and hope that maybe, just maybe, I can pull this off.

CHAPTER 45

ALARIC

We approach the Obsidian Plain and I can hardly breathe around the knot in my chest, around the spikes of fear and pain I felt from Dahlia as we made our way here. That bastard hurt her in some way, and I couldn't do a damn thing to stop it. *Never again.*

I don't know how, but I will never let him hurt her again. I will beg, I will plead, I will give him anything he desires—and really, I know that is all he wants. He wants to conquer Braxhelm, of course, but mostly, he wants to conquer *me*. He wants to see me brought low, to see me on my knees before him.

Elias is as taut as a bowstring beside me, fingers flexing and clenching on the hilts of his twin swords. Everyone is tense and thrumming for a battle that will never come. I know the choice was theirs, but I cannot help but feel the weight of their impending deaths on my shoulders. All of this is my fault. Dahlia in danger, my army soon to be in ruin, the safety of the continent hanging in the balance—all of it lies with me.

"However this ends, know that it has been my greatest honor to fight beside you, and my greatest privilege to call you my friend, Alaric. I do not regret a single moment," Elias says.

My chest twists painfully. I hold his gaze, letting his words strike at the very core of me. I nod but then try to break the awful tension hanging over us one last time.

"Not even the time that wench broke your cock and it took a week to heal?" I meet his gaze and he knows what I'm really saying: *I love you. You're my brother. It has been my great honor. Thank you.* His lips curl and soon his customary carefree smile settles over his face.

"Alright, perhaps that bit might be changed," he admits.

"Or the time you were caught fucking General Hightower's daughter and he chased you naked through the town square down in Rivendale?" Malcom supplies.

"Or the time—"

"Enough!" Elias shouts, and a ripple of laughter travels through the lines of soldiers. "As if none of you lot have ever put your cock where it didn't belong."

I laugh lightly but then Elias curses and I freeze. He whirls just as Enid rides up on what I assume is a stolen horse.

"What in the seven hells...?"

"What are you doing here?!" Elias shouts, fury and fear rolling off of him in waves. He sheaths his swords at his back and strides to the horse. He reaches out to gently grasp her waist and ease her down to the ground. She holds onto his arms and the look they share is enough to make even my cheeks flush. She swallows hard and shakes herself, pushing her shoulders back and looking so like Dahlia that I almost smile.

"You're meant to be half way to Astoria's Keep by now, damn it!" Elias fumes.

Enid juts her chin. "She's my sister, Elias. And you're my..." She cuts herself off, licking her lips and glancing around quickly before continuing. "I couldn't just run away and leave you to ride into death alone. I couldn't let that be the end..." She angrily wipes tears away and Elias seems torn between terror and elation. I daresay that we don't have to wonder if Elias will win Enid's heart any longer.

My chest clenches painfully, feeling as if a blade is driving right into my heart. They've found each other, only to have it all end in mere moments. Elias cradles her face between his hands, staring at her like she's the only thing in existence. They have some silent conversation and then he leans in to kiss her fiercely, pulling away after a few moments and resting his forehead against hers.

"Where you go, I go," she whispers. He squeezes his eyes shut in pain, and I know that his instincts are roaring at him to get her as far away from this danger as possible, to protect her at all costs. But he finally nods, kisses her forehead, and mutters something about Clayburn women and stubborn asses.

He clasps Enid's hand and we continue onward. After a few moments, Enid asks casually, "so, just how many wrong places has your cock been, Elias?"

Against all odds, I laugh. Lightly at first, but then harder, and soon we're all clutching our sides. Enid grins and leans into Elias' side and he kisses her temple, smiling. It's a strange thing to be taking the final steps of this gallows march while laughing our asses off.

We break through the final line of trees, the laughter slowly fading, and then we're on the Plain. Even the fresh snow can't hide the eternal stains of this place, the blood-sodden ground seeping up into the gathered flakes and turning them a dark rusty-black color. Thousands of Revenants wait for us, armed and ready for battle—no, not battle. They're ready for *slaughter*.

And just in front of them, in the middle of the clearing, Kilgren stands with Dahlia.

My heart explodes at the sight of her, my fangs and claws flaring in the need to destroy the one who dares to touch my mate. I study her and a growl rips free from my chest when I see her bruised cheek, the dried blood on her lip.

My vision goes red and I lose all sense of reason, not even

thinking logical thoughts. All I know is that I need to get to my mate. I feel the squeezing sensation as I try to teleport to her—only to slam into something hard as stone and tumble to the ground still fifty yards away from her.

Dahlia screams my name, eyes wide with terror. I spring to my feet and try once more, only to be thrown backwards again. The others approach behind me, sprinting forward from the edge of the Plain at what they assumed was a call to battle.

Kilgren smiles widely. "Tsk, tsk, Alaric. Already disobeying the rules of this little parlay."

I bare my fangs at him and reach out a hand, blinking in shock when it meets something solid, but entirely invisible. My brow furrows.

"What the fuck?" Elias breathes as he reaches my side. He puts out a hand, meeting that same invisible wall. I spare a moment to note that Enid is safely back at the very edge of the clearing, Takara beside her.

"What is this?" I demand, seething, though I know how foolish I've been. Of course he wouldn't have relied solely on my word that I wouldn't attack, but...how??

Kilgren holds my gaze, gloating delight sparking in those blood-red eyes.

"Come forward, leech. Show them all who you truly are."

Leech? What is he talking about? Elias curses low beside me, tensing and then I see it: fucking *Highspear* steps from behind the first line of Revenants. Rage and fury burn through my chest. His palms are outstretched, faint blue light swirling around them.

"You fucking traitor!" Malcom roars, surging forward only to run into the invisible wall. He beats his fists against it, to no avail. A rumble of disgust ripples through the soldiers, disgust and *pain*. The fact that one of our own would betray us to our greatest enemy is beyond imagining and strikes to the very heart of all of us, the bond shared between us.

"How are you doing this?" I demand, clenching my fists so tightly the bones creak. I try to force my thoughts to calm, but all I want to do is rip his fucking head off.

"He's a wielder," Dahlia says from her spot beside Kilgren, trying to step forward, but he yanks her back, keeping a firm grip on her arm. She has no coat, so I know she must be freezing, but my mate doesn't look cold. No, she looks like her very blood has been turned to fire, burning with indignation and fury and I don't think she's ever looked so fearsome or beautiful. *Our firebrand.* She glares at Kilgren but turns back to me and continues, not giving a shit about him. *Gods, do I love this woman.*

"He hid his family history so he could be turned, but apparently the prick had gifts all this time. He was the one who hid the Revenants that attacked the road."

"I told you that I was worthy time and time again," Highspear calls, a wild gleam in his eye. "But you wouldn't listen! Now, I'll make you regret it! Now, I'll bring down everything you built!"

"Well, I think *I'll* actually be doing that," Kilgren croons, looking both amused and annoyed. "I'm the one with the army, if you recall, leech."

Highspear presses his lips into a hard line but nods. Fury and disgust roil inside me to see him obeying this monster, turning on his own people.

"Now, why don't we get down to business, shall we?" Kilgren says loud enough for his voice to be heard across the whole of the field, echoing off of the sides of the cliffs that border either side. He tightens his grasp on Dahlia's arm, so tightly that his claws dig into her skin and draw blood. She gasps but bites down on her lip to keep from crying out.

"Stop!" I roar.

"I will, if you give me what I want. If you agree to my terms, no harm will come to your little *mate.*" A shocked murmur ripples through the gathered crowd. If I didn't know better, I would say that there isn't just surprise on some of the Revenant's faces but...*disgust*

—not at me or my mate, but at their own leader. I shake the thought off, knowing how ridiculous it is.

"What do you want?" I growl through clenched teeth, though I know the answer already. His eyes sparkle with wicked glee, his lips curling back from his fangs.

"*Kneel,*" he rasps.

Everything in me recoils at the word, sneers at the very thought. But I must. I know that he's lying about no harm coming to Dahlia, but I have to try. I have to do everything in my power to keep her safe.

"Kneel before me," he continues, "and surrender."

"Doona fucking dare, Alaric!!" Dahlia yells, furious and pulling against Kilgren's vice-like grip. Blood pours down her arm, but she doesn't seem to notice or care. She meets my gaze and I know she can see it in my eyes because I can feel her utter heartbreak and panic through our bond. She knows what I'm going to do. She knows that I'll give up everything for her. She shakes her head once and begs in a soft whisper, "no."

"It will be alright, Keeva. All will be well," I lie. A single tear streams down her cheek...but then she transforms, her features hardening and that steadfast determination (and stubbornness) that I love so much settling over her. She turns back to face Kilgren. I don't understand what's happening and understand even less when her next words echo through the clearing:

"I challenge you!"

CHAPTER 46

DAHLIA

*F*uck. Here we go.

Shock and incredulity and amusement ring out through the Revenants gathered around us. Kilgren stares at me blankly for a moment, as if he doesn't understand the words I've spoken, but soon enough I see the rage begin to roil inside him.

"I challenge you for leadership of the Revenants," I say again, jutting my chin. I had no idea if this would even work, if a challenge could be issued from someone who isn't one of their own, but it was the only idea I could come up with that had even a sliver of a chance. And with the way Kilgren is reacting, I'm betting that a challenge from *anyone* must be honored. I barely stop a triumphant smile from spreading across my face.

"You little *bitch*," he spits, eyes blazing and fangs bared.

"Challenge? What are you talking about? Dahlia! What the fuck is happening!?" Alaric roars, still held at bay by Luca's shield. I ignore him, keeping my focus on Kilgren. This plan is insane, but it's the only one available to me. It's the only one that has a chance of keeping Alaric and my friends safe, the only one that has a chance of saving Braxhelm.

"I won't let you use me to torture him," I say quietly. "Either way, your plan fails here and now." I shift my shoulders back. "A fight to the death now, is it not?" I ask, louder, smirking. Surprisingly, I'm not afraid. The fear is locked firmly away in that box and buried deep in the earth. Kilgren growls, a deep, unsettling sound that sends shivers up my spine.

"It's no matter. Your death will still destroy him. Without him, the army will fall. My forces outnumber his." He spreads his arm wide to gesture to the thousands of Revenants lined up behind us. It's true that Alaric's forces are smaller—I'm assuming he sent most of his men south to spread the word and evacuate civilians, or gave them leave to flee with their families. My heart swells knowing that those who stand beside him came out of loyalty and love for Alaric, but also a bit for me—but I have faith that they will survive long enough to retreat or join the others, and then they will fight back. They will not give up. They will beat back against Kilgren's forces again. I have to have faith or I can't do this.

"I will still come out victorious, you stupid little human. Soon, all of Braxhelm will bow to me." Kilgren leans towards me and adds in a low snarl, "I will still make him suffer, I promise you that." I grind my teeth and try to pull my arm from his grasp, but his claws have dug in like razors.

"A challenge has been issued," another Revenant says loudly—Xavier?—and Kilgren's lip curls in an irritated sneer. "A challenge must be answered."

Without taking his eyes from me, Kilgren calls out to his men, "I accept the challenge. A fight to the death, as is custom."

I can hear Alaric yelling, screaming his denial. He might not understand what's happening, exactly, probably not having any idea about how leadership works with the Revenants, but he surely understands the words *fight to the death*. I want to turn to him so badly, to tell him that everything will be alright one way or another, but I don't dare take pull my gaze from Kilgren's. A rumble cascades from the Revenants all around us, but not a single voice lifts to give objection. These are ancient laws, laws built into their very blood. They are absolute.

One of us will die.

Kilgren bares his fangs and they are most certainly sharper and longer than they'd been a moment ago. I swallow hard but don't cower.

"I had such plans for you, Dahlia." His eyes skate over my body and I try not to cringe. "To deny me of them is unforgiveable. But not to worry, I will visit my retribution on all of those that you love. Mark my words, little human: they *will* suffer in your place, in ways you cannot imagine." I shiver at that, my blood turning to ice at the thought, but I tell myself that it won't happen, that this will be worth it and everything will turn out alright.

I bare my teeth at him and hiss, "Let's get on with it then, shall we? I tire of hearing you speak."

He grins at that and chuckles low. He releases my arm and I take a step back, shifting my stance the way Wesley and Nova taught me.

"Leech!" he calls, "keep that fucking shield in place. Our great High General isn't going to like what's about to happen."

"Dahlia!! Gods damn it, what the fuck are you doing!?" I can hear Alaric screaming, his voice hoarse from it, and beating against the invisible barrier with all his might. All of them are, all of the soldiers that followed Alaric into this valley are shouting and clamoring against the wall, desperate to get to me. My heart surges at that, their strength bolstering mine.

I can do this for them. I take one quick, settling breath, and just hope that he doesn't take my head off instantly. That will severely derail this plan.

"Let's be quick about this. I have an army to destroy." He shifts to the right and follow, keeping him in front of me. He goes back left, stalking me casually like a big cat. "I can smell your fear. It's mouthwatering," he taunts.

"Fuck you," I say through gritted teeth, stepping forward and swinging my right fist towards his face. He grabs my wrist easily and tugs me closer, smiling. He glances down where he clutches me, claws digging into my flesh, and take the momentary distraction to lash out with my left arm. I rake my nails down his cheek, smiling when I see the black blood well. He arches a brow, completely unfazed.

"Is that it? Scratching like a feral alley cat?" Kilgren scoffs, laughing mockingly. A few Revenants around us join in. "I'm honestly a little disappointed, Dahlia. I expected more from the legendary High General's mate."

A moment later blinding pain explodes through my stomach as his claws sink deep into my flesh, ripping through bone and muscle. I gasp, trying to breathe around the pain, but it's impossible. I hear Alaric roar in fury, screaming as he feels my pain through our bond. I blink at Kilgren, trying to keep my thoughts focused. *Just a little longer. I need to hold on a little longer.*

I grit my teeth against the pain and my legs nearly give out when I look down to see Kilgren's fingers buried inside my body, blood pouring like a waterfall. He releases my right wrist and wraps his arm around my lower back, holding me upright and pulling me close to his body. It's strangely gentle, almost intimate.

"And, to no one's surprise, I am the victor of this little challenge," he muses. I cough and blood fills my mouth, dripping over my lips and down my chin. I reach a trembling hand up to his face, laying it against his cheek. His brow furrows in surprise at the touch, but he doesn't pull away.

"There was a better way," I say softly, sliding my hand down his face to the side of his neck. "You should have listened to them."

He scoffs. "Peace? You use your dying breath to speak of *peace*? How pathetic."

I lean up towards him as I press the hidden release on the band of my ring, the one da had given me all those months ago. The one that was my own design.

Discrete weaponry has always been a habit of mine.

The thin needle pops out from the side.

"Not dying yet," I whisper, and slam my hand into his throat. I feel the needle break through his skin, sinking directly into the thick vein there. The powder hidden inside the stone empties, flowing directly into his bloodstream.

He releases me, his claws sliding free from my gut. I nearly topple before steadying myself, one hand flying to my wound. I cringe at the feel of my ruined flesh, the blood and...slimy things that I don't want to think about too deeply. His hand goes to his neck, confusion clear on his face.

"Wh...what did you do?" he gasps before falling to his knees and clawing at the ground in pain. The veins in his neck and face and hands begin to turn black, like the roots of a rotten tree spreading beneath the soil. They're moving faster than they had with Alaric when he'd been poisoned. My blow was directly to the vein, where Kilgren's archer had missed by a few inches.

"Silver powder," I say with a surprising amount of strength. I know I only have so much left, know deep in my bones that this wound won't be healed, even if Alaric were to get to me in time. *It's alright. It's worth it. It will protect them all.* "You weren't the only one with a secret store of it. And I'm willing to bet you don't have a mate to come and heal you," I say, grinning wickedly at him through the blood in my mouth. There's no way the gods would be so cruel as to give this monster the gift of a mate.

He opens his mouth to say something, but the words are lost in a scream of agony that makes my ears ring. He falls to his back and writhes in pain. Cries of outrage and disbelief echo around us, but I focus only on Kilgren. My vision blurs but I force the pain away, force death itself away by sheer stubborn will. I have to see this through.

"Not yet," I whisper through gritted teeth at the God of Death. I can practically feel him breathing down my neck. "*Not fucking yet.*"

The Revenants all around us look on in confusion and unease, but no one moves forward, bound by the ancient laws to watch as the challenge unfolds, I assume. I pull my gaze from Kilgren's body as it bows and twists in pain and rage, as his veins seem to burn with poison, turning black and rigid beneath his skin, and scan the crowd, noting every scarred cheek among them. Xavier has moved forward, standing just outside the invisible ring that seems to have surrounded Kilgren and me during the challenge. He stares in shock but I see the flicker of understanding in his crimson eyes.

I look back to Kilgren as he gives one final screech of pain, eyes burning with fury as he meets my gaze one final time. The crimson is veined with black now, and dark blood leaks from the corners.

"No," he mouths and then collapses, falling utterly still. Something seems to slam into me then, right into my chest, some invisible force that fills my heart and spreads out through my entire body. It's *power*. A strange, raw, ancient power that I don't quite understand but somehow understand completely all at once. This is the bond that connects every Revenant, the power over all of them now resting in my veins.

My eyes fly wide at the same moment the Revenants seem to understand what's happened, when they feel their allegiance shift to me. A particularly ferocious looking beast bares his fangs at me.

"A human cannot lead us!" he roars.

Before he can say or do more, Xavier twists his head and snaps his neck with a sickening crack. The Revenant's body tumbles to the ground and Xavier gives me a solemn nod. I need to finish this before any others get the same idea and try to attack me—or worse, issue their own challenge. I have no more tricks up my sleeve and know that I'm keeping the God of Death waiting in the wings.

"Drop your weapons!" I call out, putting as much authority into the power thrumming inside me as I can. Weapons fall to the ground all around me and I try not to show the surprise and elation that this is actually working. "You will remain in place!" I yell, scanning the army. Though some look to be trying to push against the mystical bonds holding them in place, they all obey, most looking more confused than anything.

"Dahlia!!" Alaric roars. I know he has no idea what's happening and can feel the agony of my wound, can probably feel how close to death I truly am, but I have one more thing I have to do before this is over.

"I know some of you did not want war before Kilgren took the power as your Chieftain. I know many of you wanted peace and were punished severely for it."

A tide of confused murmurs washes through the gathered forces on both sides, Revenants and vampires alike not quite understanding what's happening. I find Malek, who has stepped up beside Xavier, and he's staring at me incredulously, but there's a tiny glimmer of hope in his eyes. *This will work. This has to work.*

"Dahlia what are you doing!? What's happening!?" Alaric yells, still beating uselessly against the shield. I'm glad that Luca seems too terrified to let it drop now that Kilgren is gone.

"They wanted peace!" I call back, gritting my teeth as a wave of nausea and pain roil through me. I glance down and see that my hand is completely coated in blood, the ground slick with it, each flake of falling snow that hits the plain instantly transforming from white to crimson. I don't have much time left.

"Any of you who do not wish for war, who only desire to live in peace with the vampires and humans, step forward!"

Malek steps forward at the same time as Xavier. All down the line, Revenants with scarred cheeks—and even some without—step away from their brethren. The others snarl and curse and rage, spitting insults and vitriol at them for wanting peace. I hold Malek's gaze and incline my head at him before turning to Alaric. Seeing him nearly breaks my heart in two, the anguish on his face sending a fresh wave of pain through my chest. The urge to run to him is nearly overwhelming, but I *will* fucking finish this.

"Alaric, vow to me that any who have stepped forward will not be harmed. They will be given the opportunity to live in peace from this day forward." His brow furrows, looking at me like I'm insane. I know he's torn between trying to figure out what's happening and the need to get to me.

"Dahlia, what—"

"Vow it, damn it! I can't explain it now, but they must obey me. If they didn't truly desire peace, they wouldn't have been able to step forward. Trust me. And fucking vow it!" I scream again.

He studies me for what feels like an eternity and the area around him becomes dark and fuzzy. I think I see my sister, but I know it must just be a sign that the end is near. Aren't loved ones something you see as death approaches? Something lovely to usher you from this world into the one beyond?

"I vow, as High General of the vampiric army of Braxhelm and as a prince of the Montclare Clan, that no harm will come to any who have stepped forward and wish for peace." I let out a shuddering sigh of relief.

"All of you," I call to the Revenants who have chosen peace, "Move over here." I point to the area near where Luca stands, shaking with fear and strain. "You're going to want to be out of the way for this," I mutter. Malek takes the lead and quickly urges them all to the area I've indicated.

"The rest of you," I call out, "Kneel!" One by one they all sink to their knees in the rust-colored snow, all snarling and cursing and looking like they want to murder me. "You will not move. You have the choice to surrender or die." I'll let Alaric and the others figure out what to do from there.

I feel myself sway but force my shoulders back.

"Xavier and Malek, you will accompany the vampires to the stronghold and carry my command with you: those who want peace will not be harmed. The rest will have to deal with the vampires." They both nod and bow their heads.

"Yes, my Chieftess," Malek says reverently.

"Highspear! Let down the shield! Let them in!" I yell.

"Like hells I will! I'll be slaughtered!" he calls back, voice shaking. He meets my gaze and his eyes are full of fear and panic.

I nearly scream in frustration. "I do not have time for this, damn it!" I reach back and pull one of the daggers free from my hair clip. I grit my teeth at the agony that I know awaits, and throw the blade the way Alaric and Wesley and Nova taught me. It sails through the air and lands true—right through Luca's right eye. He screams in pain, clawing at the hilt sticking out of his eye socket, but it's enough to divert his power and make the shield fall. With the way Highspear is screeching, I think da may have just put real silver in those daggers after all. I almost laugh.

Alaric is by my side the instant the shield falls, the rest of the men sprinting to the lines of Revenants. I don't see what they do and, really, I don't care as long as Malek and the others who wanted peace aren't harmed.

I collapse in Alaric's arms and he sinks to his knees on the blood-soaked snow.

"Keeva? Keeva, ah gods, look at me, love." I force my eyes to open again so I can look at him one last time. I know this is the end. I reach up and rest my bloody palm on his cheek.

"I'm sorry," I rasp. "It was the only way...he planned to torture me to torture you. Couldn't...let you be hurt...that way." I cough, blood thick and hot in my mouth.

"Shh, don't try to talk. I can fix this. I can heal you." I know he knows the truth, the red-tinged tears streaming down his cheeks tell me as much. "Drink," he begs, tearing into his wrist with his fangs and holding it towards my mouth. "You cannot leave me, Dahlia Clayburn. You will not!"

"Honor your vow," I whisper. "Let this be the end of the war. Take care of my family and Takara and Wesley and Nova and—" I gasp and writhe as a wave of pain crashes in to me, "—all of them," I bite out. "Take care of all of them, Alaric."

"Dahlia! No! No damn it, I will not lose you!!"

I swear I hear Enid screaming my name, swear that I see Takara running towards us in battle gear. I really am seeing things as I cross to the other side.

"I love you," I tell Alaric one last time. My eyes slide closed, my hand falls from his cheek and lands limply in the snow, and I feel the darkness coming to greet me.

The last thing I hear is Alaric's unholy roar of agony. I want to tell him that it will be ok. I want to tell him to continue on without me. I want to tell him over and over how much I love him and how sorry I am that we didn't have more time.

But I can't say any of these things.

I'm gone.

CHAPTER 47
ALARIC

N^{o.}

    No.

    NO.

"Alaric!!" Elias yells, falling to his knees beside me but his voice is coming from far, far away. There's a ringing in my ears, like after a chemical explosion.

I can't move.

I can't breathe.

I can't think.

She's...gone.

The roaring in my ears gets louder, near deafening, the pain in my chest unbearable.

"Alaric," Elias yells in my ear, somehow loud enough to be heard over the din in my head, the destruction of my entire world raining down around me. "Listen, damn you!" He shakes me hard enough to force me to obey.

My entire body jolts—a nearly silent *thump-thump* of her heart. There's still a spark left, a tiny one but...yes, it's there. There's still time. I meet Elias' gaze and he nods.

"You must hurry."

"Handle things here and at their stronghold. I'm taking her to Ashcliff."

"Good luck, brother," he says, clamping me hard on the shoulder. Enid dashes up then and he whirls to catch her, pulling her into his arms as she screams and cries. He mutters something low in her ear and I see her sink into him like he's the only thing that could possibly keep her afloat just before Dahlia and I disappear. We land in our bedroom and I immediately stagger to the bed and place her gently atop it.

"Alora!" I cry. "Alora! To me! NOW!!"

A moment later the door bursts open and Alora hurries in, shock on her face. "My Lord, we didn't—oh gods!" she whispers as she takes in Dahlia, still and bloody on the bed. Livia and Vernon file into the room behind her, expressions quickly changing into matching ones of horror. "What's happened?"

"Fire. Now," I bark, ignoring the question. I turn back to the bed but hear them scurrying behind me to obey. Triston bursts in, lagging behind the others and quickly starts taking orders from Alora. My heart is racing so fast that the beating is just a constant, faint buzz, the individual beats undiscernible, and my blood feels like cold acid in my veins. I cannot lose her. I will *not* lose her. I take the briefest of moments to steady myself and then I ease onto the bed beside my mate. My love. My everything.

I shift behind her and pull her back to my chest, wrapping my arms tightly around her. Tears prick my eyes, but I don't dare think about the possibilities. I tear into my wrist again and force it between her lips. She only needs a few drops of my blood in her system. After enough has trickled down her throat, I brush her hair aside and lean down, my lips brushing her throat.

"Come back to me, Keeva," I whisper brokenly before sinking my fangs deep into her flesh. She doesn't react and my heart clenches, but I force every ounce of will and power I can into the venom now pouring from my fangs, demanding that it work its will and transform her into one of my kind. After a few minutes, I pull away and lean back against the headboard, holding her tightly in my arms and, for the first time in a very, very long time, begin to pray.

I know it's coming, but when her heart thuds with its final beat and then falls silent, that small spark that remained fading into nothing, everything inside of me rebels, every instinct roaring and clawing like a feral beast. I hear the faintest gasp from across the room as Alora realizes what's happened, quickly whispering to the others to leave immediately. A vampire who's lost his mate is... unpredictable, to say the least. My mind reels, desperate to rip the heart from my own chest to try to stop this agony, but I squeeze my eyes shut, trying to force the clamor away. I have to hold on.

She will return.

She will survive.

She will come back to me.

And so, I wait.

CHAPTER 48

ALARIC

"We got here as quickly as we could," Elias says quietly as he sinks into a chair beside the bed. I don't know how much time has passed, but I haven't moved an inch since the moment Dahlia's heart stopped beating. The turning can take days, but...has it been too long? Is she...gone?

No.

I won't think of it.

She will return. She will wake and she will be healed and whole and mine, forever more. I grit my teeth, daring the gods to try to say otherwise.

"The stronghold fell quickly—the majority of those left behind were woman and children, or the very old, and most of them did not wish to fight. Those who tried to make a stand did not last long, most taken out by their own people, actually. I still can't quite believe it. All this time, there were so many who didn't want to fight us..." He shakes his head and clenches his jaw, and I know that he's wondering the same thing I am: how many lives were lost needlessly on both sides? How much innocent blood has stained our blades and souls?

"Anyway, we left those who surrendered there with a contingent of the army to keep watch until we can figure everything out. The rest were dispatched."

"Good," I say, hate and rage making my blood boil. Those who wanted war are the reason my mate was taken, the reason she was hurt. The fact that she not only killed Kilgren, but ended the entire fucking war, is still something I can't quite wrap my mind around, though it isn't surprising. I think that Dahlia can do just about anything once she sets her stubborn mind to it. My lips almost curl in amusement, but I can't seem to bring myself to smile.

Not until she wakes.

Elias sighs quietly, visibly relaxing just before the door opens. I know who will step through before she does, and want to laugh—was I so obvious in my affection for my mate as he is? Her eyes are red-rimmed and swollen, but she strides forward with her shoulders back and chin up.

"I want to sit with my sister," she says, voice strong with only the tiniest tremor beneath the surface. Elias tenses, knowing how fiercely a vampire guards his mate, but I try to think logically around the din of instinctual, feral possession. Dahlia loves her sister more than almost anyone else on this earth. She would not want me to deny Enid a chance to be with her now. In fact, it may help to bring her back, to coax her from the brink and back towards the light.

"Come, Alaric," Elias says quietly, "you need to drink, and Sebastian will be here any moment, I'm sure. It's only been two days." My head jerks at that. It feels like it's been an eternity. "You know the turning usually takes at least four, maybe even five or six when injuries are...severe," he adds carefully. I clench my jaw but somehow nod and force myself to slide out from behind Dahlia and lay her gently down on the pillow. Every cell in my body protests as our bodies pull apart, but I know this is right. I move to pull the blanket around her only to realize that she's still in her blood-soaked clothing. I stare at her wound, the deep gouges in her flesh where Kilgren's claws ripped her apart. I see flashes of bone and gnash my teeth, fangs and claws snapping out as rage engulfs my body, but a gentle hand settles on my arm.

I blink and force the red from my vision, looking down to realize that Enid has stepped up beside me.

"I'll get her changed and cleaned up. She'll be cross as an alley cat if she wakes still covered in dirt and blood." She forces a watery smile and I exhale roughly, so thankful for this human in this moment that I can barely even comprehend it. I nod at her and step away. Elias stands beside me and claps me on the shoulder and, as hard as it is, I walk away from the bed. Elias plants a soft kiss on Enid's temple and her eyes slide closed for a moment, looking for a heartbeat as if all is right in the world. He strides towards me and we leave the room as Livia and Vernon bring over a steaming basin of water, rags, and clean clothes.

When the door closes behind us, I lean against the wall, nearly collapsing as I try to breathe around the knot in my chest. I feel like my chest is shrinking, like my ribs are collapsing inward and squeezing, squeezing, squeezing...

I can't breathe. I can't, I can't, I can't—

Elias is there then, pulling me tight into his chest and holding me up.

"She'll do it, Alaric. I know it. She's the strongest fucking person I've ever met. She'll turn beautifully and become the most fearsome little vampire in all of Braxhelm. Breathe, Alaric," he adds quietly and I can hear the strain in his voice. "Breathe with me, brother."

Slowly, the tightening in my chest eases and I suck in deep, gasping breaths. Eventually, they calm and I find the strength to pull away from Elias, standing on my own once more. He slaps my cheek gently and smiles, though it isn't nearly as bright as usual.

"There now. Let's get you cleaned up, shall we?"

He says it nonchalantly but I know that I'm covered in Dahlia's blood and the reminder of how badly she was injured is like a knife in both of our sides. Though everything goes by in a blur and I don't quite remember actually showering or changing clothes, or even drinking deeply from the flask of Dahlia's blood that Elias holds out to me, soon enough I'm fed and in a clean tunic and pants, hair wet and dripping down my neck.

"What happened? Is she alright??" Sebastian demands as he flies through the doors of my study, Fi right on his heels looking distraught. Elias quickly fills them both in on what happened, how we were betrayed and Dahlia was taken, how she killed Kilgren and found that peace could be had with the Revenants, how she was injured and I'd attempted the turning.

Fiona storms up to me, fire in her eyes and clasps my face between her small hands.

"She *will* wake, Alaric," she says sternly, as if she's commanding it to be so. I give her a nod and she leans in to kiss me on the forehead.

"So...the war is...*over*?" Sebastian asks, incredulous.

"It appears so," I say, voice low and rough. Sebastian begins to pepper us with questions and after the twentieth one, a low growl tears from my chest. I'm anxious to get back to Dahlia's side, and am trying extremely hard not to rip my brother's throat out. Fi seems to realize how close I am to doing just that, and steps between the two of us.

"I think you should return to your mate," she says and looks pointedly at Sebastian, as if to say *stop talking, you idiot, he's about to kill you.*

"Of course, brother. Of course," Sebastian says quickly.

Elias catches my eye. "Go. I'll finish up here."

I nod in thanks and without thought, I'm beside our bed once more. Enid screams and throws herself protectively over her sister. The gesture will warm my heart later, but right now, all I can see or hear or focus on is Dahlia, still and cold and...and *dead* on the mattress before me.

"Fucking hells," Enid pants, clutching at her chest.

"Apologies," I somehow manage to grate.

"It's alright. There's been no change...which I know you know, but...I don't know what else to say," she says quietly. "I'll go." She kisses Dahlia on the forehead, tugging playfully on the end braid that she must have plaited as she stood vigil over her sister. "I'll see you soon, you little leech," she whispers and against all odds, I huff out a strangled laugh. Enid meets my gaze and gives me a small smile. She slides off the bed and as she passes me, places a gentle hand on my forearm. She squeezes reassuringly and II squeeze back, a silent communication passing between us. She nods and leaves us. I settle onto the bed beside Dahlia and take her hand in mine. I ignore how lifeless and cold it is, focus only on how perfectly it fits within my own.

I don't know what else to do, so I start to talk to her. I tell her all the things I've never told anyone. I tell her the things I'm afraid of and the ones I'm ashamed of. I tell her about my mother and my childhood and why Ahmed can go fuck himself. I tell her of training and battles and recall how I got every scar I can remember. I tell her of my friendships, of the people I've loved and the ones I've lost. Hours pass, so many that one day turns into another. Elias and the others check in periodically, but then they leave us.

I don't stop talking. I tell her how beautiful she is. I tell her how much I was dreading the Choosing but how I heard them talking in the dressing room from behind the wall and was already lost for her. I tell her how badly I wanted her since the first moment I saw her and how crazy she drove me all those months when I tried to keep her at arm's length.

"I had to run clear into the mountains the first time I heard you pleasuring yourself in your bed, Keeva," I say in a low voice, desperate for her to react. "It drove me so mad that I nearly lost all control. I almost stormed into that room and took you right there and then, hard and fast, damning all the consequences."

I freeze.

Was that...a twitch? I would swear I felt her finger move...

I wait, breath held and body taut as a bowstring, to see if my reason for living is going to return to me.

CHAPTER 49
DAHLIA

Being dead is strange.

Or, I think I'm dead, anyway.

I feel weightless and disembodied, like a spirit from an old fireside tale. I stand in the empty darkness, though it isn't a terrifying, oppressing darkness. It's peaceful. No pain. No fear. No sorrow. I turn in a slow circle, not sure what I'm supposed to be doing or why I seem to be stuck in this place. Wherever this place is. Time has no meaning here. It could be seconds. It could be years. I have no idea how long I stay in the darkness, but I'm not afraid.

After a heartbeat or an eternity, stars of every color flare to life far in the distance. They beckon, taunting me with their beauty and promised peace, and I long to go towards them.

Yes. Yes, of course I should go to them. I should throw myself into that tranquility and freedom. It would be so easy to just float away into those stars, wouldn't it? I take a step towards them, reaching out, but then I stop, my hand suspended in the air in front of me. *No.* No, something isn't right. I've forgotten something.

Something important.

I frown, trying to remember, something tugging on the very

edges of my mind when a silvery light snakes into the space all around me, swirling slowly. There's something powerful and almost forbidden in that light, something intriguing and terrifying and intoxicating. It seems to be…judging me? That seems rude, so I tilt my head, judging it right back.

"Not all can survive the gift," a breathy voice whispers from the light. The voice is inside my head and echoing from all around me all at once. It is neither male nor female, old nor young. It's a single voice and many. It's something primal and ethereal and I have no hopes to truly understand its depths, and yet, it feels as if it's a part of me and I know it as well as I know my own name.

"The gift?" I ask, turning in place as the light continues to swirl around me, a slow, assessing cyclone of power and promise.

"To change. To become more."

I gasp as realization hits me. What's happening and the reason that I can't go to the stars, why I have to keep fighting. What I've forgotten.

"Alaric," I whisper, smiling. Everything comes rushing back: the Obsidian Plain, the challenge, the agony as Kilgren gutted me… knowing that I was going to die and leave Alaric forever. But no. No, he must have attempted the turning at the last moment, when a tiny spark of life was left in my body. I feel it then, my body, heavy and lifeless around me, and I feel like I'm so far deep inside myself that I can never climb out again. A tendril of fear unfurls inside me. Am I too far gone? Was he too late?

Through the silvery light swirling around me, I can just glimpse the stars in the distance, but now I recoil from their beckoning, the thought of joining them abhorrent. *I can't leave him. I'm not ready.*

"You have the strength," the voice continues, *"but it will not be easy. There will be pain."*

"I do not fear pain," I say, shoulders back and chin jutting. The light ripples and shines brighter at that, almost as if it approves of my answer.

"You have been found worthy, Dahlia Clayburn. Now you must choose."

I wonder if this is how the turning is for everyone, if they're judged and asked to choose. Or if this is all just a strange trick of my mind as I try to fight back against death. If I survive this, I'll ask Wesley and Nova one day. Thoughts of my friends fill my mind, Enid and da and Takara and my guard and Braddock and countless others joining them, all giving me strength. I take a deep breath and stare directly into the light as it continues to swirl lazily around me.

"I choose this life. I choose Alaric. I choose the turning."

The light swirls faster, flaring so brightly that I close my eyes against the sting, and then, with no warning, it slams directly into my chest. Pain erupts as my entire self is broken down into dust. I fall to my knees as my body bends and breaks, as my blood boils and my cells turn to ash. The agony is more than a person can withstand, surely. Now I understand why the turning is a risk, why so many don't make it out alive. A part of me wants to give up, to give in and stop this pain and drift off into that peace among the stars.

NO.

I grit my teeth and chant his name in my mind, refusing to give up. He's my talisman. He's my life. He's my home. I hold on to him with everything I have, praying to all of the gods that it's enough.

Alaric. Alaric. Alaric. Take me back to him. Make me whole for him. Make me what I was always meant to be.

Power and strength and a strange hunger fill my body as the light continues to pour into me, to change me and reshape me on every level. Despite the pain ripping through my metaphorical body here in this strange in-between place, I can't seem to make my actual body move. Not yet. I hold on for seconds or hours or days.

And then, when I'm on the verge of giving up, I hear him.

Over the roar of agony in my ears, I hear Alaric. His voice fades in and out, some words lost in the storm as the light swirls and flows around me and through me, others clear as day. The pain is endless, every fiber of my being broken apart bit by bit, being burned away to ash until I don't know how there's possibly anything left, but I strain to hear him, hanging onto every word like a drowning man clings to a raft. He talks about everything and nothing, his childhood, his life, his love for his family and friends and me. He talks of battle and wounds and men lost. He talks of taking me hard and fast and I gasp, a flare of desire blooming so brightly it makes the light flash and spark around me, blocking out the pain for a moment. I want to reach for him, want to hold him so badly that my eyes burn with tears—

And my finger twitches.

"Keeva," I hear him whisper, his voice filled with a quiet hope. "Keeva, you must come back to me. I'll get on my knees and beg if I must, but I need you to open your damned eyes."

I want to. I want to open them and take the pain from his voice so badly I could scream. And then, I do. Or at least in my head I do. White hot agony spears through my heart, hotter and more painful than anything that's happened so far and I know without knowing how I know, that this is it. This is the end. I must hold on just a little bit longer. Inside my mind, I drop to my knees and claw at my chest as the heat becomes unbearable, scorching the blood in my veins. Outside, my hand twitches again, fingers curling into a fist, and my heart thuds loudly as it begins to beat once more.

"Dahlia!" Alaric gasps. "Dahlia, can you hear me!?"

"Is she waking??" I hear another voice ask. *Enid??*

"About damn time," Elias says, though I can tell there's relief beneath the humor. He huffs out a small "oof" as if someone's smacked him in the stomach.

"Come on, my Lady," Takara says. "I know how much you hate when I call you that, so wake up and tell me off about it."

"Wake, my wee firebrand." *Da.* My father's voice makes my heart twist. So many people that I love all in one place. All waiting for me.

"Dahlia?" Alaric says again, voice low and close to my ear.

Just when I think I can't take another second of the fire, it extinguishes all at once and the silvery light explodes into a shower of sparkling diamonds that float down all around me before everything turns black once more.

Welcome, the voice whispers from the darkness.

I am alive.

I am turned.

I am a vampire.

CHAPTER 50
DAHLIA

"I believe you promised to beg," I rasp before cracking open my eyes to find Alaric staring down at me, pink-tinged tears streaming down his cheeks. A broken sound rips free from his chest, something between a sob and a laugh and suddenly I'm up and in his arms and his face is buried in my neck.

"Dahlia, Dahlia, Dahlia." He says my name over and over, like a prayer. I wrap my arms around him, squeezing tightly. I can't imagine what he must have been feeling all this time while I was... dead. I realize then that I truly must have died for the turning to have been successful—and the fangs in my mouth and the burning thirst in the back of my throat tell me that it was, in fact, successful. *Holy. Shite.*

This is a lot to process all at once, so I take a deep breath and try to focus on one thing at a time.

"I'm...I'm turned?" It comes out as a question, though I know that it's true.

Alaric pulls away and cradles my face between his big hands, nodding and looking incredibly worried.

"Are you alright, love? How are you feeling? I know it can be overwhelming at first."

I blink as all the new details of his face register, all the different colors in his golden eyes, the shades of blue and black in his hair. *Holy fucking hells.* I knew vampires had enhanced senses and thought I'd gotten a glimpse when I'd taken so much of Alaric's blood after the attack on the road all those months ago, but I truly had no idea what it was really like. I can see dust mites dancing in the air, can hear hearts beating around us, can smell too many scents to even catalog or comprehend. It *is* overwhelming, every one of my senses being assaulted by too much stimuli at once, but it's also amazing. I'm in utter awe of the beauty around me, of the fact that I can see and hear and smell everything so vividly. It's like I'm seeing the world for the very first time—and what a brilliant world it is.

I don't thank the gods nearly as often as I should, but I thank them now for giving me this gift. I will be thanking them every day for the rest of...*forever*. I gasp inwardly but shake myself. The thought is a little too daunting to think about right now, so I save it to ponder later.

"I'm...ok," I say slowly, because I am. I'll get used to everything soon enough, I know. I'll find a way to adjust to these new changes in my body and mind and adapt to this new version of myself. The most important thing is that I'm alive. I'm here, with Alaric. I lean in to kiss him then, unable to stop myself, and his entire body shudders as our lips meet. *Gods.* If I thought kissing Alaric before was intoxicating, now it's downright life-altering. The taste of him. The feel of him. Lust rockets through my body, but also...*blood*lust. My fangs snap longer from my gums, extending fully and nicking my tongue. I gasp in surprise and Alaric moans softly when he tastes the blood. I pull away and cover my mouth with my hand.

"It's ok, love. It takes some getting used to, I've been told."

I stare at him, the need for blood temporarily put aside as an intense, overwhelming feeling of love for this man consumes me entirely. A voice I've never heard before echoes through my mind, sure and demanding: *yours.*

"You're mine too," I whisper in wonder, realizing what the voice is, what these feelings mean. "You're my mate. You always have been, really, but...well, now it makes sense."

"Ok, ok, he's your mate, but I'm your sister, and I need to hug you now," Enid says as she rushes forward. I huff out a laugh and Alaric brushes hair from my forehead before leaning in close to kiss me on the temple.

He whispers, "be gentle with her, Keeva," reminding me of my new strength. He pulls back and smiles before letting me go and sliding out of the way. He must have complete faith in me—Elias as well—that I won't hurt her, and I try to take that as a good sign. I don't want to be a danger to my human family and friends. I turn and Enid flies at me, wrapping her arms around me and sobbing into my hair. I can feel the strength roiling through my body and take Alaric's words to heart, being as gentle as I can as I hug her back. I can also feel the lifeblood pumping through her body, can smell the sweet perfume of it and my mouth waters, but it isn't the crazed, insatiable thirst that I envisioned. I don't feel like an animal who might rip her throat out any second. Perhaps it had been that way once upon a time after a turning, but after so many years of replicated blood, of the need to hunt all but eliminated, they—*we*—must have evolved. The thirst for blood is there, of course, but it isn't an all-consuming *need.*

"I was so scared, Lia," she whispers. "I thought you were going to leave me forever."

"Never," I promise fiercely. "Never."

We stay locked together, saying everything without saying a word, for long, long moments. Eventually she lets out a shuddering breath and I know that she's ok. I pull away and eye her critically.

"Did I imagine you at the Plain??"

"Yes," she says at the same time Elias says, "no." She cuts him a killing look but I give her a pointed one and she throws up her hands in exasperation.

"Ok, ok, fine. Yes, I was there. I couldn't let everyone else ride off to rescue you while I just ran away to safety, so I...might have evaded da, stolen a horse, and followed the army." She shrugs and juts her chin out in defiance.

"She's as stubborn as you are," Elias says, half irritated, half indulgent. It's then that I realize that I can smell Elias *all over* my sister and I arch a brow in his direction. He merely grins, but when I cut my eyes back to Enid, her cheeks flush.

"We'll discuss it later," she says quietly.

"Oh yes we will. *In detail*," I add, smiling.

"Alright, let yer old da in for a hug why don't ye?" da says gruffly, and Enid huffs out a laugh, moving so that da can wrap his arms around me. Soon, everyone is having their turns and the love I feel is nearly enough to drown me.

"I always knew you'd make a hell of a vampire," Wesley says, grinning and punching me playfully in the shoulder.

"Now we can really train you," Nova adds excitedly. "No more taking it easy."

"*That* was you taking it easy on me?!" I exclaim indignantly. "I could barely walk for the first week!"

"Oh yeah, that was nothing. Child's play," she says, waving me off and winking.

Fiona gushes about having a new sister, Sebastian greets me warmly and welcomes me to the Clan in truth now, as a vampire. Elias hugs me, thanks me for saving them all, and promises me that he'll take care of my sister.

We hug, we cry, we laugh. A flurry of chatter erupts around the room, everyone talking all at once in small groups, and while I'm beyond happy to see all of them, I meet Alaric's gaze through the throng of people, and I know that what I see in his eyes is mirrored in mine.

Need. An intense, unapologetic, all-consuming need that I've never felt before and can't deny much longer. And it isn't for blood.

"Out. Now," he says in a low, quiet command.

Elias looks between the two of us, and quickly shoos everyone from the room.

"We'll give you two some time," he says quickly, giving us both knowing looks. "Try not to break the furniture, yeah?" Alaric growls at him but Elias merely grins, winks, and closes the door behind him as he leaves.

In a heartbeat, Alaric is there, kissing me fiercely and pinning me to the bed, his big body covering mine and pressing me down into the soft mattress. His tongue delves, rolling and thrusting as I rip his shirt off: literally. The fabric comes apart beneath my fingers as if it's made of parchment.

"Fucking hells," I whisper and he chuckles lightly, using a claw to split my own nightgown down the center, the silk falling open. He quickly moves downward, sucking a harden nipple into his mouth. I moan and buck, all of the sensations more powerful than ever before. He sucks hard, then releases me only to move to the other side and twirl his tongue. He trails his hand downward and quick as lightning, slides two fingers deep inside while he bites lightly.

"Fuck, Alaric!" I cry, tunneling my fingers into his hair, begging him not to stop.

"So wet already," he growls in approval. I rock my hips upward, desperate for more, needing him to touch and taste everywhere, all at once. Everything is so new, so different. My mind is a roaring tumult of desire and need, needs I've never had before. A need to bite, a need to feed, a need to please my mate, a need to claim him. I whimper and writhe, claws and fangs flaring. I gasp as one slices into my tongue again.

"Mmmm," Alaric moans, smelling the blood, and moves to kiss me once more, my blood mixing between our tongues like it did all those months ago, but this time, I *understand* the pull. I understand the power of the blood, the desire for it. I need...I want...I can't...

"Alaric," I whisper, somewhere between a frustrated sob and a plea. I can't form the thoughts, let alone the words, but as always, Alaric understands me completely. His pants are gone an instant later, and he's above me once more, hand gripping his cock and guiding it to the right spot. I arch my hips, desperate in a way I don't truly understand. It's something primal and animalistic. Something I can't explain but need to obey.

Without hesitation, Alaric shoves his hips forward, gliding in to the hilt with one long, quick thrust. I cry out, my entire body bowing in utter pleasure. My fingers dig into the bed on either side of me, ripping the sheets and mattress beneath to shreds.

"*Fuck*," he rasps.

"More," I demand, nearly out of my mind.

He obeys, pulling back only to slam forward again so hard that my teeth clatter. It's ecstasy. Again, and again, he thrusts. I claw at his back, begging him to move harder. Faster. I feel blood beneath my fingers, but he doesn't seem to care. The scent of his blood makes my heart race and my mouth water, instincts flaring.

"Alaric," I gasp, not knowing what to say or do. He pulls back to look into my eyes and whatever he sees there makes him understand. He shifts back, pulling me up with him so that I'm in his lap, legs wrapped around his waist. He grips my hips and moves me bodily, helping me to ride him while I grip his shoulders. He kisses me hard, our chests slick with sweat and sliding against one another with every thrust.

"Do it, Keeva," he growls, his voice rougher than I've ever heard it. I meet his gaze and his eyes are practically burning in a way I've never seen before. "Take," he rasps, turning his head to expose his throat to me. I don't even have real thoughts now, just instincts roaring and directing me. I lean forward and lick his neck, making his big body shudder beneath me. I smile against his skin.

And then I sink my fangs into his flesh.

CHAPTER 51
ALARIC

Hours later, Dahlia and I lie wrapped up in each other on the floor in front of the fireplace. I gave myself over completely to my instincts for the first time in my life, losing myself with Dahlia, and I don't actually have any idea how we ended up here. Everything is a bit of a blur, honestly.

That first time was pure fire and instincts, a lust and bloodlust that I knew Dahlia would need to sate as soon as possible. After that, we took our time. Dahlia took her time to learn how her new body can feel and move and experience. I took the time to worship her, to kiss every inch of her body in thanks and gratitude. She came back to me. She came back to me and now she's whole and strong and we have all of eternity together.

And then we broke the bed...and put a hole in the wall...or perhaps several, actually, now that I look around the room. I chuckle lightly and Dahlia sighs, turning where she lies on my chest so that she can see me.

"What's so funny?"

"Have you looked around this room?"

She frowns. "Well, no, I guess not really. Everything has kind of been a haze of…oh my gods." She sits up and stares, mouth agape. "We did all of *that*?" Definitely several holes in the walls, deep gouges in the stone of the floor, a broken bed, a broken bench, and a shattered wardrobe. I grin, pushing up to sit as well to survey the damage with her, unable to resist brushing her hair aside and kissing the nape of her neck gently. She shivers.

"Gods, will this never ebb? How can I possibly want you again after we've just fucked for hours upon hours? After we destroyed half of our room for gods' sake?"

"A perk of being a vampire," I say with a shrug.

She turns towards me. "I had no idea how much you were truly holding yourself back before. How easy it really would have been for you to kill me." She pulls my hand to her lips, kissing my palm. I take a steadying breath. We haven't exactly slowed to have a real conversation yet and I need to know that she's ok. *Truly* ok with everything that's happened.

"And are you alright with the fact that we don't have to worry about that anymore?" I ask gently.

Her lips curl. "If you're asking if I'm ok with the fact that I'm a vampire, the answer is yes." I give her a dubious look and she rolls her eyes. "I swear it, Alaric. I can't explain it, but I feel as if this was always meant to be, that this is *who* I was meant to be. Plus, I was the one who wanted to attempt the turning, if you recall. You were the one being a stubborn arse, which in turn got me kidnapped—" I cut her off with a growl and a soft nip at her ear lobe. She giggles and the sound makes my chest swell.

"I'm happy with this new life, Alaric. I'll miss bacon, I'll admit, but…I feel like your true partner now, like I'm worthy of standing beside you. And you don't have to worry about protecting me so much anymore."

"Me? Worry about protecting the woman who killed Kilgren the Kinsblood Slayer and ended the war with the Revenants in one afternoon when I've failed to do it in two hundred years?" I scoff and she smiles, slapping me playfully on the chest before blinking in surprise.

"Wait, so it's really over then? What happened after..." She trails off, clearly not wanting to say the words *after I died*.

"The army dispatched any Revenants who chose not to surrender. Those who did, but did not step up declaring their want for peace will be imprisoned on Racknor Island." She shivers, imagining a prison on that frozen island and I don't blame her. It's a fate almost worse than death, I think. "Malek and Xavier and the others went to the stronghold with the army and it was a short affair there. Almost all of them wanted peace—though they were all too happy to turn on the others who tried to stand against it."

Dahlia's expression turns sad, but her eyes burn with fury.

"Kilgren did horrible things to them, Alaric. He killed their loved ones, their *mates* even, forced them to fight and kill, branded them for others to ridicule and torment at will...Well, I don't blame them for being all too eager to take up arms against the others."

"How did you figure it all out?" I ask.

"Kilgren kept me in a dungeon after Highspear took me—he's dead, I'm assuming?"

"Oh yes," I say rage burning brightly for a moment at the thought of the traitor. I wish I could have been the one to end him—slowly— but Braddock of all people took that task in my stead. The big blacksmith is typically a gentle giant, truth be told, but he'd unleashed absolute fury on the bastard. She nods and moves on, clearly not concerned with the coward's fate.

"Anyway, Kilgren liked to talk a bit too much and explained how their leaders are chosen, the power they have over the others, the talks of peace that led to his father's death."

"Very chatty," I muse, tracing shapes down her spine.

"Malek and Xavier were guarding me and they told me what happened after Kilgren killed his father, how any who wanted peace were punished." She takes a shuddering breath before continuing and I realize that this must be the first time she's really had to think about those days, about the decisions she made. "Kilgren told me how he planned to torture you by torturing me for years to come, all the things he planned to do to me while you were forced to watch…I couldn't let that happen, Alaric. I knew if I challenged him, at least he would have to kill me and he couldn't make you suffer that way. I had no idea if I'd actually succeed in killing him and even if I did, if the power would actually shift to me to control them or not, but…" she shrugs, "it was worth a try."

"And the silver?" I ask.

She smiles and holds up her hand. The ring that she's worn since the Choosing shines in the firelight.

"It's one of my designs. There's a hidden space within it for poison and a small needle that slips out when you press this little latch here." She shows me the mechanism. "Da apparently had some silver left hidden away from when he made Night's Fury and used a bit of it for powder to put inside the ring—*just in case*, he'd said."

"Genius, the both of you." I lean in and kiss her forehead. I've never believed much in divine intervention or the Goddess of Fate, but now I'll worship her until the day I die.

She blushes faintly. "So, anyway, go on about the remaining Revenants. What happens now?"

"Well, it's a long road to integrating them into life in Braxhelm, but for now they're happy to live in peace there beyond the sisters. They've all vowed their allegiance to the Montclares and Braxhlem, taken blood oaths even. Sebastian has sent official decrees to every providence telling them of the end of the war and explaining that many Revenants have wanted peace for centuries. His word on the matter will go a far way in convincing everyone else. So, some day— soon, I hope—they'll be able to live among the humans as the vampires were able to do after the Blood Peace. They're calling this the Clayburn Peace, in case you were wondering."

Her eyes fly wide and go a bit glassy, a faint tinge of pink to the unshed tears now.

"Really?" she whispers.

I brush a curl from her forehead and slide my fingers into her hair, stroking her cheek with my thumb. She leans into the touch and my heart twists in utter contentment.

"Of course. You are the reason the war is over, Dahlia. You are the reason that innocent lives have been set free and saved. You are the reason that Braxhelm will finally know true peace. *You*, love. *You*."

She swallows hard and a single tear escapes down her cheek. I brush it away and she gives me a watery smile.

"Well then, I suppose I'll have people fawning over me even more now than when I was merely the great High General's Consort," she teases.

"Oh you have no idea. There will be parades in your honor, sculptures erected in village squares, babies named Dahlia for years to come."

"What about a holiday? I believe a Clayburn Day is in order." I laugh, pulling her into my lap.

"Oh really now?" She nods, wrapping her arms around my neck and toying with my hair.

"It shall be celebrated with obnoxious amounts of chocolate, alcohol, and dancing."

"I'm sure that can be arranged. Fi is already planning a huge celebration at Astoria's Keep."

"I want Malek and Xavier there," she says firmly. "I know it will be hard for people to accept them at first, but...well, if I'm the hero of the hour and I show how much I trust them...that's got to count for something, right?"

"I think that's a wonderful idea, love. Oh! I have another idea."

"What?"

"How about those paper effigies of you where children beat you with a stick until treats fall out?" I suggest and she throws her head back laughing. The sound warms me to my core. For days, I thought I might never hear it again. She meets my gaze after a few moments.

"So...no more war?"

"No more war," I agree. I can't really imagine it. The army will persist, of course, but the number of active camps and soldiers will decline greatly. Speaking of...

"Would you like to live here at Ashcliff? Permanently?"

Her eyes light up. "Really?"

I nod. "With the threat gone from the pass, there's no reason for me to be stationed at the camp. In fact, I think the camp will be a perfect site for the first Revenant settlement within Braxhelm." She smiles at that. "I can lead the army just fine from here and we'll establish a smaller camp nearby—our lands are vast, in case you didn't know. This can be our home, Dahlia. A true home. Your family can join us, we can build them their own estates on the property if they wish, or the manor has more than enough room. We'll build a new shop for your father. What do you think?"

"I think...I think that sounds perfect, Alaric. It's everything I've ever wanted. And that will work out well since Enid and Elias are obviously gone for each other," she adds with a laugh. The two have been nearly inseparable since the day we rode out to the pass and Enid followed. I don't know what might be in the Clayburn blood that sparks the mating bond so strongly in both the vampire and the human somehow, but it appears to have worked its magic once again. I suspect that the two of them will be married soon enough, and, should they wish it, Enid will attempt the turning. Speaking of marriage...

"I'm fairly certain I know the answer, but I must ask all the same: will you marry me, Dahlia? Become a princess of the Montclare Clan, the true Lady of the Coven of the Wolf?"

"Well it took you long enough to ask me, didn't it?"

I roll my eyes and give her ass a playful swat. She squeaks and laughs.

"There was quite a bit going on, if you recall. Proposals of marriage were a bit low on the priority list of things to address."

"That's fair, I suppose," she says, pursing her lips. "Of course I'll marry you, Alaric. I'm already yours in every way, but being officially joined under the laws of the Montclares sounds appealing."

I smile and she leans in to kiss me deeply, a blazing fire igniting in my blood at the simple touch of her lips to mine, the gentle thrust of her tongue against mine. She tunnels her hands into my hair, tugging on the strands in that way that drives me mad. She nips at my bottom lip and I growl, gripping her hips tighter and tugging her harder against me. She giggles against my lips.

"I always knew you liked when I bit you, but now...well you *really* like when I bite you, don't you?"

"Yes," I say, unabashedly. Dahlia's fangs in my flesh feels almost as good as my own in hers. It's a pleasure that I can't even describe but know I can never live without again. "Plus, your fangs are quite sexy if you must know."

She waggles her brows and grins, tapping one fang seductively with the tip of her tongue. "*These* fangs, you mean?" she purrs in a sultry, innocent voice. "The ones that were buried deep in your cock not an hour ago?" A violent shudder of pleasure rolls through me as I remember the feel of her sucking blood as I came down her throat...

"Keeva," I warn.

She laughs, light and wicked, and I narrow my eyes. She yelps in surprise when I twist her around and position her on hands and knees in front of me. She may be a vampire now, but I'm still older and faster. She gasps and shivers in pleasure and anticipation.

"Wicked little leech," I whisper as I run a hand over her magnificent ass. She laughs lightly, but it quickly turns into a soft moan when I lean forward and kiss the small of her back, slowly working my way downward as she trembles and writhes. There were so many things we couldn't do when she was human, so much of myself I had to hold back in fear of hurting her. No longer. Now she can handle anything I have to give. Now her body is different...and capable of *much*.

She cries out in surprise when I spread her luscious cheeks wide and swirl my tongue around that sensitive spot.

"Oh gods, Alaric...?" she whimpers, a slight question in her tone as she realizes what I aim to do.

"Tell me, Dahlia," I rasp, pressing a finger into her pussy and thrusting gently while I flick my tongue once more. She moans loudly, rocking her hips backwards as if begging for more. "Tell me yes or no. You must always tell me."

"YES," she says immediately and I grin. I continue to pump my fingers slowly, oh so slowly, before trailing them upward, spreading her honey around her ass and pressing a finger gently inside. She makes an obscenely erotic noise, something between a growl and a moan and scream. I pump gently and she groans. "Yes, yes, yes," she chants and I chuckle.

I nip at her flesh with my fangs and she trembles, her entire body quivering when I delve deeper, adding another finger.

"Oh *gods*," she moans.

"That's my eager little mate," I whisper, my own hips subtly bucking while I watch my fingers pump slowly in and out of her.

I tease and work her body, and soon she's panting and writhing.

"Alaric, please," she begs, though there's a bit of command there too, sending a ripple of pleasure through me. *My little firebrand.* I remove my fingers and settle behind her, gripping my cock and stroking. She's so gods damned tight that I know I'll need to steel myself if I want any hope of lasting. I press her knees farther apart and press the head against her hole. She sucks in a ragged breath and then I press forward slowly. Her human body would have needed more special care before this could happen, far more preparation, but her vampiric body is ready and eager. Desperate, I'd say by the way she writhes and presses her hips backwards, sending me deeper inside.

"*Fucking. Hells*," I groan through gritted teeth.

"Oh my gods. Alaric," she pants, "it's so...full...ah gods, it feels....*so good.*" She digs her claws into the stone floor, gouging deep grooves as I slide deeper and deeper until I'm finally settled so fully inside her there's no space between our bodies.

"*Fuck.*" I shudder, my cock pulsing inside her.

"More, Alaric," she demands, turning to look at me over her shoulder. Her green eyes burn with a desire so ferocious that I lose myself completely, giving myself over to the instincts inside me roaring to satisfy and claim. I grip her hips and pull back, only to slam inside her again. The sight is nearly too much and my fangs snap free, desperate to sink into her flesh while my cock does the same. Over and over, I thrust my hips, fucking her hard and sending shivers of the most intense pleasure up my spine. She reaches between her thighs and I groan when I realize what she's doing. She moans and I grit my teeth.

"That's it, Dahlia. Just like that. Gods, you take my cock so well, love."

"Oh gods, Alaric. I'm going to...ah!" she cries out and I can feel her come, her body tightening around my cock in quick, greedy pulses.

"Oh fuck," I mutter, my own release springing forth without warning. I lean over her and sink my fangs into her shoulder as I come hard. She cries out and her body convulses, the pulses coming stronger and faster, and then the little devil turns her head and sinks her own fangs deep into my forearm. It's fucking ecstasy.

Eventually, we both collapse to the floor and lay in boneless heaps for long moments, maybe hours. I slide out of her and maneuver her so that her back is to my chest and my arms are wrapped securely around her. She sighs in contentment.

"I love you," she says quietly, turning her head to kiss my shoulder.

"I love you more than you can possibly imagine, Dahlia."

"I think you made a good choice," she says, voice thick with exhaustion and I know she'll be pulled under any moment. Her stamina is impressive for a fledgling, but it will take decades before she can keep up with me completely. I grin at the thought, of the years and years to come, of eternity stretching out before us.

I kiss her hair and squeeze her tighter.

"It was never a choice, love. You were always my path...that dress *did* help matters though," I add and she chuckles lightly before drifting off to sleep in my arms, where she'll be for the rest of forever.

Acknowledgments

As always, this book wouldn't exist without the help and support of a bunch of people, so this is the part where I scream big, giant, huge, enormous THANK YOUS! to:

- My awesome husband, Dennis, for always supporting me in this weird hobby.
- My amazing bestie for the restie, Lexie. As always, this book literally wouldn't be in the world without you.
- Kayleigh, Lexie, and Kala (ha - still funny) for being members of the best group chat in the world, for nonstop cheerleading, support, fan-girling, hype-girling, bullying, and love. Jeff Beans. Get the pudding. I love you all so hard.
- Amanda, for being an amazeballs artist and creating the beautiful cover and art work for this book, but more importantly for being an even more amazeballs friend. I love you forever.
- My amazing PA, Nancy for being a rock star and not batting an eye when I said "hey, I want to release a book in like six weeks..."
- All of my amazing ARC readers - you mean more to little indie authors like me than you can possibly realize.
- All of my equally amazing regular readers. Yeah, you, the one reading this right now. THANK YOU. I wouldn't still be doing this without you.

ALSO BY K. D. MILLER

<u>YA SCI-FI AND FANTASY</u>

- The Outliers Series (Titan Rising; Titan Unleashed; Titan Reckoning)
- Evansfire

<u>ADULT PARANORMAL ROMANCE</u>

- Veracity of the Gods Series (Dark Burning;. Sweet Tempest)
- Red

<u>ADULT CONTEMPORARY ROMANCE</u>

- Carpe F*cking Diem
- Puck the Holidays
- Wrong Place. Wrong Time. Right Viscount.